Doors of Prague

Barbara Gurney

Daisy Lane Publishing

Cover Art © 2021 Carolyn De Ridder

National Library of Australia Cataloguing-in-Publication data:
Fiction/Women's Fiction/Romance

Doors of Prague/Barbara Gurney -- 1st ed.

ISBN (SC) 9780648771883
ISBN (e)   9780648819318

For those who open doors
with a loving heart.

Other stories by Barbara Gurney

Footprints of a Stranger (2012 Ginninderra Press)

Road to Hanging Rock (2013 Jasper Books)

Life's Shadows (2015 Ginninderra Press)

The Promise (2017 Austin Macauley)

Purple and Other Hues (2018 Ginninderra Press)

Lessons of the Universe with Imogene Constantine
(2019 Serenity Press)

Dusty Heart (2020 Daisy Lane Publishing)

Seeking Self (2020 Ginninderra Press Poetry)

The Blue Book of Short Stories (2020 Black Jack Books)

The Green Book of Short Stories (2020 Black Jack Books)

'You'll have to do something. I can't keep feeding your cat.'

An explosion went off in Gillian's brain, but her body remained inert. She turned her head towards her elderly neighbour and asked slowly, 'Why are you feeding Sherbet?'

Edna snorted. 'You wouldn't have a cat if I didn't feed him.'

Gillian pushed away an empty mug; leaned her elbows on the table and placed her cheeks on her palms. Uncombed hair tumbled forward. Her muffled voice held confusion. 'I do feed him.'

'Look, lass. It's hard, I know, but … well, if there's something else I can do, you only have to ask.'

'But,' Gillian lifted her head and tucked the straggly hair behind her ears, 'I leave him dry biscuits.'

Edna sighed as she stood. 'Would you like another cuppa?' She gathered the two mugs and headed for the kitchen sink.

'But,' Gillian said again, 'why have you been feeding Sherbet?'

Edna's shoulders dropped as she flicked on the power to the kettle. 'You aren't the only one needing comfort. He often comes over the fence to visit. He was in here yesterday, clawing at my back door. I didn't have the heart to turn him away. Anyway, I enjoy his company. But, yesterday, when I tried to put him out, he struggled. I almost dropped him. Then, instead of going out he headed straight for my rubbish bin.' She walked back to the table, placed her hand on Gillian's shoulder. 'The poor little blighter was hungry.'

'No, he can't have been.' Gillian's frown covered most of her eyes. 'I fed him.'

Edna pulled a chair closer to Gillian and sat down. 'When? When did you feed him, lass?'

'Sunday night. I had baked beans. I fed him at the same time. I know I did.' Gillian's finger bumped across the tablecloth's embroidery as she ran it back and forth. 'I remember opening two cans.'

'Sunday was it?' Edna asked. 'Well, today is Thursday. No wonder he was hungry.'

After her mobile phone agreed with Edna on the passing of three invisible days, Gillian turned down her neighbour's offer of lunch and dawdled her way home, stepping over the mess of junk mail near her letterbox.

Once inside, Sherbet wound his way between her legs as she leaned on the kitchen bench, her chin centimetres from the cold stone. Surely she hadn't forgotten three days. She tried to remember Monday but couldn't. Tuesday? Esther called in. Or was that yesterday?

The phone, sounding like a police car, screeched into her consciousness. 'Go away,' she yelled. The phone continued its annoyance. She reached out and stopped the siren. 'Hello,' she whispered.

'Gilly, Esther here. Are you okay?'

Gillian walked around the kitchen bench, the phone in her hand by her side, and plonked onto the couch. Once she'd settled next to a scrunched-up rug and a coffee-stained pillow, she lifted the mouthpiece. Gillian wanted to shout at her sister, tell her *okay* wasn't on her radar; tell her, *she'd never be okay again*, but instead she said, 'Same as.'

'Yeah, but same as what?'

Sherbet padded onto her lap. Gillian ran her hand down his arching back. *I must feed him regularly.*

'Gilly, are you still there?'

'Yeah, yeah. For what that's worth.'

'Look, you need to be more positive. It's hard, awfully hard, but do something. Anything. You can't go on like this.'

Gillian's stomach jolted – turned passive anger living below the surface of hopelessness bursting through like a volcanic eruption. 'I can,' she shouted. 'I can go on exactly like this. Everyone tells me to just get over it.' She stood, used her free hand to emphasize her questions. 'Why? Why should I? Just tell me that smarty-pants. And, you're so bloody brilliant, perhaps while you're at it, you can tell me how.' Her voice quietened but now sounded accusatory.' Do you also think I should just forget it? Is that what everyone thinks? I should forget some bloody idiot ran down my husband and daughter!'

Esther gasped.

Images bounced at Gillian. Esther repeating condolences while holding her upright at the police station; words softly spoken at the hospital after the machines had stopped; the encouragement given after the funerals.

Gillian acknowledged how difficult it must have been when she, with her head resting on the organ donor documents, had swamped the written questions with her tumbling tears. Esther had managed to hold it together and guide her through the paperwork.

'Lift your head. I'll dab it dry. I'll fill it in. You'll have to sign it,' Esther had said.

When tightness in Gillian's throat had threatened to choke, Esther had been strong for both of them.

Forcing those visions back into the darkness of her mind, Gillian held the phone away from her ear. The volcano lost its momentum. The red fiery lava cooled quickly. In its place icicles formed and rain fell.

Esther's exasperation reached her sister. 'Gillian, are you still there?'

'Mm.'

'Look, of course I don't think you should forget them. I'm truly sorry it happened, Gilly. Really, I am. But it's nearly ten months.'

Gillian's mind whimpered, nine months, fourteen days and several senseless hours.

'You need to get on,' Esther said.

'On?'

'Yes, do something other than hide in your house.'

'Hide?'

'You need to start interacting more. Visit people. Or, go on holiday. Get a job.'

'Job?'

'You're young enough. But it doesn't have to be a job, just change something. Do something! You can't go on hiding away, it's not rational.'

Esther's advice clanged against Gillian's wish for solitude. She shivered despite thick track pants and a long-sleeved t-shirt. 'Bye, Esther.'

Gillian stared at the disconnected phone, contemplated her sister's advice, and wondered if visiting Edna constituted *doing something.*

'I'll do the shopping tomorrow,' she told Sherbet. Totally unimpressed, he flicked his tail and strutted to the door. 'Huh, off to Edna's?' she asked as she opened the door. Sherbet meowed his thanks and headed for a favourite sunny spot near the garden shed.

'Don't worry about me,' she told him. 'I'll be here. On my own … like it's going to be … forever.'

She retreated to Sienna's room, sat on the floor with her bare feet tucked under a fluffy mat. She cradled a photo of her family. 'Three,' she said. 'It was supposed to be three … at least until it was four.'

Esther's words interrupted her misery. *Get a job. Go on holiday.*

Could I? Definitely not a job. My resume's out of date. Anyway, who would have me in this state? Maybe a holiday, she thought. Gillian touched Patrick's nose. 'Holiday? Do you think we could manage a holiday?' She circled Sienna's face with her finger. 'Where would we go? Perhaps Melbourne? It would be your first plane trip.'

The pain hit again, wiping away the moment of distraction. Sienna wouldn't go on a plane. She wouldn't go to school or play the piano like Patrick, or favour snapdragons over petunias like her mother. Her child wouldn't do anything anymore.

At least Sienna has her daddy. Gillian held onto that thought as she banged her shoulder repeatedly against the solid wall. *They have each other.* She ...? Well, she wanted to run away from the emptiness. Away from people's pity, from their constant questions and the pressure of acceptance. Would they ever stop watching? Would they ever stop with the suggestions?

Gillian rubbed her hand up her arm, scrunching up the sleeve. The raised goosebumps nipped at her fingers. *Could I?* She stood, placed the photo back on the glass-topped bedside cabinet. *I've tried everything else.*

At her doctor's suggestion, and as relief from Esther's insistence, she'd tried counselling and therapy sessions, but the wanting, the desperate grief, smothered all of her heart. It felt shrivelled; shaken with disbelief – only beating because it knew no other way.

Maybe time away is possible, her subconscious suggested. *No, I'd still have to be cheerful to other people.* Well, maybe some place where there is no one else. *That's not possible.* A spot where there are people, but they don't want to chat. *Again, not possible. Holidaymakers are cheerful, talkative, even more than usual.* What if they spoke a different language? *Mm, that might work.* France? *No, I could manage with my school-girl French. That would defeat the purpose.* Russia? Outer Mongolia?

Gillian chuckled involuntarily. 'Get a grip.'

Over the following three days the idea of time in a far-away country teased her. Now, with her bag heavy with newly purchased milk, coffee, three apples, cat food and a tub of ice cream, Gillian lingered outside a travel agency. Her eyes flicked from one poster to another. A red and yellow poster screamed –

SALE. DISCOUNT PRICES. NEVER TO BE REPEATED BARGAINS.

Filling the remaining glass panel, several options tempted the work weary.

IRELAND FOR TWELVE DAYS. FIJI, NEW ZEALAND. SEE THE TAJ MAHAL.

Pictures of sun-soaked beaches and families having the holiday of their life beckoned and beguiled.

Yeah, fine, Gillian thought, *but what I want is somewhere to be alone.*

A twenty-something female with dangling earrings approached the window, glanced at Gillian and said, 'So many places. Hard to choose, eh?'

Gillian stepped sideways; swapped the shopping into her other hand.

'Been there,' the young woman said, pointing to a high gloss advertisement of Brazil. 'And there. New York is great. Thinking of going to Eastern Europe next time. You know, with a couple of friends. Would be awesome.'

'Oh.' Gillian frowned, wanting to disappear, or at least have this well-travelled person stop trying to include her in her jolliness.

'Yeah, now Prague, I've heard that's something else.'

'Oh?' Gillian said again.

'Well, must go. Off to earn enough for my next holiday. Have a great day.'

Gillian wasn't quick enough to respond. She watched the swinging red-patterned skirt echo the perkiness of its owner hurrying away.

Prague, where the hell is that? Gillian thought.

Checking that the consultants were busy, she slipped into the agency and stood in front of a wall-sized world map. Her eyes traced over the map locating each country: France. Germany. Warsaw. That's Poland. 'Ah, Prague, oh, Czech Republic, I wonder—'

A consultant's voice interrupted, 'Prague's beautiful.'

'Is it? Someone suggested it's worth visiting.'

'Definitely. Prague has a wonderful Old Town. Lots of atmosphere.'

'I'm not looking for atmosphere.'

'I'm Carol. Would you like to take a seat? I'm sure I can find what you are looking for.'

'Not sure what that is. Anyway, the ice cream ...' Gillian glanced at the exit.

'Prague's so close to Germany, and Poland. You can do day trips to both. I can give you some information to take home.' Carol held out a leaflet showing a cottage tucked at the foot of a grassy mountain. 'You can probably rent out a cottage in the mountains.'

Gillian often thought a mountain sat on her shoulders, pushing on her organs, making every breath laboured, every step arduous, but in this picture the mountain seemed to protect the little house.

'That's nice,' Gillian said. 'Can you really stay there?'

Carol smiled, offered the leaflet again. 'Not sure about that particular one, but I'm sure we'd find you something similar.'

'Can I think about it?'

'Of course.'

After a week of making lists, talking to Carol twice, consulting Patrick, and repeatedly changing her mind, Gillian fought against further procrastination and made an appointment at the travel agency.

'One way?' Carol stopped entering details into the computer. 'Okay. Well, the price I've given you is for a return ticket.'

'I don't know how long I'll be away,' Gillian said.

Carol's fingers tapped over the keys. 'You may be better off buying a return and paying the fee for an alteration.'

'No. One way please.'

Carol's eyes narrowed as she scrutinised her client. The thick chestnut-coloured hair had been tamed into a ponytail, revealing the tiny holes where earrings should go. Hazel-coloured eyes settled only for a moment, seemingly avoiding any contact requiring a response.

Since Gillian Middleton's first consultation, Carol had been curious as to the background of this guarded woman. She'd been keen to rent a cottage away from the city, but nothing suitable was immediately available. Then the search started for a place in an outer suburb – one that could be rented on an ongoing short-term basis. That, too, proved difficult.

Her client's continued lack of eye contact puzzled Carol. 'Do you want me to keep searching?' she asked.

'You've been more than helpful.' Gillian pulled her bag towards her chest. 'I couldn't find anything on the sites you suggested either. The internet is so confusing.' She fiddled with the zip on her bag. 'Perhaps I should just stay in a hotel. Maybe look for something once I get there.'

'That may work. You could lap up some luxury before you decide how long you're going to stay.' Carol moved the mouse. 'I'll track down an agency in Prague. You can contact them when you're ready.'

Gillian nodded. 'I think I might do that.'

'Let's get your seat secured first. Now you're sure it's one way?'

'Definitely. I can stay three months, but who knows, I might want to come home earlier.' She thought of the memorial plaques in the oft-visited cemetery.

'When did you say?'

Gillian refocused. 'Oh, as soon as possible. Next week?'

'Sure.' Carol entered information into her computer. 'Here we go – I have one on the twenty-fifth. A flight through Dubai. It's almost full. Good job you're not wanting two or three seats together.'

Gillian's head dropped and her open hand pushed against her chest. She whispered, 'Together. Nup.'

'I'm sorry,' Carol said. 'Did I say something wrong?'

'No, no, of course not. It's just … well, I'm going without my family.' Gillian placed her bag on the floor, then instantly picked it up and nestled it on her knee again. She hunched over the bag, her eyes focusing on the back of Carol's laptop as she whispered, 'Patrick would have had his nose against a window, trying to see through the clouds, enthusiastically pointing out spires, farmland or far-off mountains. My daughter would have been colouring in a picture of a fairy, making the dress a scratchy pink and purple. But …' she licked her top lip and shook her head ever so slightly, 'they aren't able to go.'

Carol shifted papers, apologised again, not daring to ask the reason for her client's sudden change of posture and attitude.

'People on long flights expect conversation.' Gillian looked up. 'I'm not sure I can cope with small talk for all those hours?' She ran her finger along the edge of the desk. 'They ask questions. Expect answers.' Her eyes glanced from Carol's face to the wall behind where happy holiday pictures loomed large. 'Business class.' Gillian glanced back at Carol. 'I think I'll go business class.'

Carol watched emotion shift from pain to dread in Gillian's eyes during this reasoning. Plenty of prospective passengers held a fear of flying, but most joked about it while booking their flight. Carol sensed this client feared something entirely different. She said, 'One-way business class is expensive.'

'I can do expensive.'

Five days later Gillian squeezed the last box of books into Esther's car.

'Are you sure this is a good idea?' Esther asked.

'A bit late now if it's not.'

The car beeped as it locked. They walked back into the house, through to the kitchen. Gillian filled the electric kettle. 'Coffee?'

'Yep, but I can't stay too long, I've a meeting at eleven.'

With a mug of coffee each, the sisters sat in Gillian's family room.

'Looks awfully bare,' Esther said.

Gillian nodded. Only essentials for tenants remained. She'd packed up her life. Patrick and Sienna's life. Into boxes. Amid heartbreak. Washed with tears. Sticky-taped with conclusions.

'I hope it works out,' Esther said.

Gillian nodded again. The rooms had lost their familiarity. Blu-Tack smudges highlighted the missing butcher's paper artistry on the fridge. I'll have to clean that.

She'd cried bucket loads of tears as she tip-tapped her fingernails across the keys of Patrick's piano. Even more tears when the removalists wrapped it in padding and escorted it to their van.

'I still don't understand why the heck it had to be Prague?' Esther said. 'Couldn't you have your holiday in Paris or London? I mean, you don't speak Czech.'

Gillian shook her head. She'd tried to explain several times. This wasn't a sightseeing tour. She wanted somewhere to disappear. Somewhere she didn't have to open her mouth and make useless small talk. Where foreigners couldn't ask why she was crying just because a child walked by holding her father's hand.

'Isn't it a bit silly not to book a return? I mean, the extra cost.' She leaned towards her sister. 'When are you actually planning to come back?'

Gillian grimaced, took a sip of coffee and ignored the question. Going was difficult, but now she'd made up her mind she couldn't face more decisions. She wanted to be far from anyone who knew her recent tragedy, and from those who openly discussed her future as if she were an absent child. All told, their over-caring only made her more unenthusiastic about life in general.

Esther gave up expecting a reply. She drank the last of her coffee, then squinted as she looked into her sister's eyes. 'You can't run away from what's happened.'

Placing the mug on the table, Gillian shifted positions and realigned her t-shirt. *The pain will never go away. But, there're too many people watching everything I do, everything I say. Pity, fuss … that's what I can run away from.*

'You don't know anyone in Prague,' Esther said, shaking her head as she sighed loudly.

Gillian rolled her eyes and remained silent. *That's a good thing. If I went to the UK, I'd be given countless phone numbers and addresses. Cousins, friends of friends.*

'Won't you be lonely?'

Gillian shrugged. 'I'm lonely here. Patrick's gone. Sienna's gone. Life is lonely anywhere I go now.'

'I'll miss you.'

Gillian looked closely at her sister, noticed the carefully applied makeup, the few strands of grey hair amongst the dark blonde. After a pause, she said, 'I know, Essie. I'll miss you too. And the others. Mira and Sandy have been terrific. But best friends aren't the same as a husband and daughter.' Gillian fiddled with her ear lobe, picking at the empty earring hole. 'Like you said … I have to do something.' She glanced at the clock, stood quickly. 'I'll have my laptop. We can email.'

'Look, Gilly. I know I fuss, but I don't want anything more to go wrong.' Esther stood, stepped forward. 'You'll be careful, won't you?'

Their lingering embrace said much. Esther wiped away Gillian's dribbling tears, then her own.

'I've got to go,' Esther said. 'See you on Thursday morning. Ten o'clock is it?'

'Thanks, Essie. I wouldn't have survived without your help. And, ten-thirty will do. Flight is at three.'

'Now make sure you eat that casserole. You'll end up looking like a stick.' Esther waved her hand towards the fridge. 'Don't leave it like the last one. Eat it.'

Gillian groaned. 'Essie, stop it. I'll get to it.'

'Promise?'

Guiding her sister towards the door, Gillian said, 'Esther, for God's sake, stop fussing. I'll heat it up later.'

'Good. Got to go. See you Thursday.'

Esther accepted a kiss before settling into her nine-year-old car. 'I'm looking forward to driving your swanky Peugeot.'

Gillian watched Esther drive away, half-heartedly waving, wondering if she could be bothered to complete her packing. She wandered around the front garden, pulled out a stray thistle and flicked it under a geranium.

Returning inside she sat with her passport and ticket on her knee, considering if she had made a lamentable mistake.

Since the purchase of her ticket, Gillian had refused to have her friends, Mira and Sandy, jolly her into a better mood. She declined their invitations to coffee and cake, lunch at Dome and an evening's concert, with explanations of the need for preparation. In truth, Gillian had willingly let Esther organise the placement of the house with a rental agency, and hire a professional cleaner and gardener. Gillian had nodded a great deal, thanked people repeatedly and generally let days pass without any major input.

By the time Esther arrived to take her to the airport, she'd wiled away the two days, ambling from room to room, storing memories, often sobbing, occasionally dry-eyed but gut-wrenchingly unhappy, staring at a silent TV. She checked her luggage in between snatches of sleep, wiped down clean surfaces and stood contemplating Sherbet's escape route to Edna's for meals.

On Thursday, silence dominated the drive to the airport, and Gillian insisted on a drop-off, rather than endure a long farewell.

As she entered the plane a wave of liberation made her sigh. *Now she could be free. Free of pressure of other people's expectations. Free to be ...*

She couldn't finish the sentence.

After returning the spontaneous greetings of the crew Gillian settled into the ambiance of her seat and watched her fellow passengers. Some produced electronic devices, others opted for reading material. Deciding they must be seasoned travellers and well-prepared for the long hours ahead, Gillian clipped the seatbelt in place, ready to experience every miniscule moment of the new experience.

Once in the air, she ignored the book in her bag, leaned back and waited for service.

I wonder what exactly this new sense of freedom will bring. She let the thought tumble around obscure images of castles, rivers, and strange languages.

By having other people make decisions while she wavered between denial and procrastination; one moment fabricating excuses, the next accepting thoughtful gestures, then shrinking away from good-intended kindness, was she inhibiting healing?

Should she have been stronger? Could she be stronger?

I'm about to find out.

As she voiced her thanks to the attentive flight attendant, she acknowledged the weight of living up to inferred expectations that had been replaced with trepidation of coping alone.

Overawed at the extravagance of Dubai airport, but willing to be seduced by the luxury of the business class lounge, Gillian tasted several of the delights generously displayed on the immaculate counters.

She boarded the flight for the second leg of her journey and converted her seat to a bed, hopeful of a few hours of sleep.

'Mrs Middleton, good morning. Would you like a hot towel?'

Gillian opened her eyes. She'd slept well but had been awake, listening to the security of the droning engines, for some time. Whispering cabin crew, and the smell of bacon, alerted her to breakfast being served. She realigned her clothes and blanket, and adjusted the seat into an upright position.

'Yes, please.'

'It'll freshen you up.' The flight attendant held out a steaming towel with tongs accompanied with a wide smile showing a flash of perfect teeth.

Gillian took the towel in her fingertips, voiced her thanks and watched him continue down the aisle with his tray before she draped her forehead with the warmth. She was wiping her hands when the flight attendant reappeared.

'Now, are you having the omelet or the French toast?'

'Could I have some tea?'

'Certainly. I'll get you one. Milk with one? Was it the French toast as well?'

'No. I mean, yes to the milk with one. Um, I ordered the omelet.'

He held out the tray for the towel. 'Won't be long.'

As she stretched her legs in the ample space of business class, Gillian acknowledged Patrick's astute decision to take out life insurance. They had initially bickered over the necessity of it.

'We're too young,' she'd said.

'Exactly the reason for it.'

'But, if anything happens, surely we're young enough to get by – financially, I mean.'

'It'd be tough. Don't you see? There'd be the mortgage. Having to work part-time or pay childcare fees if you went full-time.' His eyes had darted to Sienna's closed door. 'Social security, God knows if that'd be enough. Either way, it'd be bloody tough.'

'Yeah, I understand that, but the premiums are so expensive. And, it seems, I don't know, makes you think you might be jinxing something.'

'You said the same thing when we made our Wills. Nothing happened then.'

'I know but …'

'Look, we've got Sienna's future to think of. School fees, uniforms, music lessons. I want the best for her.'

He'd playfully punched Gillian on her shoulder. She'd pushed him away, then leaned over him, tickled his ribs until he grabbed her hands and kissed her.

'I don't intend to go anywhere, anytime soon,' he'd said, 'but, just in case, you know, the proverbial bus comes along, we're signing it.'

Anytime soon happened too quickly. It wasn't a bus, but an unlicensed idiot in a high-powered vehicle that plowed into their car, injuring Patrick so badly he lasted only a few hours, and letting Sienna suffer for three days before she succumbed.

Patrick's acumen made it possible for the business class flight, and a booking in the four-star Charles Square Hotel in the centre of Prague. Her bank account had squealed with delight when the insurance money hit the credit column, even though everything else in her life squealed in pain. However, the court case for compensation continued. Gillian replied to the insistent emails from her solicitors in as few words as possible. She told them to do what they thought was best. 'Unless it's really urgent just leave me be. I'll contact you when I get back,' she'd told them.

Her breath caught as the flight attendant spoke, 'Here you go, hot tea and your breakfast.'

Gillian pushed back into the seat, adjusted the table and watched as he placed the tray of food down.

'Thanks, looks wonderful.'

Although the advantages of business class made the process of arrival smoother and quicker, standing in a queue for immigration still had to be endured. During the uneventful taxi drive into the city, Gillian didn't bother with the scenery, she wasn't the usual tourist, the quicker she had a room to herself the better.

'Dobré ráno. Good morning.' The desk clerk greeted Gillian with a pasted-on smile.

'Good morning. I have a booking. Mrs Middleton. Gillian Middleton.' She took her purse and passport from her handbag, dropped the bag at her feet.

'Welcome, Mrs Middleton. Let's get you checked in. Did you have a good trip?'

She took a moment to react. 'Not too bad, I guess.'

'Excellent. Now, can you sign here, please?' He slid a piece of paper towards her. 'And, may I have your credit card. Excellent. Would you like to order tomorrow's breakfast now? Might be best.' He slid another piece of paper across the desk. 'Excellent. You're a poached egg lady I see.'

Gillian closed her eyes for a second. *Hurry up. I'm exhausted.* 'Yep.'

'Excellent. So, here's your electronic keys. Room 408. Fourth floor. Turn left from the lift. Room Service is available if you need something to eat after you are settled.'

Gillian didn't bother to respond to the forced smile.

'Just let us know if we can be of any further help.' He tipped his head towards a uniformed attendant. 'Barta can help with your bags. Have a good day, Mrs Middleton.'

Gillian took the swipe cards. *I don't need two.*

Barta straightened his emblem-enhanced tie, grinned, and offered assistance. With Barta handling her suitcase and hand luggage, she followed him towards the lift.

'Thanks, I'll manage from here,' Gillian said.

She dragged herself, and her bags, out of the lift and along to the designated door. What a trip. Thank goodness it's over.

Once inside, she left the luggage in the middle of the room and flung herself onto the king-sized bed. Spread-eagled across the brocade cover her feet pulsed and her head throbbed. Happy voices came and went past her locked door. She rolled over and stared at a small dent in the ceiling.

So, she thought, *I'm technically homeless. I've rented Patrick and Sienna's home to strangers.* The bile in her stomach rolled and threatened to burst into her throat. *How could I have done that?*

Does Sherbet miss me? Probably not. Edna will be spoiling him. An ironic laugh spurted out. *At least he's being fed regularly.* She tugged her shirt down and thought of Sherbet stalking between Edna's and his old home. Her home.

Won't be my home for a while. I now live in an impersonal room, in a hotel on the other side of the world. She narrowed her eyes. *And one which has a dent in the ceiling.* She pushed aside the wonderings about how the dent may have occurred, sat up and dragged her shoes from her feet.

Nothing on the room service menu appealed. 'I think I'll sleep.'

Gillian fell asleep quickly, but woke two hours later, crumpled and hungry. She checked her watch. The digital clock on the bedside table agreed: 10.30 am.

'I think I'll sleep this day away,' she told the bathroom mirror. 'I'm not a tourist. Don't need to see the sights. I can exist in this room for a while.'

After ringing room service, she showered and then returned to bed wearing pyjamas pulled from the bottom of her suitcase. She flipped indifferently through tourist leaflets: "Things to do in Prague", "Delights of Old Town", "Budget Day Trips" before letting them slip to the floor as she lay down again.

A slither of sky presented a cloudy day when Gillian startled into wakefulness. The knocking on her door wasn't the police coming to ruin her life, but her food order being delivered. Her hands shook as she accepted the tray with poached eggs, toast and marmalade, then retreated to a small table by the window and ate.

By midday she'd ignored two messages from Esther, slung her underclothes into a drawer, hung up her one pair of trousers, jeans and two blouses, and put her t-shirts, track pants, and fleecy top on shelves. With the suitcase and carry-on bag empty of all but two plastic bags, a woollen scarf, laptop and peppermint wrappers she flicked on the electric kettle, glad the upgraded room included tea and coffee making facilities.

Gillian leaned against the window frame with the edge of the curtain entwined in her fingers. The modern facades at street level below enduring stone buildings didn't attract her interest. Instead, she scrutinised the scurrying tops of heads – darting heads, heads stopping at corners. Her eyes followed a yellow cap down the street and as it weaved between chairs of an outdoor café. The kettle turned itself off. A dog pulled its owner along the cobblestones towards a pocket-sized grass area. Cars and small trucks whizzed, braked, stopped and started.

Before returning to the table, Gillian took a small journal from her handbag. Esther had pressed the flowery book into her hand, saying, 'Write a diary.'

'Humph, I'm sure I won't be doing anything worth writing about,' she'd replied, but thanked her sister for the thought.

'You never know,' Esther said. 'Take it with you. Write the things you do … it's a journal, not a novel. Just write about the things you see or do.'

As she recalled her sister's insistence it would be therapeutic, Gillian strummed her left-hand fingers on the first page, with a pen ready for action in the other hand.

Like what, she thought. *Ate breakfast for lunch.* 'It's just like Facebook … on paper. No one wants to know that.' She banged the book shut, tossed it towards the bed. It hit the edge and fell to the floor. Her shoulders slumped forward. She stared at the upended book. Pink. Esther should know I can't stand pink anymore.

The alarm clock blared. Gillian jumped. 'What the …!' She dropped the pen, strode across the room and slammed her hand against the off button. 'Stupid clock.' She picked it up, fiddled unsuccessfully with the setting, finally placing it down in its original spot.

With the room silent again, she paced back to the window. I'm certainly wide awake now. She pulled her hair into a ponytail, held it for a moment then let if fall. She blew strands of hair from her face, closed her eyes and focused her thoughts on the upcoming day.

Okay, now what? *Nothing.* You can't do nothing. *Well, I'll walk.* Good idea. Lock up, get going. *Okay, okay, I'm going.*

Gillian walked. Head down, watching feet. She didn't want to look into faces; have to acknowledge a smile, or even process a blank stare. Sharing, even just a momentary glance, wasn't an option.

Sliding into a chair in the back corner of a café, she ordered coffee by pointing. The waiter repeated her order, a large cappuccino, in English. She turned away from his mocking raised eyebrows and picked up a newspaper from a chair opposite.

She poured over an unreadable newspaper – only recognising international branded ads. Gillian ignored another insistent text from Esther. The waiter hovered several times, but finally left her to shrink away from other people enjoying their day.

Then she walked some more.

She turned corners, dodged pedestrians, waited at crossings. Saw cobblestones, concrete sections of footpaths, bitumen with potholes, smooth bitumen without holes, more cobblestones.

Heard vehicles, horns, a babble of words, laughter, sirens and music. Smelled donuts and pizza.

With each footstep she tried to empty her thoughts, but Patrick reminded her she had to look left instead of right. He said she needed water. She bought water.

When a pair of small sneakers with purple laces appeared in front of her, Sienna asked if Mummy would buy some of those.

Tears came swiftly when the purple-laced child and her mother giggled on their way. Gillian stood against a building, let the tears swamp her cheeks, cascade over her lips, some finding a way into her mouth. She breathed away threatening sobs as she fumbled for a tissue. A red-jacketed woman stopped, asked, 'Jste v pořádku?' Gillian waved away the foreign question, pretended to cough. The red jacket moved on.

After hours of wandering, without registering the delights of a foreign city, Gillian followed three women down half-a-dozen steps into a curry-smelling café, automatically seeking food.

While waiting, she reflected on her solo status. *If I was at home ... I wouldn't be eating alone. I'd have someone to eat with.* When was the last time you went out for dinner? *Umm ...* You haven't. Not after the accident. *No, but ...* Anyway, isn't that what you're here to avoid. *Yes.* Well? *I'm just so confused. I don't want pity. I don't want them watching every move.* Then get on with it. *With what?* Deciding what you do want.

Gillian wanted to punch her alter ego in the face. She didn't need to be reminded that she made no sense. Grief didn't have room for reality. In fact, grief posed two lives: one with a constant shadow, hovering, malicious, never releasing the pain; the other – the world continued, involving the suffering individual whether they chose to be included or not.

She knew what she wished for. She definitely knew. It was such a little thing. *Why couldn't the world spin backwards, rewind, and erase one horrid day? Just one unspeakable, dreadful, shattering, loathsome, repellant, ghastly day.* Gillian took a deep breath and stopped searching for more words to describe the day her world changed.

Turning her attention to the other diners, she tried to imagine if their cheerfulness covered any pain.

The waiter stepped effortlessly between the many chairs and placed a plate with generous chunks of pork in a sea of sauce, and a bowl of rice on her table. It smelt delicious. Looked inviting. Her stomach twitched as she picked up a fork. The overpowering aroma climbed up her nostrils, hit the back of her throat. The fork slipped from her hand, clattering against the tiled tabletop.

Curry meant quiet nights in front of the telly. Curry meant Patrick. Curry … it meant too many things.

Gillian paid, walked out.

She puffed air from her nostrils, wiped her nose repeatedly, trying to get rid of the memory-enhancing smell. As she passed a street stall, the sweet smell of rolled pastry with sugar and spices finally covered the aroma of the painful memory.

Further along the street, in the warmth of early evening, excited children and a few nonchalant adults queued for ice cream. Gillian joined the queue; chose vanilla, licked slowly. The cold treat echoed sunny days with giggling, splashing in shallows, and … *No!* She refused to remember those ice cream-eating days of bliss.

After finishing the cone, she tossed its protective paper into a bin, turned, and noticed a window display of books. As many of the books had English titles, she entered the bookshop hopeful of finding something lighthearted to read. She wandered around stacked tables, skimmed covers from novels in the tall bookcases, chuckled at a Harry Potter novel advertising the author as JK Rowlingová. A short thin man pulled at his tie as he directed her upstairs. White lacquered shelves held a generous selection of English titles. *Samantha's Folly* caught her eye. Surely the title echoed her situation. Esther had repeatedly declared this trip was exactly that.

As Gillian tucked the book under her arm, she wondered if Samantha's foolishness will be the characters undoing or provide an impulsive outcome?

Will my recklessness prove disastrous, or be my solution? she thought.

Just like the hints on the back cover, there were no answer to her question.

Randomly selecting another two frivolous books she returned downstairs, tapped her card over a machine and re-entered the street.

Her inattentive wandering led away from the main streets and Gillian became disorientated. The further she went the narrower the streets became. Fewer people, more parked cars, more darting traffic. She clutched her bulging handbag. The corner of a book dug into her side as she hurried back the way she thought she had come. Her eyes darted between unfamiliar street names and building facades. Wishing she hadn't thought she could survive without a Czech phrasebook she stopped a teenager and asked, 'Hotel Charles Square, that way?' She pointed towards taller buildings.

'Yes.' The teenager nodded, her nose ring catching the late sun, sparkling at Gillian. 'Yes, two streets, left, then you see Town Square.'

'Thanks.' Gillian swallowed hard, relieved the teenager spoke English. 'Two streets. Left. Thank you.'

She found the hotel but turned away from it. The day offered a few more daylight hours, so she walked some more, making sure she didn't wander too far from the centre. On passing the ice cream shop, she lingered as a couple of American tourists squabbled over their choice, and acknowledged the attraction of a simple treat by tourists on the other side of their world.

As the day slipped further into conclusion, Gillian watched snake-like lines of commuters disappearing down tunnels toward the Metro.

Bowels of the earth, Hell, she thought. She imagined frantic souls shouting, and flames laughing as they lapped against freckled skin, against blue hair ribbons. She shuddered, had to grab at the side of a kiosk to stop herself from sagging onto the footpath.

'Hej dámo! Dávejte pozor!' yelled the owner of the magazine kiosk.

She stepped away from the kiosk, averting any danger to the pile of magazines, and breathed deeply, evenly. She shoved hellish scenes away and thought of puppies playing with kittens, lions playing with lambs, children skipping through daisies, daddies hugging little girls …

Left foot. Right foot. Left… right… left… Keep walking.

She dodged a tourist group spread across the footpath, ignored an obvious request for an apology after bumping into another pedestrian, and continued mindlessly until she reached the Charles Square Hotel. Avoiding the clamour of cheerful tourists waiting for the lift, she plodded up the stairs – each footstep seemed to be sloshing through mud.

Fourth floor. Fourth floor. Fourth floor.

Relieved to have respite from the long straps dragging across her chest she removed her bag, tipped out the books, and fell face-down on the bed.

I can't do it. You must. *I can't.* You can.

When breathing around squashed-in cheeks proved challenging, Gillian rolled over and pushed a book away from her armpit. 'I've got to do it,' she said. 'Somehow.'

Her belly rumbled. 'Let's start with that,' she said, and ran her hand across her stomach. The uneaten meal of curry and rice had shattered her equilibrium, and with her thoughts still dishevelled, she resorted to ordering a BLT with chips from Room Service.

She stood next to the door, staring at the minute pattern in the carpet – following one particular grove from her feet to the wardrobe. She didn't need any more food-related memories.

After opening the door three times on the sound of the lift, she sat on the end of the bed browsing through the tourist leaflets.

With her order delivered, Gillian picked the bacon from the bun and rolled it around three salty chips. The lettuce folded nicely as she bent the top half of the bun over it. The sticky sauce escaped and clung to her chin.

When her mobile buzzed, she stopped chewing and cursed. *Damn. Bet it's Esther. Again!*

She finished the mouthful, wiped her hands, then picked up the phone. *Yes, knew it.*

You haven't answered any of my texts or emails. Are you okay?

Gillian rolled her eyes. Then spotted the last sentence in capitals.

READ YOUR EMAILS.

Worried some sort of problem had developed at home, Gillian slipped the phone into her pocket, retrieved her laptop and logged on.

God, so many emails.

Tempted to erase the lot, Gillian scrolled through to Esther's latest then read it quickly, looking for a disaster. Her pulse quickened. Her eyebrows lowered a little more with each sentence.

Weather in Perth is lousy. Peugeot's a dream.

She scanned across descriptions of appointments with this person, cancellation of another. Then ...

I know you said you want to be left alone, but I worry so much. Please, even if you don't answer this email, let me know you're there. Just send one of those predictive options on the bottom of the message on your mobile. Then I'll know you're okay. Please, at least give me that much.

Gillian grabbed the last piece of bun from the plate. She paced between the window and door as she chewed a few times then swallowed the last bite. The too-large bit fought its way down. After rubbing her chest, she pulled out her phone and opened Esther's message.

Poking at a suggested reply, she sighed. There, that's her taken care of.

This time she dropped the phone onto the bed, sat beside it, and settled her laptop on her knee again.

As she waited for the emails to reappear, memory flashes showing a teenage Esther pushing her on the homemade swing in the backyard, showing her how to thread a needle, checking her homework, made Gillian realise just how much she owed Esther.

She re-read Esther's three emails thoroughly, the content being repetitious, and with news unlikely to impact on anyone. However, Gillian replied briefly, and signed off, *with love*.

Scanning through the other emails, Gillian opened Sandy's latest with the subject line of –

Hey, this is my life without you.

Sandy's jovial notes on her latest boyfriend were expressive, and Gillian chuckled involuntarily. Something about the tone of the information caused a re-read. I wonder if that means she's finally found her Patrick.

She skipped through Mira's overly-polite one, deleted the promotional messages, and a few likely spams.

Since finishing her reply to Sandy and Mira, Gillian washed some undies, put on her pyjamas and tried unsuccessfully to be entranced by *Samantha's Folly*.

A slit between the curtains showed a moonless night. Black. Dark. Sad. Gillian sat hunched over her tightly-gripped pillow. When the description of the male character showed no imagination, she slammed the book shut and tossed it to the floor. *Tall, dark and handsome ... and incredibly wealthy. You've got to be kidding!*

Pummeling the pillow into submission, she lay down only to have dreams of Patrick's caresses disturb her sleep.

She woke several times during the small hours, one time panting after fighting monstrous doves with multi-coloured beaks. Another dream left her pulling on the sheet as she pushed a boat away from rapids, and then at four o'clock she woke frightened because she'd been falling … falling …

As she smacked the pillow again, she remembered Esther's advice when they shared a childhood bedroom. 'Think of something nice,' she'd growled. 'I can't get to sleep either, with you grunting and groaning.'

So, she thought of them sharing books, whispering long into the night, despite Mother's urging for them to go to sleep.

She recalled Esther insisting on tying her little sister's shoe-laces so they could get to school on time, pushing away bullying classmates, telling Gillian which schoolmates she shouldn't talk to, which kids she couldn't trust.

With a smile on her face, sleep snuck in until seven o'clock when Sienna's fingers tickled her feet, both giggling as they rolled together in the folds of blankets. She woke, wishing that dream was reality.

With her brain battered with hopeless wishes, she slothed off to the shower. While standing under the warm water she hoped the ache of memories would slither down the drain.

Retrieving her ordered breakfast from the pass-through, she tasted one mouthful of toast, then slammed down the knife. Time was supposed to be a healer, but for Gillian, it only meant a simple thing like breakfast threw memories in her face. With hovering resentment, she cursed emphatically and slammed the door as she left the room. Bitterness fed through her stomach and into her mind. Too angry to wait for the lift, she headed for the stairs. By the time she stomped down four floors of steps her lungs pleaded for respite. Doubting her sanity, she sagged onto a lobby couch, crossed her arms over her chest and curbed the longing to scream at anyone who dared to smile. Brushing away the desk clerk's concerns, Gillian stood, hooked the long sleeves of her t-shirt over her thumbs and hurried out into the street.

The cobblestones of Wenceslas Square were still grey, still uneven and still hard – they battered through her sneakers and challenged her to watch each step. She strode up the slight slope, stopped at the dominating statue at the top of the city square and spoke to the bronze St Wenceslas. 'How long does it take?' He stared down from his elegant repose on a majestic horse with his raised flag indicating victory. She asked, 'How do you keep fighting, eh?'

She paced down the square, ignoring men in business suits, women in high heels, tourists in floppy hats, but her eyes were momentarily drawn to a man in a kilt. After two laps of the large town square, the last lap at a more dignified pace, her anger eased and she headed back to her hotel room.

As she sipped cold water, she recalled the Scot, resplendent in red tartan, out of context, away from home. He'd been swaggering down the square, with several loud-voiced men, oblivious to her desire for anonymity, and wanting everyone to be as happy as they were.

'Hey, lass, smile, will you? Nothing's that bad,' he'd said as the five men let her pass. They turned, raised their hands and cheered as the Scot bowed and added, 'Have a bloody good day.'

She ate cold toast, loaded with strawberry jam, left the congealed egg and thought again of the Scot's advice. She tested the words. 'Bloody good day.' *How can I do that?*

She retrieved a torn chocolate bar wrapper from where she'd tossed it last night, dropped it into the bin. She smirked at the mirror behind the mini-bar. *Fake it, till you make it.*

Sandy constantly sprouted this adage. She'd made a success of her business by following this advice. And now as Gillian forced another smile into the mirror, she attempted a Glaswegian accent, 'Smile, lass. Try and have a bloody good day.'

Gillian went out again, stood at the entrance and saw, for the first time, the intricate patterns painted on the building opposite. Before putting on her sunglasses, she squinted up and down the street, realising she'd previously ignored the beauty of the medieval buildings, not even noticing the comparison between ancient and modern. However, standing on the footpath, craning her neck to take in a particularly ornate column, laughing teenagers bumped against her. Recovering her balance and accepting their apologies she abandoned the plan to observe the architecture from a stationary position in the busy city square.

Continuing down the slope, Gillian forced herself to glance at faces as she ambled past shop fronts. When a young man with a pale face returned her prolonged glance, her conscience challenged.

You don't need to search. No, you're right. *The chances of them being here is very remote.* But I can't help it. *You can. Just remember, there's no point − not here.*

Stopping at a corner, Gillian leaned against a grey stone pillar and sighed, trying to stop the argument in her head. She had voiced her fear of obsession at one of the therapy sessions set up by the hospital.

'I can't not,' she'd whispered. 'Every child, every man, especially if they look like they're recovering from illness, I feel they might be the one.' She had turned her head away, looked at the ceiling rose and inspected the dangling light fixture. 'They might be. They might.'

The somber psychologist explained it was natural for preoccupation after such trauma. 'You know you could have contacted the recipients anonymously. You've opted not to.'

With her gaze returning to his eyes, and then his mouth, she said, 'It seemed pointless.'

'Why?'

Gillian had then wanted to run screaming from the room, but her legs wouldn't cooperate. Instead, she crossed those obstinate legs and tapped her knee. 'Because ...' She looked down at her broken fingernail, fiddled with it. 'Because ...' She folded her arms. 'Sienna ... they took several ... for many ...' Grabbing her bag from the floor, she searched for a fresh tissue. He offered her the box from his broad mahogany table.' And Patrick ...' She wiped her eyes, blew her nose. 'Patrick ... I hope ... musician ...'

The psychologist waited until Gillian became calmer. 'You will come to terms with it. Just take one day at a time.'

'Humph, perhaps I should join Alcoholics Anonymous!'

His thin lips turned into a slow smile. 'There are groups.'

'No way. Don't bother to suggest that.'

After a moment of silence, where the music from the reception desk filtered through the panelled walls, he said, 'At this stage I think it's better for you not to know who received their organs.' The sound as he'd flipped over pages of notes crashed against her eardrums like a learner drummer trying out the hi-hat cymbal.

She left before her allocated time expired.

For the following fortnight she refused to leave her house. Only when Esther insisted they go grocery shopping, did she venture out.

The Scot's words came back. Agreeing to have a go at following his advice, she entered shops, slid dresses along silvery rails, tried on a hat, smelt perfume, but stayed away from the children's department. Patrick came with her when she entered a homeware store, leaned over her shoulder and told her not to buy another coffee mug. 'We have plenty,' he reminded her. She put the daisy-splattered mug down, turned – shocked that no one stood there. Hurrying out of the shop, she gulped in air, waited until her pulse slowed.

Entering a park tucked beside a child-minding facility, she drifted past the sandpit, and watched the pantomime of people. The adults sat under chestnut trees, reading, talking, watching and waiting. Two little boys fought over being captain of a ship. They sorted it out. She saw children jabbering, yelling, screaming, crying and laughing. Like kids should, Gillian thought.

As she left the park, her top lip covered her bottom lip, her tongue flicked across her teeth. She strolled indecisively, found a noisy café, ordered latte and torte – in English. Ate it quickly, ran her finger over the last spot of cream and sucked on her finger.

She returned to the hotel mid-afternoon, planning to read one of the books she'd purchased yesterday. Maybe ignore the tall, dark and handsome character and see if the plot could redeem *Samantha's Folly*.

The blurb read – Would Samantha's past catch up with her? Will Samantha live happily ever after with the tall dark stranger?

'Happy ever after?' Gillian asked the blonde-haired, blue-eyed beauty on the cover. *Of course you will. Everyone does in a book! But life's not like that. Mine was supposed to.*

Gillian lay on the bed, the book balancing on her chest and remembered meeting Patrick.

Esther had begged, 'Come on, Gilly. It's a party. Might be fun.'

'But they're your friends. They're old.'

Esther slapped her sister lightly on the arm. 'Watch it. I'm only five years older.'

'Ow.' Gillian swiped; missed. 'Well, that's quite a lot.'

'Come on. The invitation said, and "partner".' She laughed. 'I'm hoping to find one, at the party. Please come. I don't want to arrive by myself.'

'What sort of party is it? I'm not going if I have to wear a dress.'

Jeans were appropriate for the birthday party of Esther's workmate. Pig on a spit, roast potato and thick dark gravy kept the drinking youth fed. Gillian tagged along with Esther for a while, but after filling her plate she took an offered seat from a long-limbed man.

'Here, I've just about finished. Gravy's fab,' he said. 'Tempted to lick the plate.'

'Good, but I've opted out. I'm sure I'd dribble it down me.'

'Patrick,' he said as he handed her a serviette. 'Patrick Middleton. I'm the party boy's cousin.'

'Hi, Patrick. Gillian. Gillian Enderson.'

'Enderson? Did you lose the H?' His laughter trickled over her; delighted her skin.

She grinned. 'Yeah, have a lot of trouble convincing people I haven't made a mistake when I fill in forms.'

'You've convinced me,' he said. 'Can I get you a drink, Miss Enderson with the missing H?'

The pleasant memory trickled away as Gillian rolled sideways. *Samantha's* perfect world tumbled to the floor.

The sky had full reign over the wall of windows. Only a few white clouds hindered the brilliant blue. One cloud looked like a pelican, but mostly the static clouds reminded her of summer days at the river early in their relationship. Patrick's skinny legs protruding from khaki shorts, his eyes hidden behind sunglasses, his freckles smothered with sunscreen. He'd teased her about her bucket hat. 'You look like my mum, ready to do the gardening.'

Gillian took it as a compliment, secretly hoping to be someone's mum – one day. Hoping he'd be that someone's dad.

Waking from a deep sleep, Gillian stretched, wriggled her feet and checked the time. She ran her hands through her hair, rubbed a tissue over her mouth and left the room, heading for the lobby.

'Can I help you?'

Gillian peered at the array of leaflets behind the desk clerk. 'I'm looking for a map of the Metro.'

'Sure.' The desk clerk turned, picked out three, turned back. 'Here you are. One of the Metro. Perhaps you should have a city map and some places to go.' This clerk's smile reached her eyes. 'There is another selection of leaflets just down from the elevators. You should look at them. Have you been to Prague Castle yet? Where are you headed on the Metro?'

Taking all three leaflets, but opening the one showing the transport system, Gillian said, 'I haven't been on any underground before. Can you make any suggestions? Which one's best? What about a ticket?'

'Well, try the Red Line. Goes out to Letňany. There's a big centre there.'

Armed with enough information to spend the next twelve months being the number one tourist in the Czech Republic, Gillian returned to her room. She sat at the table, browsed the leaflets, putting them in piles, yes, no, maybe, occasionally glancing up at the changing sky, waiting for night to come, when one could sleep, hopefully without dreams.

The sky took forever to lose touch with the sun and when night finally came, she left the curtains open, watched a creeping fingernail of a moon slide across the southern sky.

Her mind turned to Patrick and their nights on the back patio: sipping wine, listening for a restless child, talking, sitting silently.

'Why?' she asked the midnight sky. 'Why did it have to be? Why, sky?' The rhyming words pulled the memory of Sienna's books back to her. She imagined Sienna calling out, 'Why sky? Why sky?' Then, skipping, jumping, giggling at the rhyme, making a rhythmic song out of the two words.

'Why sky?' Gillian said again. A slight chuckle escaped as she thought of Dr Seuss. 'I don't know why, but we'll get by, won't we, sky.'

The next morning, using information from the leaflets, Gillian arrived at the entrance to the Metro, purchased a ticket and absorbed the pungent smell of overcrowding and the tingling anticipation of her first planned outing in a foreign city.

The people rushing into the Metro drew her forward. Overwhelmed at the length of the escalator taking commuters to their destination, she stood with her ticket in her hand and watched. She shooed away the thoughts she'd had yesterday of the bowels of the earth and concentrated on reaching the correct platform.

She smiled as she watched people appearing to lean forward as if compensating for the steep angle of the escalator. She squeezed to the right, not left, and speculated at the fitness of those racing down the moving stainless-steel steps.

As she entered the train, Gillian noticed a tiny dog in a young woman's bag. It ignored the inevitable noises and tucked its nose under its owner's arm. Clinging to a pole, spreading her feet for balance, Gillian avoided all eye contact and watched the unfamiliar station names pull into view. When the train reached Střížkov station she eased between two women, glad to be able to sit. Both women had cane baskets on their knees, and when they stood as Prosek approached, Gillian stood too.

Baskets mean shopping, shopping means shops. She'd try Prosek. Stroll around. Eat lunch. Browse the shops. Yes, Prosek.

Gillian stopped outside a teashop. Delicately iced cakes filled most of one cabinet. A variety of bread, sugar-topped buns, and cream donuts added to the many choices.

I'll just have coffee, Gillian thought.

'Co si dáte?' said the woman behind the counter.

'Sorry. Just English.'

'What do you want?' the woman repeated.

Gillian pointed to a sign. 'Flat white, please.'

The woman asked, 'Of course. Do you require a cake?'

Gillian couldn't stop her eyebrows lifting in surprise. She expected sales assistants in the numerous souvenir shops, and in the high-end hotels and boutiques to speak English, but perfect English, here, in Prosek, in the suburbs?

Hoping the woman wasn't offended by her surprise, Gillian said, 'No, just the coffee.'

'You will wait only a little time. Have a seat, please.'

Gillian had ignored a McDonalds and chosen this quaint teashop. Its brightly coloured awning and outside seating looked inviting. Here she hoped to be ignored; left to sip her coffee, fill some time in the open air.

'Coffee for you.'

From her brief encounters, the Czech people seemed reserved. Polite. Friendly when engaged, but no one chatted endlessly like some people who weren't concerned their target didn't return their friendliness. No, Gillian was grateful for Czech boundaries.

'Thanks.'

The woman straightened the tablecloth unnecessarily. 'You are a visitor, no? Have you been to our castle?'

'Nup.' Gillian looked away. 'Not yet.'

'It is good. And our Old Town, it is special.'

Gillian kept her eyes on the cup and thought, I must put both on my list.

'Please, enjoy the coffee.'

Gillian finished her drink and recommenced walking. Yep, friendly, but not pushy. I like that.

The trip on the underground transport had brought her to Prosek. Prosek; easy enough to pronounce. She noticed modern buildings amongst the older ones. Cafes, offices, shops, tucked in unlikely spots. She strolled down grass-lined streets, tried to guess what the signs announced, wondered who lived in the charming houses, and fascinated by the prolific modern accommodation.

A group of purple-blue buildings came into view and she spotted a "K pronájmu/For Rent" sign wedged into the ground near a wall of letter-boxes. Ambling around the four-storied buildings, Gillian appreciated the neat garden surrounding the common areas, the cleanliness of the stairwell and the bonus of a lift. She scribbled down the number on the sign and her first surge of excitement since landing at Vaclav Havel airport tugged at her stomach.

Carol, from the travel agency in Perth, had given her details of an agent in Prague; someone who would help her locate accommodation, but Gillian knew it would include questions which would tip emotions. How many bedrooms? Only yourself? Where's your family? Maybe she could deal directly with this agent, cut out the middle man. So to speak.

Deciding to return to the city, she entered the underground station and joined the hurrying pedestrians. A train pulled in just as the throng reached the platform. The human tide jostled through the doors.

Ten minutes later she heard a two-language announcement, 'This train terminates here. All passengers must leave the train.' Gillian stood. That was quick. She looked around. It certainly didn't look like the winding tunnels of central Prague. The sign announced: Letňany.

Baffled, Gillian walked up the stairs to the bright sunshine. The terminating passengers quickly dispersed and left Gillian staring at an empty platform. This morning she had set out for the end of the Red Line, changed her mind and alighted at Prosek. She thought this train was going back to the city. But obviously she was in Letňany. How did that happen?

She scurried down the steps and scoured the information. 'Oh, I've gone the wrong way.' After crossing to the correct platform, she paced. Finally, the train arrived and her pulse slowed. At least I'll have a seat.

On reaching Florenc she changed to the Yellow Line. This would bring her out at Můstek, closer to her hotel.

The myriad of tunnels, crowds of people going home after their day of work, and the endless foreign words of strangers panicked Gillian. She imagined every second person was a pickpocket and every other person their accomplice. Clutching her bag tightly, she leaned against the cold tiles of a pillar. A headache built. Fear prickled. Overwhelmed by the noisy school children who jostled out of the opening doors, the signs, even the English ones, confused her. She focused on finding the Yellow directions, trying to grasp the few station names which led to Můstek.

'Můžu Vám pomoct?'

'Sorry. English.' Positive she was the only English-speaking person on the planet right now, panic rose another level.

'Can I help you?' he repeated. 'Where are you going?' The young man raised his eyebrows.

'You speak English?'

'Of course.'

'Thank goodness. I'm so confused.'

'Rozumím. I understand,' he said. 'Do you know which line?'

'Yes, the yellow one. Můstek.'

'Ah. You go this way with me. I will show you.' He reached out to take her arm, then didn't.

She strode alongside her rescuer until the crowd on the stairs forced her to fall behind. Tempted to take hold of his jacket, she focused on his blonde curls and kept going.

'You wait here. It comes this way.' He pointed down the empty track, then stepped away. 'Nashledanou. Goodbye.'

She wanted to hug him. 'Thank you. Thanks so much.'

The swoosh of air preceding the train hit her face. Her stomach relaxed. Once she reached Můstek she could find her way home.

Home? A word that conjures up so much, she thought. She glanced around at the people filling the seats and squeezing into the aisle of the train. Were they all heading home? This time of the day was peak hour in Perth, was it the same here? I guess so. She clutched a pole tightly and kept her other hand against her bag. Perth. Home?

She thought of Sienna's small room with pink walls. The teddy with its own wooden chair, the box of Lego, the growing number of books, and the fluffy purple cushion which seemed to be always in the centre of the floor.

Gillian hadn't been able to go into her daughter's room for weeks without ending up sitting on the white floor mat, hugging the cushion ... and sobbing. The door remained shut – most days, but the longing always won over the devastation of emptiness.

Esther had organised Sandy and Mira to help box up Sienna's treasures. Gillian wanted to keep every last piece of shredded purple fluff and every inch of hair ribbon, but they'd gradually sorted the precious keepsakes from items she could bear to part with.

Patrick's aura had seeped into the whole house and Gillian refused to let anything go. 'I bought that jacket.' She snatched it from Esther. 'Don't take those shoes. He wore them for our wedding.'

Her breath caught each time Mira held up another t-shirt. 'No, please, not that one. We bought that one in Auckland.'

In the end she had walked to the shops, and sat mindlessly stirring a straw in a milkshake, sucking spasmodically over an hour while the other three women filled plastic bags. She dropped the empty drink container in the bin, returned home, hoping there'd be no sign of Sienna and Patrick's belongings. However, nine black bags lined the hallway.

'No! I won't have it,' she screamed. 'My baby.' She tugged at one of the bags. 'You can't take my baby.'

'Gillian. Please, Gillian. Leave it.' Esther took Gillian's arm and lifted it gently away from the bag. 'It'll be okay.' She attempted to hug her sister.

Flapping away consoling arms Gillian cried, 'Patrick, Patrick, don't leave me.' She knelt down and wrapped her arms around the cold, crinkled plastic bag.

She heard Mira's sudden sucked-in breath, noticed her turn pale, and knew her friend was terrified simply because she didn't know how to help. Gillian didn't care, she was beyond help anyway, but she sagged against Sandy and accepted comfort.

'Come on, Gilly,' Sandy said. 'They're just things. You've still got him in your heart. You've got memories. These are just things.' She rocked Gillian back and forth. 'Come on, sweetheart. Come with me. Come outside. Let's leave these to the others.'

With the cars loaded, and Mira and Esther on their way to wherever loved-but-not-required clothes were valued, Sandy poured wine into coffee mugs and helped Gillian ease her sorrow into a mist of despondency.

The next day, while she picked indifferently at her breakfast, Gillian remembered recording the number of the agent for the Prosek unit in her phone.

Although she could hide in the city – not having to eat at the same place for any meal – she knew it was uneconomical to continue to live in a high-end hotel. Even after these few days the staff recognised her and expected her to respond to their greetings. Four stars meant they excelled at customer service. She'd have to tell them top-class service was different to different people.

She'd already become familiar with Czech greetings of ahoj and dobrý den, but the staff spoke English too well to be put off with a shrug, and it wouldn't be long before they wanted a conversation.

Pushing away negativity, Gillian dialed the agents, hoping she didn't have to fumble around finding words in the Lonely Planet dictionary.

Someone answered the phone immediately with a cheery, 'Dobrý den.'

'Oh, sorry, do you speak English?'

'Of course. How can I help you?'

Gillian sighed with relief. 'I saw your sign for a unit for rent. The one in Prosek.'

'Very good. But first, your name, please.'

'Gillian. Gillian Middleton.'

'Pleased to speak with you, Gillian. My name is Anděla. The place is still available. Would you like to see it?'

'How much is the rent?'

'It is 14,000 per month.'

Gillian couldn't convert it quickly and didn't know if it was reasonable. 'Right. Is it furnished?'

'It has some furniture, a bed, table and chairs, couch, but not fully furnished.'

'I don't need much.'

'When would you like to see it? I am able to show it today.'

Before setting out for an inspection, Gillian rang the Prague agent recommended by her travel consultant in Perth, and enquired about rental guidelines. The Prosek unit fitted within those guidelines, especially considering it came with a fridge, washer and dryer, as well as underfloor heating and air conditioning.

Both Anděla and Gillian were eager to secure the unit, and within an hour, they were sitting over coffee, signing a short-term contract.

Able to move in the next day, Gillian had dinner in the hotel lobby restaurant, deflecting offers of companionship from six Canadians, treating herself to peaches with champagne sorbet, and smiling at the anticipated solitude.

Packing took no time at all, and Gillian had only her toiletries to gather by the time a knock on the door announced breakfast.

Settling the account dragged on as the desk clerk continued to extol the beauty and history of the Czech Republic. When he raised the relatively new history of its separation from the Slovak Republic, Gillian took the receipt and turned away.

'Sorry, have to go. Meeting the agent.' She stared at her watch. 'Look at that. Yep, must get going.'

The white lie worked and the clerk finished mid-sentence, then said, 'For sure.' He pushed a few papers into a pile, as he returned to his spiel. 'Thank you for staying at the Charles Square Hotel. We hope to see you again.'

Barta smiled at Gillian as she wheeled her cases towards the front door.

'Ahoj. Have a nice day,' she wished him.

Gillian's nerves ebbed and flowed with every metre of cobblestone as she headed for the Metro, juggling both her emotions and the recalcitrant luggage.

I'm doing it. Well done, you. I'm moving forward. Esther would be proud.

Excitement covered her misgivings when a young woman offered her a seat on the crowded train. Gillian's leg jiggled under her bag, as she smiled briefly at fellow passengers.

Managing the wheeled suitcase, which refused to travel in a straight line, she literarily ran into a student as she exited the train at Prosek. Gillian apologised, altered her grip and pulled it in a full circle for a better starting point. Balancing her cabin bag on top, she lifted the recently purchased carry-all, and with her handbag slung across her chest, she stepped forward. The departing train raced past her, disregarding her resultant dishevelled hair. She tried spitting the fine strands of hair from her mouth, but in the end had to put down her luggage to push her hair behind her ears.

With the evening growing darker, she hurried along the main road, turning into the short street leading to the unit destined to be her new home. The grasses by the edge of the path, and the spreading branches of foreign trees added to her feeling of being out of place. Out of my comfort zone, well and truly. She inexplicitly wanted to run, knew the weight of her bags made it impossible. *It's okay. You'll be fine. It'll be okay.*

Gillian stood beside the letterboxes, her suitcase and bags at her feet. Her arms welcomed the relief from the strain of carrying them so far. She'd packed clean underclothes around new kitchen implements in her cabin bag and the striped carry-all overflowed with recently purchased frying pan and a pillow. The uncooperative pillow had slipped out twice. Fortunately, its plastic cover had remained intact.

As she contemplated the last struggle, up just four steps towards the lift, she relaxed. Now she could be on her own; remember Sienna when she wanted to, think about Patrick all day, and cry without anyone telling her to "get on." There'd be no one's pity to pretend to overlook: seen in their eyes, in their good intentions of talking of everything else but their family. No invitations to have to reject: a movie, a jog in the park, I don't do jogging, or some craft morning where one was supposed to exercise sombre moods.

She counted through the letterboxes until she found number fifteen – now a connection to the rest of her world.

Snail Mail! Would anyone even send her something? Esther might.

Gillian knew Esther had only wanted to help. A bossy older sister in full flight – that's what she had called Esther. Her sister had shrugged, laughed it off. Not for a moment did Gillian think it hadn't hurt. She'd meant it to.

Then, when it had been time to say goodbye, Gillian had hugged her sister and begged forgiveness.

'Nothing to forgive, Gilly.' Esther squeezed her sister's arm. 'It's all beyond belief. Your world's upside down. I do understand that.'

'Well, thanks, Essie. I really don't know why I'm mean sometimes. I can't seem to help it. I guess I want to hurt people. You know, 'cos I'm so hurt.'

Esther patted Gillian's cheek. 'Off you go. See if you can find some peace. But don't ignore us. And bring back the old Gillian.'

'That Gillian's long gone.'

'Well, find a new Gillian. A Gillian who can smile again.'

Gillian had pecked her sister on the cheek, forced a plastic smile, and joined the airport's security queue.

The lights in the foyer welcomed, and as Gillian approached the lift a soberly-dressed elderly woman appeared, her shoes clicking on the concrete path. The woman adjusted her scarf, glanced at Gillian but scrutinised the group of bags. They shared the lift. The woman nodded an acknowledgement as she alighted at the first floor. Gillian nodded back, realigned her shoulder bag and pressed the button for the fourth floor.

The musty smell of an unaired room enveloped Gillian as she entered. A pine bookcase stood in the broad hallway next to a hideous empty metal planter. *It wouldn't even be improved with a plant,* Gillian thought as she dropped her handbag on a leather couch and wheeled the suitcase into the bedroom. The queen-sized bed with a bare mattress left just enough room for a one-door wardrobe.

After emptying her cabin bag of recently purchased kitchen implements, Gillian left them on the laminate bench, then searched the unit for bed linen. The fully-tiled bathroom included the washer and dryer – both seemingly new. A plastic basket sat on top of the dryer. She discovered a rolled-up bath-mat and one towel tucked in the top of the wardrobe. Six wire coat hangers clanged together as she shut the door.

'Huh.' Apparently, I've misunderstood "furnished".' *Obviously linen isn't included.* 'Idiot.'

Frustrated by the lack of expected items, Gillian filled an electric kettle and swiped at the switch. She became mesmerised as the bubbles grew inside the glass container. Each increasing pocket of air struggled against the heat. Having burst through its anger, the sudden stillness of water had lost none of its heat, but had achieved its purpose.

Her emotions echoed those growing bubbles: her mind full of heat, and her heart ready to burst. But Gillian doubted she would ever be able to get rid of her anger enough to be useful to anyone.

It took her thirty-five minutes to unpack her suitcase of clothes, toiletries, torch with spare batteries. Esther insisted she needed these power-point adaptors. Sandy's donation, and phone charger. By the time the hour ticked over, she had half-heartedly wiped down the kitchen surfaces before depositing her meagre purchases: one knife, one fork, a soup spoon and a teaspoon, into a drawer, tucked a hand towel over the oven door handle, and found a spot for the frying pan, saucepan and a microwave-friendly bowl purchased at top price from a tiny shop in the passages of the Metro.

A spare set of underclothes, and a hand-towel remained in her cabin bag under a green fleecy top. Although the cupboards were bare of food, a Welcome Pack provided coffee and sugar sachets, tea bags and a container of long-life milk.

With a cup of tea in her one and only mug, she wandered back to the bedroom. She stood glaring at the bare mattress, sipping tea, wondering if things would ever go her way.

Sleep, I need sleep. Good luck with that. *It's summer, I don't need a blanket.* No but the room is cool. *Maybe the towel from the wardrobe will do. Nup. Too small.* What then? *I don't know. Things aren't too bad really, I'll just ...*

Gillian returned to the main room, slumped onto the couch, ran her finger along the neat stitching.

'You're right, things could be worse.' She tucked her feet onto the couch, hunched over her knees, stared at the laces of her sneakers. *You chose to be here.* Yeah, I know. But ... *but what?* It was supposed to be easier. *How?* I don't know!

After placing the half-empty cup on the floor, she rolled onto her stomach, nose against the cold leather, left arm reaching the floor. As she sucked in air through the corner of her mouth, saliva dribbled out. She sat up quickly, wiped the moisture from the leather with her forearm. *I've got to get some sleep.*

Gillian eyed the curtains. *They'll have to do.* She placed a chair next to the sitting room's window and stepped up onto it. 'Careful.'

She lifted the curtain rod off its bracket and angled it towards the floor. The dust danced off the heavy curtain as it ran off the rod. Coughing, she dispersed the dust by flapping it away from her face. 'Jeez, enough of that.'

She ripped the plastic from her new pillow and tossed the plastic onto the floor and inspected the pillow. 'Sorry, no pretty new dress for you.' After removing her sneakers and wrapped in the curtain, Gillian curled up on the bed and slept.

At four am she woke. Her bra dragged across her left breast and her jeans felt two sizes too small. As she rolled onto her back her earring caught in the raised pattern of the curtain material. 'Ow.' She removed both earrings and pushed the curtain to the floor.

Wriggling to the edge of the bed, Gillian stood. Her eyelids rasped against her eyes as if they'd been playing in a sandpit. Her dry throat threatened to cough. She released the clip of her bra and rubbed her hands across her breasts. Shower.

After standing under a torrent for several minutes, Gillian stepped out onto the bath mat, wiped her body, wrapped her wet hair in yesterday's t-shirt and went into the bedroom for her pyjamas.

For the next four days she stayed in bed until after eleven am – awake, but not wanting to move from the enveloping security of the curtain. Thoughts of up-coming miserable years, alone and afraid, encircled her efforts to empty her memory. When her bladder demanded release, she left her cocoon and sat for longer than necessary on the toilet, staring at the almost-invisible pattern on the tiles, wondering if they came in another colour but white. Sometimes, in those days of anxiety, she returned to the bedroom before remembering to wash her hands.

Between drinking coffee and staring out the window, Gillian's short mornings turned to afternoons.

Venturing out of her flat late in the afternoon, she'd watch her sneakers plop along the path, dodging chewing gum or dog droppings, only looking up when reaching a roadside curb. She called into fast-food shops where pointing achieved purchase, stopped at a bakery and bought bread without having to communicate, and selected chocolate bars from tiny cubicles where owners grumbled about credit cards.

She ate leftover pizza for breakfast, dried crusts without butter for lunch, donuts with jam at three pm, and sugar in all forms whenever her hands needed something to do.

In the long evenings, Gillian opened her laptop and watched the screen bring Sienna and Patrick to life. Forty seconds of a memory flipped open, then scurried away to allow another to fill the screen. She turned her memories into jigsaw puzzles and ignored tears as each piece added another dimension to her heartache.

Well after midnight, emotionally exhausted, she crawled into bed, only removing her socks when her feet became unbearably hot. Tomorrow, she promised. Tomorrow I'll do something useful.

Gillian had come to this European hide-away to begin the process of recovery without people constantly watching for signs of despair, or offering impossible solutions. However, after four days of virtual seclusion in the fourth-story flat, followed by a day of stubborn guilt, Gillian realised healing would have to start with action.

She cleared away the empty wrappers (KitKats, gummy bears, potato crisps, Lindt chocolate, licorice) and containers that had held take-away food, burgers and thick-shakes scattered in the bedroom and lounge room. Underwear and t-shirts piled in the corner of the bathroom had to be washed. The sink remained relatively empty, but only because of the limited selection of utensils. The lack of ants, considering the crumbs on the kitchen floor, surprised Gillian. In her Perth kitchen they'd be marching in with enough numbers for a battalion or three. Now she had the rest of the day to stock up on food. And bed linen.

Gillian set out for the ten-minute walk to Prosek's shopping centre alongside the train station. She passed few people on the way. Two women chatted happily as they gazed through the misty glass window of a furniture shop. Cars, small trucks and the occasional bus whizzed along the busy road. After negotiating the traffic lights and the increased foot traffic, Gillian decided she'd see where the path through the park led.

She strolled for twenty minutes, enjoying the solitude, scrutinizing the plants and trees. She watched a long line of school children being herded towards the Metro. Further along, three mothers chatted as they kept one eye on the sand-covered children in a play area. Her heartstrings twanged, so she hurried on.

Removing her cardigan, Gillian turned and headed back the way she had come, her mind now writing a shopping list. Breakfast needed to be more than coffee, and she'd eaten the last of the Welcome Pack's biscuits. Bread, butter, cheese, some canned tuna. Vegies, fruit, milk; the fresh sort.

Inside the small supermarket, bread of all shapes and sizes: savoury, sweet, iced, some topped with fruit, smelt delicious. Gillian bagged several eye-catchers along with a sugary, jam-filled donut. She filled separate thin plastic bags with several carrots, three tomatoes and two oranges.

'Butter?' Gillian lifted a packet with a stylized cow on its silvery covering. 'This must be butter.' She turned and spoke to a woman pushing a trolley full of cartons. 'Excuse me, is this butter?'

'Cena je na skříňce.' (The price is on the cabinet.)

'Sorry, English.' Gillian spoke louder and slower, 'Is it butter?'

'Ten modrý je se slevou.' (The one on special is the blue packet.)

Gillian put the packet in her trolley. 'Thanks. I guess I'll risk it.'

The woman rolled her eyes as she shoved the carton-loaded trolley forward.

Gillian joined the queue at the check-out, browsed the magazines, and smiled at recognising some chocolate bars. She chose one and placed it on the counter and added her groceries.

'Nemáte to zvážené,' the person at the register said.

'English,' Gillian said. She pushed the plastic bags closer to the cashier who picked up the one with carrots and spoke again, 'Nemáte to zvážené.' (You haven't got these weighed.)

She pointed towards the fruit and vegetable section. 'Támhle.' Grabbing up the bag of carrots, she thrust them towards Gillian. 'Musíte to zvážit.' (You have to weigh them.)

'Dělejte,' (Hurry up,) said the customer behind Gillian. 'Ty turisti jsou všichni stejný.' (You tourists are all the same.)

Gillian glanced from the cashier to the customer. 'Is there a bag size or something? I did get them from over there.'

The other customer held up a bag of apples to the cashier. 'Tady. Tyhle jsou moje. Jí to bude trvat celý den.' (Here do mine. She's going to take all day.)

'I was here first,' Gillian said, moving a box of tissues to the front of her pile of groceries.

The cashier reached under the counter, grabbed a basket and started putting Gillian's selection into it. 'Můžete se vrátit, až si je zvážíte.' (You can come back when you've weighed them.)

'Hey! I want them.'

'Vezměte si to a pak se vraťte.' (Take them. Come back.)

Anger bubbled. The other customer invaded Gillian's space, trying to make room closer to the cashier. Gillian leaned into the knobby shoulder, refusing to move.

'Do you think I can't pay?' She opened her purse and took out her credit card. She waved it at the cashier, then towards the other customer who had spread her shopping along the counter.

'Vemte si to. Zvažte si ovoce a pak Vám to můžu spočítat.' (Take this. Get the fruit weighed, then I'll attend to you.) The cashier held the filled basket out to Gillian. 'Vemte si to. Nemůžu to vzít dokud to není zvážené.' (Take it. I can't ring it through until it is weighed.)

Gillian took the heavy basket. She breathed slowly, trying to ease the threatening blast of useless swearing.

The other customer pushed past Gillian. 'Uhněte. Spěchám.' (Move aside. I'm in a hurry.) Another customer joined the queue. He mumbled something. The cashier mumbled in reply. The unfamiliar words merged. Gillian placed the basket down, ran her hand over her chin; flicked her hair away from her face. Should I return the items to the shelf, no, bugger them, I'll leave it here. They can deal with it.

'Uhněte z cesty.'

Gillian had no idea what the teenager said, but she didn't like his tone.

'All I want is something to eat. Is that a crime? I can pay. Surely you want my money.'

'Blbá krávo.' (Stupid bitch.)

Frustration overrode her anger. A feeling of inadequacy struck. *I'm so stupid I can't even buy food.* She leaned against the counter, looked out into the street. The sun shone, oblivious to her predicament.

'Do you need help?'

Gillian sucked up the panic in her throat and turned towards the words she could understand. A middle-aged woman peeked out from under a flowery soft-brimmed hat.

'Please. I'm at my wit's end. Just want to buy these. The cashier wouldn't take my money.'

A slight chuckle preceded the woman's next words. 'No, it isn't that. You have to get your vegetables priced before you get to the cashier.'

'Really? Where? There isn't another spot.'

'Take your basket. Follow me.'

Once at the fruit and vegetable section, the woman showed Gillian where to weigh and price her items. Gillian had seen customers weighing their fruit; she thought they were just being pedantic.

'Thank you so much. You've just saved me from starvation.'

The woman laughed heartily. 'I'm sure someone would have saved you; eventually. Most young people speak English, but not so many are here at this time of the day. The shop assistants seem reluctant to speak even the small amount of English they may know.' She tapped Gillian's arm. 'We're not so bad. Just takes us a while to warm to strangers.'

'Thank you. Hopefully I'll make it through the check-out this time. Thanks again.'

'Není zač.' And the woman walked away.

Sounds friendly. I wonder what it means.

The cashier glared at Gillian in between each beep of the machine. 'To nebylo těžké, že?' (That wasn't hard, was it?)

'Still only English.' She tapped her card on the machine, gathered her groceries and left the cashier and the next customer chattering away. No doubt, talking about ignorant foreigners.

She had to stop several times on the way back to her flat. The thin plastic handles dug into her hands. One bag threatened to spill its contents, but Gillian spotted the split and saved a can of baked beans from becoming roadkill.

The few steps to the foyer looked like Mount Everest so Gillian sat on the bench in the common area. She heard the elderly woman from the first floor approaching as the wheels of her shopping trolley announced her arrival.

Squeak, squeak, squeak.

The woman smiled.

Squeak, squeak, squeak.

I should get one of those.

The woman and her squeaky wheel kept going.

Squeak, squeak, squeak.

Except, that would drive me insane.

Gillian put the can of baked beans into the cupboard. 'Lunch, then the city.'

She opened the drawer and took out the knife, spread butter on a crusty bun and added a slice of tomato. 'Black pepper. Must write a list.' She took a bite. 'Yeah, s'pose it's okay.' Took another bite and chewed slowly. 'And must stop talking to myself.' Another bite.

After washing the knife, she held it up to the light. 'A lonely, one and only, knife. How low have I sunk that I have one solitary knife.' She placed the knife on the kitchen bench and spun it around, waited until it stopped, and spun it around again. 'Lonely Knife.' She pushed at it. It whizzed across the counter and crashed to the floor. Gillian sat down beside it, leaned back against the fridge, stared at the knife, considered its plainness, then its usefulness.

She picked it up and ran her finger down the dull blade. 'Ineffective Knife.' It took her three attempts to balance it on her bent knee. She watched it wobble, then settle. She sneezed and it fell to the floor. 'Have to keep trying.' She placed it back on her knee.

Gillian recalled her morning. A cloud of hopelessness enfolded her. She collapsed into a ball of malfunction. One twitching eye and the shallow rise of her chest the only detection of life.

None of the few shops in the centre had bed linen. *Failure.*

The newsagent didn't have any English newspapers. *Failure.*

She spotted Marie Claire and Cosmopolitan, but only the titles were in English. *Failure.*

Then the saga with the veggies.

'Total idiot. Complete failure,' she told the knife.

Her hand shook as she took the knife from her knee and ran a finger over the blade again. She placed it across her chest with the end of the blade poking into her palm.

The cool of the tiles seeped through her jeans and into her skin. Her back ached from arching uncomfortably against the fridge.

She thought of her home in Perth. *Our home. Patrick's home. Sienna's home. Now there are strangers sleeping in our bed, sitting at our table, snipping off Thyme and Basil from our garden.* ˍ

She balanced the knife on her knee again. *Balance. Balance.*

'I can't ... Patrick, help me.'

She grabbed the knife. 'Damn you,' she said and tossed it into the air. It landed in the sink, clattering against the stainless steel. She covered her ears; put her head on her knees. Somewhere in the distance a siren sounded. *Perhaps they're coming to rescue me.*

The ensuing silence scared Gillian. It was as if she was in a bubble. Nothing seemed real. Everything outside the bubble didn't relate. The torture of the vacuum reached into every organ.

She grabbed the handle of a drawer and eased herself up. Her legs behaved like her grandmother's – useless, withered; now dead.

'Bed, I'll go to bed.'

Thankfully, unconsciousness came quickly. Waking at midnight with the calmness of pleasant dreams where nothing particular happened and instantly disappeared beyond remembering, Gillian slid her feet back under the curtain and fell asleep again.

At six am she rose, turned on the radio, almost skipped to the shower. As she shampooed the tangle of her hair, she considered the change from failure to positivity. It couldn't just be a good night's sleep, could it? This morning something felt different. A lightness. A click of some switch.

She stepped out of the shower, towelled vigourously, and grinned into the mirror. 'I'll take it. Whatever it is, whatever has changed, I'll take it.'

Slices of cheese on heavily buttered bread probably ran straight to her arteries, but she wasn't cholesterol counting as she tucked into her early morning breakfast.

Gillian decided she had ignored household duties long enough. The kitchen floor needed to be swept, and the frying pan needed to be scrubbed – the crunchy bits of bacon, stuck to the rim of the frying pan, were no longer edible. *But first, I'll finish my tea.*

Picking up the notebook Esther had given her; she once again recalled her sister's suggestion of keeping notes.

'Won't you be sightseeing? All that history. Gorgeous castles,' Esther had enthused.

'S'pose. But I'll use my camera. Take photos.'

'You should record how you feel about the places. You can get pictures on the internet.'

'My feelings are pretty much … you know, all over the place.'

'Anyway, keep a record. It'll give you something to do.'

Gillian flicked open the notebook. "Gillian Catherine Middleton" she'd written. That was the only legible entry. Biro scribblings could hardly record her bungee-jumping feelings.

After finding a pen in the bottom of her handbag, she wrote: another knife, cutlery, bowl. *I'm sick of sleeping under a curtain.* Sheets. Doona. Pillowcase. *Um, I wonder if anyone has vegemite.* Vegemite, peanut paste, more food, she added to the list. *Ah! I'll shop via the internet. Won't have to go out.* Don't you dare. *Why not?* Brooding. Lonely. *So.* Just go out. *Yeah, I should.* 'I wonder how early the shops open.'

Travelling on the Metro had become easier, and the repetitiveness triggered familiarity. This morning, commuters remained solitary, while Gillian tried to guess when the travelling statues, most of them with their attention firmly on a mobile, would suddenly spring to life and alight.

After returning from a few hours in the city Gillian leaned her new shopping trolley against the kitchen counter and unloaded her purchases. Moving through the city, trailing the trolley like an old person, had been embarrassing, but it would've been impossible to carry the queen-sized Doona, sheets and towels as well as the dozen other items now cluttering the benchtop. Grannies have shopping trolleys. Gillian wasn't ready to apply for the pension just yet.

She unwrapped the bed linen and carried it through to the bedroom. The curtain can go back up.

After dropping the sheets on the bed and the Doona on the floor, Gillian turned to put the new pillowcase on the bedside cabinet.

Oh, my gosh! She grabbed the silver-framed photo and kissed it. *I'm so, so sorry.* She sat on the bed hugging Patrick and Sienna to her chest as she rocked with small quick movements.

How could I? I'm so sorry.

Gillian realised she'd spent the morning without thinking of her loved ones.

How could I?

She ran her finger over Patrick's head and let it sit over his ear. She loved that ear.

He had teased her for her flat ears. 'How can you hear properly?' he'd asked. 'Look at mine. Huge. All the better to hear you with.'

She laughed, pushed aside his dark hair and peered into his ear. 'Mm, daylight.'

'That, my dear, is how I can think so clearly. Plenty of space for original thoughts.'

She had loved listening to his quirky composition expertly played on his upright piano. He'd convert well-known pop tunes into marches, marches into lullabies, lullabies into pop music. She'd waltz around the room partnering a cushion as he played Strauss' Blue Danube, changing tempo to try and catch her out.

They'd dreamed of three, maybe four, children. 'A quartet,' he said. 'We'll play gigs together, stun the audience.'

'Can I be in the quartet?'

'Technically, no. In fact, we'll be a quintet. Four kids and me.'

'And me, playing the triangle, will make six.'

But they didn't make a family of six. Years came and went. They didn't make a family of three either. They watered down their dreams, worked hard and achieved much: mortgage free, two new cars, boutique clothes and a new black lacquered piano.

Gillian spoilt her friends' babies, said how nice it was to hand over a grizzly child to its parent, and loved Patrick a little more to make up for being a family of two.

Patrick volunteered at a local youth centre, umpired an under-eight footy team and went fishing with two dads and five kids in the school holidays. He regularly told Gillian a family of "you and me" was perfect.

When Gillian turned thirty-five, they decided the stork had lost their address and they'd be better off with a puppy.

But while they were deciding if they'd rather a boisterous hound or a tiny indoor dog, the stork obtained a new road map.

After a perfectly ordinary day in the garden, a microwaved dinner and satisfying, but no bells-and-whistle sex, Sienna was conceived.

Sienna's smile shone through the glass of the photo and pierced Gillian's misery, shattering it into happy memories. She remembered so clearly the moment they'd become a family of three.

Patrick had groaned with relief as he cut the umbilical cord. He hugged a bemused nurse before having to sit down to let adrenalin realign in his veins.

It had been a relatively straight-forward birth, particularly pleasing for Gillian; especially after warnings from concerned friends about the dangers of being an older first-time mum. With her newborn on her chest, Gillian crooned, saying words of wonder; words she'd given up thinking would be in her vocabulary.

Never for one moment did she plan to return to work. Someone else could manage the office; keep the staff on their toes. The stationery wholesaler would have to find another Product Manager.

Patrick and Gillian no longer talked of terriers and dachshunds, but again day-dreamed about a quartet.

'Perhaps a drummer next time,' Patrick said as he extolled the piano-playing quality of Sienna's long fingers.

Gillian wrapped her arms around the photo and lay back on the bed. She closed her eyes and remembered the Saturday afternoon Patrick had offered to take Sienna to the swings at a local park.

'You stay,' he said to Gillian. 'We'll get out of your hair for an hour. Go take a bath. Read a book. God knows you can do with a break.'

No! She opened her eyes and stared at their photographic smiles, driving away the rest of that tragic day. Then closing her eyes again, she recalled the song Patrick had written for Sienna. There were few lyrics, mostly just a melody, suitable for a piano with violin accompaniment. *For the Love of Sienna* calmed her, and by the end of the chorus, where those few lyrics promised "forever," she fell asleep.

The day turned cold and Gillian woke from the nap, shivering. She sat up quickly, rubbing a sore spot in her shoulder where the corner of the photo frame had dug in.

'I need coffee. Fresh air.' She placed the frame back on the bedside cabinet and stood for a moment taking in Patrick's long fingers draped around Sienna's tiny shoulder.

With a mug full of hot coffee, Gillian went down in the lift and out into the blustery wind. She needlessly checked her letterbox, then settled on the bench in the common area oblivious to the wind trying to dislodge her scarf. She placed the mug on the seat and tugged the sleeves of her jacket down.

The squeaky wheel of her neighbour approached. Gillian turned and watched as the elderly woman struggled against the wind.

'Hello, Dobree daan,' Gillian said, her Australian accent highlighting the newness of her pronunciation.

The woman stopped next to the bench. 'Dobrý den. Proč jste tady v tom větru?' (Why are you out in this wind?)

Not knowing if yes or no would be the correct answer, Gillian pursed her lips and shrugged.

'Nastydnete.' (You will catch cold.) Then the woman pointed to the mug of coffee. 'Tohle Vám také vystydne.' (It, too, will get cold.)

Gillian picked up the mug and looked away from the woman. She realised they couldn't converse, and hoped the woman would leave, but the old woman pulled her trolley forward and lowered herself beside Gillian.

'Je zima na to, že je duben.' (It's a cold day for April.)

Gillian moved away from the woman. She tucked her chin under the folds of her scarf and with her free hand rubbed her leg.

'Jste také sama, jako já?' (You are alone like me?) the woman asked.

Gillian didn't turn towards the question.

'Nemáte rodinu?' (You don't have a family?) The woman tapped Gillian's arm. The coffee wobbled in the cup as Gillian jumped. She moved a little further along the bench.

'Jmenuji je Hana. Jak se jmenujete Vy?' (My name is Hana. What is your name? You?) The woman pointed to her chest. 'Hana.'

'Hana, okay. Nice to meet you, Hana,' Gillian said. She looked towards the lift, hoping the woman would get the hint.

Hana pointed at Gillian, repeated her question. 'Jak se jmenujete?'

Gillian gulped down another mouthful of coffee before giving in. 'Gillian.'

'Gillian.' Hana sounded out the name. 'Gillian, máte děti?' (Do you have any children?)

'Sorry.' Gillian looked away again.

Hana tapped Gillian's knee. When Gillian glanced back, Hana cradled her arms and rocked them as if she held a baby.

Gillian put the mug on the ground, opened her handbag and pulled out her phone. Flipping it open to her favourite one of Sienna as a two-year-old, she said, 'Sienna.'

Hana leaned over and looked at the photo. 'Je moc hezká. A kde je?' (Lovely. Where is she?)

In the next photo Patrick's face peeked out from behind Sienna dressed in a fairy costume.

'Manžel?' (Husband?) Hana asked as she pointed to Patrick.

Gillian assumed, held out her left hand and pointed to her rings.

'Ah.' Hana held up her bare hand. 'Můj manžel zemřel. A prsten je teď moc malý.' (My husband died. My ring is too small now.) She touched the photo and raised her eyebrows in question. 'Kde jsou?' (Where are they?)

Gillian moved the phone away from Hana, wanting to stop the speculated questions. She knew what the woman was asking. She didn't need to get out her phrasebook to know Hana was wondering why a married woman, a mother of a small child, would be sitting in the biting wind on her own. Placing the phone back in her handbag, she stood and lifted the mug from the ground. She forced a smile at Hana and walked towards the stairs. If she was quick, she could take the stairs and avoid having to travel in the lift with this nosy neighbour.

'Gillian,' Hana called. 'Je to krásná holčička.' (She is a beautiful little girl.)

Suffering an evening of impossible wishes, Gillian closed down the array of stored photographs, turned off her laptop, and with expectations of another restless night, went to bed. Sleep came amid moist eyes and a longing heart, but morning arrived with a fresh mood of determination.

With the tourist leaflets tucked into the side of her bag, Gillian set out early, keen to tick off some of the "must-see" attractions of Prague.

Leaving the lift, Gillian took a deep breath. The morning brewed cool but clear, ideal for walking. She spotted Hana leaning against the wall of letterboxes. Oh no, surely she hasn't been waiting for me.

'Ahoj. Ahoj, Gillian.' Hana reached into her shopping trolley. 'Doufala jsem, že se dnes potkáme.' (I hoped you would come out today.) 'No, pojďte a podívejte se na mého syna.' (Come, look at my son.)

Gillian re-aligned her handbag and slowed her step. This is getting difficult, she thought. 'Hello, Hana. How are you?'

Hana took hold of Gillian's arm and encouraged her towards the bench. She sat in the middle of the seat and motioned for Gillian to sit beside her.

'Já mám také dítě. Podívej.' (I, too, have a child. Look.) She held out an elaborate frame with a picture of a young couple on their wedding day.

'Is that you?' Gillian pointed to the bride and then to Hana.

Hana laughed, shook her head. 'Ne, ne. To je manželka mého syna.' (No, no. This is my son's wife.)

Gillian frowned, tipped her head and shrugged with question. 'Who?'

'Můj syn. Jeho svatební den.' (My son. On his wedding day.) 'Pavel.' She tapped on the photo of the groom, mimed a pregnant stomach, grinned so broadly Gillian could see a missing tooth, then Hana pointed to her chest.

'Oh, is that your son? How nice. Does he live in Prague?'

'Praha? Nevím, na co se mě ptáte.' (I don't know what you are asking.)

Gillian took the picture and pointed to the dress, grinned excessively while nodding. 'Lovely.'

'Krásné.' (Beautiful.)

Conversation stopped. Hana mumbled to her photo. Gillian fiddled with the zip on her bag, struggling with the barrier of language. She wanted to leave, but Hana obviously expected company. She tried again, 'Where is Pavel?' Gillian held out her hand, imitated a handshake. 'Pleased to meet you, Pavel?'

'Pavel?' Hana queried. 'Nemůžete ho poznat. Je mrtvý.' (You can't meet my son. He is dead.) She pretended to shoot herself and then leaned against Gillian with her eyes closed.

'Oh my goodness. Was he shot? Was it suicide?'

Hana straightened, stroked her chin. Her smile held memories.

Gillian placed her hand on Hana's knee. 'I'm so sorry. It isn't fair to lose a child.'

Covering Gillian's hand with her own, Hana said, 'Bolest se zmírňuje, ale vzpomínky tu jsou pořád. A my musíme žít dál.' (Pain diminishes, but memories never go. We must keep living.) Making soft noises of effort, she eased to her feet. 'Promluvíme si jindy.' (We will talk another day.)

Gillian stood and smiled broadly at Hana. 'Thanks, Hana. Have a good day. Dobrý den. Ahoj.' She hoped her scant Czech was appropriate.

Gillian watched Hana walk away using her shopping trolley as support. She groaned softly as she battled with the few steps near the lift. Just as Gillian stood, ready to offer support, Hana negotiated the steps, turned and waved. As the lift door closed, it struck home that this elderly woman had survived the loss of a child, probably endured many difficult years, but still remained cheerful, and determinedly friendly to a foreigner. Gillian stood for several minutes, contemplating if she would, could, be so cheerful when she became a senior.

Deciding she should make an effort to enjoy her new surroundings, she checked her bag for the tourist leaflets and headed for the Metro.

Alighting at Muzeum she watched the umbrellas and tourist guides' flags bobble above the heads of their obedient followers. Mobile phones made happy snaps an easy action, and Gillian marvelled at modern communication. In a few seconds, selfies would be seen on the other side of the world.

She took her mobile phone out of her pocket and snapped holidaymakers as they gathered around the large statue at the top of Wenceslas Square. When the tourists moved away, Gillian, with the help of a translator app, read the inscription on the base of the statue: St Wenceslas, Leader of the Czech Lands, our Prince, do not let us die nor those yet to come.

She knew nothing of Czech history, but assumed the inhabitants would have seen many wars, just like all ancient countries; invaded from the north, south, east and west. How horrible.

"Do not let us die", she read again. She ran her forefinger across the cold stone of the statues' base and thought of Sienna. *I would've walked on molten lava through the jaws of hell to save you.* She remembered the tubes trying to bring life to a broken body and the constant beeping hiding the background hideous silence. The doctors and nurses did their best, but they could do nothing except let Sienna die. "Do not let us die, nor those yet to come". The words pulsed across her eyes. *Imagine,* she thought, *having your husband ... your sons ... leave for war. While you could do nothing. Horrific.*

Dawdling away from the horse and its rider, Gillian scanned the photo she'd taken of the statue. In the background, behind the youthful tourists, a mother and child stood. The mother had her hand on the child's shoulder. *That should be me,* Gillian thought. *That should be Sienna and me.* She stabbed at the keys and deleted the photo.

As she walked down the slope and into the centre of the city square, Gillian re-assessed her day. The sun played hide and seek behind the clouds, casting shadows across the cobblestones. But the brief spots of sunshine at least brought promise. I need "spots of sunshine" in all my days. Otherwise? She didn't want to put options into words.

She decided to have a day of cheerfulness. She would pretend Patrick and Sienna had reached the playground.

Sienna would slip down the slide; ride on the yellow and red swings. She'd lose her breath as she begged her father to push her even higher. Higher, Daddy, higher.

When she tired of that game, Patrick would grasp his daughter's waist and hold her up as she made her way across the monkey bars. After Sienna reached the other side Patrick would tickle his child and they'd fall onto the ground poking each other, laughing with companionship.

Mellowed by this illusion, Gillian stared at her reflection in H&M's window. *Yes*, she thought, *I'll go shopping, but first, coffee, and a huge slice of cake.*

Late in the afternoon Gillian stepped from the Metro, up the stairs, out into the street towards her flat.

Gillian spotted Hana as she approached the lift. Oh no, not again. It's so difficult.

Hana waved. 'Gillian, Ahoj. Gillian. Pojd'te, prosím. Musím Vám něco říct.' (Please come. I have to tell you something.)

While she appreciated the older woman's friendliness, Gillian found it unrealistic to continue to mime their conversations. She stopped and put her parcels down. 'Hi, Hana.' Gillian smiled, nodded, indicating pleasure in their meeting.

'Koupila sis něco hezkého na sebe?' (Did you buy something nice for yourself?) Hana asked, pointing to the bags beside Gillian's feet.

'I indulged in make-believe today. Stupid thing to do. But I needed a day without feeling so bloody miserable.'

Hana grinned as Gillian started talking, then frowned when she slowed her words and spoke in a sad tone. 'Nebyl to hezký den?' (Wasn't it a happy day?)

'Would you like to see what I've wasted my money on? Don't know what I'll do with them. Do you have a grandchild?' Gillian lifted one bag onto her knee. 'God, I'm so stupid!' Lifting out a Pinocchio puppet, she held it towards Hana. 'Would you like it?'

Hana took the puppet and made it dance. 'Podívejte Pinocchio tancuje.' (Look, Pinocchio is dancing.) She laughed, turned to Gillian and asked, 'Tančíte ráda?' (Do you like to dance?) Hana stood up and danced a few steps with the puppet jiggling in front of her. 'Pojďte, zatancujte, Gillian.' (Come, dance, Gillian.)

Removing the empty bag from her knee, Gillian stood. She took the puppet from Hana and made a complete mess of making him move. Hana took Gillian's hand and they made a trio of dancing partners. It was the first time in almost a year Gillian had laughed so heartily.

'Staré dámy by neměly tančit.' (Old ladies shouldn't dance.) Hana plopped down on the bench clapping her hands at Gillian who tried to make the puppet bow. She gave up and let Pinocchio drop back into the bag. With Hana still clapping, Gillian curtsied then sat down beside the old woman.

'I haven't danced for ages. If you call that dancing. Fancy dancing in the street. Good thing there's no one else around.'

Hana placed her hand on Gillian's knee. 'Čekala jsem na Vás. Moje vnučka přijede na návštěvu. Řekla, že bychom si mohly dát odpoledne čaj. Pak můžeme mluvit.' Hana delved into her pocket and pulled out a piece of paper. 'Ona mluví anglicky.'(She speaks English.)

Gillian shook her head slowly. 'Nup. I can't read Czech either.'

'Podívejte, Elena mi řekla co mám napsat.' (Look, Elena told me what to write.) Hana held out the paper.

Taking the paper, Gillian saw child-like writing in English.

Hana pointed. 'Přečtěte si to. Pochopíte na co se chci zeptat.' (You read it. It will tell you what I want to ask.)

I am to visit my grandmother on this Saturday. She would like us to meet. Elena. 'Oh, your granddaughter. Elena. Right. Yes. How old?'

Hana beamed. 'Elena přijede v sobotu a zůstane tu se mnou dva dny.' (Elena is coming on Saturday. She'll stay one night with me.)

'Elena. Okay.' Gillian read the note again.' Saturday. Tomorrow. Okay. Bloody hell this is awkward. Hope she's not just a little kid. How old? Elena? Damn.'

Hana kept smiling, nodding and repeating her granddaughter's name.

'Right, I'm going. I guess I'll see you ...' Gillian pointed to the paper. 'When Elena visits.'

'Ano, Ano. Elena. Elena.' Hana indicated that Gillian should keep the paper. 'Naobědváme se u mě doma. Vyzvedneme Vás. Až přijede Elena.' (We have lunch at my house. We will come and get you. When Elena comes.)

'Bye, Hana. Thanks for the dance.' Gillian picked up Pinocchio, the other two bags and headed towards the lift. 'You going up, too?'

Hana followed Gillian. They waited silently for the lift. Gillian juggled her bags while Hana's head bobbed as if she was agreeing to continuing thoughts.

In a light-hearted mood, and with Pinocchio grinning from top of the bag, Gillian strode into her unit. Her keys clacked into the planter; she placed her shopping on the kitchen bench. Opening the curtains, she smiled towards the pedestrians, watched the passing parade for several minutes before turning on her laptop.

Gillian now checked her emails most days, returning a few messages with brief accounts of her day. She avoided exposing her dark moments, not wanting to record her unstable feelings, so simply explained the sights, sounds and differences of a foreign country.

Esther enquired about practical matters. Ever the older sister, Gillian thought, as she pondered Esther's latest diatribe on the rental market in Perth, which might affect Gillian if her tenants moved on.

Sandy sent jokes: banal, inappropriate jokes, which Gillian supposed was an attempt to disregard anything serious.

Opening Sandy's email headed MEN! Gillian grinned and thought of her friend's often expressed opinion on the opposite sex. 'A smorgasbord is more appealing than a set menu, and I like to try all the dishes.' Sandy never understood the attraction of marriage. 'Boring! Must be bloody boring,' she said when Gillian had announced her fifth wedding anniversary.

Sandy's email started out with:

Have you tried out any of those Czech men? Should I catch the next flight over? Come on, Gilly, let me know ASAP!!!!!

Gillian chuckled as she hit reply. Nup. Not likely. And you needn't bother to ask again, she typed, then paused, deleted her typing, deciding against answering her crazy friend in favour of making dinner.

She nibbled on toast between slurping through canned soup. *Evenings are the worst*, she thought. *I'd hire a telly, but I couldn't understand the programs.*

As the evening dragged on, she gave up on the books from the bookstore as trite rubbish, downloaded three novels and only read two chapters of each. Life depicted in fiction seemed to be either about the rich and famous who had everything, or some poor soul who had nothing. Each book solved all problems by the last chapter. Happy Ever After was something Gillian knew didn't happen in real life.

She closed her laptop and listened to outside noises. The soft humming of traffic in the main road a block away meant people had somewhere to go, something to do or someone to visit. *I have nothing to do, nowhere to go, no one who wants to see me.*

A door slammed somewhere in the building.

Uh, my choice. I wanted to be alone.

Footsteps approached; went past.

At least here I have no one to pity me.

The lift door opened; closed.

But I still pity myself.

That thought hit like a slap; a sharp blast on her forehead, or across the back of her head. Any minute now her head would cave in.

She ran her fingers through her hair, gripped the ends in her right hand and let her other hand fall to her knee. The jagged edges of her fingernails and torn cuticles exposed lonely hours when she couldn't bear to think of the future.

Gillian walked to the window and stood where she could glimpse the main road and watch the traffic. All going somewhere; going away from where they've been. She remembered the day she'd purchased her flight. One way, she'd insisted.

Have you run away forever? Maybe. *Could you really leave Perth?* Possibly. *Stay here?* No, I don't see it as being my forever place. *Then what?* I've only just arrived. *Mm. So what are you going to do ... tomorrow, and the days after that?* I don't have a plan. *Hadn't you better start one?* Definitely not. *I came to get away from plans.* Yes, but other people's plans for you. *True.* Then what?

The streetlights shone; she could see two men striding towards an intersection.

Don't know. Don't care if I never have a plan.

The men didn't wait for the green light.

Sounds like self-indulgence, self-pity.

A motorist blared his car horn.

Mm.

One man turned and gave the driver the international "get stuffed" signal.

A snort of a laugh escaped Gillian. *Maybe that's what I need to do. Show people "the finger." Tell them I'll do my grieving my way. In my own time. If I want to feel sorry for myself, that's what I'll bloody well do.* So, who exactly are you telling to get stuffed? *Everyone!*

Gillian remembered Esther comforting her on that life-shattering day. The police had rung Esther after delivering the shocking news to Gillian. Then in the following hours, which somehow became days, Esther's comfort included driving Gillian to the hospital, sitting through police interviews, holding her hand at the solicitors and seemingly being there every moment of each day.

Esther. Well, Esther could lose a leg and she'd be a Pollyanna over it. She'd have a replacement ordered by the time anyone noticed it was missing. Hang on, her husband died. Yeah, and she hardly missed a beat. Now that isn't fair. Guess not, but, he was older. Not a child. She lost her husband! Yeah, but, she knows about losing someone. Still no reason to expect me to be the same. No, but give her credit. Yeah, but she's not the only one who won't leave me be.

Gillian knew Esther had organised a roster for laundry and shopping. How else did clean clothes appear on her bed? How else did the fridge always contain fresh milk?

After those first weeks, Esther bullied Gillian into action. 'Here,' she'd say, 'You sweep, I'll water the pot plants.' Or, 'Let's go through this mail.' Or, 'Can you butter the bread, I'll find some tuna.'

Remembering her friends who had also fussed over her, Gillian struggled to reconcile those difficult days with her current situation where she could choose to engage in "deep and meaningful" contact or not.

Mira had rung every day for three weeks, except for Tuesday and Wednesdays when she'd arrived exactly at two o'clock and leave at two forty-five to do the school run. After clearing dishes, sweeping floors or picking up tissues, Mira always made a hot drink for Gillian and declared, 'Taxi duties. See you next time.'

Mira's phone calls petered out, but she still came Tuesdays and Wednesdays. She avoided mentioning Patrick or Sienna, and Gillian couldn't share her heartbreaking emotions with this gentle soul.

Anyway, Mia's only ever lost a dog. Since you've known her. She certainly doesn't do tragedy well. Perhaps because she's been hurt. Possibly.

Even so, I can't put my grief on Mira, Gillian decided. She'd end up in tears, and I'd be comforting her.

Sandy?

Despite her internal misery, Gillian chuckled. Sandy couldn't be serious for a moment. Try explaining loss of love to Sandy. She'd say, "Poor you. Move on". Not pity, just expectation that love shouldn't hurt so much.

Yeah, but Sandy is the one person who does call it as it is. True. *She's the one you can be truthful with.* Not so sure about that. *Why not, she'll deal with it.* Yeah, but putting my emotions into words isn't the easiest thing to do. *Why not?* Bloody hell, piss off.

With her playlist on so she wouldn't have to argue with her annoying conscience, Gillian had her second shower for the day, put on her pyjamas and prepared for bed.

However, her alter ego poked and prodded a little more.

Your friends are your support system. Don't need one. *Yeah, right!* Go away. *Not until you decide to be sensible about this.* What "this?" *Sharing.* Don't want to. Came here to stop sharing. *Stand up for yourself then. Use those size nine feet. Stand tall – figuratively.* That's total shit. It's okay to decide to stand up for oneself, but it's impossible when the pain hits. *They're only doing what they think's best.* Yeah, I know, but it's still shit. *Give it a go. Haven't you noticed you're in bloody beautiful Prague? For goodness sake, get out and see it while you can.*

Gillian gave in to that directive, found the pink notebook, the half dozen tourist leaflets from the souvenir shop and a pen.

'Right, let's make a list. Instead of just wandering, I'll do something decisive. How do I get to the castle? Where the hell is this Charles Bridge that bloke recommended?' She glanced through the leaflets. 'Ah, maybe I don't need Mr Google after all. And … I really do need to stop talking to myself.'

Late the next morning Gillian discovered a note protruding from under the front door. It read: *Arrive today. Elena. Můžeme vás pozvat na oběd?* With the help of her phrasebook, Gillian understood an invitation had been extended for lunch.

When she heard the metallic groan of the lift door as it opened, Gillian drank the last of her coffee and placed the mug on the bench. She hoped Hana and Elena wouldn't expect her to invite them in. She still only had one coffee mug, and yesterday she'd eaten the chocolate biscuits she'd purchased. In fact, her stomach rumbled, not used to being without food, junk food, corrected Gillian, for so long. She'd ignored breakfast, having only black tea.

She'd meant to get out of bed earlier, but because of another restless night she had tucked up her legs, pulled the Doona over her head and went back to sleep. After the initial panic on waking, she hurried through showering, dressed carefully, adding perfume for the first time since moving from the hotel.

A soft tapping, followed by a prolonged buzz of the doorbell made Gillian jump, despite her expectation. She picked up her handbag and went to the door.

'Hi, Ahoj,' Gillian said as she opened the door to Hana and a teenager.

'To je Elena.' (This is Elena.) Hana placed her hand on her granddaughter's arm.

'Počkej, babičko.' (Just a minute, Granny.) Elena turned to Gillian. 'Ahoj, it's nice to meet with you. Please excuse my grandmother, she's forgotten her manners.' Elena's braces showed behind her broad grin.

'To je moje vnučka,' (This is my granddaughter,) Hana said. 'Musíte přijít na oběd. Budeme moct mluvit pořádně. Elena umí anglicky velmi dobře. Má jedničky ze všech zkoušek. Ona s Vámi může mluvit. Řekne, co chci říct já Vám. (You must come to lunch. We will talk properly. Elena has learned English very well. Top marks in her exams. She can speak to you. Tell you what I want to say to you.) She nodded at Elena. 'Řekni jí to.' (You tell her.)

'Ano, babičko.' (Yes, Granny.) Elena took her grandmother's hand, but spoke to Gillian. 'Did you get our note? I hope she wrote the English as I told her. Can you come today?'

'I figured it out.' Gillian reached for her keys in the planter. 'I wasn't entirely sure if you meant lunch today, or some other time, but as you can see, I'm ready.' Gillian stepped back. 'Should I come with you now?'

'It is not too soon?' Elena asked. 'It can be tomorrow.'

Gillian shook her head. 'No. I don't plan my days. It'll be nice. We can go.'

During Gillian and Elena's conversation, Gillian sensed Hana watching their faces intently. She assumed Hana was looking for an immediate connection.

'Doufám, že máte ráda knedlíky,' Hana said as she watched Gillian lock the door.

'Hana says she hopes you like dumplings,' Elena said. 'She makes them for me every time I visit. Papa tells me he has eaten enough to last his life so we don't have them at home. Have you had dumplings since being here?'

Gillian stood aside for Hana to enter the lift. 'Yes, but I'm sure Hana's will be better. Home-made usually is.'

Hana poked Elena, asking quickly, 'Má ráda knedlíky?'

'Ano, babi, už se těší na ty tvoje.' (Yes, Granny, she's looking forward to having some of yours.)

The lift stopped at the first floor and Elena ushered Gillian towards Hana's flat. Letting Elena use the key, the elderly woman stood aside, nodding and smiling.

'Come in,' Elena said. As she opened the door, the smell of cooking greeted them.

'Vítejte u mě doma. Asi to vypadá podobně jako u Vás. Myslím, že většina z těchto bytů jsou stejné.'

Gillian smiled at Hana, then looked at Elena for translation.

'She said, welcome to her home. She thinks it's the same as every other house.'

'Thanks, Hana. Your home is much nicer than mine.' Gillian paused and let Elena repeat her words. 'I make do with very little.' As she removed her shoes and accepted slip-ons, Gillian absorbed the cosy atmosphere of the small hallway. An elaborately carved hallstand with a circular mirror filled one wall. A sun hat hung on one of the three porcelain knobs and a row of women's shoes stood neatly on the bottom shelf. 'I'm afraid I haven't any pretty things.'

Hana, relying on Elena's translation, proudly pointed out her mother's favourite cup and saucer, a tiny china dog, a tall crystal vase, and several family members in a variety of silver frames. While Elena explained who was who, Hana poured three glasses of ale. After offering Gillian a seat, Hana disappeared, with her beer, into the kitchen.

'Cheers,' Gillian said.

'Na zdraví.' Elena clinked her minute glass against Gillian's tall one. 'How long are you in Prague?'

'Nearly two weeks.'

'Where did you come from? Where is your home? Grandmother said she didn't know.'

'Ah, yes. Perth. That's Australia. On the west coast.'

'Australia is far. You are brave to come to here.'

Gillian debated her bravery, shrugged.

'Is it first time?' Elena asked.

'Yes. I must get out and see the sights. I have plenty of information.'

'Babi said you are married. Did work make you be here?'

Gillian's mind danced around answers. *Should she lie? Could she tell the truth to this teenager?* She drank half the glass of beer, wiped her hand across her damp lip, before answering. 'I was married. My husband and my daughter died in a car crash. I …' She took another mouthful of the amber liquid.

'I am sorry. You don't have to tell me of it.'

'It's still difficult.'

'I will check on babi.' Elena left her beer on the small table and darted out to the kitchen.

Gillian peered into one of the cabinets, counted vases, all decorated with roses, trying to slow her pounding pulse. 'I can do this,' she whispered. She listened to Hana and Elena talking, their tone low and questioning. Returning to a velvet chair next to a TV, Gillian sipped the last of her beer.

'Lunch is ready,' Elena called from the kitchen, then appeared around the dividing wall and repeated, 'Lunch is ready. You are to sit here.'

'Doufám, že máte hlad. Udělala jsem spoustu knedlíků. S vepřovým. Doufám, že máte ráda vepřové.' (I hope you're hungry. I've made many dumplings. There's pork. I hope you like pork.) Hana carried a large pot and placed it in the centre of the dining table. 'Eleno, zeptej se jí, jestli má ráda vepřové.'

Elena glanced at Gillian. 'Do you like pork?'

Gillian squeezed between the wall and the chair, sat down; nodded.

'Vezměte si talíř. A nandejte si sama,' Hana said.

'Take a plate. Help yourself,' Elena repeated.

Eating eased the awkwardness of a translated conversation. Between mouthfuls, they talked about Elena's visit, the people who used to live in Gillian's unit, the weather, and the way to make a perfect dumpling.

With a platter of cheese and a pot of brewing coffee on the embroidered tablecloth, Hana passed a cheese knife to Gillian. 'Máte ráda sýr? Eidam je můj oblíbený.' (Do you like cheese? There's my favourite; Edam.)

'Thanks. I'm too full.' Gillian waved away the knife.

'Tak kávu?' (Coffee, then?) Hana asked. 'Eleno, řekni jí, že ona potřebuje kávu.'

Elena chuckled and lifted the coffee pot. 'Babi says you need this.'

Gillian forced a laugh, held up her cup. 'I think I can fit in one cup.'

Elena filled the three cups, leaving no room for milk. Gillian inwardly shrugged, and sipped slowly.

'Jsem ráda, že jste dnes přišla,' (I'm glad you came today,) Hana said. 'Ráda bych se zeptala na manžela a dceru. Ty, na Vaší fotografii, kterou nosíte u sebe v kabelce. Elena mi řekla, že zemřeli. Je mi to moc líto. Je těžké pohřbít dítě. A manžela také. Já to vím. Sama jsem to prožila.' (I want to ask about your husband and daughter. The ones in your photograph you keep in your bag. Elena said they died. I am sorry. It is difficult to bury a child. A husband, too. I know, I have done both these things.) She patted Gillian's arm, looked down at her hands and nodded ever so slightly.

'What did she say?' Gillian asked Elena.

Elena glanced from her grandmother to Gillian and back again, avoiding Gillian's gaze as she answered. 'She said she's glad you came today.'

'But that wasn't all, was it?'

'No.'

'What did she say? Please tell me.'

'She said she was sorry you have lost your child. Her son, my uncle, died when he was twenty-eight. Her husband, many years ago now.'

Gillian sucked in a lung full of air, held it, then let it out slowly. 'Tell her, thanks.'

'Bude to lepší. Musíte se s tím vyrounat sama, ale nechte své přátele, aby Vám pomohli. Měla byste je nechat.'

Elena translated, looking at her grandmother, not at Gillian. 'She says, it does get easier. You have to work it out yourself, but don't shut out your friends. They can help. You have to let them.'

'That's why I'm here. In Prague. Trying to work it out. My sister is too … you know, she wants to help but …' Gillian shrugged, left the sentence unfinished.

'I have a sister,' Elena said. 'She always is trying to be the boss of me.'

'I guess they have their useful moments.'

'Co? Co povídáš?' (What? What are you saying?)

'Že máme obě panovačné sestry,' (We are agreeing we have bossy sisters,) Elena said.

Hana laughed. 'Máš štěstí, že máš sestru. Já mám jen Františka a Karla. Byl k ničemu, když jsme byli děti.' (You're lucky to have a sister. I only have Frederic and Karel. They were no use when we were children.)

The mood changed with Elena's translation and despite intermittent silences, they manage to amuse themselves for another hour. As she slipped her sandals back on, Gillian thanked Hana and Elena for their kindness.

'Měla byste zase přijít.' (You should come another time.) Hana held out a dish of left-overs.

'Thanks for that. I haven't exactly been eating properly.' Gillian took the tea-towel-wrapped dish carefully. 'Thanks.'

'Zkuste to a ať jsou Vaše vzpomínky šťastné. (Try and let your memories be happy ones.)

'You must let me have the recipe. Mira would love them.'

'Jednoho dne si dovolíte být opět šťastná.' (One day you will let yourself be happy again.)

'Thanks again. Perhaps I can shout you lunch at a café next time Elena's here.'

'Krásná, mladá dáma jako Vy, by měla být šťastná.' (A lovely young lady like you should be happy.)

'Bye, Hana.' Gillian looked passed Hana to Elena, who had remained away from the other women. 'Thanks, Elena. Nice to meet you. Thanks for translating. Must be difficult.'

'Ještě přijdete, ze ano. Eleno, zeptej se Gillian jestli mě znovu navštíví.' (You will come again, won't you? Elena, ask Gillian if she will visit again.)

Elena stepped forward, placed her arm around her grandmother's waist and looked pointedly at Gillian. 'I hope I didn't upset you by telling her about the car accident.'

'No, it's okay. I have to face up to it, maybe it'll get easier if I tell enough people. Anyway, that's fine, I wanted to tell her, but didn't know how.' She tipped her head as she added, 'You've been great.'

Hana frowned and asked, 'Je všechno v pořádku?' (Is everything all right?)

'Ano.'

' Zeptala ses, jestli mě ještě navštíví?'

Elena said softly, 'Babi asks if you will come another time. I hope you will. She likes you. Perhaps when I visit. I come in few weeks.'

'I don't know how long I'll be here, but, sure, let me know next time you come. I'd like that.'

'Přijde?' (Will she come?)

'Ano, babi, přijde znovu.' (Yes, Granny, she'll come again.) 'Ahoj, Gillian. See you then.'

'Bye, Elena. Goodbye, Hana.' She kissed Hana on one cheek, then the other as Hana turned her head.

'Děkuji, Gillian. Bud' k sobě laskavá.' (Thank you, Gillian. Be kind to yourself.)

Taking the stairs slowly, so as not to spill the gravy-covered dumplings, Gillian examined her emotions. Hana had lost a son and a husband, and she'd managed to become an old woman. She must have managed somehow.

Life keeps happening despite disasters. I guess I should just take one day at a time. You're not a frigging alcoholic. *No, not exactly, but I'm an emotionalalcholic.* You made that up. *Yeah!* It's not quite the same. *Yes it is.* How? *Well, I keep doing the same thing even though it hurts me. Crying, shutting myself away, eating that rubbish.* Why do you do that? *It hurts even more not to.* You mean you're scared. *Um, maybe.* Scared of what? *Not sure scared is the word.* Picky, picky. What then? Frightened. *Scared, frightened, same isn't it.* Maybe. *If one is frightened of something, shouldn't one face it full on?* Guess so, but how do I do that? *One step at a time.* I've been doing that. *Mm, maybe, but you need to take bigger steps.* Like what?

Gillian unlocked her door, let her handbag and keys fall into the empty planter, took the dish to the fridge, went into her bedroom and picked up the tourist's leaflets and her notebook. She read the list she'd made last night. 'Prague Castle, yep, tomorrow I'll start with the castle everyone says I have to see.'

Impressed by the size of Prague Castle, Gillian wandered through the buildings, constantly gasping at ancient displays of grandeur and modern adaptations. It took a moment to comprehend that this building had commenced in the year 870.

She read the flyer: *The castle was a seat of power for kings of Bohemia, Holy Roman emperors, and presidents of Czechoslovakia – and remains the residence of the President of the Czech Republic today.*

The next line of information made her giggle. *Prague Castle is the location in the second level of Indiana Jones and the Emperor's Tomb video game.*

Yep, modern technology is everywhere, even in this ancient place, she thought.

Standing in front of a guard in his pale blue uniform, she managed a selfie before three giggling tourists bustled her out of the way.

After wandering through the towering hall of St Vitus Cathedral, running her fingers in the water of Kohl's fountain and taking another look at the verdant view over St Wenceslas' Vineyard, she headed for a café.

With her feet rested and her thirst quenched, Gillian followed a gabbling group, behind a waving orange flag, along a street, listening to, but not understanding their excited words. She skirted the group as they gathered for further instructions.

Leaving the tourist route, she turned left and then right, crossed the road to the shade and continued walking in the shadows of the stone buildings. In a holiday mood, she grinned at passersby, watched children playing in a park with only a sigh. Strolling up an incline, past a small grocery store, she stopped in front of a shop and admired the rainbow-coloured scarves and guessed at the advertising signs.

She'd never been to a country that didn't have English as its first language. Patrick and she had honeymooned in New Zealand, spent two weeks in Hawaii, holidayed at a ski lodge near Mt Kosciusko, snorkeled on the Great Barrier Reef, and planned to ride The Ghan from Darwin to Adelaide.

She had tried talking him into New York for their next vacation. She'd even shown him a You Tube video of a Central Park concert hoping it would be one more encouragement. 'Dollars, English, sun, music,' she listed.

'Twenty-four hours on a plane,' he moaned.

The negative won out. They went "overseas," whole 20 kilometres to Western Australia's Rottnest Island instead.

Patrick never truly enjoyed holidays. His idea of relaxation included wine, piano, sharp pencil and a blank manuscript. As a music teacher those items were also his tools of trade – apart from the wine!

Gillian always had to cajole him into living in a hotel, using someone else's bathroom. He refused to battle language obstacles, exchange money, worry about passports and visas.

As Gillian dawdled past old buildings with modern facades, she puffed her chest out; gratified with her confidence. Her plan had been to hide away, lick her wounds, ignore everything and everyone, and although that was a miserable existence, she had survived. She'd overcome the language barrier, although not very well, she admitted, dealt with the money difficulty, used her tap-n-go, mostly, and had got used to wearing a close-fitting shoulder bag.

Today she'd caught a tram, followed maps and asked for a černá káva. The black coffee had been a little too strong, but černá it was, káva it was, so her minute foray using Czech had worked. She chuckled at her previous attempts to pronounce other items on the menu, usually using the English version printed underneath.

Approaching a building flying an Australian flag, she noticed the impressive door and stepped closer. Huge. The fabricated door reminded Gillian of the pressed metal of early Australian walls and ceilings. Replica pressed metal as kitchen splash-backs had now become fashionable, but this double door looked heavy, intricate and definitely not a replica. Its metallic beauty twinkled in the top corner where the sun caught it, and stood cold and defiant in the shadows. She pulled her phone from her pocket, stepped closer and snapped.

'Ne! Ne! To se nesmí.'

The urgency of the gruff voice made Gillian fumble her phone. She turned towards the footsteps. A broad-shouldered man put out his hand. 'Dejte mi Váš fotoaparát.'

'Sorry?' She frowned, tipped her head back in order to match his stare. 'What did you say?'

'You are not to take photo. You must give to me.' His accent emphasised his insistence.

'No way. I'm just taking a photo of the door.'

'This is Australian Embassy.'

'I guessed it was. And, I'm Australian.'

'You are still not to take photo.' He held out his hand. 'You give to me.'

'I'll just go.'

'You are to not go. You must give. I will delete the photo.'

Gillian pushed her phone into her bag and gripped it. A second man ducked as he came through the doorway. She peeked up at him. Her voice squeaked as she attempted confidence. 'No.'

'You will come with me,' the second man said. His instruction wasn't open to discussion.

They escorted her to a marble-walled reception area inside the intimidating door. 'Wait.' One man turned away, then over his shoulder added, 'Please.' The other stood, with splayed legs and folded arms, by the front door.

Baring my escape, Gillian thought, then asked, 'Why do I have to wait? Surely, I haven't done anything wrong. Just taking a simple photo.' *Just when I was enjoying myself. That'll teach me.*

'Hello, can I help you?'

She turned towards an Australian voice. 'Well, I certainly hope so. I don't exactly like being held hostage.'

The Australian spoke in Czech to the man by the door but kept glancing back at Gillian. At one point he gripped his lip with his teeth.

Hope that's a smile he's trying to hide.

He tapped the other man on the arm, spoke, pointed towards a long corridor. The man nodded and walked away, his shoes clacking loudly on the parquetry floor.

'Right,' the Australian said to Gillian. 'Let's get this straight. You've been caught taking photos of our building. Is that correct?'

'I guess.'

'We'll need to check your passport.'

'Really?'

'It's protocol. My staff would usually attend to such matters, but I heard your accent. Had to stop.' He stroked his chin. Gillian noticed his neat fingernails. 'See if I could help a fellow Aussie.'

'But, I was just taking a photo. Not of the building. Just the door. It's so beautiful.'

'There are many beautiful doors in Prague. Why ours?'

'Ours? Is it your family's?' Her sarcasm fell flat.

His eyebrows moved up, then settled over his intense brown eyes. 'This is the Australian Embassy. I'm Max Barkley. Ambassador to the Czech Republic. Taking photos of embassies is not recommended. One is under immediate suspicion. Especially these days.'

Gillian glanced around the room, back to Max Barkley and then down at her feet. 'Sorry.' She glanced up, faking confidence again. 'Shouldn't there be a sign.'

'They are there, I can assure you. In Czech and English. Didn't you see the Australian flag?'

'Yes, but, well, I …'

'Where are you from?'

'In Australia? Perth, actually. You?'

'Adelaide. But it's been a while.' He looked past her shoulder, back at her, then asked, 'Are you here on your own?'

Gillian thought about her answer. *What did the Australian ambassador need to know? Not much, I expect. Just enough for me not to be a threat to international security.* She inwardly chuckled.

He noticed her slight smile. 'I'll have to lock you up. If you pose a threat.'

Her smile vanished. Her eyes showed instant fright.

Max reached out, laying his hand lightly on her forearm. 'I'm sorry, that was my poor attempt at humour.' He removed his hand. 'We'll check your profile. After that, you'll be free to go, once you've shown me the photo, and assured me you're a tourist.'

Gillian's shoulders sagged with relief. Taking out her phone she tapped the screen until the photo of the door appeared. 'I'm not a tourist in the true sense. I'm staying. For a while at least.'

Max checked the photo. 'Okay. I won't need to delete it. It's not security-sensitive.' He paused as Gillian slipped the phone into her bag. 'Now your passport, please.'

'Is this really necessary?'

'You've ignored the signs, taken photos.' He paused, looked towards the security man. 'Yes, I'd say it's necessary.'

Gillian turned her back on the Ambassador, reached under her t-shirt, fiddled with the zip on the pouch next to her perspiring skin and pulled out her passport. 'There,' she said as she held it out. 'What is it you want to know?'

Max ignored her question, turned the cover over and read the details. 'Gillian Middleton.'

'It's in order,' she snapped.

'It is.' He closed the passport and handed it back. 'Where are you staying? In the city?'

'No, out at Prosek.'

'Right. Prague 9.'

'Prague, nine?' Gillian's frown showed her lack of knowledge.

Max shrugged. 'Yep, like the local councils in Australia. The city is Prague 1. Further out, the higher the number.'

'Oh, something else to know.'

'It's endless, but you'll catch on. Are you enjoying your stay?'

'Enough.'

'Enough what? Enough people, enough highlights?'

'My time has been a bit of a sabbatical.' Gillian hadn't previously thought of it as such, but hopefully he'd realise she was trying to avoid giving personal details.

'Prague's as good a place as any to get away from the usual.' He seemed to drift away with a private thought.

'Have you been here long?' When he didn't answer, she added, 'In Prague. In the Australian Embassy, as Ambassador.'

'Mm. Long enough.'

'There's that word again.'

'What word?'

'Enough.'

'Right. Right.' He glanced at his watch. 'Look, I've got a meeting.'

'Okay.' Damn, she thought, I was beginning to enjoy this interaction.

'You didn't say, are you with a group, or on your own?'

She looked towards the exit. 'No group. All alone. Me, just little old me.'

'Good.' He glanced down the passage, then back at her. 'Gillian, it's nice to meet you. I don't see too many Aussies. At least, not ones who aren't in some sort of trouble.'

Gillian's face beamed with a sugary smile. 'So, does that mean you're not going to arrest me?'

He tapped her shoulder. 'You're in luck. I'm very generous on Sundays. So, no jail cell for you today.'

The spot, where his fingers had so briefly been, seemed to burn at his touch. She took a quick breath and let it out slowly. 'That's a relief.' She slipped her passport into her bag, realigned the strap across her shoulder and sighed. 'Should I just go then?'

The ambassador raised his hand and beckoned to the security man who hurried over.

'I'll get Marco to show you out,' the ambassador said. 'That way no one will pounce on you again. Once you're past the barriers, the ones with the signs you didn't see, you'll be safe.'

'Right.' She tried to imitate his accent: Australian, but edged with upper class. 'I guess I'll go.'

His eyebrows lifted as he noticed disappointment in her voice. 'Gillian, look, it's totally against usual protocol, but may I have your number?'

'Perhaps.' Her smirk revealed her teasing.

'Only perhaps? Is that all I get for letting you off an espionage charge?'

'Well, since you put it that way.' She grinned again. 'I guess.'

Max pushed the sleeve of his shirt up and revealed his watch. 'Ten past. Look, I'm sorry, I must go. Could you give your number to Marco? Please.' As he stepped sideways, he said, 'Tell him you'll stamp on his toes if he doesn't pass it on.'

Gillian frowned. The security man towered above her; he'd hardly feel any lightweight stamping.

The ambassador laughed, and as he moved away, added, 'He's got frostbite.'

As she returned to the tram stop, she tried to erase the image of Marco's enormous frostbitten toes.

Noticing the smell of fresh bread, she turned the corner and entered a bakery. The aroma reminded her of Esther's baking: carrot cake, muffins, cupcakes, pancakes, enough to satisfy any sweet tooth. Every second day her sister would call in. 'Just on my way past,' she'd say before dishing out repeated advice.

'You've got to keep eating. And … I know you won't treat yourself.' Then Esther would detail the where and what of the course, or important meeting, she was rushing to.

Gillian purchased an apple and walnut roll, and bit into it immediately she left the store. It had amused her to see school-children on trams, in the streets, biting into plain bread rolls. Sienna would've wanted butter and Vegemite.

As she swallowed the warm bread, she realised it was the first thought of her daughter which hadn't been accompanied by the threat of tears. *Sienna. My darling, Sienna. I miss you.*

By the time she reached the tram she had noticed several fascinating doors – none attached to any building likely to be "security-sensitive". Sprawling ivy dangling from a lintel hid half of an aqua door, and a solid oak door stood out behind a puny wire gate. She dug her phone from her pocket and took a photo of another door, its detailing reminiscent of a door at Prague Castle.

'Gorgeous. Nothing like that back home.'

Feeling pleased with the day's happenings, she Googled Prague Castle and compared her snaps to the professional angles. While she sat motionless, examining her reactions to the charming Ambassador, and considering her response if he did contact her, the screen saver flashed unnoticed memories across the screen.

When Max rang on Monday with an invitation to dinner, Gillian stammered out her excuse, 'I'm sorry; I don't think I can go.'

'It doesn't have to be tomorrow. Can be next week, if that suits better.'

'Um, not really.' She leaned against the fridge and closed her eyes. This is so hard. 'I don't think I can do this.'

Max remembered Marco commenting on Gillian's rings. 'Third finger, left hand. You know what that means.' Max thought she'd covered that issue by saying "just me". Now he realised she might only be in Prague on her own, not without a husband at home. He tried to cover his embarrassment. 'Okay, sorry, I should've realised. Marco mentioned, well, your rings, and …'

Gillian's eyes jumped open as she said, 'It's not that.'

'You don't have to explain.'

'Um, no, but perhaps I should,' she said. 'I'm a widow. Recent. Finding it hard.'

'I'm sorry.'

'Thanks.' Saying anything more became difficult. 'Sorry.' She knew she wouldn't cope with any implied sequence of events which often started with dinner.

'It's okay. I certainly understand.'

'You too?'

'No, I'm divorced. Long time ago.'

'I'm sorry.'

Max thought of a shredded wedding photo he'd thrown in the bin six years ago. 'It's okay.' He knew of heartache and pain, and wanted to reach out to this woman who'd made him think of quiet dinners and long walks. 'What about coming to a barbecue? Poshed-up one, of course.' He heard a murmur of interest, so continued, 'It's our way at the embassy to get to know the who's who, the up and coming, the powers that be. A total social cliché I know, but a necessity in this business.'

'It might be a bit too posh for me.'

'I shouldn't think so. It's Saturday afternoon.' He chuckled. 'I could do with another Aussie. Keep the percentages up.'

'I don't think I could do it. All those people; strangers.'

'Gillian,' his voice became softer, 'I can only imagine how hard it is, but may I suggest you have to start somewhere. Your heartache will be safe. It's a promotional event. Those strangers will only want to hear about sunshine, beaches,' he chuckled before continuing, 'kangaroos hopping down main streets. That sort of thing. And, everyone will be on their best behaviour. You can tell them anything. Just polite conversation. Think of it as a start.'

She listened to his Australian accent, smoothed with European influences, and realised how far from eucalyptus trees over the proverbial billabongs she'd travelled. She confirmed her decision, 'That'd be nice.' Patrick won't mind.

'I'll send an invitation; it has the details. You can come and go as you please.' Gillian sensed him smile. 'You'll have no drama from Marco – this time.'

'Is there a dress code?'

'Not really, but it won't be jeans and t-shirt. Mostly it's the top end of society. You know, politicians, business people, and other ambassadors. Smart casual I believe is the buzz word, but they'll be out to impress. Don't doubt that for a moment.'

Gillian's thoughts flashed over her clothes in the wardrobe. Jeans, t-shirts, trousers, track pants, more t-shirts. Nothing "smart" amongst them. Damn. 'Second thoughts, maybe I'm not up to it.'

'Please, don't write it off just yet. I'll send the invitation. Ignore the RSVP. We always have no shows, and last-minute acceptances. The business of diplomacy is like that. Just let me know, so I can look out for you.'

'Maybe.'

'Promise you'll give it some thought.'

My brain is already arguing with itself, Gillian thought. 'Okay, I'll promise to think about it.'

'Good. I'll put my direct number on the invitation. Ring me, either way, please.'

A little while later Gillian knocked on Hana's door and stood back, one moment hoping Hana would be home, the next preparing to scurry up the steps to the safety of her own flat.

'Dobrý den. Moc ráda Vás vidím.' (Hello, how nice to see you.)

'Ahoj. I hope I'm not bothering you.'

'Pojďte dál, pojďte dál.' (Come in, come in.) Hana ushered Gillian into the sitting room. 'Kávu?'

'Yes, please.'

Hana's head bobbed repeatedly as she spoke softly while filling the kettle. She motioned for Gillian to sit. 'S něčím si děláte starosti, že?' (You have something that is worrying?) She accentuated her frown, hoping this might interpret her words.

Gillian said, 'I really shouldn't be bothering you, but I have no one else who knows my story.' She shrugged, pursed her lips. 'Can you read this, please?' She held out a piece of paper which Hana took and put on a chair opposite Gillian.

'Ale nejdříve si dame, kávu.' (First the coffee.) After she placed two cups and some biscuits on a low table, she read Gillian's note with a smile playing around her lips as she said, 'To je dobře, že jste to zkusila.' (It is good that you've tried.)

Gillian had written: *Muž ptát se mi na jídlo – Australia ambasáda – já jít?* and underlined the double-sized question mark.

'The translator ap only helped to a point,' she explained. 'No barbecue in there. Didn't want to put "date". It isn't a date. Dinner might have been. This isn't. It's just a barbecue.'

'Barbecue? Embassy? Měla byste jít.' (You should go.) Hana nodded furiously.

Pointing to her wedding ring, Gillian frowned. 'I don't know if I'm ready.'

'To je v pořádku. Váš manžel by chtěl abyste byla šťastná.' (It's okay. Your husband, he would want you to be happy.) Hana pointed to Gillian's chest, her rings, grinned excessively, nodded some more. 'Je čas, abyste byla znovu šťastná. (It should be time to be happy again.)

'This is so stupid,' Gillian said. 'I mean, I don't even know what I expected from you. Permission, perhaps.'

Hana shook her head, picked up Gillian's empty cup. 'Ještě kávu.' (More coffee.)

Gillian laughed, nodded. 'Hana, you're wonderful.'

Gillian argued with herself half the night and most of the next morning. When the formal invitation arrived, by courier, Gillian wondered at Max's enthusiasm. Deep end, she thought. Well, I know how to swim.

Thursday. She texted Max. *Thanks for the invite. See you then.* After hesitating over an appropriate parting expression, she rolled her eyes and pressed send.

Friday. Gillian spent the morning at the Palladium Shopping Centre searching for something suitable for a posh barbecue. Huh! she thought, in Australia that'd be an oxymoron.

Marks and Spencer provided black tailored slacks and a muted green jacket. She splashed out on a leather handbag with a long shoulder strap, the subtle black stitching and gold clasp catching her eye as she rode down the escalator past the accessories counter. A tucked-away shop gave up shoes with low wedges.

Her card suffered even more after Gillian realised she'd need new cosmetics. She had tossed hers in a rubbish bin one miserable day when she thought she'd never use lipstick again.

Saturday morning. She ignored breakfast, spent time shaping her eyebrows before leaving the unit, still arguing about her sanity.

I've spent all that money. And, I'll never get another chance to mix with the hoi polloi. And, I've told him I would go. And, he'll be expecting you. *Do you really think he just wants someone else from down under?* Well, it has been planned for months. You're probably just an add-on. *But, he sent the invitation by courier. Who does that?* Someone who wants the other one to get into bed, that's who.

When that thought hit, she reached out for the back of the park bench, gripped it while she let the idea bubble around.

No. I wouldn't. You might. *Not yet. Too soon.* That means you will. *Go away.* Nuh, you have to consider it. *I said ... someday.*

'But, not for quite a while,' Gillian informed the park bench.

A few hours later Gillian watched her lipstick-enhanced mouth smile back from the mirror. She examined the smile closely. *Would it convince people she was just another person wanting a free feed?* The smile disappeared. She wiped the lipstick away with a tissue and sat down on the edge of the bath and checked her watch. *Eleven thirty. If I'm going, it's time to go.* Standing in front of the mirror again, she bared her teeth and ran her tongue over them. Clean. She checked for stray eyebrow hairs and after finding none reached for the lipstick tube and replaced the smudged colour.

Gillian repeatedly checked her reflection during the train journey. *Was she overdressed; underdressed? Too much makeup?* An elderly man looked her over before he sat down next to her. His face revealed none of the required answers.

Her stomach complained. With only coffee to feed on, the butterflies were competing for space, demanding attention and generally misbehaving.

She dawdled the short distance towards the embassy, arriving with the butterflies having gone into all-out assault mode. Spotting another guest with similar clothing her level of anxiousness decreased a little.

Marco greeted her with a grin. 'Ahoj, how are you this day?'

'Ahoj, hi, Marco. Fine thanks.'

'Please go in. Go and turn left. You'll find the outside through the big doors.'

'Thanks.' Her stomach continued to gurgle, her palms dampened and her heartbeat bounced in her throat. It reminded her of being sent to a school Principal's office. Entering the patio already pulsing with conversation overwhelmed her. She glanced around. Nup, no Max. She wanted to go before anyone could see the panic in her eyes.

'Would you like a drink? Wine? White? Red?' Gillian turned towards a smiling face. 'There's soft drink, if you'd rather.'

Gillian checked the young woman's name badge. 'Thanks … Madison. White, please.'

Madison grinned. 'Oh, good. Another Aussie. Where from?'

'Perth.' Gillian took a glass, concentrated on sipping without spilling it. 'Mm. Smooth.'

'It's from the Barossa.'

'South Australian. Good. And you?'

'Queensland actually. Been here six months. Love it. What about you?'

'Just a short while. Haven't seen much yet. But I must.'

'Awesome. There's lots to see.' Madison nodded towards the glasses. 'Got to keep going. Enjoy the day.'

'I'm terrified really. Don't know a soul.'

'See that group over there.' Madison tipped her head left. 'The lady with the striped top. She's Australian. Head that way.'

'Thanks, Madison. Don't work too hard.'

Gillian eased into the group, her accent assuring a welcome. After a few trivial introductory explanations, it was easy to nod and murmur along with the conversation. Gillian glanced around several times, finally spotting Max. His animated face and expressive eyebrows enhancing his words.

With three tiger prawns, a tangle of mango and rocket salad, and a well-grilled sausage on a plate, Gillian found a spare seat at a table and tucked in.

'Here you are.' Max's hand rested briefly on Gillian's shoulder. 'Managing?'

Gillian looked up at him. 'Yes, thanks. This salad is great.'

'Good. I'll get some and come back. Don't go anywhere.'

After he thanked a waiter for finding another chair, Max placed his plate down and wriggled into the spot next to Gillian. 'You didn't get any tomato sauce. How can you have a burnt sausage without tom sauce?'

Gillian laughed and pushed her fork into the sausage. 'I didn't see it. But I think it'll be okay without.'

Max grinned. 'Have some of mine. I think I've got too much.'

'No, thanks anyway.' She was sure the sauce would end up on the front of her jacket.

In between eating, Max answered many questions from the guests around the table. He impressed Gillian with his enthusiasm and ability to converse, occasionally in Czech, often with a German phrase or a French expression thrown in amongst the precise English.

When they'd finished eating, Max asked, 'Do you like pavlova?' He pulled a face and whispered, 'No matter how many times we have these events, everyone expects pavlova. It's like the sausages. Anyone would think that's all Aussies eat. Don't like to bring up the fact that New Zealand claim pavlova as theirs. Who knows? Anyway, they devour the prawns and kangaroo steaks, but if we don't have a burnt sausage on the menu we've failed in our duty.'

'It's the smell,' Gillian said. 'I mean, a barbecue wouldn't be the same without the smell of onions and charred sausages.'

Max chuckled. 'You're right. And we'll probably smell it through to Monday.' His left eyebrow went down. 'So, want some pav?'

Gillian's smile had broadened throughout Max's explanation. 'I love pavlova, but at the moment I'm too full. Is there coffee?'

'Sure. Come with me, we'll get some. It'll give me a moment to thank you for coming.' He caught the linen serviette falling from his knee as he stood. Gillian wiped her mouth and stood too.

'I'm glad you came,' Max said, as they accepted a cup of coffee from a busy waiter.

'I nearly didn't.'

'That would've been a shame. You've enjoyed it, haven't you?'

'Sort of, but I'm not used to so many strangers all at once. I nearly bolted.'

'We're not so bad, are we?'

Gillian took a sip of coffee, licked her top lip before answering. 'Of course not. But this is out of my usual league. And then, what with everything, it's been a challenge.'

He touched her arm, for just a second, and then said, 'Well done for rising to the challenge. Not easy, I guess.'

'No. So many people enjoying themselves. It isn't ...' She was about to say "fair", but hesitated long enough for Max to interrupt.

'We're here to enjoy ourselves, certainly, but many have problems to go home to. We see so many difficult situations at the embassy. Some tourists bring the problems on themselves.

But, well, others? Life doesn't seem to spare many countries some sort of trouble these days. Today is a chance to forget that, share the good things in life.' Max saw Gillian's mouth sag. 'Good things,' he said with a smirk, 'like burnt snaggers.'

Gillian's impending sadness departed; she grinned. 'With or without tomato sauce.'

'Exactly. Now are you up for some pavlova?'

Gillian refused the pavlova and said goodbye. Max made her promise to stay in touch. 'Not many Australians in Prague, apart from the tourists,' he said. 'Ring me.'

As she moved away from the entrance, Marco muttered a quick goodbye, fiddling with the cuffs on his jacket. He looked tired.

I bet his feet are aching. 'Bye, Marco.'

On the train, Gillian rehashed the event, wondering if she'd played the role of enthusiastic Australian and the interested tourist successfully. A smile teased her lips as she travelled up the lift to her front door.

A note, written in Czech, had been slid under her door, and Gillian recognised the signature. 'Ah! Hana.' Closing the door, Gillian retraced her steps to the lift and pressed down.

'Ahoj, Hana.' Gillian waved the note as her neighbour peered through the security peephole in the door.

Hana, opened the door, grasped Gillian's arm, ushered her into the room. Hana's head bobbed as she motioned for her visitor to sit. 'Jaké to bylo? Našla jste ho?' (How did it go? Did you find the man?)

'Hana, it's okay. Wait, wait.' Gillian sat and dropped her bag to the floor.

Hana's head stopped bobbing. She sat next to Gillian and clapped her hands like an excited child. 'Ano, ano.'

Gillian allowed herself to agree with Hana's enthusiasm. Her inquisition didn't need translating. Yes, it had been okay, she'd survived the hoi polloi. Max was nice, lovely, in fact. But Gillian didn't think past that.

'Čaj? Kávu?'

'No.' Gillian held up her hands, indicating refusal. 'No, thanks, Hana. Full. Totally.' She patted her stomach.

Hana pointed to the note on Gillian's lap. 'Elena. Elena, přijde.' (Come.)

'Elena? Is she here?'

'Elena, přijde.' Hana counted her fingers. 'Jeden, dva, tři, čtyři.'

'Four? Wednesday? Is Elena coming on Wednesday?'

Hana shrugged. Counted her fingers again.

Gillian nodded, frowned, then giggled. 'Oh, Hana, it really is like a horse talking to a cow.'

Without knowing the reason for Gillian's laugher, Hana joined in. They giggled like frivolous teenagers. Gillian's cheeks hurt. Hana's eyes leaked.

Gillian wrapped her arms around Hana. 'Děkuji, děkuji, Thank you, Hana.'

'Není zač, mé milé děvče. Musíte se víc smát. Sluší Vám to víc, když se smějete.' (Please, my dear girl. You need to laugh more. You are so much prettier when you laugh.) Hana touched Gillian's face as she said goodbye.

'Thanks, Hana. Send Elena up on Wednesday.'

'Elena?'

Pointing to four fingers, Gillian said again, 'Elena.' She knocked on Hana's door and pointed to her own chest. 'Elena, tell her to come and get me.'

'Ano. Elena. Čtyři dny.' (Yes, Elena, four days.)

Am I the cow or the horse? Gillian thought as she entered the lift with a broad smile.

Spread-eagled across the queen-sized bed, Gillian considered how, without routine, one day can seem the same as the next. Acknowledging her daily schedules had "gone to hell in a hand-basket" since arriving in Prague, she stretched noisily, and considered not getting up.

However, as the warm Sunday didn't encourage snuggling under a Doona, she shook free of the sheet and headed for the bathroom.

Once showered, dressed, and with a half-eaten bowl of cereal in one hand, she turned on her laptop, eager for any news from Perth. The computer obliged, and spooning milky Weetbix into her mouth, Gillian read the emails from home.

Hi Gilly,

Did you hear the one about the man going into a bar and finding a gorgeous, hilarious, witty, spectacular, red-haired forty-year-old sitting on her own? No? Well, I'm telling you, this particular red-haired wonderland is having a very, sexy time with that man who came into Welling's Bistro last week.

Anyhow. He's taking me to the Como. You know the one on the Terrace. Six stars. When? I hear you ask. Soon. Don't worry, I'll tell all.

So, my dear Gilly, how's your love life going? I know, I know, Mira rang yesterday. Her usual doom and gloom. She said I shouldn't be going on about Magnificent Murray – that's his name BTW – when you're, you know. But I always let you live vicariously through me and my men. Mira's worried I'll upset you. I told her you're upset anyway. Maybe I can make you laugh. Seriously though, I miss you. Hope you are sorting things out in that lovely head of yours. Smile, smile, smile. You know what they say, fake it until you make it.

Your sage friend. Me, of course, who else says it works? Done it many times. Even the times when "making it" never happened. But that's another story and maybe too much info.

Have to go buy something to wear to stun the stunning Murray. Will of course let you know EVERYTHING that happens.

Xxx Sandy

Grinning through Sandy's eccentric email, Gillian imagined Mira and Sandy at odds with each other over their approach to a grief-stricken widow. It was impossible to be unhappy while hearing about Sandy and her latest conquest.

She opened Mira's email, knowing her news would be carefully tempered.

Hi, Gillian,

Hope you're okay. I've been busy. Kids are driving me mad. Both of them have colds. Lily is still at home. Rohan went back to school today. How is it possible for them to have so much snot?

Jamie's working in Melbourne at the moment. It's the devil trying to do everything.

Saw Sandy yesterday. Mum came and stayed with the kids while I did some shopping. Called in at Sandy's on the way. She's working from home with this new contract. Did you know that? Did you also know she has a new car? It's silver. BMW. Lucky her. Guess she doesn't have school fees!

Also, she has a new boyfriend. This one has heaps of money. (Don't they all) I hope she hasn't been going on about him to you. I told her you don't need to have it put in your face. Sorry for bringing it up, but not much else happening.

I hope you're enjoying the sights of Prague. Make the most of it. Thinking of you.

Love Mira.

Gillian read both emails twice, poured a glass of cold water and read Sandy's again before pressing the reply button.

To my egotistical friend.

Of course I want to live a six-star life through you. You must tell me everything on the menu. And something about the night out.

BTW Mira emailed.

Is this Murray so spectacular that you didn't even think to mention your new car? Boy, he must be something. BTW what were you doing at Welling's? I remember you saying something about it being SNOB CITY.

Like I said, let me know SOME of the details of your evening.

Mira's worried you'll upset me. It might as I'm sitting here wishing I was there with you, debating your single life against my happy-married-with-baby one. The ache is still there. But then it might not be. Not too much, anyway. I'll be okay. The pain will NEVER go. I know that, but I think I've turned a corner. I don't feel like throwing my laptop through the window anymore when I think of the times Patrick and I went to places like that. I no longer pace around this little flat trying to get rid of the panic that seems to touch every nerve. I've even stopped looking at my one and only knife and ... well, I can't put those thoughts down.

You see, I'm healing. Some days, I don't want to heal I mean. Not if it means memories will fade.

Enough of me. For heaven's sake, don't listen to Mira, (only her sensible stuff. You should definitely take notice of the sensible bits)

I EXPECT you to tell me how many calouries you ate, the price of your scotch and soda, and what happens NEXT.

Love Gilly.

After she pressed send, Gillian took her empty cup to the sink and opened the cutlery drawer and picked up the knife. 'Nice Knife.' She ran her finger along the flat edge of the blade, smiled, and replaced it in the drawer. 'Not-a-dagger-anymore Knife.'

Returning to her key-board, she considered her reply to Mira, then began.

Dear Mira,

Nice to hear from you. Perth seems a long way away. I'm finally getting out and seeing something. Prague is gorgeous. Jamie would love the architecture of the place. Old Town is so, old – adorable. And their famous clock. Look it up on Google. Do you know they poked out the eyes of the man who designed the clock so he couldn't build another one? Yuk, gruesome. Maybe it's not true. But everyone says it is. Sort of thing your Rohan would be into. Ten-year-old boys love blood and gore, don't they?

I've discovered some fab doors. The intricate details, the ancient handles, and even some of the unloved ones seem to have something special about them. I'll send you some photos.

You'd love the cafes. Often tiny little shops, but, oh my, the cakes, buns. You'd never be able to decide.

Sorry to hear about the kids. Hope their colds clear up soon.

I heard from Sandy. Glad you two are still getting together. I've always thought you two clashed … and without me to referee … anyway, you have to lend some normalcy to her life. Get her to watch the kids. Now, that I encourage!!

Please don't worry about me. I seem to have turned a corner. Have been out and about. Went shopping. Not entirely successful, but a good start. Remember those shopping trips we did together, buying clothes for Sienna and Rose. I should have asked you if you wanted Sienna's clothes. Sorry. Head not clear that day.

Prague is working its charm on me. There seems to be a settled aura about it. Like it knows it's survived the years of many invasions and turmoil and now all it has to do is put up with the hundreds, no, thousands, of tourists.

Stay in touch.

Love Gilly.

After the internet had snatched the messages away, Gillian watched the screensaver search through her files of photos.

Twenty seconds. Patrick at the beach disappeared and Sienna in her stroller filled the screen. Gillian's smile came unexpectedly. *No tears!* A photo of Esther with Sienna on her knee. *You're a good aunty.* Gillian frowned. *Were. You were a good aunty.* Next photo – Patrick and Sherbet. *I bet the silly cat has forgotten me. Sienna and Gillian – matching skirts.* Gillian chuckled. *Ridiculous. Sienna and Gillian – hugging. Never. Won't happen. Never again.*

Gillian slammed the lid of the laptop down, stood, walked to the window. NEVER. It seemed tattooed on her tongue as she tried to swallow. *Horrid, horrid word.*

She dropped down onto the couch, arms tightly folded, bottom lip between her teeth, a frown so deep she could hardly see her tapping foot.

Two minutes. I'll NEVER kiss Patrick again.

Five minutes. I'll NEVER hold my daughter again.

Seven minutes. NEVER! It'll NEVER be "we" again.

Ten minutes. Damn, you. You bastard. I hope you rot in hell.

Twelve minutes. Gillian put the other foot on top of her tapping foot. I hope your feet rot.

Thirteen minutes. I hope your feet smell.

Thirteen minutes two seconds. *What! Your feet smell?* She smirked. *Gillian Middleton, is that the best curse you can invent for that speeding, drunken bastard?*

She returned to the window and stared down at the silent, empty courtyard. She fingered the thick hem of the curtain, experienced the fabric's strength as she wrapped it around her body, enjoying the comfort of being hidden.

Seventeen minutes. Gillian left her cocoon, closed her door and hurried down the steps, strode across the empty, silent courtyard, onto a concrete footpath and tried to fathom the anger which was overtaking her grief.

Two hours. Gillian forced her feet to climb the four flights of steps to her front door hoping the effort would erase the internal pain. She toasted stale bread, added cheese and ate it without tasting a crumb.

After an hour of wandering under a cloudy sky of mid-morning, Gillian headed for the main street, deciding to stop for an early lunch. A bite of wind hit her neck as she approached a café and she immediately understood the true purpose of scarves.

With a smoked salmon salad finished, she devoured banana bread slathered with butter. Heading the long way back to the Metro, she stepped back out into the cool afternoon. It was pleasant to meander through the suburbs, be delighted by the wrought-iron gates, elegant facades and towering windows in a collage of interesting buildings.

An unmaintained house caught her attention. Tall weeds poked through a graffiti-covered fence.

Even in this pretty area, vandals can't leave well enough alone. What a shame.

Further on, impressed with a cream-coloured house with a crimson door, Gillian focused her camera on the brass door-knocker. She'd snapped three different angles before child-like singing diverted her attention.

Gillian turned towards the happy sound. A young woman held the hand of a child who sang as she skipped. The girl's singing slowed and then petered out as they approached Gillian. The woman spoke, 'Dobrý den. Jste z agentury?'

'I'm sorry, I don't speak Czech.' Gillian slid her phone into her pocket.

'Are you from the agency, too? A photographer came yesterday. I thought they only wanted inside shots.'

Gillian didn't understand the question, even in English. 'I'm not from any agency. I was just admiring this house. The door is very eye-catching. Is it yours?'

The child tugged on her mother's hand, pulling her up the path leading to the red door.

'Ještě okamžik, Izzy.' (Just a moment, Izzy.) 'Yes, it is. We wanted something cheerful.'

'Are you selling?'

'No.' The woman's furrowed brow showed they were talking at cross purposes.

'I just wondered. You spoke of an agency.'

The woman's face relaxed. 'Not that sort of agency. We have an oven which is new in the market. The supplier wanted pictures for promotion.'

'Oh.' Gillian tipped her head towards Izzy, who had dropped her mother's hand and now jumped up and down the steps. 'Is your daughter four; five?'

'Izabela? Yes, she is soon to be five.'

'She's tall.'

The woman nodded. 'And never sits still.'

'That's good.'

Izabela's mother looked Gillian up and down, taking in her sneakers, and the jumper tied around her waist. 'Why were you photographing my house?'

Gillian remembered Marco's interrogation. 'I'm just visiting Prague and I've noticed how many gorgeous doors there are. Especially around here. I've taken quite a few photos. Your red door and its handle caught my eye. I wanted to add it to my collection. I hope you don't mind.'

The young woman's eyes narrowed as she looked Gillian over again. Then she turned, still frowning and watched her daughter pull on the door handle.

'Pojd', mami. Potřebuju na záchod,' the child called. (Come on, Mummy. I need the toilet.)

The woman stepped toward Gillian. 'Could I see the pictures?'

'Of course.' Gillian took her phone out of her pocket, tapped on it.

Izabela ran from the steps and tugged her mother's hand. 'Mami, já chci jít na záchod.' (Mummy, I want to go to the toilet.)

'I'm sorry, I'll have to go.' The mother turned to her child. 'I'm coming.'

Gillian nodded, acknowledging the child's desperation.

As Izabela's mother unlocked the door, a butterfly tattoo became visible on the pale underside of her right arm. The child pushed the door open, ran past her mother and along a corridor.

'She's lovely,' Gillian said. 'Sienna's about her age. I mean … she would've been …'

Izabela's mother caught the sudden sadness in Gillian fading voice. 'Could you wait a moment?'

'I guess,' Gillian said.

'Better still, come in. Izzy can manage. Come in. You can show me the doors.' The woman dropped her bag on a stool, removed her shoes, then hung her coat on a peg. Gillian copied the etiquette of changing outdoor shoes into slip-on ones.

'It is cool today,' Izabela's mother said. 'You must have been walking for a while.'

Realising the woman was tactfully seeking information, Gillian replied, 'Yes, I'm living over in Prosek, but love this area. I indulged at lunchtime and thought I'd better walk off some of the banana bread.'

'Where are you from? London?'

'No. I'm from Perth. In Western Australia.'

'All this way? Now, would you like coffee or perhaps tea? But first, we haven't introduced ourselves. I'm Petra Lakrinová. My daughter is Izabela.'

'I'm Gillian Middleton.' Gillian placed the strap of her bag over the back of the chair, twisted a strand of hair around her finger. 'I had a daughter, Sienna.' She looked at Petra. 'Coffee would be nice, but could I have a glass of water first, please. Tap water's fine.'

Petra's face showed a flash of speculation at the past tense in Gillian's information. 'I'm sorry. It's always hard, isn't it?' She turned away, filled an electric kettle, poured a glass of water and passed it to Gillian. 'There is no pain like losing a child.'

'Mami, mami, můžu si pustit televizi?' (Mummy, can I watch telly?) Izabela bounded into the room. 'Prosím, prosím.'

Gillian wondered how to extricate herself from this kindly person's warmth. Soon she'll be expecting the full story. I've got to get out of here.

'Izzy, Izzy, stop it. We have a guest. Where are your manners?'

Izabela clasped the hem of her mother's shirt, stepped behind her and looked shyly at Gillian.

'Say hello to Mrs Middleton.'

Izabela whispered hello before looking up at her mother and repeating, 'Prosím mami! Můžu si na chvíli pustit televizi?'

'Excuse me, Gillian. I'll get Izzy settled and we can enjoy a hot drink in peace. Come on, Izzy, let's see what's on.'

Gillian didn't want to sit. If she did, she'd be trapped.

Why not stay? her annoying alter ego prodded. *Because.* Because what? *Well, for instance, she's already asked about Sienna.* So, tell her. *No way.* Why not? *I came here to avoid talking about Patrick and Sienna.* That was then. *They're still gone.* Yes, but this person seems to know about losing a child. *But she has a daughter.* So? *Well, she can't know what I've been through.* Why not? *She's got a daughter!* Give it a try. *No!* Yes! *I'll regret it.* Maybe, maybe not. You won't know if you walk out. *But if I—*

'How do you want your coffee? White, sugar?' Petra's question interrupted Gillian's self-arguing.

'What? Oh, sorry, yes. No sugar. A little milk. Thanks.'

Gillian listened as Petra explained the enhanced features of her new stove, before accepting a mug of coffee and sitting at the table.

'You speak English very well. Did you learn at school?' Gillian asked.

Petra grinned. 'Of course, but my mother was born in Wales. She worked in London and met my father when he was on holiday there. My husband and I speak both languages and I teach Izabela. Sometimes I get caught out, but not often.'

'Are your parents still alive?'

'Sadly, no. But they had a life worth counting. Full of love. My brother and I were most lucky.'

They sat silently for a while, then Petra asked, 'How long have you been in Prague?'

'Umm, three weeks or more, yes, nearly a month.'

'Have you come for something special?'

'No, not really.'

Petra shook her head. 'I'm sorry, it is rude to question you when I've just met you, but your eyes show a shadow. I saw that when you looked at Izabela. You spoke of your Sienna as if she was not with you anymore.'

Gillian sniffed, but her eyes remained dry. She pulled a tissue from her sleeve and twisted it. 'I came to get away. My family, my husband and daughter … killed in a car accident. I'm trying to … I'm not good at … It's hard.'

'Yes, always.' Petra reached across the table and let her hand stay a moment on Gillian's forearm. 'It doesn't go away. But I can promise you it does get easier to stop the tears.' Petra stood and took a photo frame from a low cabinet. 'This is Bridget. Izabela's older sister.' She spoke these words softly with heartache showing on her creased forehead. She passed the frame to Gillian, who took it gently.

'How old?'

'Almost three.'

'When?'

'Six years ago.'

'I'm sorry.'

'Thank you.'

Gillian placed the frame on the table. In between sips of coffee, the women glanced at Bridget's tiny face.

'Does it really get easier?' Gillian asked.

'Eventually. The pain is strongest on anniversaries. But you have to continue, don't you? You have to. You must.'

'But I won't have another child. My husband died too.'

Petra shook her head and closed her eyes for a moment. 'I can't imagine. When Bridget died ... They couldn't save her. I ... we ... didn't want another child. The pain of losing one was too great. We almost lost our marriage, but Ivan was the only one who truly knew how I felt. We clung on. Then Izzy came. I don't know what else to tell you, but you must keep going.'

'I'm surviving.' Gillian grunted. 'I guess I'm improving. Slowly. Awfully slowly.'

'Good. It's just like they say, one day at a time.'

'Like alcoholics. That thought has already crossed my mind.'

'Well, it's a good idea. But, you were going to show me your doors. You must, before you go.'

Gillian took this as a subtle sign and pushed her empty mug towards the centre of the table. 'I shouldn't keep you. I've probably ruined your day already.'

'Of course not. Anyway, Ivan won't be home for some time. All you're stopping me from is housework. I always welcome an excuse for delaying the ironing.'

'If you're sure.' Gillian pulled her phone from her pocket again. 'I've taken quite a few. This is the first one. At the Australian Embassy. I nearly got arrested.'

'Really?'

Gillian related her encounter with Marco and Max, but didn't mention the follow-up invitation. They looked through the photos, discussing the attributes of all seventeen doors.

'Mami, mám hlad!'(Mummy, I'm hungry!)

'Okay, Izzy, I'll be with you soon.'

'I better be going. Let you get on with it.' Gillian stood, put on her jumper and picked up her bag. 'You've been very kind.'

'Not at all, I don't get to chat in English much. I have enjoyed it.'

'Thanks, Petra.'

'Mami, mám hlad. Mami,' Izabela repeated.

'Wait just a moment. Say goodbye to Mrs Middleton.'

Izabela bobbed down behind a chair and peeked through the strutted back. 'Goodbye.' She waved her hand. 'Goodbye, lady.'

'Goodbye, Izabela.'

Gillian offered her hand to Petra, who, instead, pulled her into a quick embrace. 'Perhaps you could call again.'

'That would be nice,' Gillian said. 'I'll knock next time I'm wandering past. If that's okay?'

'Of course. If I am home, I will be pleased to see you.' Petra followed Gillian towards the front door. 'Keep taking your photos. It's good to have a reason for walking.' Petra released Gillian from another tight hug. 'You know about doors closing and then opening. The next one might be your special one.'

As Gillian stood in the crowded train, she thought about that. *One closes. One opens. Yes, and who knows what's behind the next.*

'Co myslíš, že děláš?'

Gillian's hand jerked. Damn, that'll be another photo spoilt. She hadn't suddenly learned Czech, but she knew this bent-over chap wasn't happy.

'English,' she said, her voice clipped.

'Na co?' His grey eyebrows jumped with each word.

'Look, I'm just admiring the door. Is taking a photo of a wooden door paramount to espionage?'

'Co tady fotíš?'

Gillian shrugged. 'Bye.' She walked away. *Pity,* she thought. *It's a great door, and his neighbour's would've been worthwhile, too.*

Another day and another street turned out to be a gold mine of intricate doors, lintels and door jambs. She'd added nine to her collection before turning the corner. Gillian was sure Mira's husband, Jamie, would love the five finely detailed wooden doors she'd emailed, but neither he nor Mira had replied. Surely, as a carpenter, Jamie would appreciate the work involved.

The plain wooden door, now in front of Gillian, looked dwarfed by the huge concrete surrounds.

'Made in the sixteen hundreds. Amazing isn't it?'

Gillian turned, lowered her camera. 'The door's so plain.'

'The fussy lintel needs a plain door, don't you agree?'

'Mm, I wouldn't call it fussy.'

'Pretty?' His grin oozed sarcasm.

'No way,' Gillian said. 'I was thinking intricate, elaborate.'

'Okay.' He dipped his head. 'You win. Elaborate it is.'

'Is it yours?'

'Yes.'

Gillian raised her eyebrows. 'I guess you want to know why I'm taking a photo of your door.'

'No.'

'You don't?'

'It's obvious. Tourist. I'd say from … mm … Australia somewhere. Everything's too new over there. Here. Old. But definitely not fussy … elaborate.' His emphasis irritated Gillian. 'You'll go home, rave about us. Never come back. Am I right?'

Obnoxious sort, Gillian thought. 'Not a tourist. Right about the nationality bit.'

'There you go then.' He rattled his keys as he stepped towards the entrance.

'I've been here long enough to know you aren't Czech.'

'Miss know-it-all, eh?'

Obnoxious and rude. 'Somewhere … I don't know … south of say, Buckingham Castle with all the upper class, but false knobs on.' She copied his English accent as she added, 'Eh?'

'What?' He laughed, opened the door, stepped into the hallway and called out, 'Take as many photos as you want.' Then he shut the plain wooden door.

Gillian wanted to bang on the door and ask for an apology, knowing curtesy had failed from both of them.

Cursing as she took six photos: one, rude; two, impolite; three, impertinent; four, obnoxious; five, doubly obnoxious; six, I hope he's watching.

She retraced her steps towards the tram. The house on the next corner had a similar door to the obnoxious Englishman's. She stood on the footpath across the road and laughed until her breath caught.

Bloody hell! I enjoyed that.

Another car whizzing past ruined Gillian's second attempt at recording the aqua panels of glass in the window above a tall metal door. After waiting for a break in the traffic, she crossed the road and stood next to a leafy shrub in front of number 5. She aimed her camera at the patterned door and pressed. The door opened and ruined her shot.

A yapping dog announced Gillian's presence. She shoved her phone in her bag, acknowledged the dog's owner and turned to walk away. The dog, still yapping, strained on its lead, sniffed at the air.

'Hey, wait up.'

Gillian stopped. This is getting a little repetitive.

'Were you looking for me?' The dog's owner held the lead tightly, but the dog strained forward and sniffed Gillian's shoes.

'No.'

The young woman tugged the dog to her side. 'Sorry about the dog's interrogation. Likes people. Won't hurt you.'

'That's okay.' Gillian bent down, offered her hand and let the dog lick it.

'You're an Aussie, aren't you?'

'Yep.' Gillian's eyes widened. 'You too?'

'Yeah.'

'Do you live here?'

'At the moment. My sister and I are working our way through Europe. Love Prague. Been here a while. Might even stay a bit longer than planned.'

The dog pulled its owner towards the corner. Gillian walked alongside.

'Plenty is taking me for a walk. We're meeting my sister at the park. You want to keep us company?'

'That'd be nice. Thanks. I've already worn a track through Stromovka, but I'll come with you for a bit.'

After exchanging names, they let the eager dog lead them towards the park.

'So, Morgan, how did she get the name Plenty?'

'Well, *he* has plenty of fur. Drops it everywhere. He poops plenty, eats plenty, sleeps plenty. What else could we call him?'

Gillian chuckled as she looked at the mixed-breed dog, its tail working "plenty". 'You chose well. Dogs are great, aren't they? Takes a lot for a dog not to be happy.' Maybe I'll get a dog when I go home.

'Yeah, Maddy couldn't resist him. Someone dumped three puppies at her work. Plenty was so tiny. Anyway, she brought him home. He's always up for a walk.'

'Maddy, she's your sister?'

'Twin actually.'

'Okay, and where are you from? In Australia, I mean?'

'Brisbane. Holland Park. You?'

'South Perth. WA.' Gillian let the image of her far-away home fade before she said, 'So, you're a twin. Guess you must get on really well.'

'Yeah, mostly.'

As they reached the grass Morgan released Plenty. He scampered away, circling back over an inviting smell, then recommencing his run towards a mound of decaying leaves.

'Thanks for the walk, I'll be on my way,' Gillian said.

'You don't have to go, do you? Stay and meet Maddy.' Morgan looked at her watch. 'She'll be here soon.'

'You sure you don't mind. I'd hate to be a nuisance. Take up your time together.'

'I see her all the time. And, I don't get to talk to another Aussie; like, not often. Maddy does, but I don't. Not many at the hospital where I work. Please stay.'

'Okay, just for a while. Are you a nurse?'

'Nup, just push around a mouse mostly.'

'A mouse? Oh, you mean a computer mouse.'

'Yeah. I work in administration. Same as I did in Brissy. It's hard work, but I don't mind. Pays the bills.'

Gillian's mind flashed to the sterile white walls of a particular hospital. Morgan's shrill whistle broke Gillian's thoughts from spiraling towards blood transfusions and plasma drips.

On Morgan's repeated whistling, Plenty headed back, but then darted towards someone appearing from behind the boundary hedge.

'That's her. Good.' Morgan waved her arms and called out, 'Maddy, over here.'

Plenty raced back to Morgan, jumping up at her as if he hadn't seen her for hours.

'Stop it, you stupid dog,' Morgan said. 'Hi, Maddy. How'd your day go?'

Madison pushed Plenty away from bounding against her legs. 'Go take a run, Plenty. Leave me in peace.'

'Maddy, this's Gillian. She's from Perth. On holidays.'

Gillian and Madison nodded a welcome. 'You look familiar,' Madison said. 'Have I met you before?'

'Don't think so,' Gillian said, pausing as she examined Madison's face. 'But, yes, you do seem familiar. I haven't been in Prague long. Don't know where it could have been. Do you work in a café?'

'Yeah, in Florenc. And part time at the Australian Embassy.'

'Ah, that's where I've seen you,' Gillian said. 'I went to the barbecue.'

'Right, that's where I've seen you. You wore a green jacket.'

'Fabulous memory. Yeah, green jacket. And, you saved me from being a wallflower.'

Morgan asked Gillian, 'How did you get an invite?'

'I was nearly arrested. They thought I was a spy.'

Morgan laughed. Madison's eyebrows shot up. 'No way,' Madison said. 'Surely, they wouldn't have done that.'

'No, they gave in eventually.' Gillian gave a short version of her encounter at the embassy as the three women continued their walk around the garden beds and along a path by a pond. They sat on a bench in the shade and watched children toss bread to squabbling water birds. Plenty had exhausted his adventures and now lay at their feet.

'I was dying to go to that do,' Morgan said.

'You knew I couldn't get you in.' Madison pushed her sister's arm.

'I reckon you could've if you tried harder.'

'They said next time.'

'Yeah, well I believe that when I'm hob-nobbing, next time!'

Madison raised her eyebrows at Morgan and shrugged as she turned to Gillian. 'Sisters! You can't live with them—'

'Could live without one,' Morgan added.

Gillian wriggled forward, preparing to stand, but Madison gripped her arm. 'Don't go. We're often like this. Do you have a sister?'

'Yes.' Gillian leaned back. 'Yes, one sister. Esther's nearly six years older than me.'

'You know, Maddy and I argue a lot, but really, is there anything better than a sister? Like, you don't have to explain stuff to a sister, do you?'

'Yeah,' Madison added. 'Morgan's a pain, most days.' She smirked, but her eyes softened as she glanced at her twin. 'Bossy, my god, can she be bossy!'

Morgan slapped her sister on the arm. 'I am not.'

'Esther's bossy,' Gillian said quietly. 'Thinks 'cos she's older, you know, older, wiser, she can tell me what to do.'

'Exactly!' Madison said.

'Two minutes. I'm two minutes older.'

'Yeah, but still a bossy older sister.'

Plenty decided he had rested long enough and stretched into a standing position. Morgan stroked his head. He moved away, and, as if he hadn't been watching the ducks for almost ten minutes, started yapping at them. As the ducks flapped into the air, the children glared at Plenty, blaming him for their lost friends.

'Time to go,' Madison said. She grabbed Plenty's lead, stopping him from upending a child as he chased a stubborn duck from the edge of the pond.

'Will we see you again?' Morgan asked.

Gillian shrugged, 'I—'

'Maybe at the embassy,' Madison said.

'You might,' Morgan said. 'I'm not on the invitation list.'

'I told you, next time.'

'Yeah, right!'

They turned as Gillian spoke, 'I'm sorry. I didn't mean to cause a row.'

Morgan put her arm around Madison. 'Don't be,' Morgan said. 'We like taking the piss. Don't we, sister dear?'

Madison grinned, leaned into her sister. 'Yeah, who else would we argue with?'

'I really must go,' Gillian said.

'Yeah, we better get going too.'

'Catch ya.'

Following the path away from the pond, Gillian recounted the twins' banter. Good-hearted. Sparing. They must get along if they spend their spare time together. Even while complaining about her being bossy, Morgan hadn't been angry with Madison. *More like teasing*, Gillian thought.

As she strolled towards the tram line, Gillian thought of Esther.

Their mother died just after Esther's nineteenth birthday. Harold Enderson mourned Ruthie completely, but refused to let it rule his life or alter his business momentum. He returned to work immediately after the funeral and placed his wife's responsibilities on Esther.

He handed out money like it was home-grown parsley from under a lemon tree. 'Just get someone to fix it,' he'd say to Esther. Whether it was a blown fuse or Gillian's declining school marks, Harold wanted nothing to do with problems.

'I have enough people demanding my time in the office, ' he said. 'I just want a quiet life at home.'

Harold expected his elder daughter to be as proficient as his secretary. His accountancy practice didn't skip a beat – he didn't want his household to be any different.

Esther became an expert at diverting problems. She organised a neighbour to keep an eye out for thirteen-year-old Gillian after school, paid a gardener and a cleaner, wrote a roster for laundry and kitchen tasks, and spent time re-learning algebra and geometry.

No wonder she fusses, Gillian thought.

She remembered a few of Esther's boyfriends. Thoughtful Clive, Sporty David and Italian Joe with a red mini which kept breaking down – apparently. Forty-five-year-old Tony married twenty-nine-year-old Esther after a brief romance. She became a step-mother to Carmel, who immediately moved to Melbourne to be closer to her mother. Tony and Esther managed a successful handyman business until six years later when Tony died. After selling the business, Esther became a perennial volunteer; prodding and poking every unsuspecting person on her mailing list to donate to her latest pursuit.

Esther's a problem solver – loves getting her teeth into society's problems, Gillian thought. *And, she still thinks she can solve all my problems.*

Not this one. But her heart's in the right place. *Maybe, but she doesn't let me stand on my own two feet.* Can you? *Eventually I will.* Essie doesn't do "eventually". *That's for sure. She can't help interfering.* Surely it's not interfering when you're sisters. *But, I don't need it.* Don't you. *Maybe at the start. Not now? But ... she won't let go.* Of course not, she's your sister.

Gillian sucked in a breath, let it out slowly. 'Yeah, she's my sister.'

Gillian opened her laptop as soon as she returned home.

Hi Essie,
Hope you are well.

Deleting the second line, she tried again.

How's the latest fundraising going?

Gillian stood, went to the fridge, stared at the jar of pickles, pushed aside a container of cheese, picked up the vegemite, changed her mind and put it back. She watched the door close slowly before returning to her computer. Her fingers danced lightly over the keys, not pressing any in particular as she decided what to type.

I miss you.

There! She'd said it.

Thought of you today when I spent time with some twin sisters. Walked to the park with them and Plenty.

I can hear you asking, what twins, who is Plenty? And then you'd be saying it's good that I'm going to a park, with people. I bet you'll want to know everything they said / I said.

Plenty is their dog. I met Madison at the embassy. She's a waiter. Should that be a waitperson? I came across Morgan when I was taking a photo of her door. Did I tell you I'm collecting pictures of doors? Probably not. There are so many stunning doors here. Think I've got about fifty now. I just go walking and see them and take a picture. Thank goodness Patrick got me that new phone. Anyway, Morgan caught me outside her flat. Actually, I don't think she knew about my camera. They're from Qld. Working around Europe.

So, I'm doing okay. Improving one might say. Not there yet. Tears are less. Pain isn't.

Miss you

Your sister, Gilly.

Gillian read the email, resisted the temptation to alter or delete it and sent it before she could change her mind.

The streets around Prosek didn't offer enough varied doors to add to her collection, so the following day Gillian boarded the train and rode through to Florenc. The enormous length of the escalators, as they carried passengers from the depths of the earth, amazed her. She stood for a moment watching in awe. The noise of an arriving train caught her attention. Making an instant decision, she hurried over and stepped on board, deciding to explore the Green Line.

In contrast to Prosek station, Depo Hostivař was claustrophobic and unwelcoming. Leaving the platform and exiting via the stairs, Gillian took only a few minutes before regretting her decision. The end of the Green Line didn't look like a place to wander. She decided to return to Letná.

Recognising the tree-lined streets alongside the tram terminus, Gillian walked towards the park. By happy co-incidence she reached the street where Petra and Izabela lived. The crimson door stood out against the shadows cast by a huge chestnut tree next to the footpath. Gillian knocked on the door and stepped back, stumbling on the step. After waiting a minute, she knocked again. Disappointed, Gillian decided against leaving a note and recommenced her search for more doors.

Coming across only one she hadn't previously snapped, Gillian realised she was covering streets she'd already explored and returned to the shop-lined main street. The aroma from a patisserie she'd ignored last time attacked her senses – probably cinnamon, and of course, coffee. The cool interior, the sparkling tables and an extensive array of cakes welcomed her.

She chose a berry tart and ordered an iced coffee. The creaminess of the custard sitting below the berries caressed her mouth. 'Yum,' she said to the person who placed the iced coffee on the table. 'This is so smooth.'

'Yes, it is made of the best cream.'

'Did you make it?' Gillian sucked on the straw. A shot of cold coffee hit her tongue.

'No, a husband and wife make them. They live quite close, I am told.'

Gillian wiped the serviette over her mouth. 'I think I'll take one home.'

'Sure. Wait until you finish. Maybe you can be tempted with some more.'

While enjoying the tart, she eyed the many delicacies in the display cabinet, continually changing her mind on which ones she'd buy to take home.

She left the patisserie with four different cakes in a container balancing in her bag, and decided to see if Petra was now at home.

Gillian could hear Izabela singing as she reached out to the doorbell. A happy sound, despite being a little flat in tone. A flash of Patrick encouraging Sienna to listen to the key he tapped out as they sang through the doh, ray, me's, made her hesitate. She let the memory form a tender glow before ringing the doorbell.

Petra welcomed Gillian instantly. 'Hello, how nice to see you again. Please, come in.'

Noticing a tea towel in Petra's hand, Gillian asked, 'You're not too busy?'

'Of course not. We've just got home. Izzy is supposed to be changing.' Petra laughed. 'She'll take her time. Come in.'

Replacing her shoes with slip-ons, Gillian put her bag down, lifted out the container of cakes and followed Petra into the large family room. 'I bought these.' She held out the container.

'Ooh, lovely. Would you like tea or coffee?'

'Mamí,' called Izabela as she raced into the room. She stopped and eyed Gillian, then asked her mother, 'Můžu mlíčko?' (Can I have some milk?)

'Izzy, do you remember, Mrs Middleton? Say hello.'

Izabela leaned against the back of a chair. 'Hello.' She turned and opened the fridge.

'Kids.' Petra rolled her eyes. 'Tea or coffee?' she asked again.

'I had a huge iced coffee not long ago, so, black tea, please.'

'Mami, můžu dort?' (Can I have a cake?) Izabela had already lifted the lid of the container and wiggled her finger into a vanilla slice.

'Wait, Izzy. They're not for you.'

'Mamííí.'

'I don't mind,' Gillian said. 'I brought them for you. I'm too full for another one.'

'Já chci čokoládový,' demanded Izzy. (I want the chocolate one.)

Chocolate cupcakes are Patrick's favourite. Oh, were. The thought flashed uninvited through Gillian's mind as she listened to the exchange between mother and child.

With Izabela sitting at the table, nibbling at a piece of sliced cupcake loaded high with vanilla icing, Petra poured the hot water into a teapot.

'Do you always use leaf tea,' Gillian asked.

'Often for guests.'

'How lovely. I never go to that trouble. Teabags are quicker.'

'Yes, they are, but I once went to a Japanese Tea Ceremony. They used powdered green tea, and it seemed so elegant, the process makes it wonderful. I think it adds something to the tea.'

Even though Izabela continually interrupted, 'All five-year-olds do,' Gillian said, the women chatted over the world's problems, favourite books, good recipes, hairstyles and the weather.

Petra didn't brag about Izabela's certificate for spelling, or tell of tomorrow's school picnic she still had to prepare, or the plans for Izzy's fifth birthday.

As Petra poured a fresh cup of tea, the butterfly above her wrist peeked out from the long sleeve of her blouse. Gillian hesitated, waited until Petra sat down again.

'Your tattoo is lovely. Did you have it done when you were a teenager?'

Petra placed her cup in the saucer. 'No.' She pulled up her sleeve and extended her arm. 'It's Bridget's butterfly.'

'It's beautiful.'

'Yes.' Petra traced the edges of the wings with a fingernail. 'Yes, it is beautiful. I had it done on the first anniversary of Bridget's ... when we lost her.'

'Is there a special reason ... for a butterfly?'

Petra stood, disappeared down the passage. Gillian didn't know if she was expected to follow. She remained rigid with procrastination, glad when Petra returned.

'This is Bridget's favourite book. *The Dance of the Butterfly.* I'm sure I could still tell it without looking.' She sat and slid the book across the table.

'How wonderful. The colours are spectacular. The illustrator has done a wonderful job.'

'The story ends with butterflies dancing on the petals of sunflowers. The first time I read the book, Bridget wanted to dance too. Of course, mostly she was in bed, so I invented a kind of dance with our hands. Even when she was so desperately ill, she asked to dance with the butterflies.'

Gillian ran her finger over the sunflowers, around the gossamer wings of the butterfly at the top corner of the page. 'This is like your tattoo.'

'Yes, Bridget called it Tora. She couldn't say Flora at first, but Tora stuck. She was Bridget's favourite.'

Petra sipped her tea while Gillian read the happy story of dancing butterflies from the beginning. 'It's lovely.' She looked at Petra. 'Was it painful, the tattoo?'

'Only for the moment.'

'If only other pains…' Gillian closed the book. 'You're very strong. I'm so glad—'

'Prosím. You are so welcome. You've brought back many emotions, some that have been buried, and now I know for certain that I'll, we, Ivan and I, will be okay. I hope you, no, I know you will survive. You too are stronger than the pain.'

They finished the cooling tea, each with thoughtful contemplation.

The clock above the oven struck half past four.

'I must go.'

'I must start our dinner. You're welcome to stay.'

'Thanks, but I won't. Perhaps another time.'

Petra stood. 'I'm so glad you came. It's been lovely.'

'It has. Very special, once again.' Gillian carried the cups and saucers to the sink, picked up her bag and headed for the door. 'I hope you don't mind me just dropping in.'

'No. You must come again. I'll give you my number. Save you travelling if I'm not home.'

'Thanks, Petra. I love this area. I have so many doors from around here.'

'Have you tried a little further over? The embassies are fabulous.'

'Mm, I might avoid them.' Don't want to be arrested.

'That would be a shame. So many have wonderful doors. You must have them in your collection.'

Armed with directions of several embassies, she caught the tram and then the Metro back to Prosek.

Gillian sat down to chicken pasta, and opened her laptop to choose something to read.

The next morning, still in her yellow pyjamas, Gillian made tea, swiped vegemite across a piece of toast and then opened her laptop. Six new emails sprang to life.

She opened Sandy's first after it demanded her attention with a little red flag, and the worrying subject line of **HELP**.

> Gillian, you have to help me.
> Oh dear! Things are going so wrong. I don't know where to begin. Remember Murray? Of course you do. You have no men on your radar so I know you haven't forgotten my last email. Or do you? Have a bloke I mean. Perhaps you're hiding him from me. You shouldn't, I could... Oh bugger I was going to say I could advise you. Me with all my experience. But not now. Have my own dilemma. In the men department. So, getting back to Murray. HE PROPOSED. How the hell did that happen? I certainly didn't see it coming.
> We went to the Como. You know the one on the Terrace. New and expensive! Had a great eat. Miniscule servings, but delish. Coffee, liqueurs, then Uber back to his place. The place REEKED of good taste. It even had a bidet. West Perth. Classy. Modern.
> Anyway, the sex was good, great. And no, I'm not expanding. Har, har, har.
> The next morning, he cooked breakfast. Then he PROPOSED. Over breakfast. MY GOD!
> You know something, I almost said YES straight away. Well, my dearest friend, he is a good catch. After nearly dropping the gold-ringed mug, I did manage to say I was flattered, and I'd think about it. Think about it!! I've done nothing else.
> HELP!
> BTW: have you heard from Mira? I'm not supposed to tell you, so I won't. She has NEWS.

AND your sister. She didn't actually tell me not to say anything to you. Anyhow! She's been in the paper, society page no less. Ah, now I've caught your attention.

PLEASE tell me what I should do about MURRAY.

Desperate Sandy

Gillian had paused after the first two lines. *No men on my radar. Of course not. The bloke I really want is, is dead.* She read on. Giggling at her friend's comments at Magnificent Murray's proposal, she didn't understand why Sandy would be surprised. It certainly wasn't the first proposal she'd received. Gillian remembered at least three long lunches where Sandy had casually mentioned she'd turned down another luckless man. Sandy knew more than one way to say no, and her heart was only ever dented, never broken.

Gillian's eyes widened when she read that Mira had news. She scanned the rest of the list of emails. Esther being out-and-about didn't rate the same questioning. She minimised Sandy's email and opened Mira's.

Hi Gillian,

Hope you are well. I hope you are sorting things out. I think of you a lot. I miss you at aerobics. Wednesday nights aren't the same. Eleanor strained her ankle and we have a new instructor. She's not switched on. Most of us are tired of doing the same thing. Eleanor is due back in two weeks. Thank goodness. Maggi and Pip says hi. Pip's mum is visiting from Adelaide, so she won't be there next week. Sally lost her job, so she's miserable. She didn't come for coffee afterwards last time. I might have to quit soon. I've just found out I'm pregnant.

What! Gillian read the last line again. Trust Mira to try and sneak the news in between other stuff. Gillian read on quickly, looking for details.

Did Sandy tell you her latest boyfriend proposed? She can't decide. Funny isn't it. She makes decisions for her importing business every ten seconds of the day. Did you know she's just sealed a deal from India? She gave me one of the samples. A shimmering mauve and gold table runner. I bought a vase with artificial pansies. They match perfectly. Lily wants one for her bedroom.

I've cut out a photo of Esther from the paper. She's with a chap, Theo Weaver, and some other people. Theo is a journalist, so the article says. Do you want me to send it or keep it until you get home?

Rohan is due at football soon, so must finish.

Hope you are doing okay.

Love Mira

Gillian started her reply immediately.

Mira,

How exciting. Pregnant. Lucky you. But, you shouldn't have just snuck it in. SHOUT about it. For goodness sake!

Gillian meant it, but she sighed, glanced across at the photo of Patrick and Sienna. *Not fair!* Wrapping her arms across her chest, she rocked sideways and considered what else to say to Mira. Her friend had obviously downplayed her news, tucking it between gossip and Sandy's problem. *Huh! Nice problem.*

You must be over the moon. I guess Jamie is bragging. I remember when Rohan and Lily were born. He thought he was the only man who had ever become a father. Have you told the kids?

Gillian thought of the plans she and Patrick had made. *A bigger home when Sienna's siblings were born – one with a large backyard. No pony, but perhaps a puppy to add to the goldfish Sienna wanted to feed six times a day.* She banished those thoughts and started again.

I received Sandy's plea for help. What a laugh. I don't understand why she hasn't just done her usual and said no. Perhaps she's tired of smorgasbord! Keep me updated. Please. Although I'm sure I'll get a full report from hers truly. She's certainly never shy in spreading her own gossip.

BTW I want to hear about the bean in the womb. Don't you dare think I won't want to? I'm managing not to cry all the time. Met a lovely lady, Petra, who lost a child to illness. She's helped a lot. Just because I feel someone else has been through it. She's survived. I think we'll be friends, even when I come home. Keep sending your news. It might even help me if you do.

Give the kids a hug. Tell Jamie congrats! (Despite him only doing the easy bit)

Love Gilly

Oh, say hi to Maggi and Pip and Eleanor and Sally. I'm afraid I haven't done one scrap of exercise. Except lots of walking.

Oh, don't send the photo; I'm sure Esther will have it filed already.

After reading through Sandy's and Mira's emails, and her replies again, Gillian thought of the times they had argued over the simplest of things: Sandy's new hair colour, Mira's choice of wall paint, the benefit of gerbera's in the ground or in a pot, and countless other trivia.

She remembered both her friends attending her wedding. Mira had married three years previously. Sandy returned from New York especially for the wedding. Both refused to be bridesmaids. 'Too old,' Sandy said on a distorted Skype connection. Mira couldn't imagine standing in front of "all those people", despite Gillian's encouragement. Esther also refused bridesmaid status saying, 'Even if you call it Matron-of-Honour, I'm still not doing it.' She did agree to be a legal witness and spoke admirably for their deceased parents at the reception. Gillian settled for Patrick's cousin's six-year-old daughter as a flower girl. 'She's old enough to hold my bouquet while I accept Patrick's ring,' Gillian told Sandy in an email. Patrick's friend and fellow teacher was best man. Glen made sure there were no embarrassing incidents at the buck's night, but teased Patrick continually throughout his eloquent speech.

Together the three friends had been through Mira and Gillian's pregnancies, Sandy's romances, Sandy's career highs and lows, Mira's parents' struggle to achieve Australian citizenship and the death of Gillian's father. Gillian knew these were special people and she missed them. *I should think about going home. Yes, I'll think about it ... soon.*

Gillian deleted the email request from someone who was willing to share their fifteen-million-dollar inheritance, and opened the email from Esther.

Gilly,
Sorry I haven't been in touch for a few days. My latest fundraiser took a huge effort. We raised over $12,000 for Telethon.

A journalist, Theo Weaver, was most helpful in getting the event publicised. This increased the numbers significantly. We've had lunch at Crown a couple of times. He's promised to help with my next one.

I've checked on your house. I think you should ask the agent about how often the lawn is being mowed.

Saw Mira last week at the farmer's market. She looks like she's put on weight. I've always thought she's a bit thin. So that's good. Haven't heard from Sandy. Suppose I wouldn't with you not being here. I did run into Mr Hawkins, remember him, he had a limp we used to copy as kids. He looks the same, but must be at least ninety. He had someone with him, and then I wasn't too sure it was him – so I didn't stop. Strange how some live to be old, others don't. Mum's birthday is next week. I'll visit her grave. Dad's while I'm there. I'll stop at Patrick and Sienna's. I can get flowers and leave some on each plaque.

Have you decided when you're coming home? I think you've been away long enough. You could fly via Singapore. Have a real holiday. Maybe I could meet you there.

Stay positive.

Ess

Reading the email slower the second time through, Gillian knew her eyebrows were at an all-time high. While Esther's bossiness showed through, the last line left Gillian amazed. She would meet me in Singapore!

While she ignored the reference to the cemetery and concentrated on imagining holidaying with her sister, Gillian went to the fridge and broke off a piece of celery.

For a holiday? Just the two of us? We've never done that! She pulled the celery through her teeth, letting the stringy bits hang on the piece between her fingers. *It's possible, I guess.*

She walked around the room and stopped by the window. People strolled, children ran, cars stopped at the lights, trucks went on their way.

Flowers, flowers for Patrick. He'd want kangaroo paws. Or something native. Sienna? Roses. After all, she is Sienna Rose. Gillian tossed the remaining celery at the bin. It missed. She didn't pick it up.

It should be me. I want to take those flowers. But you're not there. *No, but I'm going home.* When? *Soon.* When's soon? *Not yet. Not quite yet.*

Dear Essie,

I'm so glad the fundraising went well. Do I sense something special with this Theo? You should grab the chance with both hands.

I remember Mr JENKINS, not Hawkins. I had a good giggle when I remembered you with that toothbrush under your nose, and a hand-towel around your shoulders, limping along the passage. What horrid kids. But I guess we were pretty normal. I also remember Dad giving us a whack on our bottoms when he saw us imitating Mr Jenkins. Fancy him reaching ninety. He seemed so old when we were teenagers. Funny how "old" changes.

Thanks for the offer of flowers. Yes, please. But they have to be fresh. I don't want plastic ones. Let me know how much. You make me feel guilty – about Mum and Dad's. You are always more diligent. Perhaps I'll go more. Now.

See, no tears. I'm healing.

Am I? Gillian thought. *Just because the tears have stopped.* Are you? *A bit.* What's a bit? *Well, the panic has gone.* Panic? *Yes, the fear of the fragility of my life ahead.* That's understandable. *Mm, but can I live with the uncertainty. Don't think I can.* You have to get on. *Yes, so everyone keeps saying.* Put it behind. *I can't.* Well, bear it, and keep going. *Yes, I think I'm starting to do that.* Good.

Mira is pregnant. So she will get fatter. Much fatter. I bet Jamie is already bragging. He's a good hubby and father. They'll be okay as long as fate leaves them alone.

I'll give Singapore some thought, but I'm not ready to come home just yet. Have a few more doors to photograph. Joking aside, I feel I have more to see, more to do, more something to achieve before I can come home.

Oh, and don't worry about the house. It'll be fine.

Tell me more about this Theo Weaver.

Gilly.

While thinking about the process of going home, Gillian remembered the gifts she'd bought for Patrick and Sienna. It brought a jelly-like feeling to her stomach, which turned into warm custard around her heart. The warmth made her smile. Prague had been kind to her. Prague had opened a door – several doors – greeted her, smiled at her, despite her initial response of misery and disregard.

If they'd been alive, I would never have come to Prague. If they'd been alive, Pinocchio wouldn't be hiding in the bottom of a wardrobe in Prosek.

'Ah, Pinocchio. I can't have you staying in there.'

She pulled the large paper bag from the bottom of the wardrobe, a string of beads wriggled onto the floor as the bag caught
on a shoe.

Tipping the remaining contents on the unmade bed, Gillian
clenched her bottom lip. She took a deep breath, picked up a
man's t-shirt with "I bought this in Prague" emblazoned across
the front and held it against her chest. 'Might be a bit big.'

She dropped the t-shirt and untangled the strings of the puppet from glittering hair clips. 'Izzy can have this.' And these.

Dialing Petra's number, Gillian paced around the bedroom.

'Ahoj, hello, Gillian.'

'Petra, ahoj. How are you?'

'I am well. You?'

'Yes, I'm okay. Look, I was wondering if you're at home.'

'Not at the moment. I'm at a shop. Are you near here?'

'No, I'm at home, but if you're going to be there later, could
I come over?'

'Yes. I'll be about another hour. It will be nice to see you.'

'Thanks, Petra. It's just that I remember you saying it was
Izzy's birthday soon. I have a parcel for her.'

'How lovely.'

Gillian ran her tongue over her top teeth. 'I hope I'm not being a nuisance. I mean, I should have brought it yesterday, but
it only just occurred to me.' She paused, then added again, 'I
don't want to be a nuisance.'

Petra answered carefully. 'Of course you are not. I would
like you to visit again. Come before school finishes. We'll be
able to talk without being interrupted.'

'Thanks. Thanks, Petra. I'll see you soon.'

After disconnecting, Gillian gripped the phone, breathed
deeply. *I can do this. I have to do this.*

Gillian scurried to the shop, bought wrapping paper, sticky tape and pink curling ribbon. The custard around her heart threatened to curdle as she read the cute messages in cards for five-year-old girls. *It's okay. It's for Izzy.*

Once back in her unit, she hastily wrapped the gifts. Pinocchio's hat broke through the butterfly-laden wrapping paper requiring a wad of sticky tape to repair it. The beads and hair clips caused less trouble and a gala of decorating ribbon dwarfed the smaller packet.

With her eye on the time, Gillian hurried to the train, glad to have made a decision which just a few weeks ago would have been impossible.

The train journey became one of squeezing to the left for departing passengers, then shuffling right to allow a pram and a bike to be pushed into the carriage.

Hoping the tram wouldn't be as crowded, she boarded the next one through to Petra's stop.

Unable to dodge the personal space of the many commuters on the tram Gillian squeezed between an old woman and a teenager. Avoiding the impertinent gaze of the old woman who struggled for balance, Gillian kept her eyes on the floor, but as the tram negotiated a bend her bag with Izzy's gifts slid from between her feet.

As she hooked the bag back with her left foot, she recalled choosing the puppet on the day she'd been pretending she'd be taking it home to her daughter. She'd imagined performing some sort of dance with it to Patrick's tune for Sienna. *For the Love of Sienna* whispered over the noises of the tram and the murmurings of passengers. She rummaged for a tissue and sniffed into it.

'Co sakra fňukáte?'

An elbow hit her ribs. 'What?' Gillian asked as she moved away, bumping against the teenager on her left.

'What the hell are you snivelling about?'

The old woman's perfect English shocked Gillian as much as the offensive question.

She sniffed again, and glared at the woman.

'Got a cold then?'

'No.'

'Well, girl, nothing's worth crying over.' She thumped her walking stick into the floor, emphasizing the word "nothing".

Gillian clutched her bag tighter, stared straight ahead.

The woman's elbow struck again. 'Nothing,' she growled.

'Shut up!' Gillian's whispered retort reached the intended ears. 'You have no idea. Just shut up.'

The old woman's unplucked eyebrows frowned, the multitude of wrinkles on her forehead reacted. Then her eyebrows shot up and her cracked lips smirked. As the tram pulled into the station, she bumped against scowling teenagers, pushing forward in her attempt to alight first. Gillian juggled her possession into position and waited for the platform to become accessible. She strode away from the tram stop. The slow thud of the woman's stick followed.

Anger rolled around Gillian's stomach as she hurried towards the street corner, stepping between strolling schoolchildren and suited men. The throng of pedestrians stopped at the lights. She ignored the rattly breathing of the old woman who pushed between Gillian and another pedestrian.

'Huh! Hit a raw nerve, eh?'

Gillian turned, snapped, 'What's it to you?'

The woman's bulbous neck jiggled in time with her cackle.

Gillian closed her eyes for a moment, heard cars braking. Someone brushed past, but she refused to react when the woman tapped her arm, laughed again and plodded across the intersection.

The lights turned red, green.

Red again.

Gillian frowned as she watched the old woman, now ambling on the other side of the street, brandishing her stick at a child on a wobbling bike.

What's her issue?

The lights turned green. Gillian's aggressive stride enabled her to overtake the fresh swarm of commuters across the intersection as she headed towards Petra's.

Why should she care what I do? So what if I sniff? So what if I even cry? What's it to her?

At first Gillian strode defiantly, cursing the old woman for insensitivity. Then, remembering the woman's creased dress, matted hair and a total lack of grooming, thought, *I hope I never get like that.*

She placed her hand around her ponytail, lifted it and then let it drop. *When did I last have it trimmed?* She looked at her chipped fingernails. *Mm.*

It just shows, doesn't it, she told her inner voice. *There's a lesson everywhere. As for one person I'll never see again telling me nothing is worth crying over, well, of course there is. Silly old cow!*

By the time she reached the familiar red door, Gillian chuckled at the encounter.

After closing the door Petra hugged Gillian. 'I'm glad you came.'

'I'm glad I came.' She removed her shoes, replaced them with the offered slip-ons. It was a custom she found unnecessary when the floor was tiled, but she certainly didn't voice her opinion.

'Tea? Water?'

'I think I need coffee.' Gillian placed her bag with the gifts on the table.

'Need? What has happened?'

'Nothing really. Just an old woman making fun of me.'

'When?'

'On the tram. Just now. She … her English was pretty good.'

'What did she say?'

'I was sniffing. No tears, but she assumed … She just … I guess, teased me. But it's okay now. I think she actually prodded me along a bit. How do I explain – a kick up the backside us Aussies would say.'

Petra chuckled. 'I like that saying. But, are you okay?'

'Absolutely. Lesson learned, and anyway, I have nicer things to think about.' Gillian slowly tipped the two parcels out of her bag. 'I remember you saying it's Izzy's birthday soon. I thought she might like these.'

'That's kind of you. It must have been hard to choose them.'

Gillian accepted the coffee, sat and stirred in some milk. She'll understand. Gillian placed the spoon down slowly, made sure it aligned perfectly with the straight edge of the table. I know she will. 'I bought them for Sienna.'

Petra's eye flicked from the gift to Gillian's solemn face. She put her hand on Gillian's shoulder. 'Then they are even more precious.'

Gillian paused, thinking about Petra's words. 'Mm, yes. I bought them in a fit of denial. I can see that, but ...' She picked up the gift-wrapped puppet. 'Hana and I danced with Mr Pinocchio, so he does have some happy memories.'

Petra pulled out a chair, sat, raised her eyebrows and asked, 'Danced? Now you have to tell me about that.'

Telling of her friendly neighbour and how they'd danced with Pinocchio, further softened Gillian's mood. During a second cup of coffee, Petra asked if Gillian would like to attend Izabela's birthday party. 'Could you manage a couple of hours with six little children? There will be Izzy's cousin, two girls and two boys from school. You are most welcome. What do you think?'

'When is it?' Gillian's calendar lacked appointments, but she wanted the time to let the invitation sink in. *Could I? Could I watch happy children when Sienna is ... No don't go there. Perhaps it'll harden me. Against what? Pain, loss.*

Gillian's mouth tightened.

'I understand,' Petra said. 'It's okay. I just thought ... Her birthday is Monday, so the party is on Saturday. I don't want you to feel you must.'

Gillian ran her finger around the rim of the cup. 'No, it's okay. I might.' She looked at Petra. 'Do you think I should? Do you think it would help?'

'I have no clue.' Petra shrugged. 'Some days, nothing helps. You just have to get through to the days where something nice happens. Like your time with Pinocchio.' She folded her arms across her chest. 'Izabela looks a lot like Bridget. Sometimes I imagine how it would be to have two daughters.' Petra looked up quickly and a grin immerged. 'Imagine trying to get a word in with two like Izzy?' She reached over and held Gillian's hand for a moment. 'I don't know if it would help, but you're very welcome.'

'Could I ring you?'

'Yes, but you could just arrive. Around two o'clock.'

'No, I'll ring.' Gillian drank the last of her coffee. 'Do you need help? I seem to remember children's parties require a lot of work.'

'Ivan will be here, and his sister, she's making some biscuits. No, I think I will be prepared. You'll be our guest.'

'I'll let you know.'

'Six children!' Petra rolled her eyes and chuckled. 'Heavens knows what we're in for.'

'I'll let you know tomorrow. And now I must go. I've held you up enough.'

On her way home Gillian remembered each of Sienna's birthdays.

When she turned one, they had fairy bread, party pies and saveloys, wine and beer, with six adults and no other children. They celebrated Sienna's second birthday at the zoo with Mira and her family. Esther called around in the evening with a huge teddy bear and a cupcake which almost toppled over from the weight of the two candles stuck in the mountainous frosting. Sandy sent a card from London, backed it up two weeks later with an embarrassing amount of money.

As a three and four-year-old, Sienna grasped the idea of a day of spoiling, even if she wasn't totally aware of the significance of the day. Numerous gifts, cake, and adoring adults taking many photographs, filled a day of celebration.

Yes, we had lovely birthdays. No more, though. *No, none.* Well, should you forgo Izabela's because Sienna won't have her fifth birthday? *Fifth, sixth, tenth, twenty.* No, none of those either. But Izzy's fifth is on Saturday. *Yes?* Go, then. *Yes, you're right. I will go.*

The day of the party came soon enough. Gillian skilled herself to think of Izabela as she left the tram.

She took a deep breath, straightened her blouse and rang the bell. Excited chatter and Petra yelling in Czech reverberated. Gillian knew she'd be in a sea of indistinguishable words. Her phrasebook would be of no help with kids probably all speaking at once.

'Come in. Watch out for the hordes. Ticho, děti! Buďte potichu a pozdravte paní Middleton.' (Quiet, children, be quiet and say hello to Mrs Middleton.)

'Ahoj,' two children chorused. Izabela waited next to her mother; the others rushed back down the hallway.

'Hello,' Izabela said. 'Your parcels I have not opened.' She paused. 'Thank you.'

Gillian bent down. 'I hope you will like them.'

Izabela looked up at her mother. 'Můžu si to otevřít hned?' (Can I open them now?) She ran off without hearing the answer.

'Come through. We have wine, lots. What would you like?' Petra took Gillian's bag. 'Go through. Don't worry about your shoes today. The children have already spoiled my clean floor. I'll put your bag in my bedroom.'

As Gillian entered the main room, Izabela grabbed her hand. 'Daddy says I am to wait. Can I open it now?'

'Of course. Let's see what's in it?'

Izabela let go of Gillian's hand and took the two parcels from the dresser, plonked down on a floor rug and ripped open the larger gift. Adults leaned over her, children knelt or squatted on the rug. One wriggled closer to Izabela and pulled the wrapping paper from her hand. The happy chatter smothered Gillian's anticipated hurt.

The puppet was an instant success and with Ivan's dexterity in making it come to life, it kept the children amused while Petra, Ivan's sister, Lydia, and Gillian completed the last of the preparations for the birthday feast.

The children's noise ebbed and flowed with the games and consumption of party food. With a second glass of wine half finished, Gillian stood back and watched.

Then with a natural conclusion hovering, children, prompted by their parents' arrival, thanked both Petra and Ivan as they said goodbye.

Izabela wanted another piece of cake, and grizzled when Ivan said no. She brought one of her new English books and asked Gillian to read it to her.

'Yes, go. Read it. We'll clear up a bit. Then we can have coffee,' Petra said.

With a flip of sadness turning into pleasure as Izabela snuggled up against her on the couch, Gillian opened the book and started reading.

The story ended and Izabela put her head against Gillian's body. 'It is nice story,' Izabela said, her eyes drooping. Gillian wrapped her arm around the child. Her heart warmed; snuggly as the cuddly five-year-old.

The dishwasher hummed, the kettle boiled and the adults sighed, appreciating the almost quiet. Ivan carried Izabela to her bed. A disjointed sleeping pattern could be managed later.

'Success,' he said as he re-entered the room. 'I think it was a great success.'

There were scraps of happy dreams. Mostly of giant cakes, tumbling children and for some unknown reason, a skipping rope Gillian mastered like a professional from Cirque du Soleil.

Sunday. Refreshed from a decent sleep, she searched the internet, re-read the tourist leaflets and tucked a couple into her bag for later.

After walking through Old Town again, Gillian spotted the seven-foot-tall sculpture of the world-famous psycho-analyst Sigmund Freud hanging with one hand from a metal beam high above the cobbled streets. The leaflet explained: "The unusual artwork had proven so popular it has been exhibited in cities all over the world including Chicago, London and Berlin. Often mistaken for a suicide attempt, the sculpture has also been responsible for several calls to emergency services."

As other pedestrians dodged her, Gillian stood, engrossed in the profound art. Her mind wandered from fragility to stubbornness – while Freud hung on relentlessly, oblivious to those who ignored him, those who stared without contemplation or others, like Gillian, trying to fathom the message. With a deep intake of breath, she flipped over the leaflet and left Freud to his battle.

She found her way through to the Jewish quarter – information read: "Its history began in the 13th century when Jews living in Prague were ordered to vacate their homes and settle in this one area."

Feeling the aura of Jewish struggles, she headed away from the sad tombstones, pausing at the Franz Kafka monument of a huge jacket with a small man on its shoulders, before entering an outdoor cafe.

With the assistance of an enthusiastic waiter, she ordered pickled cheese and a large Pilsner. Sharing a long wooden table, the other patrons buoyed her mood, nominating other landmarks she must see, and by the time she left the café she was ready for more cheerful pursuits.

After being puzzled by the odd statue, The Franz Kafka Museum was a must. The displays included several first editions of Kafka books as well as original letters, diaries and drawings created by Kafka.

Gillian bought a bookmark with Kafka's quote, "Prague never lets you go… this dear little mother has sharp claws."

As she wandered through to the Metro, she knew it would be true. She'd remember this dear little country forever.

Monday. Gillian opted for a river cruise to the zoo. Tourists from all corners of the earth happily included her in their day as they stood at close quarters on the boat, experiencing the rise and fall of water as they passed through the locks, waving to the numerous small craft on the Vltava, and seemingly shouting Na zdraví before every mouthful of lager.

Her day quietened as she strolled around the zoo on her own. Compelled to photograph the Czech kangaroos, – 'Hi, Skippy,' she giggled – acknowledging how ridiculous it seemed that many creatures she'd seen for the first time, weren't recorded. The astounding number of giraffes, surprised Gillian. 'We've got two, maybe three, in our Zoo,' she commented to a couple also admiring the tall elegant creatures.

'I've never seen so many,' the man replied. Gillian snapped many of the twenty-or-more herd.

After hours enjoying the numerous exhibitions, and reading most of the presented information, her brain wouldn't absorb any more except how to enjoy a tall glass of orange juice.

The seventy-five-minute return cruise was low key with most patrons succumbing to the exhaustive day, although some were convinced one more lager was necessary.

Satisfied she'd played the role of tourist satisfactorily, she returned home ready for something to eat.

Finishing a bowl of pumpkin soup and a crispy roll, Gillian nibbled some cashews as she scrolled through Facebook before falling captive to Solitaire. When the screen finally yelled "Success" she shut her laptop and prepared for bed.

Deciding on a slow Tuesday, Gillian had a leisurely breakfast and curled up on the couch to finish *Samantha's Folly*. Leaving even the worst of stories unfinished always played on her mind – *the author had made the effort, so should the reader!* It took an hour of headshaking and eye-rolling as she struggled through the last chapters, grimacing at the tackiness of the love scenes and sniggering at the perfect ending where the two lovers gazed into magnificent eyes and murmured clichéd promises. While considering how she would have written the ending, her mobile rang.

Gillian scrambled through her bag, locating it just in time. 'Hello.'

'Gillian, Max. Max Barkley. From the embassy.'

'Hi, Max from the embassy.'

'Are you making fun of me?'

She grinned as she replied, 'Yeah.'

'I wasn't sure you'd remember my name.'

'I did. How are you? Busy?'

'Bit of a lull at present, but there's always paperwork.'

'Good. Hate to have the ambassador not being able to ambass something.'

He laughed. 'That's not a word.'

After a short silence Max spoke first. 'I wondered if you're up for another posh outing.'

'Maybe. What is it?'

'The Canadians are putting on a dinner. I've been invited, plus one.'

'Okay, when?'

'I've left it a bit late, it's this Thursday.'

'Are you saying I'm a plus three, four?'

'Three, four?'

'Max, have you asked others and I'm last on the list.'

Silence.

'Max?'

'No, Gillian. It's taken me a while to build up the nerve to ask. You're definitely my plus one.'

'Okay, sorry.'

'Well, yes or no?'

'Do I need a posh frock?'

'Afraid so.'

Silence.

'Is that a yes then?'

'Yep.'

'Good.'

Silence.

'Will you send a formal invitation or do I have to guess the details?'

'Sorry. No. Um, I'll pick you up Thursday evening. Seven. Is that okay?'

'Sure.'

'I'll come up. Don't wait downstairs.'

'Oh, okay.'

Silence.

'See you then,' Max said.

'Okay. Yep, see you then.'

That was awkward, Gillian thought, as she shut her mobile and placed it on the kitchen bench. *Thursday, right, two days to find a dress. Wish Sandy was here. But right now, I need some fresh milk.*

Returning from the local shop with milk and cherries, Gillian spotted Hana sitting on the bench in the common area, her shopping trolley propped against the end.

'Hana, Ahoj,' Gillian said. She sat down next to Hana, tapped her on the hand, raised her eyebrows in question. 'Hana, dobře?'

'Není mi dobře. Teče mi znosu. Asi jsem nastydla.' (I am not so good. My nose runs. I think I am getting a cold.) Hana forced a sneeze, pretended to blow her nose, shook her head as she frowned.

'Not so good, eh?' Gillian placed her hand on Hana's shoulder, trying to show sympathy. Cow, horse, here we are again. Damn! I'd love to tell her about Izzy.

Hana reached into her bag. 'Elena.'

'Elena? What?'

'Elena mi dala mobil. Tady někde je. Elena,' she said again as she held out a phone towards Gillian.

'Is it Elena's? Why do you have it? What are you trying to tell me?'

Hana opened the phone, tapped a few times, waited for a connection, then shouted into it. 'Já tu sedím s Gillian. Promluvíš sní? Řekni jí, kdy přijdeš.' (I am sitting with Gillian. Will you speak to her? Tell her when you are coming.) She didn't wait for a reply, but thrust the small phone towards Gillian. 'Elena.'

'Hello? Elena?' Gillian asked.

'Ahoj. Babička has asked me to say I am to visit on Thursday. You are to go to her house for lunch.'

'Thursday? Oh, I've been invited out for dinner. I wouldn't be able to eat lunch as well.'

'That will disappoint, but it is all right. Let me speak to her.'

Gillian reacted silently. Isn't it always the way? Nothing on one's calendar, then two the same day. I suppose I could go to Hana's and not eat much. Impossible. Hana would be insulted.

Elena finished talking to her grandmother and spoke to Gillian again. 'Babi said she's pleased you are to go for dinner. Is it with the nice man from the embassy?'

Gillian said yes, then handed the phone back to Hana.

Their conversation continued, Hana glanced at Gillian in between sentences and finally passed the phone to her again.

'Do you have a dress?' Elena said. 'And earrings? She has
many. She doesn't mind. Wants you to be nice.'

'Thanks, Elena, I haven't got a dress yet. Planning to go to
the city tomorrow.'

'Let her show you her things. It will please her.'

'It's just so difficult. I don't know enough Czech.'

'This does not matter. Babi likes you. You can do it.'

'Okay, I will, but will it be okay with Hana?'

'I'll ask.'

Grandmother and granddaughter chatted for several minutes
before Hana gave the phone to Gillian again.

'Yes?' Gillian said.

'Babička says you to go to her when you get your dress. She
will give you a, how do you call it in English, something to
keep you warm at evening? Anyway, she will be home.'

'Good. Let's hope I can find something suitable. I'll go down
and show her. Let her help. Thanks, Elena. By the way, should-
n't you be at school on Thursday?'

A short silence ended with Elena assuring Gillian that she
wasn't missing anything important at school, and that permission had been granted. Without knowing anything about school
procedures, Gillian could only take the teenager at her word.

After a brief chat with Elena, Hana ended the call grinning
broadly. 'Skvělé, skvělé, budete mít hezký večer, ty a ten milý
muž z velvyslanectví.' (Lovely, lovely, you and the nice man
from the embassy will have a nice time.) She gripped her trolley, eased onto her feet and pointed towards the lift. 'Pojďte,
půjdeme společně.' (Come, we go together.)

They rode in the lift to the first floor. The warmth of Hana's departing hug made Gillian respond. She touched the old woman's cheek. 'Bye, Hana. I hope your cold doesn't get worse.'

The desire to present a good impression at a level of society she wasn't used to created stress. During Wednesday morning's search, Gillian had two supposedly calming coffees in between several stores and countless unsuitable dresses. Finally, a helpful salesperson found a midnight blue dress that fell comfortably over Gillian's small stomach bump.

Arriving at Hana's Gillian hoped the dress would still be gorgeous away from the lighting of an upmarket boutique.

'Ahoj. Pojďte dál, pojďte dál. Máte šaty.' (Come in, come in. You have a dress.) Hana ushered Gillian into her room taking the paper shopping bag from her.

'Ahoj, Hana. How is your cold?' Damn the language barrier. Her brow wrinkled, she coughed and pointed to Hana.

Hana shrugged. 'Ne, nezhoršilo se to. Ale stále mi teče z nosu.' (It hasn't developed. But my nose still runs.) She placed the paper bag on a chair and eased the dress from the tissue.

'It cost me a fortune,' Gillian said.

'Krásný, krásný,' Hana murmured. (Beautiful.) She held it in front of her chest and took a few halting waltz steps. 'Krásný.' Then she passed it to Gillian. Nodding exaggeratingly while pointing towards her bedroom, Hana made her request clear.

'Okay, but I don't have the right underwear, and I'm not going to put these on.' Gillian pulled out a smaller bag from the shopping bag and revealed black bra and panties.

Hana raised her eyebrows, covered her mouth with her hand and giggled shyly. 'Oo la la,' she said in a high-pitched voice.

'Right.' Gillian disappeared behind the half-closed bedroom door and changed into her new dress. She emerged and waited for Hana to say something. Hana instructed Gillian to turn around. She realigned the broad shoulder strap and fondled the skirt. 'Pana velvyslance určitě ohromíte. Ještě pojďte sem. Najdeme pro vás nějaký šperk.' (You will stun the ambassador. Now come in here again. I will find some jewel for you to wear.) She led Gillian into the bedroom where she opened a box with gold-leaf lilies decorating the lid and lifted out a chain with one pearl. 'Tohle?' (This?)

By the time they had worked their way through Hana's box of semi-precious and costume jewellery, they had a collection of options on the bed. Gillian had mixed emotions after agreeing to Max's invitation, but now as Hana's excitement rubbed off, she was looking forward to the event. Hana offered a fur stole, which Gillian refused, but accepted a gossamer wrap of the palest mauve.

After changing back into her jeans and blouse, Gillian stayed for a cup of tea, bread, cheese and some cold sausage. 'I won't have to have dinner,' she said as she patted her stomach and headed for the stairs.

A habitual walk through the park filled the early part of Thursday morning. Then she returned for a toast-and-coffee breakfast.

Gillian held the new dress at arm's length in shaking hands. Her mind somersaulted through the positives and negatives of such an outfit. Twisting the hook of a wire hanger she hung the dress on the outside of the wardrobe. With Hana's wrap draped over one shoulder of the blue dress, Gillian stood back and admired the effect.

It's a perfect dress. For romance. *No!* Well it is. *Yes, but romance isn't on my mind.* Really? *No way.* Why are you going then? *Because he's a nice man.* And? *I'm allowed, aren't I?* Of course, but ... *But what?*

Gillian ran her hand down the soft material, picked it up by the hem and placed it against her cheek.

Oh, Patrick, it's okay, isn't it? You don't mind, do you? A prickle of tears built. *I'll be good.* Tears disappeared with a *throaty giggle. I'm just going to dinner. There'll be dozens of people. Shit!*

Thinking about making small talk with strangers, and dignitaries at that, Gillian's stomach flipped. But, at the Canadian embassy, she shouldn't have to battle the language barrier. Most would speak English. Of sorts, she added with a condescending grin.

With the day settling into evening Gillian checked that Autumn Blush hadn't smudged onto her teeth. She tried to check the back of her dress in the small bathroom mirror with little success. She experimented with Hana's wrap over her arm, around her shoulders, then gave up and dropped it over the back of a chair. Opening her small handbag, she checked that tissues, comb, phone and keys hadn't, by some means, disappeared since she'd put them there ten minutes ago. At seven o'clock she tucked the bag under her arm, picked up the wrap and stood by the door. No, too obvious. She put the wrap and her bag on the kitchen counter and went to the window. Although she couldn't see the carpark, she watched the road for a car she wouldn't recognise.

At five past seven Gillian leaned against the door, listening for the lift. She heard someone sneeze; a dog bark. When the lift door finally swooshed open, she scurried away, paused a moment longer when Max knocked, smoothed the already smooth skirt, took a deep breath and let it out slowly before opening the door.

'Sorry,' Max said. 'The driver was held up.'

'That's fine,' Gillian said as she closed the door behind them.

He grinned, held out his arm. 'Posh suits you. You look lovely.'

As the car darted through traffic Gillian asked if there was protocol to follow, any subjects to avoid, and would she be out of her depth? He offered assurances on all counts and they arrived before they had to resort to discussion on the warm weather.

'Have you got your camera?' Max asked as the car pulled up outside the Canadian embassy. The driver jumped out and opened the door for Gillian.

'Um, yes. I've got my mobile. Why?'

'You might want to get this door. They've blended the beautiful old building with a fairly new one. You won't get this style in the other areas.'

She raised her eyebrows at him over the roof of the car. 'Might I get arrested?'

Max came around the car and took her by the arm. 'Not while you're with me,' he teased.

Spotting the security men and the CCTV cameras, she pushed her elbow into his side. 'Diplomatic immunity is it?'

He laughed. 'Comes in handy.' He spoke to the driver and led Gillian towards the entrance.

With a gregarious Chilean ambassador on her left, a German businessman (with eyebrows like past Australian Prime Minister, Robert Menzies) and his wife sitting opposite, and Max to her right, she reminded herself to look interested. Through the entrée Gillian kept her elbows in and scooped from the far side of the bowl. During the main course she managed to chuckle appropriately at a tale told by the German. By the time they served pancakes and maple syrup (presented haute cuisine style) Gillian had given glowing descriptions of Kings Park and its expansive views of Perth. The guests then moved to another room with large settees and small marble-topped tables where hovering waiters offered coffee, and liqueurs in tiny crystal glasses.

'Not so bad, eh?' Max settled himself next to Gillian in the back seat of the embassy car.

'I must admit I was a little nervous. It's the swankiest event I've been to.'

'Really?'

'One can hardly compare it to the musician's annual dinner, can one? I mean, they book a local restaurant, talk quavers, crotchets, tension of violin strings. Far cry from the German economy or the state of Chilean education.'

'You weren't bored, were you?' Max put his hand over hers. 'I mean tonight.'

Gillian turned her hand over, put her fingers through his. 'No, I enjoyed it. Anna Schroeder was delightful. She's promised to send me the recipe for sauerkraut. I'm sorry but I didn't have anything to write my contact details on. She said she'd send it to you. Email. You don't mind?'

'Not at all. It'll give me an excuse to see you again.'

She squeezed his fingers. 'You could send it on by email.'

'We're here, sir,' called out the driver. Once again, he jumped out and opened Gillian's door. 'You going up, sir?'

Max got out the other side, shut the door and came around the car. 'Yes,' he said to the driver.

'You don't have to,' Gillian said. 'I'm okay from here.'

'I can wait, sir. I have my book.' The driver grinned; stepped towards his seat.

'No, I'll see you up. He's used to waiting.'

As they rode up in the lift, Gillian struggled with Max's closeness. She could feel his eyes on her face, but she concentrated on the red indicator light as it announced each floor. She pulled her keys from her bag, fumbled with unlocking the door, opened it a fraction before she said, 'Thanks, Max. I had a lovely time.'

He took her arm and gently pulled her towards him. Her resistance remained so he kissed her cheek. 'I did too.' His voice softened, sounding like creamy mousse to Gillian as his hands lingered around her waist. 'A lovely time.'

Apprehension made her pull away. 'I'm sorry, Max. I can't ask you in.'

He let her move further towards the open door, but he held her hand, pulled it to his lips for a quick kiss. 'That's okay. I couldn't drink any more coffee tonight. I'll give you a ring. I can, can't I?'

So ... diplomatic, Gillian thought. 'Yes, I'd like that.'

'Goodnight, Gillian.'

She stood with her hand on the doorknob and listened to his footsteps run down the stairs.

You're an idiot. No I'm not. *What did you expect?* Nothing. *Nothing!* You're so naïve. Man takes woman to dinner. Man expects reward. *It wasn't like that.* It will be. *No, it won't.* Yes, it will and you know it. *Damn. Why are things so difficult?* Because you have Patrick. *Did.* Yes did, but you have to realise ...

No, I don't. Yes, you do. *I'll never forget Patrick.* You don't have to. *Damn. Life is much too complicated.*

Gillian threw her keys into the planter, shoved the door closed with her hip and stalked through to the kitchen. With her mind full of argument, she slammed on the switch for the kettle, stood like a statue and waited for the dancing bubbles. *Damn, damn, damn.* The kettle switched itself off. *Damn, double damn.*

Deciding she didn't want another coffee after all, Gillian paced into the bedroom and plonked onto the bed. Her new shoes refused to be released by using the toe of one to flick off the other, but she persisted, ending up with her dress bunched up around her waist. The left shoe suddenly shot into the air, landing heel down on her bare thigh.

'Ow.' She shoved the offending shoe to the floor; rubbed the spot. 'Like friggin' buttered toast.' She sat up and eased the right shoe over the beginning of a blister, then tossed it towards its mate.

'What a night.' Gillian stood, removed her dress and draped it over the wardrobe door.

Laying under the cool cotton sheet she reflected on the evening; acknowledging she'd thoroughly enjoyed the banter, the party mood and Max's company. She pulled off her wedding ring and slipped it on her right-hand pinky, with a question teasing her future. *Will I ever be able to think of another man like I did Patrick?*

With a knot building in her stomach she returned the gold band to her shuddering left hand. Her mind jolted with furious resentment.

Why did that stupid, stupid idiot have to choose that day, that park? Was it fate? Karma? Sienna was just a child. Patrick? Patrick was a good man.

Karma? She couldn't swallow. Her eyes refused to blink. *It was my Karma! But what have I done to deserve all this?*

Red and orange flashed like a neon sign; broadcasting a painful memory.

Many years ago, when Patrick suggested adopting a child, she'd yelled at him; slapped unsuccessfully at his arm. She didn't want another person's discard, she'd cried.

She walked out of the house, paced around the block, cursing everyone's god, cursing Patrick, wishing him dead so she didn't have to face up to the options he'd given her.

Karma? It was only once, her mind screamed, *and I didn't want him dead, I truly didn't.*

What about the wonderful things I imagined? Patrick and I becoming fuddy-duddies, with our Zimmer frames and pureed food. Teasing each other about our forgetfulness, our aching bones and our wrinkles.

Gillian unclipped her bra, tugged it away from her body, pushed it to the other side of the bed. The empty side.

She cupped her hand around her breast. They'll end up droopy. She ran her hand across her stomach. I'll have granny knickers eventually. She imagined hanging "saggy baggies" on the line when she became seventy, eighty. Patrick won't get old. Her hair rubbed across the pillow as she shook her head. "They shall grow not old". She recalled the ANZAC day message, "as we that are left". *I shouldn't have been left, I should have gone to the park. I should be dead, too.*

After lying straight and stiff for a few minutes, Gillian got out of bed, headed for a shower.

The clock showed 3 am, Sunday 9 May, before Gillian finally fell asleep. Her last thought was of Mother's Day last year when Patrick and Sienna brought to her bedside a lukewarm cup of tea, buttered raisin toast and an aqua patterned scarf wrapped in tissue paper.

Emerging from the cocoon of sleep, it took a while for Gillian to remember she'd woken up to this special day.

Flowers, books, cups and saucers, along with more unusual suggestions had been displayed in shops throughout Prague in the weeks prior to the second Sunday in May. Just like in Australia, retailers encouraged everyone to spend abundantly – in a show of adoration to motherhood. She purposely avoided the invasion of feminine gifts threatening her resolve to have it come and go like any other day. However, three days ago Gillian had run her fingers across white fluffiness on a pair of slippers, swallowed building saliva, and hurried back into the street for fresh air.

Now as she pushed the sheet from her body, Gillian exhaled deeply. Resigned to melancholy, but determined to stay above sadness, she dangled her feet out of bed and slowly made the rest of her body respond. She stood for a moment, sighed again, then headed for the bathroom and the comfort of routine.

It is what it is, she thought as she wiped her hands. *Mothers all over this country will be waking up to an emotional morning – either a joyous moment or one of disappointment; even sorrow. I wonder how Petra is managing?*

Leaning over the handbasin, Gillian peered at her image in the mirror. Aunt Anne had commented on many occasions about the resemblance to her mother.

'Spitting,' Aunt Anne would say. 'No doubt about it. You are your mother's child. But Esther ... no doubting she's from your dad's farm.'

Gillian chuckled, trying to imagine her refined father being enamoured by an animal reference.

She tilted her chin for a clearer view of her face. Minimal recent attention meant her eyebrows hinted at her mum's heavy ones. As she straightened up the moving reflection caught the similarity between mother and daughter.

'Determined. Stubborn,' her father had often said. 'Just like your mother. Shows in your pert noses.'

Gillian looked back, trying to catch the fleeting resemblance. Her mother had been determined to survive, but couldn't. Gillian ran her hand across her chin, pushed the end of her nose up. *Stubborn?* she thought. *Determined? It doesn't always matter how much you try it's not always easy. I guess I have to keep at it.*

While blow-drying her hair, Gillian recalled the touch of her mother's hands on her hair. As a three-year-old she hated hair-washing days, but grew to delight in the intimacy of the occasion. It always took time to tame Gillian's long curls and inconsequential chatter, often accompanied by giggles, made it more pleasant. Even when she outgrew the necessity for cajoling, Gillian often asked her mother to brush her hair.

Gillian lifted the weight of curls and looked for a hairband amongst the paraphernalia on the vanity. As she picked up a white elastic hairband the memory of Sienna wriggling under Gillian's attempt to tighten her ponytail hit like a bullet into glass. Dropping her hair and the hairband, Gillian sucked in air, holding for seconds before releasing it noisily.

No, I won't. I just won't. She peered into the mirror again, rubbing away the frown with a shaking forefinger. *Let's not go there. I'm going to think of happy Mother's Days. There were lots. There must have been.*

Over toast and tea Gillian recalled a picnic organised for Kings Park being relocated to the lounge-room – complete with blanket, thermos, sandwiches and lemon cake – after the weather didn't co-operate. Her mother's delight with a home-made card meant Gillian had imagined a future in design until her mum removed the card from the mantle – out of sight, out of a child's mind.

From when Esther was twelve the sisters spent weeks deciding on a gift for their mother. They had to save their pocket money for family gifts – their father's rule. It wasn't until a few years later when Gillian questioned how their meagre joint funds could purchase a petticoat, recently advertised beyond their budget, that Esther exposed the additional money from their father. Gillian stamped her ten-year-old foot and spat words she wasn't allowed to use at her sister – annoyed at being tricked, angry for being gullible – then cursed her father, who fortunately was miles away in his office, immune to the sensitivities of growing girls.

Father doubled their already generous pocket money and insisted they each open a bank account, starting it off with one hundred dollars. Gillian knew they were being placated with their father's usual style of resolution and refused to spend any of it … until teenage years saw the benefit of not having to explain unsuitable purchases.

With memories still hovering, and sitting over a difficult electronic jigsaw puzzle, Gillian cast aside the melancholy and, forcing a smile, endeavoured to be satisfied with the many Mother's Days shared with her mother, and the few shared with Sienna.

At first Gillian ignored the soft tapping. When it became stronger, she stopped trying to find the correct place for the jigsaw piece and hurried to the door.

'Hana! Sorry, didn't realise … Is everything okay? Dobré?' I really should know more Czech than the word for good.

Gillian's neighbour waved two leaflets, accompanied by a burst of words.

Placing her hand on Hana's arm, Gillian ushered her forward. 'Come in. Come in.'

Hana's eyes worked overtime as she shuffled around the coffee table. 'Ah,' she said; placing her walking stick down and picking up the Traveller's Guide. 'Ah,' Hana said again as she held the book and leaflet towards Gillian.

'What?' Gillian took them and sat down, pointed for Hana to do the same.

Hana giggled. 'Kráva, kůň.' She pointed at Gillian. 'Moooo.' Her grin spread as Gillian whinnied.

The leaflets, one in English, one in Czech, detailed the Church of Our Lady Victorious – Infant Jesus of Prague.

This Early Baroque building, dating back to 1611, was rebuilt from 1634 to 1669 by the Carmelite order. The church is famous for its statuette of the Infant Jesus of Prague, originally from Spain and donated to the Carmelites by Polyxena of Lobkowicz in 1628.

'Wow! 1600's. That is old.' Gillian turned the leaflet over, looking for a location.

Hana flicked through the Traveller's Guide. 'Přijít.' She poked Gillian's arm. 'Go. Gillian, Hana go.'

'To this church? Sure. Ano. When?' Taking the book and searching for the translation, she asked again, 'When, kdy?'

Hana eased onto her feet. 'Dnes.' She walked towards the door. 'Gillian, Hana … Go …' She beckoned, nodded. 'Go. Ano?'

Gillian looked back at the open page; a sentence caught her eye. Considered a special place for mothers, pregnant women, and those having difficulty falling pregnant.

Special place for Mothers. Mother's Day. That's why Hana wants to go, Gillian thought. 'Hana, Ano. We'll go. Just give me a minute.' She pointed to her bare feet, desperate to be successful at miming. 'I need to put some shoes on. Ano. Yes. We go.'

Hana absently turned the pages of the little book while Gillian combed her hair, changed her shirt, slipped on some sandals and gathered her bag.

'Let's go,' she said as she helped Hana stand. 'Hana and Gillian, the cow and the horse, will go. Moo.'

'Boo,' replied Hana. 'Hana, kráva.'

Many smiles and much nodding accompanied the predominantly silent journey. Hana pointed out the scenery as trees and buildings flashed by. Gillian read the leaflet; in awe of the elaborate decorations of the church's interior. The happy chatter of passengers built an aura of pleasantness around a minute niggle of sadness in Gillian. She'd tried all morning to curb the longing of Mother's Days of the past. Now Hana and this train hurtled her towards celebrating the very thing she still struggled with. *Could she participate without falling into the dark hole of yesterdays?* Her throat dried. She had trouble swallowing.

Hana cupped Gillian's hand, tapped her finger. With a shake of her head, and a concerned frown, Hana asked if her young friend was okay.

Without having to translate, Gillian's slow smile below distressed eyes gave Hana her answer. 'Not really.'

'Modlíme se k Ježíšku,' Hana said. (We pray to Jesus.)

'Jesus? Yeah bit late for him to intercede.' Gillian gripped Hana's hand. 'I'll be okay. I'll get to be dobré. One day.'

Gillian only released Hana's hand when the train pulled into the station.

With a subsequent tram ride completed they finally stood inside The Church of Our Lady Victorious. Gillian's eyes widened. 'Wow! How beautiful.'

'Šuš,' Hana whispered, her index finger covering her mouth.

Dropping her voice Gillian repeated, 'Wow, you'd never know from the outside. I mean, the stonework is lovely, in an old-fashioned way and the—'

'Šuš,' Hana insisted.

'Sorry.'

Hana slipped her hand into Gillian's and they stepped towards the back of the pews where people were seemingly in prayer. Gillian continued to gasp at the elaborate gold-enhanced statues as she and Hana moved slowly down the side aisle.

'Heavens, Hana. What's that word for beautiful, ah! Krásné. Definitely krásné.'

Hana's broad grin agreed with the sentiment.

They slipped into a side pew. Hana closed her eyes, clenched and unclenched her hands as her lips moved silently. Gillian watched women: old women, young women, pairs of women, women clutching a male's arm – all with reverence etched on their faces.

Are they remembering lost mothers, departed children, too? Are they pleading with the baby Jesus to ease their sorrow? I wish I could believe that was possible.

Gillian stood and moved towards the statue. After waiting for a gap in the throng of visitors, she gripped the cold steel of the wrought-iron barrier and stared at the indulgent icons.

After agreeing with the chatter of the other softly spoken tourists, Gillian browsed part of the leaflet in her hand. "The statue is a 19-inch (48cm), wooden and coated wax representation of the Infant Jesus. The statue of Infant Jesus is studded with diamonds and crowned with gold." Gillian glanced back at the miniscule diamonds. Gold embellished so much of the interior of the church it could go unnoticed on the tiny Jesus.

'I'm glad I came in,' said a tourist to no one in particular. 'I nearly didn't. The outside is so plain.'

A tiny woman smothered by a vivid red scarf hushed her. The tourist wouldn't be hushed. 'They've got a beauty here. I'll be telling my friends back home. Now where can I buy a baby Jesus?'

Gillian strolled around the church, tempted to ignore the signs and take a picture or two, but instead dropped a coin in a box and took another leaflet. Hana finished her contemplations and waited with Gillian, nodding and pointing at various alcoves, the arched ceiling and finally at a sign displaying Mass times.

'Not for me.' Gillian shook her head. 'Nup.'

After visiting the gift shop, purchasing a book detailing the interior of the church and its history, a bookmark, and making a donation for the upkeep of the building, Gillian stood outside with Hana watching the moving stream of people.

'Líbil se ti kostel našeho Jezulátka?' Hana asked.

'What?'

Hana nodded vigorously. 'Ano?'

'It's impossible, Hana.'

'Excuse me.' A young woman touched Gillian on the arm. 'You do not know what your friend asks?'

Gillian turned. 'No, I don't speak Czech. Hana doesn't speak English. It's absurd really.'

'That is so for many. Your friend asked if you liked our church of the Infant Jesus.'

'Yes. Yes, I did.' Gillian turned to Hana. 'I did. Thank you for bringing me. Děkuji.'

Hana spoke to the young woman with a flurry of Czech.

'Gillian, your friend asked if you are ready for coffee.' She dipped her head before continuing, 'She said I may come too. But you are friends. You will not want a stranger to interrupt your day.'

'Coffee is a must. And, yes, please come. You can save us having to speak in one-word sentences. And that's with the aid of the phrasebook! Yes, please, if you're prepared to be a translator, it'd be lovely.'

'I am studying English, so it is perhaps rude of me. But I would enjoy to talk with you.' She offered her hand. 'My name is Martina.'

After further introductions, they strolled to a nearby café. The cool afternoon provided an ideal prerequisite for steaming coffee and a croissant. A little awkward at first, but as Martina provided prompt interpretation, the women drifted into a three-way conversation.

Hana explained how she visited this church every Mother's Day, said a prayer for her husband, but especially her son. 'A mother should never bury her child,' Martina repeated.

The softness of Martina's English after the sadness in Hana's voice, sounded like silk wrapping a broken cup. Gillian placed her hand on Hana's arm. 'No. It is not the way of things.'

Martina let the comfort of shared grief linger before speaking to Hana and then turning to Gillian. 'My mother is difficult. We argue many times. She is traditional and expects her daughter to be the same. Today I see why. Today I must make good with her. This is why the Baby Jesus had us come together.'

While Gillian felt it was nothing but an opportunistic coincidence, she mumbled an agreement. Martina spoke of her hopes for a new job and her desire to travel. Gillian described the vastness of Australia and some of Perth's attraction, before the conversation wandered inevitably through to the changeable weather. With the difficulty of translating every discussion bringing awkward silence, Gillian said to Hana, 'We should go. It's a decent trip back to Prosek.'

Martina walked to the tram with them. After a polite hand-shake, Gillian pulled her into a hug. 'Good luck with your dreams. It's been really lovely chatting. Thanks for translating.'

'It is a pleasure for me,' Martina said. 'You must also be happy in your future.'

Aware of Hana's fading energy they negotiated the return journey slowly, waiting in a nearby café instead of at the tram stop, accepting a seat in the tram from a ripped-jean-wearing teenager, until strolling arm in arm from the Prosek station to Hana's door.

Keen to rest after the long outing, Hana kissed Gillian's cheek before saying goodbye.

Pulling the Traveller's Guide from her bag, Gillian opened to a page with a turned-down corner and pointed to several Czech words she'd written while on the train. *Zvláštní den. Šťastné vzpomínky. Nikdy nezapomenu.*

As Hana read, Gillian said, 'You've created happy new memories. Thank you. Děkuji. I'll always remember today.'

Mother's Day petered out into an evening of more memories between chores.

Gillian clicked through photographs of Sienna: from birth to the last one – Sienna pulling a silly face and holding up a half-eaten apple.

'My darling,' Gillian said. Her eyes stayed dry, but as she loaded dirty clothes into the machine, longing tumbled around every speck of every atom of her body.

She emptied the last of a bottle of red wine in a glass and spent an hour playing online Sudoku.

Two late breakfasts, lonely wanderings, and avoiding Hana and her squeaky shopping trolley, added anxiety to the approaching day.

Evenings of reliving memories as the laptop screen flashed cute baby photos, serious piano-playing teacher images, and happy two-some – three-some family snaps.

Gillian cuddled her memories close to her chest, wondering if memories could ever be enough.

Tomorrow – Sienna's birthday. She would have turned five.

Gillian knew the 12th of May would be difficult – a fifth birthday that would never be.

After humming *For the Love of Sienna* in the shower in a pretense to be upbeat, Gillian decided to go out for brunch. She wandered through the park, reached the park café and ordered pancakes with maple syrup. As she greeted the other customers with a quick nod, and spoke about the cold wind to the lad behind the counter, she realised she had chosen to leave her flat, the safety of my flat, and be amongst people.

With the sweetness of the maple syrup on her tongue, Gillian remembered the Canadian Ambassador proudly relating the myths and history of maple syrup. 'We think it goes back to the 1500s,' he'd said. 'But the early inhabitants were definitely harvesting in the 1700s.'

Gillian put her fork down, sipped her orange juice, pulled out her phone, and pressed Petra's number.

'Hello, Gillian,' Petra whispered her greeting.

'Hi, have I caught you at a bad time?'

'Yes, a little. I'm waiting for my appointment. Is anything the matter?'

'Oh, sorry. I just wondered if you are at home this morning, but obviously you're not.'

'I'm in the city. Did you want to meet? I'll be finished soon.'

'Would you mind? I need some company.' Gillian frowned, then added, 'Today.'

'Why don't we meet in about an hour? Under the horse's tail.'

Morgan had laughed heartily as she told Gillian of the name of this popular meeting place. 'Under the horse's tail,' she'd said. 'Not a great place to test your luck!'

'Yes, I know it,' Gillian said to Petra. 'In an hour. Okay. and, if I can't find you, I'll ring again.'

'Of course. But I have to go now.'

Gillian finished the orange juice, paid, and strolled towards the Metro. Three minutes later she hurried onto a train and found a seat. While stations flashed by through the windows and people read iPads or talked on mobiles, Gillian remembered Petra had said she was in a waiting room. Waiting for what? Or whom? One "waited" in a doctor's surgery. I hope she's not ill.

A voice announced, 'Příští stanice Muzeum.' Gillian stood, held her bag tightly and waited for the doors to open.

One could get fit living in a city like this, Gillian thought as she followed the hurrying mass up the stairs and out onto the footpath. She couldn't explain the excitement in the back of her throat, the eagerness with which she perused the dozen or so happy people around the Town Square statue. *I thought I'd be devastated today. Where has this feeling come from?*

'Gillian, Gillian, here.' Petra waved enthusiastically.

Squeezed tightly in Petra's hug, Gillian absorbed her friend's perfume. 'I'm so glad we could meet.'

Petra squinted at Gillian, tried to uncover her emotions. 'You sounded sad, but now … I don't know … you sound more cheerful.'

'I did. I do. It's Sienna's birthday. Or would have been.'

'I'm sorry. Anniversaries can be complicated.'

'This morning I expected to be miserable. I've found I'm not.' Gillian grabbed Petra's hand. 'Come with me. I need to walk.'

The two women ambled down the slope of the square, past shoppers, around groups of tourists, avoided scampering children, without talking. Stopping outside a shop window full of children's clothes, Gillian dropped Petra's hand and spoke softly, 'I would have bought that yellow dress for Sienna.'

Petra nodded. 'Gillian, can we sit for a while? Let's have a drink.'

'Yes, my shout. For destroying your day.'

After they'd ordered tea, Petra thanked Gillian for paying.

'My shout, as thanks for meeting me. I needed company. Probably would have been sulking away under the bedclothes if I hadn't come out.'

'Maybe.'

Gillian hesitated, then said, 'You seem distracted. I assume you were in a doctor's waiting room when I rang.'

'Yes, I was.'

Gillian watched Petra frown, but her eyes seemed to be dancing. 'Bad news?'

Petra avoided looking at Gillian while the waiter placed their order on the table. Gillian continued to scrutinize Petra's face as she poured the tea, added sugar and stirred more than necessary. Gillian waved a spoon towards Petra. 'Is it bad news?' she asked again.

Without looking up, Petra said, 'No, not at all.'

'Oh, good.' Gillian blew on the hot liquid. 'If it's not bad news, you should look happier. Is there a problem?'

Petra finally looked at Gillian. 'My insides are … jumping with joy. I just don't want to upset you. Especially today.'

Gillian chuckled. 'You mean it'd be okay to upset me tomorrow?'

'No, of course not.'

Gillian patted Petra's arm. 'I'm joking. God knows I'll be happy to hear some good news.'

Petra whispered, 'I'm pregnant.'

Gillian's face froze. She remembered the moment her egg turned from hope to announcement. Then a grin spread across her face. 'That's wonderful news.' Petra's frown confused Gillian. 'You are pleased, aren't you?'

'We've been trying for so long. Since Izzy no longer wore nappies.'

'Why aren't you happy? For heaven's sake, don't waste a moment of joy for this baby.' Gillian stood, walked around the spare chair and hugged her friend. 'I'm truly pleased. It's just a shame we can't celebrate with champagne.'

'Thank you, Gillian. I was so worried. When you told me about Sienna's birthday, I was unsure if I should tell you.'

Returning to her seat, Gillian shifted the empty cup and saucer, placed the tiny spoon into the cup. 'I understand. Do you know that this morning something shifted? I've been dreading this day. Watched it approach on the calendar. Tried to, I don't know, tried to pretend it didn't matter. Then, I chose to leave my flat, the cocoon of misery I've made it. I chose an option that wasn't about crying, about sadness.' She slapped her hand on the table. 'Do you know something? I'm going to buy that dress. That yellow one. I'm going to buy it and give it to the first little girl I see in the street that it might fit.'

'Gillian?'

'I'm going to do something silly. Something I wouldn't have done even if Sienna was alive.' Her grin suddenly disappeared. 'I have to start doing things differently. Somehow. My life is not going to ever be the same.' The grin came back. 'Are you up for it?'

'Maybe, but I have something I want to ask you.' Petra sounded wary.

'Ask away.'

'If our baby is a girl,' Petra let her hand drop to her stomach, then looked at Gillian tenderly. 'If my baby is a girl, may I call her Sienna?'

Gillian's eyes widened. She stared at Petra; noticed a small pimple on her left cheek. 'Wow,' she whispered. 'Are you sure?'

'It's a pretty name.'

'Wow.' Gillian picked at her thumbnail, testing her emotions, trying the idea out. 'Come,' she said. 'Let's go and buy that dress. Let's see what else we can find for your Sienna.'

Petra grinned. 'But it might be a boy.'

The day Gillian had been dreading turned into a celebratory, carefree day shared by two friends. They ate pizza and sipped icy cold lemonade, sitting for nearly an hour before ending the afternoon with green tea and a shared raspberry slice.

The following morning, buoyed by her optimistic outlook, Gillian left the dishes in the sink and walked to the café for a cappuccino. Reading an English paper, with worldwide news that didn't include Australia, she frowned at how the human race still didn't know how to be kind to each other.

'Have you been to the Zoo?'

Gillian looked up at the grinning face of Morgan. 'What are you doing in Prosek? And on a week day. Thought you'd be at work.'

'Nup, day off. Worked Saturday.'

'So, why Prosek?'

'At the moment, same as you. I've just ordered a coffee. Take-away though.' Morgan pulled out a chair, sat and flapped a leaflet in front of Gillian. 'Have you been to the Zoo yet?'

'Yep, been there, done that.' Gillian took the leaflet, glanced at the front and passed it back. 'I enjoyed it. And I've been playing the tourist a lot more. I'm trying to see as much as I can before I go home.'

Morgan's face showed surprise. 'You're going back already? Gosh, I thought you'd be here longer.'

'Well … not going just yet. Anyway, what are you doing in Prosek?' Gillian asked again. 'I didn't think it'd be somewhere high on your list of things to do.'

'Nup, but Marianne, the Scottish girl in the office, said it had a great park. I like to make the most of any sunshine on my day off. Got off at Střížkov, walked through the park. She was right. About the park. Anyway, I'm heading for the Metro again. Going through to Letňany.'

'What's there?'

'About to find out. I've been to the end of the other lines, so this is my last one.'

'I've been to Depo something or other,' Gillian said. 'End of the Green Line. Disappointing. And, I've been to Letňany. By mistake. Got on the wrong side of the station.'

'Ha! Easy to do.' Morgan accepted the cardboard cup from the waiter, took the lid off and fingered the froth to her mouth.

'I'm told there's a decent shopping centre at Letňany. Shopping and Morgan are a good match.'

Gillian thought about her mistaken trip to the end of the Red Line. She shook her head, frowned. 'I didn't see any shopping centre. Just a lot of buses. It was peak hour. Lots of people rushing. Definitely no shopping centre.'

Morgan put the cup on the table, held the lid with her teeth, opened her phone, tapped, wobbled her head sideways as she waited for the requested information. She placed the lid back on the cup, closed the phone and slipped it into her pocket. 'All good. It's just a bus ride away. Shouldn't be hard. Want to come with me? That's if you've got nothing else to do.'

'I was going to go into the city again, but somewhere different sounds good. I need to get gifts to take home. Sandy will kill me if I don't take her back something.'

'Awesome. You finished?' Morgan checked the security of the lid. 'Let's go.'

After a quick ride on the Metro, a slow crowded bus ride, and a short walk, they entered Letňany's shopping mall.

'It's the biggest in Prague,' Morgan announced.

'Really? Are you after something special?'

'Yeah, need new shoes for work. Just going from our office to another department requires a trained hiker. What about you?'

'Sandy's rather particular. Likes quality. Can afford quality. I'll probably look for a handbag. Something gorgeous, and by that, I mean colourful and flashy.'

'Cool. Marks and Spencer's?'

'Let's try them.'

They visited many of the shops in the centre, laughing at greeting cards they couldn't translate, smelling candles and perfume, and admiring jewellery. They also tried on ridiculously expensive outfits, practical jeans, large hats, small hats, hiking jackets, prickly scarves and finally Morgan purchased some sneakers.

They entered an up-market accessory boutique and browsed handbags of differing shapes and sizes. Morgan slung the straps of an orange tote over her shoulder and, imitating Elle McPherson, strutted the length of the shop.

'Yep, definitely Sandy's taste,' Gillian said.

Watching Morgan swap the orange tote for a shiny black number with gold "dangly bits" and pose in front of the mirror, Gillian and the assistant curtsied, then broke into giggles. 'You're the limit,' Gillian said.

'We have show ponies, on many times,' said the assistant in her sophisticated voice, 'but I am not amused until today has come.'

All shopped out, Morgan and Gillian had another coffee, before tracking back to the Metro.

As she balanced bags containing Sandy's gift, a Krtek mole for Rose, a jar of hand cream, and a container of cannelloni for dinner on her knee, Gillian's mood remained upbeat. *Patrick, you don't mind, do you? I miss you, to the depths of the ocean and back, but I can still be happy, can't I?* She nodded to her reflection in the window. *Yes,* she thought, *Patrick would approve.*

Morgan gave Gillian a quick hug as the train pulled into Prosek station, and demanded they meet again. 'Before you leave. Madison will be cross if you don't. Promise, promise.'

Ignoring the message tone of her mobile, Gillian hurried out of the lift, put the name-emblazoned plastic bags at her feet, and unlocked the door of her unit.

Over a glass of water, she read Max's text.

Do you need coffee? With me?

Gillian's mind wandered. *Max. Not too tall. Blow-away hair. Divorced. Important work. Nice laugh. Large hands. Flat ears.*

Then she remembered Patrick and their first date at some forgotten movie. Choc tops – his spearmint, hers vanilla. She remembered months later when they spent a night together. Long piano-playing fingers. On her skin. Arousing her. Soothing her.

Max. She sipped her drink. Recalled his joke-revealing eyes. His fondness for teasing.

Another sip.

Patrick. Pedantic-art/music-teacher-husband explaining the subtle difference of paint colours. Ice Blue. Misty Blue. Lotus Aqua.

She picked up the phone again, located Max's number and pressed call.

'Gillian.' Max's silky voice floated through the phone.

'Hi. Sorry, not up for coffee just now, had too many already.'

'You're out?'

'Nup, at home. I've been shopping.'

'Shopping? I didn't think you liked shopping,' he teased.

Gillian filled in enough of her morning with Morgan for Max to comment, 'Sounds like you enjoyed yourself. Excellent, but she's done me out of a job.'

'You wanted to take me shopping?'

'Look, I'm about to go into a meeting,' Max said, 'but I have a rare day to myself tomorrow. Can I pick you up, go somewhere you haven't been?'

Patrick liked driving to the country. Gillian flinched as her mind took her away from Max's question. 'I haven't seen anything beyond the city.' She thought of footpaths, cafes and shopping centres. 'Although I've been to The Castle, Charles Bridge − seen lots of doors. Some more memorable than others.'

Ignoring the reference to their first meeting, he said, 'Good. What about the Bone Church? Kutná Hora. Not a bad run.' As soon as he'd spoken Max realised it was a bad idea. Bones, skeletons, Gillian's family. 'Or,' he said quickly, 'I can take you to the countryside. Have lunch. Drive back.'

The small house below a mountain, on the travel brochure, re-appeared. 'Country, I think.'

'Great. It'd have to be reasonably early.'

'Sure.'

'And, Gillian.'

'Yes?'

Max laughed into her ear. 'No posh frock or high heels.'

She thought of the blue dress on the outside of her wardrobe, one she'd probably never wear again. 'I have sneakers.'

'Good, see you about eight. I'll come up.'

The clock had just shuffled over 7.45 am when Max arrived.

'No driver?' she teased as she settled into the passenger seat. He pretended to sulk. 'I do know how to drive, young lady.'

He drove, talked of castles, spires, clocks, ancient invasions. She listened, made companionable noises, stared at the greenery. 'Not the olive green of our gum trees,' she said. Patrick would love the challenge of finding the right green, she didn't say.

Gillian interrupted his telling of Král Václav, Wenceslas, the Czech king, 'about the 10th century,' after whom the city square was named, by singing, 'Good King Wenceslas once looked down.' His faultless voice joined in, 'On the feast of

Stephen ...' They laughed their way out of the end of the Christmas carol.

He pointed out a prayer hut and the mountains in the distance. She experimented with the Czech names scattered on the map that lay across her lap. He encouraged her to try again, knowing his knowledge impressed.

At a wooden tavern, with a goat in the front yard, a rotund woman at the counter and a lanky cook who brought the food to the table, they ate tender roast duck and potato dumplings with delicious creamy sauce. The cold beer she chose matched perfectly. He told of some Czech beer history as he drank lemonade. Budweiser and Pilsner coming from the towns of České Budějovice and Plzeň. He told of the city of Brno which had the right to brew beer since the 12th century.

After lunch they drove further while he espoused the beauty of Karlovy Vary. 'A spa town out west, popular with Tsars.' Of Český Krumlov. 'Great place, great castle. We can go another time, perhaps.'

Gillian folded the map and watched the view slip by. 'Are we going to the real mountains?'

He pointed across the mint green fields; talked of the winter snow still to come. Skiing. Falling. Cold. Necessity for gloves, scarves and beanies. Highlighted frostbite – Marcus' frostbite that came from his trip to the high mountains.

They walked part-way up a challenging slope, the rest of the mountain reaching into the sky – much taller than the Darling Range in Western Australia, taller than a skyscraper, smaller than others Gillian could see on the horizon towards Salzburg.

On their way back to the car he rested his arm around Gillian's shoulder. She hesitated before snuggling closer.

In the car he leaned towards her, kissed her cheek. Gillian's skin turned warm and chocolatey. She turned towards him. 'Home is it?'

'We can probably stop for afternoon tea.'

'You've got to be kidding!' She patted her stomach. 'How come you're not huge?'

He raised his arm and flexed his bicep. 'Would be if I ate like this all the time. Our kitchen staff has strict instructions to keep me on the straight and narrow.'

'Works,' Gillian said. *I bet he has nice muscles.*

They stopped at a small town, bought cold drinks, gave in to a shared slice of strawberry tart. He wiped cream from her lip. She touched his shoulder on her way to the gift shop. She could sense his eyes on her hands as she picked up trinkets and used her right hand to pick up the next item.

She purchased a wooden plate, said it was for Esther, but as she slipped it into her bag, she thought how nicely her breakfast toast would sit on it.

After refusing Gillian's offer to pay for the tart and drinks, Max spoke at length to the woman behind the counter in Czech, and then rattled his keys towards Gillian. 'Back to reality I'm afraid.'

She forced her eyes to stay open as the car eased along the narrow road, onto wider ones, and into rows of traffic. The sun dipped behind the multitude of flats, determined to stay in this northern sky way past Sienna's seven o'clock bedtime.

Max talked of meeting Chinese, Cubans, Vietnamese, Bulgarians, Greeks. He told anecdotes: some amusing, others culturally fascinating. 'Proving we're all the same, yet all different.' He acknowledged her grinning appreciation.

As she slipped the key into the lock, Max asked, 'Do I get an invitation today?'

Images of lips pressed together, bare feet, tossed clothes, hands on her breasts, flashed in front of words of an affirmative.

She delayed further as she thought of strong arms, a hairy chest, grunts, caresses, climaxes.

Max raised his eyebrows at her. She frowned. 'No pressure,' he said.

'Right.' She opened the door, ushered him in. The clatter of her keys on the metal planter sounded like an announcement. 'Right,' she said again. 'I can offer you wine.'

He came up behind her, ran his hands around her waist. 'Is that all?'

'No.' She swivelled in his arms, faced him. 'You deserve a kiss.'

The hands on her breasts, the climax, happened after a hesitating start. For one miniscule moment, Max's fine hair and Patrick's strong auburn hair tangled in her fingers. She sat up, shook her head, wondered if it was really her, in this bed, with this man with a hairy chest. *I want, I can, I will,* she thought as she ran her recently painted toenails along the length of Max's leg.

In the small hours Gillian drifted from the euphoria of Max's closeness to the realisation he might want to stay. She stroked his arm as they spooned.

'Will you stay?' she whispered.

He leaned over and kissed her lightly. 'I shouldn't. I might never want to leave.' He swung his legs out of bed. 'Bathroom? Can I shower, please?'

Curled up under the sheet, listening to the water washing away their lovemaking, she refused to think of anything but the pleasure of last night. After the quickest of showers, Gillian offered him toast, tea, coffee, water.

With a smidgeon of awkwardness, he refused all offers and took her in his arms. A prolonged kiss, a promise of phone calls, preceded one last lingering hug before Gillian gently closed the door behind Max.

She returned to bed and slept for several hours.

Darkening clouds fought against the blue morning sky as Gillian stood by the window finishing off an overripe banana. Ignoring any argument with an alter ego always keen to be devil's advocate, she poured boiling water over a heaped spoon of coffee, took the mug to the couch and opened her laptop.

The subject line of Sandy's email read: **YES!** Gillian grinned, opened the email expectantly.

Hello, dear friend of mine.
I can't believe it. I'm getting married. So, no more single friend. No more living through me. You'll have to do it on your own. I'll be old and MARRIED, you'll be living the single life.
Mira thinks I'm heartless. Thinks I should avoid, you know, the "single" comments. God knows what Esther would say. Only she won't get the chance because I haven't seen her. AND she definitely won't be privy to these emails.
But it's a fact. So, forgive me once again. Now to some other things – MURRAY.
Murray, ah! The epitome of richness. Yep, filthy in folding stuff. Also in gorgeousness. Is that a word my learned friend? He's been married before. Ex-wife has long gone. Living in USA, I think. Wasn't concentrating, thinking of his, well anyway.
Won't be pressing for my eggs. Think we're both good on that front.
Wedding? Big party. Soon.
When are you coming home? I can't get wed without you. No tacky bridesmaids dress involved.
OTHER NEWS: Business going well. Don't forget to look out for anything that could be suitable for me to import. Local handicrafts. Make sure the label stays on. Info is always on labels.

MIRA: She's battling on. Sick most mornings. Lily is still delightful. Rohan! God! Boys! Then they turn to men! Jamie apparently is building a room on the back. She's got a good one. Mind you, Murray is too, except he'd just buy a new house. Ah! Money. Lovely stuff.

MY GIFT. If you could bring home some of those cute glass nail files. Twenty please. I can hear you asking right now. What'll you do with them? I DON'T KNOW. But they'll come in handy. Ha! Ha! See, that's clever. You know, nail files for hands – handy. Well, maybe not. But bring some. I'll even let you off for anything else.

SERIOUS STUFF. Dear Gilly, I hope you're going okay. It's alright for me to bumble on, but I hope that my (delightful, clever, amusing) ways help. I remember you saying that you didn't want pity. Didn't want people to fuss. I DON'T DO FUSSY. But I do care. A LOT.

Miss you.
Lots of love
Sandy

PS: You still haven't told me what Czech men are like.

Huh, Gillian thought. *Czech men. She should be asking about one particular Aussie man. That I could tell her about.*

Hi (delightful, clever, amusing) friend,
Congrats. Fancy that. I'll have to change my description of you. Instead of "you know, my single friend," I'll be saying, "Sandy, the one with the rich husband."

Will you have "room for a pony" in your new MARRIED home with MURRAY? I just know how much you loved Mrs Bucket!

Sorry to hear about Mira's morning sickness. I guess that's why I haven't heard from her in a while. Must email.

I've seen a little more of this country. Did you know it would fit into Australia ninety-nine times? Funny that they don't say 100 times. I mean who's going to measure it? Max took me for a day in the country. Perth is so flat. Here is so NOT flat.

Gillian paused, wondered how long Sandy would take to pick up a man's name. Probably two seconds – no, only one – Sandy's "man radar" is always finely tuned.

But Gillian deliberately didn't expand. She wanted to cling to the memory of Max's tenderness, his sex-laden voice, and his last lingering kiss on departure.

Now, hovering over the keyboard, she remembered standing under the shower, running her hands over her breasts, not shocked when she thought of Patrick and Max within the same moment.

She typed. I've, about to type, a man, but then changed her mind; instead she typed;

I've already got a present for you. However, with much expense to the management.

I'll also get 20 nail files. Hope customs don't want to know why. I guess I might have 20 friends.

Yes, since you asked, I am moving on. Strange to type that. But I have. Not around the corner yet, but at least started up the street. Who knows where it will lead, this new life of mine?

Single? Yeah, funny that. You married. Me single. This MAGNIFI-CENT MURRAY won't stop you from doing stuff with your SINGLE friend will he?

You know, the thing is, Patrick is everywhere. Still hovering in every corner of my life. I guess he always will be. Sienna is somewhat different. She belongs in pockets of my life. My "mummy" life. People have four, even twelve kids. Love them all. So, her existence won't be replaced no matter what. Maybe complemented, added to, with, say, Mira's new one, but never replaced.

It's Patrick who will be harder. My new life is replacing his exist-ence in my old one. Maybe some important things will come to be supplanted, like a lover's love. I'm not saying it will, I can't imagine that right now, but it might. I already will have to replace the things he did. You know, when I return to everyday bits and pieces. Paying the bills, car servicing, gutter cleaning, tree pruning. Does that wipe out his life within mine? It has to, doesn't it? Not the emotional things, but the actions of everyday life.

Does that make sense?

It's just another struggle to contend with.

I'm thinking about coming home. First step. Can't advise on the second step of buying a ticket. Not yet. But I feel it's close.

Thanks for being real, couldn't stand it if YOU GOT FUSSY.
Lots of love back at you
Gilly

Reading through the email before sending it, Gillian knew she couldn't CC anyone else this particular email. Sandy held a particular place in her life. Sandy didn't cringe when faced with reality, wasn't fazed by too much, too little.

She pressed send and opened Mira's previous email, clicked reply.

Mira dearest,
I hope that new bean isn't being difficult. Remember when we took those photos of our bellies. Sienna and Lily. They were big fat beans by that time. Have you got a short list of names yet? I guess you won't be finding out the gender. I don't know how you can wait. Remember the list you had last time? Will you use it again? Olivia, Breanna, James. They're the ones I can remember. We always wanted Sienna. It just popped out at Patrick from a computer list. He spent a whole Saturday afternoon repeating the name. It was a wonder I wasn't sick of it. We had a "discussion" with her second name. Rose for my mum, Sylvia for his mum, but SS Middleton sounded like a boat, so I got my way.
Listen to me ramble on.
I must tell you about a yellow dress. I saw it in a shop window. It was the cutest dress. I would've bought it for Sienna. Actually, it was her birthday that day. Anyway, I told Petra, a friend I've made through my door pictures, I wanted to buy it and give it to a child in the street. She thought no one would accept it. I was a little concerned, but I needed to do something I wouldn't normally do. Something cheerful, a little silly and spontaneous. Something to change my dreary thoughts.
Anyway, I bought the dress and asked four mothers. Petra translated. I almost gave up, but we found a woman sitting on a bench next to a little girl of the right size. The child was swinging her legs, telling a great tale to the older woman. Turned out to be her grandchild. The grandmother accepted the dress, said the little girl would like it. I think she was more excited about it than the child. The

grandmother told Petra one of her grandnieces died aged two, so once again the universe delivered a like-wounded soul. Petra bought some baby clothes. She's expecting. About the same time as you. I intend to stay in touch with Petra. She's helped so much. Did I tell you her Bridget died in hospital, just three years old? Too much to tell in an email. Boy, we're in for a talkfest when I get home.

I'm healing. Can now talk about them both without tears. But not always.

Please don't think you have to avoid talking about your pregnancy.

As I said before, I do want to hear about your growing bean.

What can I bring back for Rohan? Boys are difficult. What's his latest thing? Something not too heavy, or big.

Bye for now
Love
Gilly

I might as well do the trifecta, Gillian thought. Now what to say to Esther? Gillian hadn't had another email since the suggestion of meeting in Singapore.

Hello Ess,
Hope you're doing okay. Is winter over yet? I've checked the WA weather a few times. I guess my house survived that storm as I didn't hear from the agents. The heat comes and goes here. I'm lucky this building has cooling. Lots don't. The trams are so hot. Bodies crammed in, doesn't make for a pleasant smell. Think the weather laughs at us foreigners. A bit like everyone expecting Australia to be always hot. Here a little of the reverse. We had three days where I could have done with a swim at Cottesloe. Fancy Czech not having an ocean. Can't imagine not being able to go to a beach.

Had a trip to the countryside. So green. Primary green colour. I can hear Patrick yelling that green isn't a primary. Well, you know what I mean. Not our dusky grey-green.

I want to visit another castle. I've seen Prague Castle, but there are so many tourists. Did you know they call Prague the City of Spires? Yeah, there are lots. Then there's Karlstein Castle, which looks impressive. Then I've read about the Bone Church. Thousands of skeleton bones made into decorations. Sounds a bit gruesome. And a cathedral, St Barbora's Church. She's the patron saint of miners. I did go to an ancient library in a monastery. Bit of a walk, but well worth it. Hang on, I've got to find the info. Strahov Monastery Library. You wouldn't believe how old or how beautiful. Check it out on the internet. It really is overwhelming. But I reckon you could get a little blasé after too much of it all.

You see, I have "got on". I intend to make the most of the next few weeks. Then I'll come home.

She thought of her home. The honeysuckle on the trellis Patrick had planted, Sienna's bright red and yellow rooster statue stuck in the bromeliads, the goblins painted on the side fence – painted by Patrick for Sienna.

She accepted that she'd have to make new memories. Perhaps with Mira's bean; when it was a child – a child who didn't know Sienna. Perhaps this new child of Mira and Jamie will like brightly coloured roosters.

You didn't answer about Theo. Is he still helping you? What is your next grand function? Maybe I could help when I get home. I'm pretty good at typing. I could be of some use with the boring stuff you hate doing.

Anyway, I'll let you know about Singapore, but it might be a distraction too far. I think when I'm ready I'll want to get straight home. I can feel that pull already. Maybe we can go after I settle back. When you have some empty spaces in your diary.

I thought I saw Auntie Anne the other day. Of course it couldn't be, but they say everyone has a doppelganger. This woman had as many double chins and leaned forward as she walked. (Another walk we copied) The thing that stopped me speaking to her – apart from being in Prague – was the woman's bright orangey hair. Obviously dyed. Our prim Auntie Anne would never have done that. Seems I must be channeling family.

Must go, have my favourite take-a-way to pick up.

Bye for now

Love Gilly

Ps: pizza. From a bathroom-sized shop five minutes away. At least I get a walk!

When her phone pinged, revealing a message from Max, Gillian's smile was automatic. Then remembering *Samantha's Folly,* the novel with the sugary ending she'd tossed into the bottom of the wardrobe, she wondered if Max would be her folly. Unsure of how to answer the innuendo-heavy text, she hesitated.

She revisited their day in the country, analysed the plot she'd cast on agreeing to go, realised how the sexual tension had built, understood the ending had been written when she lowered her eyelids, smiled coyly after he asked if wine was the only thing on the menu.

It was pleasing to think another man, apart from someone who promised "in sickness and health", thought she was beautiful. Hadn't Max said so in the moment she stood naked before him. Max made her feel desirable, not a widow; a leftover from tragedy.

When Max texted a half hour later, Gillian opened her phone, read the new message and replied.

Yes, she typed. *Great day. Greater night. Yes, tomorrow night, dinner okay.*

Good, he typed back. *Pick you up at 7. Wear what you wore to the bbq.*

Okay.

She flipped the phone shut and decided she wanted something new to wear.

'And I might as well go now.'

As Gillian left the stairwell, Hana's squeaky wheel approached. Gillian waited by the lift and waved as Hana walked towards her.

After their greetings Gillian put her arm around Hana's shoulders, squeezed lightly. 'Dobré?'

'Ano.' Hana's head bobbed. 'Gillian, dobré?'

'Ano, yes, I am well.'

Hana placed her hands gently on Gillian's cheeks; looked into her eyes. 'Máte úsměv v očích. To je to moc dobré. To jsem ráda.' (You have a smile in your eyes. This is very good. I am pleased.) Her head continued bobbing.

Gillian grinned. 'Oh, Hana. It's impossible.' She took Hana's hands, held them, caressed the thinning skin for a moment and then released them slowly.

Hana laughed, pointed to her chest, then to the lift. 'Půjdu.' (I am going.)

'Bye, Hana. Ahoj. See you next time.'

When her phone beeped again, Gillian expected another text from Max. She waited until she was seated on the train before flipping open her phone.

Are you in the city today? We could meet.

She dialed Petra immediately, but the phone rang out.

On my way right now, Gillian typed.

The train arrived at Muzeum and Gillian tried the phone again. Petra answered, 'Hello, Gillian. Sorry, but I was just leaving the tram when you rang.'

'Where are you?'

'At Muzeum. Coming up the stairs.'

'Let us meet at the horse's tail in five minutes.'

After dodging slow-moving pedestrians Gillian greeted her friend with a hug. 'It's so good to see you,' Gillian said as she slipped out of Petra's firm embrace.

They found space in a busy café and ordered. 'And,' Petra asked, 'what about this smile that plays with your eyes? You must tell me why it is so.'

'Ah,' Gillian said. 'Is it obvious?'

'To me. I could often see your pain because I knew of it. How sorrow does more than hurt the heart, but reaches down every vein to all parts of one's body. I see these tentacles have been snipped off. It is the very best of things to happen. You must tell me every moment of it.'

Gillian told of Max, their day in the country, how Patrick hadn't gone completely, even that day, but Max had eased her self-doubt, took away the thought that life couldn't be changed.

'Hope,' Petra said. 'I think you can call it hope.'

'I suppose that's it.' Gillian picked up the paper napkin, rolled the edge around her finger. 'I mean, he's not going to be the love of my life. Patrick still holds that banner. But ... well, Max has definitely helped. Made me feel ... I don't know; it's a bit of a cliché, but ... like a woman again. Does that sound stupid?'

'Of course not.'

The waiter placed their lunch on the table, asked them if they wanted to order coffee, promised to come back when they'd finished their meal.

'You know,' Petra said as she folded the melted cheese around her fork, 'I remember after Bridget died, we couldn't touch each other. We didn't know how to explain our hurting. One night Ivan cried so much I left our bed, stood in the back garden praying that one of us would know what to do. I visited my grandmother and asked her if I could stay with her. But she said no. She said we should give ourselves permission to be angry, to be scared, to be anything we wanted, but we should just be those things together. That helped so much.' Petra spoke softly, her head down, the fork resting on the remainder of the meal. 'I do worry about you, on your own, not having someone to talk through things with. I can't imagine how you do it.'

Gillian gripped Petra's arm, whispering her words. 'I don't know either. I guess I'm a bit of a loner. Stubborn, Father used to say. Probably, it's true. I didn't really want help. Not after the fog of the first weeks lifted. Everyone seemed intrusive. While I was trying to hang on to every single memory of Patrick and Sienna, I thought they wanted me to forget them. Get on, they kept saying. I couldn't get on if it meant forgetting.'

They ate in silence as they filled their forks and nibbled the crispy edges of the lasagna.

Gillian let the fork hover over the next piece of pasta. 'I know. I just know I couldn't have got this far without you. That day you spoke to me, changed everything. All those doors I have on my thumb drive. It's thanks to those doors. I met Max. I met you. And you've helped so much.'

'I'm pleased.'

'Finding someone else who knew, really knew, what it's like to lose a child.' Gillian nodded slowly. 'I just can't thank you enough.'

'Není zač. Prosím. I am sure Izabela has gained an auntie.'

'I've certainly gained a friend.'

The waiter approached. 'Are you ready for coffee, tea? Do you want desserts?' He glanced from Petra to Gillian, unsure if tears were responsible for the shining eyes. He tucked the dessert menu behind his back. 'I can come back.' He was relieved when they smiled and Petra said, 'Lattes, please.'

Gillian's shopping trip had been aborted as Petra and she dawdled through streets, chatted over a milkshake in a recently opened café and ended up sitting in a tiny park talking of nothing and everything.

The next day, as the train sped towards the city, Gillian assessed her time in Prague. In the six weeks, she'd started the three books she purchased, finished one, *and* would probably leave the other two in the bookcase – with a significant part of the stories unread. None of the novels on Amazon's "recommended reading list" made it to her reading list. Concentration wasn't proving to be her strong point. However, she seemed to have mastered the art of wasting time. She played Solitaire late into the night, promising to log out at the end of the next successful game – then played another two, or three. Jigsaw puzzles made from snapshots of Prague filled lazy hours.

Playing tourist, seeing castles, art galleries, ancient buildings made more recent days slip by.

But you didn't come to play tourist. Definitely not. *Then the
beauty of the place has been a bonus.* I suppose. *Something to
talk about.* Mm. *When you go home.* Mm. *Well isn't it?* Of
course, but have I really achieved anything? *What did you want
to achieve?* Nothing. I just wanted to get away. *Done that!*

The train pulled into the next station. People pushed their
way into the crowded carriage. Gillian shifted closer to the man
on her left. A teenager squeezed into the available space. No
one acknowledged their travelling companions. As the train
picked up speed again Gillian surreptitiously scanned the faces.

Is the school lad's scowl because of his dread of school, or
just the annoyance of being bumped by a pram? Is that old lady
travelling to see family? What story is the woman with the
smudged red lipstick hiding? Do they all have a sadness to endure?

Gillian recalled the first time she met Petra. She'd seemed a
lucky mother with a gorgeous child, lovely home, happy marriage. But underneath: the hidden pain of loss.

So, what's the answer? What was the question? What did
you want to achieve? Oh, yes, that! And?

Gillian remembered wanting to run away from the pressure
of acting as others thought she should. She knew it wasn't possible to run away from heartache.

Solitude, that's what I wanted. Being alone? *No. Yes. Perhaps.* Make up your mind. *Okay, I don't know what I wanted. I
just needed things to be different. I wanted to be able to react
to my memories without someone making comment. Esther giving me leaflets on grief management did not help. Or Edna,
telling me how she managed when her husband died. For*

goodness sake, he was eighty-three! And, I didn't need Sandy putting on her cheerleader face, buying me things, inviting me to stuff.

Gillian held back a rising giggle. One evening Sandy had arrived with tickets to a live comedy show to see a friend's performance. When Gillian refused to go, Sandy performed a ridiculous tap dance, told two ribald jokes, then pulled a stuffed toy rabbit from her handbag and advised they were invited to the after-show party and, 'We'd be mad to miss this opportunity.'

They were trying to help. Yeah, I know. *You should be grateful.* I am. Well, up to a point. *What point?* Um, don't know. But I got to visit Prague. That's something to treasure.

Gillian let the rush of the passengers pass, then left the train and hurried down the square towards a frequently visited café. The waiter acknowledged her, asked, 'Something to eat today?'

'Maybe, but a cappuccino first. Thanks.'

He held out a menu. 'You take time. I will bring coffee.'

Several groups, chatting noisily, filled the café. Gillian leaned back, looked around the room, returned a smile as a young woman caught her eye. Three suit-clad men juggled their glass of beer between iPads, printed material and conversation.

If I was in Perth ... Gillian sighed. *I'd be having morning tea with Sandy. Finding out about her wedding plans.* She read the menu, decided against anything to eat.

The waiter placed her coffee on the table. 'Anything I can get for you?'

'No,' she replied. 'Watching the waistline.'

'Let me know if your mind is changed.'

Gillian had come to the city to choose something new to wear for her date with Max. As she browsed the rack, her stomach twitched with anticipation. After trying on unsuitable options, budget-breaking creations, she settled on a long-sleeved, two-toned silky top to wear with her black trousers.

The doorbell rang at exactly seven o'clock. Gillian imagined Max standing outside, checking his watch, waiting for the last few seconds to tick over. After opening the door, she tapped her watch. 'Timing is everything.'

'Yep, thought I'd better make up for the other times.' His eyes travelled from her mouth, over her body and settled on her face. 'You look great. Is it new?'

'Thanks. Just the top this time.' Gillian stood back from the door, not sure if she should ask Max in. 'Do you have a driver tonight?'

'No. I'm driving.'

'Want to come in?'

He shook his head. 'If you're ready we can get going. I've booked for seven fifteen.'

Gillian glanced at her watch. 'Doesn't leave much time. Where are we going?'

'There's a place in Prosek that's been recommended. Just a little further on than the shopping centre. It's new. Worth a try.' He looked at her feet, considered the height of her heels. 'Can you walk in those?'

'Yes, as long as it's an amble.'

'I don't mind taking the car, if you'd rather.'

'Nup, a walk will be good.'

After locking the door, they headed out. As the lift descended past the first floor, Gillian told Max a little about Hana and Elena. How the old woman had befriended her, despite the language barrier. How they'd shared their sorrow with minimal communication, and then with Elena's translations.

'It's amazing how it's both difficult and easy at the same time.' She added, 'I've never had to do that before. I guess you've got it down to a fine art.'

'Most people I deal with speak English. Sometimes as their second, or even third, language.' Max shrugged. 'But it does make one break down language to a common denominator.'

'What do you mean?'

Max slipped his fingers through hers. She relaxed her hand into his.

'Using straight-forward words, not obfuscating and byzantine ones.' He chuckled at her frown. 'Exactly!'

She slapped him playfully on his forearm.

'And, one has to forget slang and any ockerisms. It's amazing how even the phrases we think are everyday English trip people up.'

'Well, I have a new appreciation for mime. Getting good at it. And reading body language.'

'Ah,' he said, 'body language. That's a lesson embassy staff need to perfect.'

Max dropped her hand, held open a glass door. 'We're here,' he announced as he let her enter.

The low-lit room, with a modern chandelier over the reception desk, smoky-coloured drapes and soft music, oozed ambience. An attentive waiter settled them in comfortable leather chairs and presented a wine list and menus.

'A bit up-market for Prosek, isn't it?' Gillian whispered after the waiter departed.

Max shook his head. 'Not really. The area's become quite popular since the Metro came this way. That was a while ago, and now, the ongoing business development has helped.'

'I've not come this far before. I either just go to the small shopping centre or catch the Metro to the city. Oh, I once went out to Letňany with a girl I met.'

'You've been making friends then?'

'Some. You might even know one of them.'

'Really. Who?'

'Madison. Actually, I don't know her surname. She works part-time at the Embassy. She served the drinks at the barbecue.'

Max considered the information. 'Sorry, can't place her.'

'She has a twin; Morgan. They're Australian.'

When Max frowned and shook his head as she described Madison, Gillian added, 'Oh, and she took Plenty. He's a dog. Apparently, someone dumped puppies at the Embassy. She took one.'

'I remember the puppies. Yes, one of the kitchen staff … I remember her, young, dark hair, long nose – rather like mine.'

'I hadn't thought of that. But, yeah.'

'So, you went to Letňany. You sound like you've settled in well?'

Gillian took a deep breath, wondered how she should answer, but the waiter appeared at the table.

'Have you decided?' the waiter asked.

Max chose a red wine, and requested a little more time. The waiter returned with the wine and took their orders. Gillian opted for grilled fish. Max decided on roasted pork.

'So, Prague's treating you decently?'

'Prague's beautiful.'

'You said you came as a sabbatical. Has it been worthwhile? Have you got what you came for?'

Have I? Gillian thought.

Max's eyes narrowed, he stared into hers, trying to see the answer before she replied. 'Well?'

'I guess.' She looked down, fiddled with a napkin. 'I didn't really come for answers. I didn't expect there to be any. I came to get away from questions, expectations.'

Max turned away quickly, looked across at another couple laughing over a shared amusement. He sipped some wine, took time to swallow and then placed the glass down slowly. 'I didn't mean to pressure you.'

'That's okay. I mostly put the pressure on myself. I've figured that out at least.'

'The last thing I wanted was to upset you.'

Gillian didn't want to look at Max. His expressive eyes would show his concern, his growing fondness. She didn't want to see his emotions. She let go of the napkin, sipped the wine, still avoiding his eyes.

'Have you ever been to an opera?'

Gillian appreciated the change of topic. She looked up. 'Never. Have you?'

Max relaxed his shoulders. 'A few times. Quite a good company here. The building is spectacular. Carmen's on next. Some friends of mine are making up a group. Would you like to go?'

Their meals arrived and after nodding at Max's question, Gillian tasted the fish before adding, 'I'd like that. Some culture before I go home.'

'Ah, you've decided.'

Gillian shrugged, put another piece of fish in her mouth.

They ended the meal with coffee and a shared cheese platter, Max naming each type, teasing Gillian into declaring she knew little of the names, but a lot about the eating.

'I've moved on from the plastic slices,' she said. 'I'm always buying something different, but I can't remember the names. Patrick liked ...' She closed her eyes, held her hands still. A moment later, she opened her eyes again, tipped her head, said, 'Sorry.'

He reached for her hand. 'It's okay. He was a big part of your life. It's natural to recall him, speak of him. You shouldn't be sorry.'

'But, I ...' She pulled her hand away. Had she ruined the evening by bringing a third person to the table?

'What was his favourite cheese? Tell me.'

Her throat refused to swallow the last drop of coffee. She let it swill around her mouth until finally it went down. 'Mersey Valley cheddar,' she whispered.

'That's from Tassie, isn't it?'

'Yes.' She remembered a night, not unlike this one, where Patrick and she had giggled their way along the foreshore of the Swan River after eating at the Casino in Burswood. They paddled their feet, kicked at the foam on the edge and ran like children back to the car. 'Yes,' she said again.

'Gilly, I don't mind. We all have memories that linger. We're not teenagers. All of us come with backstory. Some better than others.' He grunted out a laugh. 'My ex-wife hated cheese. Said it was bad for the digestion.' He picked up the last piece of Brie. 'But, good for the flavour buds.' His eyes showed kindness. 'You want it?'

'You have it.'

He bit it in half, offered the remaining half to her. 'Go on, you know you want it.'

She leaned forward; let him place it into her mouth. 'Mm.' *He's a nice man,* she thought. *A really nice man.*

After dinner, they ambled around the block of closed shops, pointing out things they liked in the windows, being amazed at an array of door handles, shocked at the prices of vases and pretended to choose a new mirror for the embassy foyer.

As they stood outside a furniture store, grimacing over a lime green sofa, Max put his arm around Gillian's shoulders. She snuggled into his side. 'It's been a lovely evening,' he said.

'I guess,' she said.

He turned her towards him. 'You didn't enjoy it?'

'Yes, of course I did. You're wonderful company. It's just … well … I hope my mood didn't ruin it for you.'

'What do you mean?'

'Everything reminds me of my previous life. There's always something triggering me off. Like the cheese.'

'Gilly, you don't have a "previous" life.' He placed his hand on her hip. 'You have one life. A life that throws all sorts of scenarios at you. A life that is you. You can't deny the stuff that's happened.'

Gillian put her head on his chest. He wrapped his arms tightly around her.

'It's okay, Gilly.' He tipped her head up, kissed her chin. 'You can let him be part of the rest of your life. Let him share it. It doesn't mean you can't do different things. Things you wouldn't have done with him. But you don't have to forget him to move forward. Do you understand what I'm saying?'

'I think so.'

Max took Gillian's hand, stepped forward. 'My wife, my ex-wife, she still comes into my thoughts. We were together for nearly fourteen years. One shouldn't wipe away years of one's life. I know your situation is a little different from mine. Patrick and you had so many plans. I can't imagine the emptiness. Just let that pain be part of your life for as long as it takes. Don't deny your feelings, they're part of you. Part of what makes you a lovely person. That pain may help someone, someday. Don't push it away altogether.'

The sentences bumbled over each other. Each making sense, but some needed time to hit home. Others reached Gillian immediately. Her eyes jumped to Max's face. 'Max. Did I tell you about Petra?'

'The lady whose child died?'

'Yes.'

'And?'

'You said about my pain helping someone else. I guess that's like Petra. She's helped me so much. And the same with Hana. Her son died when he was an adult, but still, one shouldn't bury your child at any age.'

'No. It's not the natural way of things.'

Gillian pressed the button for the lift. 'Do you want to come up?'

'Do you want me to come up?'

She stood with her back holding the lift door open. 'I think I'd like to go up alone tonight. You understand, don't you?'

'Of course.'

'It's not how I imagined the evening would go. I'm sorry.'

Max leaned forward, kissed her mouth, lingered until she responded. Finally, he pulled away. 'No, but there's always next time. You still up for the opera? I'll find out the details and let you know.'

'Thanks, Max. That'd be great. Love to find out what I'm missing.' When he raised his eyebrows and smirked, she added, 'The opera, Max. The opera!'

He kissed her again, enjoying the spread of excitement reaching his groin, but willing to let her go. 'Be kind to yourself, Gilly.' He kissed her cheek and gently pushed her into the lift. 'Bye, I'll ring you.'

He's such a good man. Patrick would have liked him.

Tears welled as she stood in the lift, even after it reached the fourth floor. Then she stood in the open doorway ignoring the door as it tried to close. It bumped against her shoulder several times before she stepped away, walked to her flat and opened the door. She let the tears flow as she cuddled the picture of Patrick and Sienna while recalling Max's advice. You don't have to forget the past to move forward.

Finally, some advice I can do something with. But everyone has said the same thing. *Not quite.* Almost. *Not the bit about sharing with Patrick. Maybe I'm just ready for the advice now.* That's it! You are ready.

The words, *I'm ready*, echoed around her brain as she filled the next morning with chores, then a brisk walk in the park, stopping for fresh bread at the supermarket before heading home for a cheese sandwich.

With an apple in one hand, Gillian held the phone tightly against her ear as she exchanged greetings with Petra. 'The reason I rang, could you come for lunch next Saturday.'

'Saturday? Yes, I think so. Is it a special occasion?'

Gillian nodded ever so slightly. 'Yes. Hana is coming, and Elena. I'd like to treat you all.'

'How nice. I'd love to come. And to meet your Hana. I'll check with Ivan. He can be with Izabela.'

'I don't mind if you bring her.'

'I would like to come without her.' Petra paused. 'If you don't mind ... she's just a little girl. I think it would be too long.'

'Okay then. But you will come?'

'Of course. Where do we meet?'

'I'm going to book at a place where Max took me. It's up the road from me – in Prosek. We won't be rushed there. And Hana will be okay to walk that far. I'll text the details.'

After catching up on Izabela's latest antics, the call ended amid laughter.

Gillian hoped the next phone call would be successful. She tapped numbers into her phone, waited for Max to answer, replied to his greeting then asked, 'Max, could you do me a favour?'

'More cheese lessons?'

'Over the phone?'

They both chuckled. He responded quickly, extending the joke. 'Cheeses. Many. Let me list them. Edam, Jarlsberg, Camembert, Mozzarella, Feta—'

'Max!'

'What? You don't like Feta?'

'Max, about this favour I need.'

'Right. Fire away. If it's within my powers.'

'Good. You know I spoke about Madison, the one with the puppy, who works at the embassy.'

'I have a puppy working at the Embassy?'

'Max!'

He laughed, apologised briefly. 'Couldn't resist it. I'm constantly having people correct my Czech. Wanted to sound knowledgeable for a change.'

Gillian chuckled again. 'You're forgiven, but only if you help me out.'

'Okay, what's up?'

'I want to get in touch with Madison. I forgot to get her number and I don't have time to go to the house. Do you think you could find out from your records?'

'Possibly, but I don't know if it would be considered correct.'

'Oh, I didn't think of that.'

'I could ask her to ring you. Madison wasn't it? You don't know her surname?'

'No, but there shouldn't be too many Madison's on file.'

'Shouldn't think so. I'll track her down and ask her to ring you. Won't be straight away. I have one of those inevitable meetings in a few minutes.'

'That's fine. Thanks. And Max, any news about the opera?'

'Seems they're still working on it. I'll let you know.'

'Great.'

'Got to go. I'll be in touch.'

When Maddison rang the next morning, she spoke without waiting for Gillian's greeting. 'Is everything okay? I got a weird message from some clerk at the embassy. Said to ring you.'

'Oh, thanks for ringing back. Yep, I'm fine. I didn't have your number, so I asked Max to get you to ring me.'

'Thank goodness. I was worried.'

'Sorry. I just wondered if you and Morgan would like to come for lunch on Saturday.'

'Saturday? I'm good. Have to ask Morgan. She's got a boyfriend. Might be busy.'

'Okay then. Can you text back later? I want to book.'

'Sure. Where are you going to book? Somewhere nice?'

'It's fairly new. In Prosek. I'll send the details. And, Maddy, what's your surname?'

'Didn't we say?'

'Nup.'

'Rosich.' Madison spelled it out.

'Okay. And now I have your number, no more weird messages.'

'Awesome.'

Madison's text came through twenty minutes later: *We're both good for Saturday. Send the where and when. We'll be there. Cool.*

'We shouldn't have left it so long,' Max said as he grinned at Gillian over the top of a menu.

'It's only been three days.' Gillian raised her eyebrows.

Max signalled to the waiter; turned back to Gillian. 'You've been counting?'

Gillian's eyes darted from Max's face to the tablecloth and spoke softly, 'Sort of.'

'Oh, that sounds ominous.' Not receiving any further explanation, he scanned the drinks menu. 'Are you okay with red?' he asked Gillian, who nodded without catching his eye.

He turned to the waiter, pointed at the list of red wine. 'This one, please.' Once the young man had walked away, Max asked, 'Are you okay? I mean, you don't sound very cheerful.'

Gillian pretended to read the menu.

Max studied her face. 'Gilly, what's wrong.'

She placed the menu down, pointed to the blackboard displaying the specials. 'The pasta looks good.' She glanced at Max. 'Have you decided?'

'Um, well.' He scanned the menu quickly. 'Maybe I'll have the pasta too.' Max watched Gillian fiddle with the serviette. 'Gilly, please, what's up?'

'I ...'

The waiter appeared with the bottle of wine, offered it to Max, then with his approval, half-filled two glasses. 'Are you ready to order, sir?' He looked at Gillian.

'The pasta special, please,' Gillian said.

'Yes, I'll have that as well,' Max said.

The waiter gathered the menus and moved away.

Gillian picked up a glass, held it towards Max. 'Na zdraví.'

He clinked glasses, sipped, let the smooth red run around his mouth; swallowed. 'Not bad.' Max placed the glass down carefully. 'You were saying ...' He tipped his head sideways, his eyes pleading for her answer.

'Um, you asked if anything was wrong.' She paused, sipped the wine without tasting it, then said, 'I've decided to go home.'

He looked down at his plate, shifted position, licked his lips and wriggled his head. Then raising his eyes to Gillian, asked, 'When?'

'I'm not sure.' She scrunched the serviette into a ball, then opened it and placed it across her lap. 'Soon.'

'Shouldn't you be celebrating?'

She rearranged the serviette again. 'Yes, I suppose so but–'

He caught her gaze. 'I was hoping you'd stay.'

'I know.' Gillian averted her eyes, then looked back to him. 'That's why it's so difficult.'

Max straightened his shoulders, realigned the left sleeve of his jacket. 'It's not about me,' he said. 'If you're ready to go, then the trip to Prague must have been a success.' His voice quietened. 'I'm pleased for you.'

'Oh, Max, ever the diplomat.' She smiled. 'You've been wonderful. Most men would have run a mile. I'm just sorry I couldn't be what you wanted.'

'Don't say that!' his whispered exclamation surprised her. 'You opened your heart to me. That doesn't happen often. Not to me, anyway. I don't want you to go, but I understand. Prague isn't your home.' He closed his eyes for a moment, opened them, grinned sheepishly. 'More's the pity, eh?'

The waiter's interruption saved Gillian having to reply. He said, 'Your pasta. Enjoy the food.'

As she pushed the pasta around the bowl, Gillian knew her explanation wasn't complete. 'I have to explain,' she started.

'Not if you don't want to.'

She speared a piece of pasta, put it in her mouth, and chewed slowly. When her mouth was empty, she said, 'Yeah, I do. We've shared a lot. And, under normal circumstances we might have continued, built a more permanent relationship. I could see that. But ...' Gillian shrugged, scooped up another mouthful of food.

Max, aware of Gillian's struggle, said, 'It's okay, Gilly, really it is. Let's enjoy each other while we can. We can cry on each other's shoulder when you're at the airport. Please, you don't have to explain. Not here, anyway.'

'See!' Gillian said. 'That's what I mean. You're too good to be true. How come the departed Mrs Barkley didn't appreciate what she had?'

'Ah! Now we're on different ground.' Max jabbed his fork into a piece of pasta, wiped it around the bowl before putting it in his mouth.

'Oops, foot in mouth.' Gillian smirked.

'Not really.' Max spoke around chewing the pasta. 'Different kettle of fish. She wanted the high life, complained about the means to get it. He wanted to make a difference, worked at everything except his marriage. Result − divorce.'

'So now you've made it. What's next for Max?'

He wiped his mouth, put the serviette down and grinned. 'Ever think of going into politics, 'cos you sure know how to change a subject for your own advantage.'

'Learning from an expert.'

The waiter hovered. 'Coffee, dessert?'

'Not for me,' Gillian said.

'No thanks.' Max glanced at Gillian, back to the waiter. 'I'm hoping to entice this young lady for a walk, then coffee at my place.'

'Good, sir. Have a good evening. I'll bring you the account.' The waiter's grin lingered all the way to the front desk where he whispered to another waiter.

'Oh, so, you're enticing me, are you?'

'I didn't think he'd cope with me adding seduction to the list.'

Gillian dropped her head, struggling with her emotions.

Seduction, mm, why not?

They ambled to the parked car, listened to a late-night music show as he drove; spoke spasmodically, until they reached the back entrance of the Australian Embassy.

'No flag?' Gillian teased Max into stopping at the gate and considering this question.

'I'll organise one.'

'Immediately!'

He made a poor attempt to salute her. 'Immediately, madam.'

Even though no one was around, they tip-toed across the parquetry flooring in the hallway and up the stairs to his private accommodation. Gillian's mouth opened as she took in the tall ceilings, modernistic artwork in the sitting room, a stained-glass window high above the kitchen sink, and the sleek granite benches.

'Wow, a lot more modern than I expected.'

'They've done a good job. Apparently, the chap before me was a bit of a spendthrift. I'm benefitting from it.'

'His artwork choices?' She tipped her head trying another angle to the splashes of colour on the canvas.

'Nup, that would be mine. I thought the vibrant colours cheered the place up.'

'They do.'

'Coffee? Or would you rather something stronger?'

'What's the stronger option?'

'How about ...' Max led her to the sitting-room, opened a cabinet. 'Whisky, port? You name it, we've probably got it. It's the preferred option for gift-giving – so, name your poison.'

'Glayva?'

'Ah, any other choice?'

'Um, Johnny Walker?'

With drinks poured and music selected, Max sat down next to Gillian on the couch, snuggled back into the soft leather and sighed. 'Delightful.'

As Sting's Fields of Gold started, Gillian let the soft burn of the whisky ease its way down her throat. She tilted her head back against the headrest and agreed with a sigh of her own. 'Nice.'

'Very,' Max said.

Gillian leaned sideways, her shoulder touching Max's arm. 'I bought Patrick the sheet music for this. He played it at the school's wind-up. His last solo performance.' She hummed along to a stanza. 'Sienna often played the simple pieces Patrick taught her.' Gillian chuckled. 'My limit is chopsticks.'

The tune finished and a classical piece followed.

'Can you play an instrument?' Gillian turned to Max, shocked to find tears on his cheeks. 'Oh, Max, what's wrong?'

'It's okay.'

'No, it's not. Tell me.'

Max slipped his arm around Gillian's shoulder, pulled her against his chest, and kissed the top of her head. 'Gilly, dear Gilly.' He put his hand under her chin and gently tipped her head up so he could look into her eyes. 'It's just, well, life seems so unfair. Patrick and you, your daughter, it makes no sense. Such love shouldn't be taken from anyone. Especially one so young.' He brushed his tears away with the back of his hand. 'But, such a love, I reckon you should hang on to it. Don't let it go, for anyone.'

'But, Max, I have to. Let it go, I mean. How can I move on otherwise?'

He stood, walked to the other side of the room, his eyes on a painting, obviously trying to have the thoughts in his head make some sense. He turned. 'So they say.'

'Come here, sit with me, Max. I want to ask you something.'

He sat down and took her hand. 'Ask away.'

'Could you live with someone who had a husband lurking in every corner of her being?'

He thought of saying yes immediately, but knew Gillian expected discussion, not a one-word answer. 'It would be complicated.'

'It would be.' She turned her hand over, gripped his hand, caressed it with her other fingers. 'I think I'm still working things out. I mean, Patrick will always be there. But I have to have some portion of my heart ready for someone else, if it was to work. I haven't got there yet. Patrick still has it all. Maybe in time, he'll let me have a bit back.' She frowned and asked, 'Does that make any sense?'

'Of course it does.' He kissed her hand. 'Do you think I might steal just a corner, for the rest of the time you're in Prague?' He leaned towards her, pulled her closer. 'Even the tiniest of corners?'

She leaned forward and kissed his lips.

'Is that a yes?' he asked.

'A smidgeon of the bottom tip perhaps.'

'And can I tempt you to stay the night? I want to see how much a smidgeon is?'

She pushed him away. 'Max!' She flapped her hand in front of her face and blinked rapidly. 'Stay the night? Well, I never!' She tried to prevent a smile. 'Mm, what would people say?'

The next morning, wrapped in Max's bathrobe, Gillian entered the small kitchen. 'Morning, Max. You should have woken me.'

He turned, smiled broadly, and said, 'I wanted to make you breakfast. Hope you're up for bacon and eggs.'

'The smell hit me the moment I woke. You can't beat it, can you?'

He poured a glass of orange juice and held it towards her, his eyebrows lifted in question.

'Yes, please.' She drank half the juice, licked her lip and peered into the frying pan. 'Are you feeding an army?'

Max grimaced. 'Too much? Wasn't sure how hungry you'd be.'

'An egg, a bit of bacon will do me. Have you any bread?'

'Right, bread coming up. I assume you want it toasted?'

Gillian nodded, watched him drop white bread into the toaster. She fiddled with the prepared cutlery. 'Max, I—'

'How about you choose your egg.' He offered her a plate, avoided her serious look as she took it. 'Let's eat. Don't want the pigs sacrifice going to waste.'

They took their plates to the table. Gillian, acutely aware of her naked body under Max's robe, watched his mouth, noticed that he'd shaved, then looked away quickly when he glanced at her. She dipped the toast into the soft yolk and nibbled at it.

It had been some time since Max had a breakfast companion. He realised Gillian hadn't come prepared and he battled with the etiquette. He'd offered her one of his t-shirts once they'd satiated their desires. This morning he found a packeted toothbrush and left it on the bathroom cabinet.

'Max, I'll have to go soon.' Embarrassed by last night's appetite for sex, she struggled with light conversation.

A few months after Patrick's death, Sandy had teased her. 'I'll find you a man,' she'd said. Gillian, shocked, had answered, 'No way, Sandy. Don't even joke about it. I'll never have another man. Never. Not after Patrick.'

'Course you will. Women of our age,' Sandy had lifted her chin, pursed her lips, put her hands on her hips and finished off the sentence, 'need sex. Doesn't have to be love-ever-after, my dear girl, but sex − we need.'

Now, as she tugged the robe across her thighs, Gillian didn't quite know how one should act after a night of total abandonment. 'I'll…' She stabbed her fork into the crunchy bacon, it snapped in two, one piece shot off the plate onto the table. 'Oh!'

Max laughed. 'I love crispy bacon, but perhaps I overdid this lot.'

Gillian picked up the wayward bacon, about to place it on the edge of the plate, but instead held it up, pouted at it. 'Can't waste good crunchy pig.' Every little shard stabbed against her tongue as she crunched it, but the enjoyable flavour lingered.

'Coffee or tea?' Max asked.

'I might get dressed first. Then, coffee. Then I'll go.'

'You don't have to.' He grinned. 'Go, I mean.'

She stood up, wiggled her toes on the tiles. 'I'm getting cold. I need to get something else on.'

He came up to her, put one hand on her shoulder, the other on her waist. 'Or not.'

Gillian kissed his nose and then stepped back. 'I won't be a moment. I'll have coffee, please.'

After a three-minute shower, a quick scout through the cabinet for toothpaste, Gillian finished her ablutions and dressed. As she stared into the mirror, she asked, 'Have I created a situation?' She sighed. 'Good one, Mrs Middleton.' She combed her hair with her fingers, thinking about the comb and lipstick in her handbag that she'd left in the sitting-room. 'Oh well, better than nothing.'

As they drank hot coffee, and Max finished another piece of toast with marmalade, he asked, 'Have you booked your ticket?'

'No. Not yet?'

'Is the procrastination significant?'

'Mm, big words so early in the morning.'

'Well, is it?'

Gillian swished the last of her coffee around the cup. *Procrastination,* she thought. *Perhaps.* 'Not at all,' she told Max. 'I'll probably go to the agents tomorrow.'

'And book for when?'

She shrugged. 'Depends on what's available.'

'Look,' Max said, 'are you sure about going. It seems to me you're hesitating. Are there things you're still avoiding? You know, back at home.'

'Good question. I don't think so. But, well, Max, to be honest, you've complicated things a bit.'

Max pretended to look guilty. 'Who me?'

'I came here wanting to get away from pressure being put on me. Now ... well ... not that you've put any pressure on me, but I'm feeling it anyway. Perhaps because I'm unsure about how to go forward. How to...' She put her head in her hands, leaned forward on the table and sighed. 'It's so hard.'

He wanted to hug her, tell her he'd look after her, beg her to let him, but instead he said, 'I hate to say it, but I think you do need to go home. Go back and get a firm footing with your sister, with your life back there. Then you can decide what you want for your future.'

Gillian looked up; laid her hands on the table. 'Bloody hell, Max. I bet you could sort out a quarrel at the United Nations.'

He closed his eyes for a moment, shook his head. 'That's the easy bit. It's the personal stuff I'm shit at.'

'Oh, Max, don't be so hard on yourself.'

He stood, took her empty cup, rinsed it before placing it in the dishwasher. 'I'll run you home.'

'Thanks, I'm a bit crumpled even for the good old Metro.'

As he pulled up near her flat, he asked, 'When will I see you?'

She opened the door, turned back to him. 'How busy are you?'

'Fairly, but my evenings are mostly free. And depending if you're rushing off, I can do this weekend.'

'Can I ring after I've been to the travel agent?'

'Sure.'

Gillian eased out of the car, stood up, then leaned down again. 'Max, I had a lovely time. You're a special person.' Then she closed the door and walked away without looking back.

On Saturday, as she ran down the steps to meet Hana and Elena, Gillian's stomach flipped with a mixture of excitement and nervousness – today she'd be putting into words – saying it out loud – her decision to go home.

After greeting her elderly neighbour with a quick hug, and acknowledging the teenager's smiling nod, Hana, Elena and Gillian strolled to Boehme Prosek together.

Slipping her hand around Gillian's arm, Hana explained she usually used her shopping trolley for confidence, adding with a chuckle, that without the squeaky trolley people wouldn't recognise her.

They reached the intersection just as Petra came out of the Metro's exit.

'How's that for timing!' Gillian hugged Petra and introduced her to Hana and Elena who spoke Czech as they shared information about their connection to Gillian.

They'd been seated in the restaurant for a few minutes before Morgan and Madison burst through the door, their cheerfulness evident in their smiles. Their greetings surprising the overwhelmed maître d'.

'This way,' he said as he regained his professionalism.

'This place is awesome,' Morgan said. 'Maddy and I have tried out a few places. There are so many gorgeous old hotels. You should try Slavia Café and the Imperial Hotel, my god, the tiles on the wall. You've got to go there. We'll take you.'

Madison jumped in, 'There's the one in the city, beautiful, can't remember the name. It's near the Old Town Square. It's awesome. The chandeliers, wow. And, they really know how to do food.'

Elena and Petra took turns translating for Hana. Gillian tried to get her guests to decide what they wanted to eat, but the twins couldn't be restrained in their compliments for the food they'd had in Prague.

'Take a breath,' Morgan finally said to her sister.

'Yeah, okay.' Madison asked Gillian, 'Are you really paying? What can we have?'

Gillian laughed, waved the menu at Madison. 'Anything, anything at all. Let's have three courses. We can always skip dinner. This is a celebration. And yes, I'm paying. Acting like a millionaire today. No restrictions. It's all on me.'

Hana tugged Elena's arm, asked why Gillian was so happy.

Elena caught Gillian's eye, told her what Hana had asked then translated for her grandmother. Hana picked up the menu, read quickly down the list, told Elena she wouldn't have entrée because an old person can't eat like young ones.

The waiter brought a carafe of wine, and one of juice. Both were refilled during the afternoon. Hana sat quietly, soaking up the joy of the other women, occasionally asking for translation, often being given it by Petra. Elena revelled in speaking English with native speakers, often forgetting the need to translate for her grandmother. Morgan tried out her smattering of Czech. Madison laughed at her own attempts and goodheartedly teased Gillian and Morgan as they pronounced the selection on the dessert menu.

'Now, you lot, hush for a little,' Gillian said. 'Who wants coffee or tea?' She looked at Morgan. 'Or more wine?'

Petra suggested no one needed any more wine. 'There is the Metro to negotiate.'

They ordered coffee and the chatter quietened as they unwrapped chocolates while waiting for their hot drinks.

'I want to thank you for coming today.' Gillian leaned forward, tapped Hana on the arm. 'Děkuji, Hana.'

Hana forced a smile, but then turned to Elena and asked why she was being thanked. Elena's quiet translation enhanced the formality of Gillian's expression of thanks to her new-found friends.

'My stay in Prague has been made a lot easier because I met you lot. Petra, you'll never know how much you've helped. Just to have someone who knows about losing a child. It made all the difference. Thank you, so, so much.'

The twins whispered questions to each other.

Gillian took a deep breath. 'Morgan, Madison, I didn't tell you the underlying reason as to why I'm here. It was too painful at the time, and it was nice to have someone who didn't know. You see, I … well … my husband and child were killed in a car accident.' She pushed her hair behind her right ear and spoke determinedly, 'I admit to running away. This is where I ran to.'

Morgan put her hand over her mouth, her eyes wide with shock. Madison said, 'We're so sorry, we—'

'No need to be sorry at all. I was grateful not to have to tell you. And, Plenty, well, his tail says it all. It was good to be happy, just a stroll through the park when I so needed it.'

Petra filled in for Hana. Elena eyed off the last chocolate.

'And Hana, my dear friend. Elena, you've been so helpful. It was like a cow talking to a horse until you came along.'

Hana laughed heartily when Elena translated. The others chuckled.

'I'm going to use the cow horse thingy,' Morgan said.

'Elena, please tell Hana that I want to thank her. That's why we are here today. My way of showing my new friends how grateful I am.'

'And does this mean you are going home? Is it a farewell party?' Petra asked.

'I think I'm ready to go,' Gillian said. 'I honestly don't know exactly when, certainly haven't booked my ticket, but I wanted to get you all together at least once before I do go.' She clenched her bottom lip, shook her head, stayed silent for a moment. 'It's still hard, but I think I can move forward. Anyway, today we're to be happy. Does anyone want anything else?'

'No way,' Madison said. 'I'm fully stuffed.'

With the seriousness broken, conversation recommenced. Petra spoke softly to Hana, telling her about Bridget, Izabela and the baby still to be born. Elena wanted to know where Morgan had bought her "cool" shoes, while Madison asked the waiter if there were any jobs going. Gillian relaxed, finished off the last of the coffee from a pot in the middle of the table, and knew she would miss these people when back in Perth.

Hana asked if it would be rude for her to go. Elena slipped the last chocolate into her pocket as she stood, explained that her grandmother was tired, and offered a goodbye. But Gillian declared the party finished, and helped Hana to her feet. They all spilled out onto the footpath, waiting for Madison to take a business card from the counter before re-joining the group. They strolled towards the Metro in a ramble of chatter.

Petra draped her hand across Hana's shoulder, talked of comfortable shoes. Hana gripped Gillian's arm, keeping her eyes on the uneven path. Morgan, Madison and Elena hurried ahead, pausing outside clothing shops, teasing each other as they pointed out favourite pieces. At the entrance to the train station, Petra embraced Hana and then Gillian. 'My friend, it's been a lovely day. Thank you. Will you ring me soon?'

'Yes. Don't worry, I won't leave without telling you.' Gillian stepped out of the embrace, but held onto Petra's arm. 'Today I refuse to feel sad. Thank you for coming. I'll be in touch.'

The others waved as Petra descended the steps. 'Ahoj,' she yelled.

'Aren't you going too?' Gillian asked the twins.

'Yeah, we should,' Morgan said. She turned and poked her sister on the arm. 'Come on, stop jabbering, I'm going out tonight.'

'Morgan, you won't...' Elena's eyes narrowed as she stopped mid-sentence.

Morgan held out her phone. 'I've got your number. I'll let you know the name of that shop. Promise.'

Hana, Gillian and Elena ambled back to their homes, commenting on the cooling weather and a speeding motorist.

Gillian broke the silence in the lift. 'I had a good time.' She turned to Hana. 'Dobré. I had a good time. Děkuji, both of you.' The lift doors opened. 'Elena, thanks for coming today. It made it a little less awkward.' She chuckled. 'My Czech hasn't improved much. I think I know about five words. And overuse each one of them.'

'It was nice. I like your friends. Morgan is to tell me about where she bought her shoes. Maybe I can get my father to give me money.'

'I'm sure she'll remember.'

Hana pulled on her granddaughter's arm. She nodded at Gillian. She tugged Elena's arm again, speaking softly and slowly.

Elena frowned at her grandmother, turned to Gillian, said, 'Granny said she enjoyed your lunch, and that Petra is a kind person, and you should stay friends.' She shook her head at Hana, turned again to Gillian. 'She is tired. We must go. I'll ring you when I am coming to visit. Unless already you have gone.'

'No, I will let you know,' Gillian said. 'Ahoj, Hana. Thanks again, Elena. See you next time.'

Gillian flopped down on the couch, kicked off her shoes and sighed. 'How exhausting can a lunch be?' She let her mind wander over conversations at lunch, amazed at how much Czech Morgan and Madison knew, pleased they included Elena in their teasing, and remembered how Petra had made sure Hana kept up by translating the mixture of English and inaccurate Czech.

After a five-minute nap, Gillian yawned, stretched, licked her dry lips and stood. 'Cuppa time.'

As she waited for the kettle to boil, she opened her laptop and scrolled past a list of commercial emails. 'Got to do it,' she said as she settled the machine on her lap, a cup of tea close at hand.

Hi Esther,
I think I'm about ready to come home.

There you've done it! Wasn't too hard. Yeah ... but ... *Now what?* Well, I'll be saying goodbye to Petra. *So?* I'll miss her. *Of course you will. She's helped so much.* I'm definitely going to keep in touch. *Easy peasy with emails.* Yeah, but ... *You keep saying that. What's the but?* Well ... there's other stuff to finalise. *Like what?* The stuff that won't be easy peasy. *Just say it.* THE conversation with Max. *THE conversation?* Yeah, you know, nice knowing you. Got to go.

Gillian closed the lid, slid it onto the couch, stood up and walked to the window.

During lunch, when the others were asking Hana to explain what made her dumplings special, Gillian had wondered how Max had coped with the position of ambassador before he had a conversational command of Czech. Her thoughts had then turned to Max's empathy, and his caresses.

It's going to be hard, she thought again.

She watched the slowing traffic, the changing of amber lights to red and sighed. 'Oh, well.' She returned to her laptop and continued her email to Esther.

I haven't booked yet. Will let you know the exact date soon.
I'm going to email the agents, get them to give the tenants notice. They'll need a month. So, I was wondering if I could land at your place for a while. Would you mind? It'd just be until the month was up.
If I leave here in a couple of weeks, you won't have to put up with me long.

Anyway, see what you think. I guess if it's difficult, I could ask Sandy. Although … Is Murray living with her or is she with him? Maybe her place would be empty. I'll ask and get back to you.

Lots of love
Gilly

She changed into her pyjamas, determined to have a relaxing evening, then started another email.

Hi Sandy,
Hope arrangements haven't got out of hand. Are you going to be a blushing, white bride? Can't imagine you blushing at anything! White was never your colour. Are you going to be wed in burgundy then?

Look, I've decided I'm ready to come home. (No need for that cheering) Haven't booked yet. Just getting things started as it's not simply a question of lobbing back there. I have to give the tenants a month's notice for starters.

I've asked Esther if I could stay with her until I can get back into my place. But I was wondering if you are staying with the MAGNIFI-CENT MURRAY and have an empty bed at your own place. It might save me upsetting Esther, unnecessarily. Or more to the point getting a 24hour grilling from her.

Anyway, what is the state of play? Let me know soon.
Love Gilly

Sunday passed slowly. Gillian spent most of the morning wandering around the park. Making excuses not to return home to a sandwich of leftovers, she ate at a café while reading texts from yesterday's guests, pleased they'd all enjoyed themselves.

Several times she hovered over Max's texts, but only answered them with reciprocal light-hearted banter, deciding to wait until she had a firm date to announce her imminent departure.

Acknowledging procrastination was the theme of the day, she caught the Metro to Depo Hostivař, wondering if a second visit would prove more appealing. It wasn't, but as she skirted the nearby buildings, one striped door at the rear of a corner shop caught her eye and she pulled her phone from her bag. 'There, something to prove I made the end of the Green Line.'

Despite a lazy day and a good night's sleep, the emotional effort of what was to come left her weary.

Unable to find a travel agent in Prosek, Gillian headed for the city. On her way towards the Metro, she had planned to grab a take-away coffee, but stopped to admire a patterned caftan in a tiny shop at the base of the stairs.

'Hello.'

Gillian turned at the sound of the heavy accent in the English greeting. 'Um, hello.'

'Have you … Can you do your shopping with everything being good?'

Gillian's brow crinkled with the effort of recognising the angular face surrounded by curly greying hair of the woman standing next to her.

'Your carrots gave you trouble.' The woman laughed. 'I helped you.'

'Of course. I didn't recognise you without your hat. It was rather large.' Gillian smiled generously. 'You certainly did save me.'

'Yes, yes. My good work for a day.'

'Look, I'm about to get a coffee. Would you like to join me? I owe you one. Please.'

The woman swapped her shopping bag to her other hand and glanced at her watch. 'I have a little time. Yes. We can enjoy together.'

'Good. By the way, I'm Gillian.'

'I am called Lettie.' She grimaced as she held out her hand. 'The name my mother gave me was foreign and hard for a child to say. My father was Russian, you see. You are ... English, or perhaps from America. I have yet to decide.'

As she shook Lettie's hand, Gillian replied, 'Australian. Perth. Western Australia.'

'Ah, yes, there is a difference. Now I can tell.'

Gillian refused Lettie's offer to pay for her own drink. 'My shout.' She waved away the money. 'I certainly owe you.'

'It was nothing. You were a person needing help. But if you are sure, I will accept.'

After they ordered and settled at a table near a window, Lettie asked, 'Why did you come to Prague? It is a great distance from your home, is it not? And, I think, you are on your own?'

Gillian considered her answer. Did she really need to keep telling her tale of woe?

'Your eyes, they now have just a little pain. It was big the first time. I thought it just the carrots.' Lettie shrugged. 'But there are no carrots today.'

Putting her open hand across her chest, Gillian said, 'It's hard for me to talk about ... everything.'

'I see it is. Everyone has something deep that is hard to bring to the top. It is okay not to tell, but, sometimes a comfort.'

'Mm.' Gillian nodded. 'Yes, sometimes it is.'

They stopped talking while the waiter put two mugs of coffee on the table and spoke in Czech. After Lettie shook her head and replied, he headed back to the kitchen.

'I ran away,' Gillian whispered, her eyes remaining on the mug.

'From something you couldn't bear?'

'Exactly.'

'Can you now?'

Esther's face, nodding, encouraging, flashed across Gillian's memory. 'Maybe.'

'"Maybe" is a good place to start at.'

Gillian looked up. Remembered the smile she'd seen under the floppy hat; remembered how kind Lettie had been. 'I ran away from, amongst other things, the love and care of my sister.'

'It is a shame to go from that.'

'Esther was overwhelming me. I was drowning in her fussing. She watched me constantly. It felt like she recorded everything, thought about it and then lectured me because she thought I should be … ' Gillian paused, clenched her lip, shook her head before continuing. 'Perhaps the same as I'd always been. It wasn't − it isn't, possible.'

'Did you tell her?'

The hot coffee scalded her tongue, but Gillian didn't notice. 'Tell her what?'

'Very few sisters are brain readers. Did you tell her?'

'Often. And sometimes not so nicely.'

'But did you say to your sister what you wanted?'

'I …' Gillian thought of the many times she had hung up the phone, refused to reply to Esther's questions, ignored valid suggestions, constantly insisting her sister stop fussing so much. 'Now you mention it, I never did. Not exactly.'

'Perhaps you should.'

Gillian turned away, looked, without seeing, out the window. *I didn't, did I.* No. *But I didn't know what I wanted. Not then.* And now. *Maybe.* Like Lettie said, maybe is better than a no. *Yes, it is.*

She placed the mug down, faced Lettie. 'You're right. I'll have to decide what I want first.'

'Then talk. It is something we should all do.'

'Are you speaking from experience?'

Gillian could tell Lettie's thoughts had now drifted. 'Yes,' Lettie said, 'but I was lucky. It was okay for my problem to go away.'

'Good.'

'And now, I must go. Thank you for this.' Lettie stood, gathered her bag from the floor. 'I am pleased to see you again.' She grinned as she stepped towards Gillian. 'Glad that you can buy carrots without me.'

Gillian chuckled as she stood, accepted Lettie's momentary one-armed embrace. 'You've been like a fairy godmother,' Gillian said as she stepped away.

'A fairy godmother! Look at me, no magic wand.'

'You saved me … ' Gillian smiled, 'and my vegies. Now, today, you helped me see a way ahead with my sister. I'd say very fairy godmother like.'

'Well then, this fairy godmother must now disappear. We might not see each other again, but I wish only for your dreams to come true. I'm sure if you keep believing in fairies, then magic will come. One day soon, that is what I hope for you.'

'Thanks, Lettie.' Gillian kissed her on the cheek. 'Thanks again.'

Gillian stood, watched Lettie walk away, and let her mind wander to Cinderella's happy-ever-after. *Fairy godmothers! Everyone should have one.*

Considering Lettie's advice as she travelled to the city and bought her ticket, Gillian formulated several options, but discarded them all. I'll wait. Get home – before I decide what I want for the future. Right now, I've got to ring Max.

Grimacing with reluctance, with her newly purchased ticket sitting on her lap, Gillian punched in Max's phone number.

'Max, have you got a minute?' Gillian spoke into her mobile.

'Hi, Gilly. Yes, but can you hang on just a moment.'

Gillian could hear Max issuing instructions. 'The situation needs to be formalised. Make an appointment for him.'

She wondered if she should have sent a text.

'Right. I'm free now. How are you?'

'Good, sorry to interrupt state secrets.'

Max laughed. 'Much of what I do is dealing with dignitaries wanting information about Australia. Not many secrets, but, yes, this one is a little delicate. May require some significant attention. However, all in a day's work. Now, tell me if you're free for dinner tomorrow night.'

'Sorry to disappoint. I've said I'll visit Petra then.' She paused, then added, 'I promised I'd ring you after, well, I've booked—'

Max didn't let her finish. 'Your ticket? Damn, I was hoping you'd change your mind.'

'No, Max. I have to go. You said so yourself.'

'You sound different. Have I upset you?'

'Of course not. I just feel … I think it's because I've made the decision. I feel in control again.'

'Okay, that's understandable. When's the − I was going to say, happy day, but it's not for me. When are you going?'

'Next Monday.'

'Damn. So, if it's Petra's tomorrow, when can I see you? Unfortunately, tonight is out for me. What about the weekend?'

'Well ... I want to see Morgan and Maddy – might have to be the weekend. But, yes, we've got to have some time together.'

'Is there something you wanted to do, that you haven't done? We never got to the opera, did we?'

'I was waiting for you to organise that. Did your friends end up going?'

'They're still planning to. Option twenty-five still being discussed. Sorry, looks like you'll miss out. But, is there anything else? Can I tempt you to a trip to Karlovy Vary?'

'Maybe.' She paused. 'There is something I wanted to do. Is Karlovy Vary in the mountains?'

'Sort of. It's in a valley really. Why?'

'I have this picture. I might have said already – got it from the travel agent at home. A huge mountain looks like it's protecting a cute cottage. It's the reason I chose Prague. I always hoped to find that little house. Does that sound crazy?'

'No, but I doubt we could find that particular house. It's probably photo-shopped. But let's see … Opening diary. Um, no, Thursdays out. Oh, yes, the diary has two lovely blank spaces. So, all good.'

'Friday or Saturday?' Gillian asked, then waited while Max rambled out his decision.

'Yeah, let's see. I've got something, no, Friday's out. Meeting at the … okay.' His attention turned back to the phone. 'Sorry, about that. Thinking out loud. We could get away late on Friday. Say, eight. That would give us all Saturday and most of Sunday. I'd have to be back for, let's see. Um, Sunday is problematic. Bloody essential meeting with … anyway.' He paused. 'Oh, are you still there? Sorry, rather disjointed.'

Gillian chuckled. 'I think I got that. Leave Friday, eight o'clock, back Sunday afternoon. Sounds like a plan. Will you book?'

'I'll get the office to book something. Apart from a cottage, any other requests.'

'No. But must be in the mountains. I want to huff and puff up something I can brag about.'

'Sure. I'll get right on to it. One huff-and-puff mountain with a cottage. Done.'

'You'll confirm, won't you?'

Max's chair squeaked as he swivelled back and forth; answered cheerfully, 'Sure. I'll let you know a-sap.'

'Thanks, Max. You're a sweetheart.' She bit her lip. Damn, that's not ideal.

Max grunted before he said, 'I've got to go, state secrets and all. Bye.'

Sighing several times, Gillian gripped her silent mobile, stared at it as if it might offer an insight into her tumbling thoughts and her somersaulting feelings.

'Right, Morgan next.' She punched buttons, connected to Morgan's number and waited.

'Hi, Gillian. What's happening?'

'Morgan. Great. Glad I caught you. Is this a bad time?'

'I'm at work, so I'll have to be quick.'

'Oh, sure. Look I'm going home Monday—'

'Monday? Already?'

'Well … Anyway, are you and Maddy available after work Thursday? Maybe a walk with Plenty. We could eat at the café. Letná Park.'

'Sounds good. Let me check with Maddy. I never know when she's working. I'll ring her when I go for my break. Afternoon or evening?'

'Either or. Whatever suits.'

'Awesome. Spreadsheet calling. Going now.'

Gillian made a tomato sandwich, then opened her laptop. 'Right, now Esther.'

She re-read her sister's expansive email from a few days ago. It seemed overly enthusiastic. Esther had assured Gillian she could stay as long as she wanted in her spare room. Even suggested a long-term arrangement. As she pressed "reply" Gillian shook her head. 'Nup, that isn't going to happen.'

Hi Ess,
Thanks for finding a bed for me. It's a relief not to have to scramble and find accommodation. I heard from the real estate people. They've given the tenants notice, so I won't have to stay with you too long.

And I don't think I want to retain my house as a rental. Good suggestion though. I might want to think about moving at some point, but, no, not right now. And, yes, I think I'll cope okay.

This time away has been good. Not exactly "over it", I don't think I ever will be, but let's just say I can actually plan a few days ahead. That has to be an improvement.

Prague is beautiful. I didn't get to Poland or Germany, despite them being neighbours, but met people from all over. Travel certainly broadens the mind. We'll have lots to talk about when I get home.

Thanks again. Don't go to too much trouble. I'll text when I land. You'll probably still arrive before I get through customs, so don't rush.

Love Gilly

Now, who else needs to know, Gillian thought. *Sandy, yep. Mira, yeah. No one else? No, they'll find out soon enough.*

Getting-hitched Sandy,

I can't believe I'm typing that. Are you counting the days? Are you scared or excited? Big step, my dearest friend. Can't wait to meet the Magnificent Murray.

I have a bed at Esther's so you don't have to feel guilty about not sharing your abode with me. I understand the need for renovations. NOT! Your place is fine. Okay, maybe not up to a millionaire's standard, but pretty damn good by mine, and I might add yours, previously. But, hey, I'll forgive you. I'll even still give you the gift I bought especially because you're my BFF. (Do I sound like a teenager?)

Seriously though, I'm doing okay. Looking forward to a long chat when I get home. You'd better schedule some Murray-free time and buy several bottles of wine.

Esther is picking me up from the airport. BTW thanks for offering. I'll ring you when I get to her place. We can organise something then.

Gilly

xx

Not enthusiastic about anything in her freezer, Gillian walked to the shops to buy something fresh for dinner. After strolling in the park, enjoying a coffee at the café, and browsing the range of toys in the shop next to the supermarket, she bought a pork chop, a container of prepared salad, brie and a bottle of wine. On her way to the counter she stopped at the freezer and added honeycomb ice cream to her trolley.

Later, with a bowl of the ice cream beside her laptop she wrote to Mira.

Hi Mira,
Won't be long now. I'll soon be home. Esther is picking me up from the airport. Thanks for offering. I'll be staying with her until I can get back into my place. I hope there's nothing damaged.
No, I haven't put on weight. Even though I've eaten so many pastries. You would love Prague. The bakeries, the cafes, the cake shops, my goodness. I guess it's the walking. They walk everywhere. Well, at least as far as public transport. I've developed a love of walking. Had to buy some decent shoes. Fortunately, there is a great choice of flat shoes in Prague. I mean, they really do walk everywhere. And there are just so many parks.
Well, anyway, you can stop frowning. (Yes, I'm psychic) Stop worrying about me. I know you do. Even though you don't say anything. It was tough for a while, but I've enjoyed the last couple of weeks and I know I can manage, mostly anyway.
Lots to tell you. I'll ring asap.
Gilly
xx

Just as she plugged in her phone to the charger the phone beeped and made her jump. 'Shit. Ah, Morgan.'

Thursday 4.30 is good. Letná Park outside the café. We'll have Plenty.

Gillian replied immediately. *Looking forward to seeing that happy tail.*

While brushing her teeth, she went through a mental list. Max: wait for his call. Petra: dinner tomorrow. Maddy,

Morgan: Thursday 4.30 Maybe early dinner. Still have to get a gift for Rowan, something for Elena. And … the boring stuff; packing, cleaning. She rinsed her teeth, spat the water into the basin with force. *I have to see Hana. For the last time. Damn! It's going to be hard all over again.*

After another day of ambling through streets, shops and parks, while constantly checking her mobile for any message from Max, Gillian set out for Petra and Ivan's home.

On arrival, and before knocking, Gillian took the ninth photo of the red door, this time incorporating the branches of the chestnut tree. She heard Izabela running down the hallway and Petra calling to her daughter. Izabela pulled open the door and launched into Gillian's body, her greeting muffled by Gillian's stomach.

'Ahoj, Izabela.' Gillian knelt down, giving the child her full attention. 'Hello, Izzy. What an enthusiastic greeting.'

'Izzy, let Mrs Middleton get in the door.' Petra gently eased Izabela to the side and spoke to Gillian. 'She's been waiting for you. Asking the time every five minutes since we had lunch. Please, come on in.'

Once Izabela had showed off new pencils, a drawing she'd done, and a magnet displaying a cat with wobbly eyes, she was content to look through a book Gillian had bought her.

'Finally,' Petra said as she placed cups of tea on the table and sat down next to Gillian. 'Now I can ask if you are okay. Although I can see your eyes smile. This is good, eh?'

'Yes, I am smiling much more. Even when I think of Siena and Patrick. It's strange isn't it?'

'You mean, to smile around misery?'

Gillian nodded. 'When I think of just a few weeks ago …'

'It isn't so strange. I often smile when I pick up Bridget's photo. But sometimes there are tears. Yes, sometimes there's no stopping the tears.'

'You know, I just couldn't see that I would ever smile again; never be happy when looking at photos of us. But I do see that now. Sometimes I think of Siena and my chest responds as if it's being hugged – like a glow of memories is filling the space.' She shrugged, took a sip of tea. 'Does it happen that way for you?'

Petra agreed with a quick nod. 'I like that explanation. I feel it too. And, the tears are many times less, but sometimes … sometimes they are furious all over again.'

After nodding her agreement, Gillian asked, 'Are you keeping well? This new baby, is it behaving?'

'So far it hasn't made me sick. That's different this time.'

'Maybe you'll have a boy this time.'

'Perhaps. We would like that.'

During a few minutes of silence Gillian ran her hand over her abdomen, thought of the lost chance to have a son with Patrick. Her eyes moistened, she bit hard into a biscuit and stared out the window at a moving tree branch.

'Gillian,' Petra frowned as she asked, 'do you like pasta?'

Gillian swallowed the biscuit, took a sip of tea to wash it down. 'It's okay, Petra. I'll be fine. Just one of those moments. And, yes, I like pasta.'

'Good, I've made a huge pan full. We can fill our stomachs. I seem to be always hungry these days. Ivan will be home soon.'

After dinner, Ivan offered to escort Gillian to the tram. 'No, I'll be okay,' she protested.

'It isn't always safe,' Petra explained. 'Visitors either are scared of every sound, every movement, or, they are oblivious to the same dangers they'd be wary of at home.'

'I guess,' Gillian said.

Tiptoeing into Izabela's room, she gazed wistfully at the sleeping five-year-old before kissing the child's cheek.

'Come,' Petra said, 'Ivan will go with you.'

'Thank you for a lovely time. Again, you've inspired me to keep going.' She took Petra's arm and they walked to the front entrance. 'Bye. I'll ring you.'

'Prosím. It was a joy to have you here.'

Gillian and Ivan walked silently for some time before he spoke softly. 'I wish I could say the right thing to make your heartache go away forever.'

'I don't think there are such words, are there?'

'No, perhaps not,' he said. 'And … if there are, I haven't found them yet.'

Their pace slowed as they approached the tram stop. Ivan turned, stopped, looked at Gillian. 'It's been hard for my wife, but …' he shrugged and shook his head, 'people expect a mother to cry, to be … zranitelný … ah, vulnerable, but a man, a father, he must be strong. For so long, I could not be so.' He hung his head, sucked in a long breath. 'I could not be so.'

'Oh, Ivan, I'm so sorry.'

He straightened up, smiled weakly. 'I was lucky. Petra knew my pain caused the distance between us. We struggled, but we got through it together.'

Gillian thought of her "together". *Their together was supposed to last a long time.* She slipped her hand through Ivan's arm. 'Ivan, can I ask you ….' She knew Ivan had turned towards her, but she kept her vision straight ahead. 'Did you ... I mean, were you asked to ... did you offer Bridget's organs?'

Ivan stopped. Gillian let her hand drop from his arm, and faced him, shocked at seeing tears in his eyes. 'I'm sorry, Ivan. I shouldn't have asked.'

'It's just another moment of pain. I'm okay.' He wiped the back of his hand across his cheek, dispersing the tears. 'We considered it. But ... you see, she ... Bridget was too ill for them to want ... and then ... we took too long to ... Petra couldn't find the strength to sign the papers.' His shoulder bumped against Gillian's; he gripped her arm. She could see pools of ignored injury in his eyes. She reached out and touched his damp cheek.

'So, so hard,' she said. 'I signed those papers.' Stepping away from him she cleared her throat. 'I signed those ...' She turned back to him. 'That was harder than the rest of the decisions I had to make. I did it all in a daze: caskets, flowers, music, pallbearers ... all those things. But those papers ...'

'Come, Gillian.' He took her hand. 'Your tram is here soon.'

'Yes, I have to get going.'

They walked hand in hand. People went by, probably thinking they were lovers, sharing their evening, strolling with joy. But their shared emotion was much stronger than romance.

They continued in silence.

Turning the last corner, he squeezed her hand then released it. 'You are amazing, Gillian. So much to bear and you do it all alone.'

'I wonder sometimes about that. Esther, my sister, looks after me, but ... the pain makes one lonesome, isolated, don't you find?'

Ivan mumbled an agreement before saying, 'If you need someone to bear your pain with you, Petra and I can be that someone.'

'You know, that day I stopped to take the photo of your door, it changed everything. I found out, really understood, that I'm not the only one with this unbearable loss.' A gentle smile turned up the corners of her mouth. 'And, I'll remember your offer. I know I'm healing, but I also know that, just as you said, the words can't be found ... the pain is stronger than any words, isn't it?'

'It is.'

'But, well, thanks, thanks for everything.'

'Není zač.' He pointed down the road. 'You must go, your tram is coming.'

'Bye, Ivan.' She followed other passengers towards the tram.

'Stay in touch,' he called out.

'I will, I will,' she called back.

She clung on to the handrail, ignoring the empty seats, battling with the tram's maneuvering as fiercely as she battled with her tumbling emotions. Her glassy stare out the window didn't see the dwindling daylight.

The conversation with Ivan had proved cathartic. She hadn't spoken to anyone about the trauma of those urgent few hours, but now she realised it was one of the reasons she fled from the familiar streets of Perth: streets, shopping centres, parks, where the next little girl, or the next adult, could hold a part of Patrick or Sienna within.

Esther had guided her through those demanding questions that blurred before tear-filled eyes and foggy brain, but it was she who had put her name on the last page and hesitantly handed it back to a clerk.

By the time she stepped from the tram her attempt to stay cheerful gave way to defeat.

Will it never go away? I guess not. *Please, please make it go away.* Only you can do that. *I ... I know, and I'm trying.* Okay then, this is just another challenge. *Well* ... Come on, you have things to do, things to look forward to. *I guess.* Good, it's only a glitch, you've survived this far. *Yes, I have, haven't I?* Go, girl.

A snort came out with an involuntary laugh. *Honestly! Go girl? That's ridiculous.* There! A smile. *Right, I'm good to go.*

Gillian realigned the shoulder strap of her bag and pulled an artificial smile at her reflection in a shop window. As she scurried towards the Metro, she wondered why she hadn't processed that particular pain before. Saving another child, maybe two, and three or four adults was a sacred gift – at least that's what a surgeon had said when he left her standing in the office holding a copy of the consent form like a ready-to-explode grenade.

'In all your anguish, know that someone else will be forever grateful,' he'd said, before shaking her hand and advising her to ask for help when she needed it.

Was that the plus hiding in the minuses? The gratitude of an unknown family. That Patrick and Sienna's organs provided life to a mystery child; a nameless adult?

Was her decision to put her name on the consent form the only worthwhile action tangled amongst the sorrow and loss?

Perhaps talking to Ivan, not just having it bite away at her other progress, was the last hurdle? The one requiring extra energy to get over and leave behind on the way to the finish line? Perhaps.

While waiting for the train she checked her phone again. Nothing. She hoped Max would contact her soon. She still needed to clean the flat, see Hana – packing wouldn't take long – but she had planned to keep the weekend free for him.

The phone remained silent during the train trip, through her hurried walk along the darkening streets of Prosek, and well after she reached her flat.

Despite Gillian checking repeatedly, the phone never rang. Her concentration wavered as she thumped the keys while playing Tetris, and a late-night coffee did nothing to aid sleep.

In the morning she picked up the phone twice, but thought better of ringing Max. From the moment her eyes opened she'd battled with expectations, without resolution. A weekend with Max. Her mind twisted and turned, finally allowing excitement to build. She'd Googled a couple of bed-and-breakfast cottages but without knowing anything of Max's, or his office's choice of towns, it'd been a wasted search.

'He was the one who promised to ring,' she told her reflection as she tackled the tangles in her hair, a result of tossing and turning throughout the night.

Her phone eventually caught her off guard as she paced along the path between Prosek and Střížkov Metro stations.

'Max. *Good morning*,' she said, instantly regretting the emphasis.

'Gillian. Yes, sorry. The evening slipped away. Everything is in panic mode, I'm afraid.'

'What's happened?'

'It's, well, I won't go into the drama, but suffice to say, it's messed up our plans. I'm really sorry.'

'What do you mean? Max, what's happened?'

A huge sigh came down the line, and Gillian rolled her eyes and waited.

'I spent the evening swearing like a pirate, I tell you. None of it helped. Result is, I just won't be able to get away. Everything has turned into mush.' He paused, before apologising again.

'But, it's only Thursday. Surely you'll have it sorted by the weekend.'

Max humphed. 'Yeah, one can only hope. I'm expected in Germany, and I suspect this particular issue will take more than a few days.'

Gillian's excitement washed away, with the tide of anticipation following. 'Can't be helped, Max. I guess it's not meant to be.'

'Don't say that, Gilly. I've tried everything. That's why I didn't ring. Busy trying to sort something out. Still at it. And, I'm afraid today's also out of the question. I'll try—'

'Look. Let's just see how it pans out.' Gillian stared at the rubbish bin and back to the phone in her hand; shrugged. 'If it can't be helped, then it can't be.'

'Maybe I could—'

'Max, don't promise anything else. Just ring when you can. I've got to … I'm going now.' She hung up as Max apologised again.

She strode into the park's café and ordered pancakes with maple syrup – yes, four, yes, ice cream and cream – a long black – yes, large mug – dragged a chair out, all but threw her bag on the floor, and slumped across the small table.

Knew it. Knew what? *I'm not supposed to be happy, ever, again.* Of course you are. *Doesn't seem so.* Really? *Did you not hear Max. He can't make it.* Exactly. How does that relate to not being happy – ever? *Piss off.* What now? *Look, you might be my alter ego, but you really are stupid.* Clarification required. *It's the universe telling me I'm not supposed to be enjoying myself.* Stop wallowing. *Go away, will you.*

'The pancakes.' A teenage waiter waited for Gillian to remove her sagging body from the table before sliding a plate in front of her. 'And coffee. Is that all you have to come?'

Gillian blinked, glanced at the food, then looked up. 'Yep, nothing else.'

Her thoughts grew bleaker as she stuffed the pancakes dripping with syrup into her mouth. *Never going to get to my mountain house. Not fair.* She jabbed the fork into a blackberry. *Life's not fair.* When she accentuated the stabbing of the next berry and accidentally bumped the mug, coffee slopped over the table. *Damn!*

'I fix for you.' The attentive waiter mopped up the spill, his smile lasting throughout the process. 'There,' he said.

Gillian forced a smile; returned with less vigour to eating. Leaving half the food, but none of the coffee, she ambled back to her unit, a cloud of despondency building with each step. As she turned the key in the lock, the picture of the little house being protected by a mountain sprang to mind. She hesitated, then rushed to her computer.

Enthusiasm built further when she located *Siesta Haven*, a bed-and-breakfast within walking distance of a country village, Vysoké nad Jizerou.

'Ah! Can't go, eh, Max? I'll bloody well take myself. Maybe the mountain is just for me.'

The website claimed the owner spoke English and evening meals could be provided on request.

'Perfect. But Petra first.' With telephone guidance from Petra, Gillian booked accommodation for a Friday night stay and bought a bus ticket through the internet.

Now to tell Max.

Amid several attempts to text an explanation, Gillian pushed away her emotions.

I shouldn't feel guilty about going without Max. No way! He can't take you, so why the guilt? *Don't know. Shouldn't be.* Maybe it isn't guilt. *Mm, maybe.* What then? Disappointment? *Um, nup, not that either. Well, maybe a little.*

Her stomach continued to churn, and twice she left the unfinished text, walked to the window, looked at nothing, before returning to the keyboard.

'This is ridiculous!'

She typed: *So sorry you're stuck with work. Totally understand. I needed ...*

Deleting needed, she typed: *thought I'd take these last days to sneak in a visit to the mountains. Booked at a B&B in Vysoké. If by some miracle you get away, text me.*

Two hours later, a text came back from Max.

Good for you. Vysoké is lovely. You're bound to find your mountain house. Sorry it isn't the two of us. The State Secrets thing isn't going to be solved soon, so don't expect good news. Enjoy yourself. I'll contact you when I can.

Thursday hurtled its way through existence, and Gillian arrived a little late at Letná Park where Plenty greeted her by sniffing her crotch. His paws indicated a rush through the shallow end of a pond.

'Hah!' Madison said. 'Don't know how to stop him doing that.'

Morgan pulled the dog away, giggling an apology.

Straightening her clothes, Gillian chuckled. 'Glad we don't greet each other that way.' She stroked Plenty's ears and scratched his muzzle. 'How are you two? Everything going well? How's the boyfriend, Morgan?' She stood up, accepted a ball from Madison and threw it for Plenty to retrieve.

'Boyfriend is pretty awesome,' Morgan said.

'She's got a winner,' Madison said. 'He's bought them matching bikes. Talk about—'

'He didn't,' Morgan disagreed.

'Yes, he did.'

'Well, I'm paying him back, so technically he didn't buy it.'

'Picky, picky. Anyway, I have to climb over it every time I come in the front door.'

'Where else can I keep it? Mrs P would have a fit if I left it in the shared laundry.'

While throwing the ball several times for the enthusiastic dog, Gillian listened to their banter. 'Anyone listening would think you two don't get on.'

The sisters looked at Gillian then at each other, raised their eyebrows in mock horror, then grinned and agreed.

'But we do really,' Morgan said.

I should be kinder to my sister, Gillian thought. When I get back—

Morgan interrupted Gillian's thought, 'When are you going? Monday is it?'

Before Gillian could give details, Madison ushered them towards the seating outside the café. 'Come on, I'm famished. Didn't have a lunch break so I could knock off early. Let's get something.'

The three women chatted for twenty minutes about differences between Prague and Australia. The sisters amused Gillian with their comical tales of misunderstandings. Gillian shared her episode at the supermarket. Plenty accepted titbits while lazing under the table.

'Are you glad to be going home, Gilly? I mean you've settled in well here, haven't you?'

Gillian hesitated. 'Mm, yep, but I really couldn't live here. I mean the language barrier is okay as a tourist, but … no, don't think it would work for me.'

'What about the bloke you've been seeing?'

'Yeah, aren't you cosy with the ambassador?'

'Cosy!' Gillian laughed. 'I guess you could call it that. Max is really nice. Is he a good boss?'

'He's okay,' Madison said. 'I mean, I don't have much to do with him. Seen him a bit, you know, when I'm working, but, yeah, he's okay. Everyone seems to like him.'

'Right,' Gillian said.

'So, you two had a fling? Will it go anywhere?'

'He's an Aussie,' Morgan said. 'Maybe he'll go back there. That'd be cool. For you.'

Gillian sighed. 'Happy ending, eh? Well life doesn't always turn out the way you want. I know. Just ask me.' She ran her hand around her chin; let it rest on her chest. 'Nup, that's one thing you should learn, girls. Life sucks some times. Good and proper.'

Morgan glanced at her sister. Madison grimaced, then said, 'Sorry.'

'Oh, it's me who should be sorry,' Gillian said. 'Didn't mean to lower the mood.'

Madison reached over and put her hand on Gillian's arm. 'We're so sorry. Sorry terrible things happen to someone so nice. Life's not fair, is it?'

'Yep, certainly had my share of unfair.' Gillian's eyes narrowed when she caught the flash of pain in Madison's eyes. Morgan's shoulder sank forward; she resembled a balloon that had suddenly lost air. 'And, I'm guessing you have too,' Gillian said.

Madison looked down. Morgan sipped at her empty cup. Gillian's gaze darted between the young women. 'Didn't mean to put you on the spot. Forget I spoke.'

Morgan put down the cup, pushed it away, cleared her throat, and wiped her mouth with a paper serviette. 'Auntie —'

'Let's change the subject,' Gillian said.

Madison folded her arms, glared at her sister. 'We promised.'

'Well, I know, but …'

Gillian shifted in her seat, straightened the collar of her top. 'Do you want another drink?'

'See,' Morgan explained, 'we came on this holiday because—'

Madison interrupted. 'It's a family thing.'

'Okay, I—' Gillian started.

'Look, as far as life being fair, we haven't had it so bad. I mean you've had it way worse than us. It's just that Auntie —'

'We promised,' Madison said again.

Gillian leaned on the table, looked down at her hands and shook her head. 'You don't have to tell me. Everyone has secrets. Some little, some not so little. I don't want to—'

'Auntie died a year ago.' The following words tumbled out in quick succession. 'Breast cancer. Gran died of it too. When she was fifty-eight. Mum's already had a scare. Our odds are high.' Morgan grabbed Madison's arm, frowned as she spoke to Gillian. 'It's scary.' Her eyes glistened with threatening tears.

Madison sighed. 'Life sucks big time.'

Gillian shook her head in disbelief. 'Sure does.' A picture of two burial plaques hovered. 'Pain doesn't have to be physical to hurt like the devil.'

'Absolutely.' Morgan shrugged. 'That's why we're here. To forget about it. You know, just for a bit.'

'Do stuff,' Madison said.

'Before it's our turn.'

'But we decided not to speak about it. Like, while we're away.'

'Yeah, we did, but it's always there,' Morgan said.

Madison confirmed, 'Life sucks if you let it.'

The three women avoided looking at each other as they struggled with their own life-sucking anguish. They watched a toddler hurry past, his mother pushing a pram behind him. A teenager popped a can open, the fizz catching her by surprise. Two cyclists wearing Lycra zoomed along a nearby path. A sudden breeze tossed a discarded wrapper high in the air.

'Have you been checked?' Gillian asked softly.

Morgan fiddled with a teaspoon, while Madison sighed again. 'Yeah, so far, so good. Now if you don't mind, I'd rather talk about something else.'

'Of course, but you're both so cheerful. Makes me realise ... I've got good health ... can do what I want really ... shouldn't complain ... I should ... I don't know ... more like you—'

'Yeah, but losing a baby. That's really ...' Morgan tipped her head towards Gillian. 'It was awful losing Auntie Jen. She wasn't that old. Just when they thought they'd got it all. Bam!'

'Mum's finding it hard. They were close.' Madison's eyes jumped to her sister. 'Close,' she whispered. 'But Mum and Dad insisted we still do this.'

'They said we had to live our lives and forget about ... like ... the cancer ... Auntie Jen ...'

'Actually, it's impossible,' Madison said. 'How can you forget? I mean, I bet you know that.'

Gillian said, 'I agree. One can't. You just have to carry on the best you can. It's hard.'

Morgan pushed her chair back a little. Plenty stood, his tail flicking back and forth, hoping for action. 'Sit, Plenty.' Morgan drew a long breath, let it out slowly. 'We love it here. Prague's terrific, but we can't stay forever.'

Madison grinned. 'Just long enough to catch a good-looking bloke.'

'Jealousy doesn't look good on you,' Morgan said.

'Jealous? No way.'

'Maybe just a little, eh? I mean, you're the one without a boyfriend.' Morgan pointed to her sister. 'You're not trying hard enough.'

'Don't want complications. We'll be going soon.'

Gillian's mind went immediately to Max.

'Yeah, Gilly, what are you going to do about the Ambassador?'

Turning to Morgan, Gillian shrugged, didn't answer.

'Well?' the sisters said.

'I'm going home. He's staying here. Nothing to decide.' Gillian knew that wasn't entirely true.

'No way,' Madison said. 'I'd be hanging on to someone like that. He must be rich.'

'Maddy! I can't believe you said that.'

'It must be just as easy to fall in love with a rich bloke, as a poor one.'

Gillian chuckled. 'Certainly. But I have too much baggage for anyone, rich or poor. Got to go home.'

'Anyway,' Madison said, 'we still have half of Europe to see, we don't want … baggage.'

'Where will you go next?' Gillian asked, glad the conversation was moving away from Max's potential.

'We'll go to Croatia next. See where Dad's grandparents came from.'

'They went to Australia just after they got married. Can you imagine what it was like then?' Morgan said, not expecting an answer. 'Bet it was tough.'

Plenty pushed his nose into Morgan's hand. 'For God's sake, Plenty, you've eaten half my sausage roll already.'

Covering Madison's hand with her own, Gillian said, 'I'm glad I met you both. And of course, Plenty.' She leaned back, ran her tongue over her bottom lip, then asked quietly, 'What will you do with him, you know, when you leave Prague?'

Madison sighed. Morgan shrugged. 'Don't know,' they said in unison.

'I suspect you can't take him with you,' Gillian said.

'We've thought about it. Like, taking him to Croatia. We'll have to ask about the rules,' Morgan said.

'Yeah, but Mrs P might keep him. She's already said he's a good guard dog.'

'Well, I hope it works out.' Gillian fed the last of her crust to Plenty. 'Just look at him. How could anyone resist those soppy eyes? Not sure about the soggy coat and the muddy paws. Glad it's you two taking him home.'

Plenty didn't understand why his humans were suddenly giving him attention, but he'd take another titbit and more patting anytime.

'You've got my email,' Gillian said. 'And if you ever do get to Perth, I really expect you to come and visit. You would, wouldn't you?'

'Yep,' Madison said. 'We could even go home that way. We've not seen any of the West.'

'Yeah, we should. Maybe when we're done with Europe, after Croatia, of course. Yeah, we'll do that,' Morgan said. Her smile broadened as she brushed crumbs onto the bricks. Plenty tried to catch the miniscule pieces and then licked at the dots of pastry before begging for more.

'Go chase a cat,' Madison said. Plenty woofed as if replying. The women laughed as the dog gave up and wriggled under the table, thumping his tail when Madison added, 'Good boy.'

After another coffee each, and a stroll through the park, with an exuberant Plenty chasing lowering shadows as well as his ball, the three reached the main street and agreed it was time to part.

'We could come to the airport. Give you a proper send-off,' Madison said.

'Yeah, fill in your waiting time.'

Gillian shook her head. 'Not necessary. Anyway, I hate prolonged goodbyes.'

'You sure? This feels a little anticlimactic. Today's Thursday. What are you doing for the rest of the time?'

Morgan smirked. 'She wouldn't want to fill the time with us. Come on. One sexy Aussie bloke, I'm guessing.'

Gillian sighed. 'Nup, not this weekend. He's tied up. Business.' She tipped her head in a half shrug. 'However, I've organised some "me" time. In the mountains. Do you know Vysoké?'

Neither of the twins did, but talking over each other, they voiced their opinion about "me" time.

'I'm looking forward to it,' Gillian said. 'However, it's time to go. I'll be in touch.'

Madison hugged Gillian tightly, then as she released her, said, 'Have a safe trip. Hope you get some sleep.'

'I expect I will.'

'Spectacular,' Morgan said. 'Have a good one then.'

Gillian hurried for the tram, turning several times to respond to calls of goodbye; waving as melancholia descended. Privileged to have met these particular Aussies, Gillian knew she wouldn't have made friends with anyone of their age at home.

We probably won't ever see each other again, Gillian thought, *but then again, you never know.*

Early Friday, Gillian packed quickly as butterflies of expectancy danced around the coffee and toast in her stomach. She greeted the other early morning commuters with a forced grin as she waited at the Metro. She'd been to the end of the Yellow Line before so locating the appropriate bus stop at Černý Most went without a hitch.

After a fast drive along the freeway, and a slower trip along winding roads connecting several country towns, Gillian alighted at the broad town square of Vysoké nad Jizerou.

Petra had explained Jizera is the river that starts near the border of Poland and winds through Czechia.

So, Vysoké nad Jizerou is like the Czech version of Stratford-on-Avon, she thought as she glanced around hoping to spot part of the fast-paced river the coach had followed for several kilometres.

Not seeing the river, Gillian scanned the front of the buildings: a restaurant, a sports store, a cute shop with plants and racks of cards, amongst the dozen shops. Two people sat on a bench – a young lad held a multi-coloured ice cream, and the elderly lady took a final lick from hers before dropping it to the ground for her dog. Gillian wondered if she had time to dart into the café before Karla from *Siesta Haven* located her.

'Gillian, Gillian Middleton?' a woman called. 'Excuse me, Gillian?'

Gillian turned as a woman in green trousers and a patterned t-shirt, with a broad smile across her freckled cheeks, came hurrying across the grass.

'Karla? Siesta Haven?'

'Yes, yes. I am pleased to find you.' Karla's handshake conveyed strength. 'Have you had lunch?'

'I ate an apple on the bus.' Gillian turned her head in the direction of the café. 'I was just thinking an ice cream would hit the spot.'

Karla frowned, then her smile returned. 'Ah, it would. The café has ice cream that is very good. Let us have some. Then we go home. It is not far.'

They sat in the square, people-watching, enjoying the ice cream, while Karla chatted about the town, and cheekily pointed out a local businessman who, it was rumoured, had a younger mistress, as well as a wife and three children.

With their sugar-hit complete, Gillian followed Karla across the grassed area to her car.

The trip was over before Gillian had soaked up enough of the scenery flashing by. She'd wanted to stop at every corner, ask a thousand questions, but instead listened to Karla's running commentary, which finished with instructions about the myriad of walk trails in the area, three starting near the bed-and-breakfast.

After turning another corner and creeping up a steep narrow road, a picture-perfect bungalow appeared in front of the car as it bounced over a rough driveway.

'Sorry,' Karla said, with a giggle. 'It is not so smooth.'

Gillian shrugged. 'But, the house – it's gorgeous. Even better than the website pictures.'

'Yes, it is pretty. I do think. We painted last year. You see more inside. Come.'

Gillian ooh-ed and aah-ed as Karla led her up three steps, across a covered forecourt and towards a side door which opened into the attached bed-sit. Karla's home was too large to be the little mountain cottage from the travel brochure, but the wooden ceiling beams, and the rug-covered slate floor, together with two small windows dressed with dainty lace curtains oozed the charm displayed on the website.

After placing her bags down, and dropping her jacket on the bed, Gillian ran her finger across the intricate carvings on the door of a wardrobe, and asked, 'How old is this?'

'It came with our cottage. But many years old. Maybe hundreds of years.'

'Staggering. So beautifully made. And matches the headboard.'

Stepping away from the bedroom alcove, Gillian looked over the rest of the room as Karla talked.

'Everything for making tea, or coffee, is here.' Karla waved her hand theatrically towards the dresser where a blue china bowl held shiny red cherries and two apples. 'There is fruit.'

'Cherries are so expensive at home. I've eaten a ton while I've been in Prague.' Gillian took one and closed her eyes as she savoured it. 'Yum. It's so fresh.' She took another and inspected it before popping it into her mouth.

'Cherries are from my friend at the hill.' Karla rolled her eyes. 'Apples I have to buy.'

'Oh, okay. Do you, I mean the Czech Republic, export cherries?' As Karla considered her answer, Gillian added, 'I knew nothing about your country before I came.' She chuckled. 'Now I still know next to nothing.'

'That is normal, I think. Czech is tucked away. We are not Russia, or Germany. But there is much history. There is some to see in books on the shelves. Sadly, I do not know if we export cherries.'

With an awkward pause hovering, Karla rubbed her hands together and walked towards the door. Turning back, she said, 'I bring breakfast at time to please you. You have choice of food.' She picked up a booklet from the small dresser. 'Here, you can read. It shows the walking ways we talked about in the car. And breakfast. Do you like early or to sleep more?'

Gillian took the booklet. 'Um, maybe seven-thirty. Is that okay?'

'Of course, and I'll bring you some dinner at – is seven to be suitable?'

Gillian had packed some cheese, a half-empty vegemite jar, and a bread roll into her bag for backup. Something hot, and no doubt more sustainable, now being offered, certainly sounded inviting.

'Thanks. Just something light. Seven will be good.'

With many hours of sunlight remaining, Gillian refilled her water bottle, packed an apple and a warm jacket in her backpack, and headed along a narrow road.

'That way is towards Poland,' Karla had said.

Three children waved as she momentarily interrupted their ball game with a greeting. The older lad bounced the ball against a wall as he yelled back in English. The younger two echoed his response, their accents more pronounced.

Karla had told her to be on the lookout for wild strawberries growing by the roadside, but Gillian's eyes feasted on the quaint buildings, the abundant garden flowers and, most of all, the fantastic views. Peeping between the tall trees and slanting roofs, the valleys dipped between enormous mountains unlike anything Western Australia had to offer.

Watching the scenery instead of the pebbly, narrowing road, Gillian stumbled in a pothole. 'Shit!' she cried as her hands hit the ground. Grazed and tingling from the impact, her hands needed attention. She perched on a low rock and spat into her palm. With a careful rub with a tissue, she managed to clear the grit away. 'No real harm.'

Behind her: one delightful two-storied house with fireside-sized wood stacked against the side wall, and red geraniums cascading from window boxes. Across the road: a tall crumbling building without windows, a waist-high field of grass and a tumbling-down fence.

Gillian paused. Her mind discussed the obvious opposites. *I feel like that.* What? The crumbling or the delightful? *Both.* Surely not. *Yep. One moment I'm getting by. Have the appearance of being presentable. Then, wham, bam, turn me around, and I'm a mess again.* Surely not that severe a difference. Maybe a pretty cottage and an ordinary one. Not the one needing demolishing. *Possibly. Maybe my windows do have glass, but my walls are still shaky.*

Absentmindedly checking her hands again, she twisted her wedding ring, took a deep breath and sighed out the next breath. 'And then there is Max. I should let him, oh, and Petra, know I've arrived safely.'

Leaving thoughts of Max and the disappointment of two days together in a figurative ditch beside the road, she strode up an incline towards the mountain path, determined to soak up the ambience of this spectacular place.

Forty minutes later she reached the top. Far in the distance haze hid the mountain top where one could descend into another country.

She imagined families trudging to safety over these vast distances like the Von Trapp family, immortalised in film. 'Not to Poland,' she whispered, 'but mountains like this.' *How did they find something to eat? With children to look after! With fear and dread hovering. Danger all around.* Gillian trembled. It seemed an impossible predicament.

Forcing away the sombre thoughts, she twirled around the steel structure which in winter became part of a ski lift, kicked playfully at the grass, and raised her arms to the glorious blue sky.

With delight soaring, Gillian dropped her backpack to the ground and plopped alongside it.

Life is good. Told you. *Go away, I don't need you.* I'm just saying— *Yeah, like you're a perfect specimen.*

Gillian didn't want to argue with her alter ego. Not today. Certainly not right now. This moment showered contentment on her and she eagerly accepted it.

The disappointment of not having Max's company had blurred into realisation she could be happy – on her own. Doing something as simple as puffing up a mountain.

As she sipped warming water from her bottle, she nodded slowly. *Yeah, my life sucked big time, with a door slammed in my face – even smashing into my face, but maybe, just maybe, another door is creaking open. Maybe, a tiny, tiny, wee little bit.*

Her broad smile matched the colourful balloons juggling for space in her mind. Pulling her mobile phone from her bag, she grinned as she texted Max and Petra with a brief message. An immediate smiley emoji came back from Petra.

After watching a couple of clouds chase across the sky, she closed her eyes and drifted through drowsiness into a mist of relaxation. When her leg muscles involuntarily jumped, she rose, stretched her arms towards the sun and prepared for the descent.

She whistled as she ambled down the slope, delighted when she spotted a bunch of tiny strawberries. The sweetness belied their size.

'Yum.'

Returning to the cottage, Gillian showered, snuggled into lightweight trackpants and t-shirt, and scoured the bookcase.

'History or romance?'

She settled for a book, *Czech Fables*, where the preface quote said: Prague, a city worth knowing. Then the author went on to discuss where the city's name originated. Some said the city was named Praha – "threshold". Some disagreed, and maintained its name came from the prahy – "rapids" or "shoals" – formed in the river Vltava. She let the pages argue amongst themselves and flipping through, read a few sentences from a variety of stories.

A light knock on the door brought her back from ancient fables of celebrated priests and spooky coincidences.

With Gillian holding the door open, Karla entered with a tray of food: braised rabbit, crispy potato portions, a green salad, homemade lemonade, and a flower-patterned plate holding sugary biscuits.

'I hope you enjoy this,' Karla said. 'Something light, as you asked.'

Gillian grinned. It looked like a banquet. 'Gosh, I didn't realise how hungry I am. It looks terrific.'

After enjoying every mouthful of the other portions, the biscuits remained untouched until Gillian changed into her pyjamas, made a weak black tea, and settled against a pile of pillows in bed, ready to continue reading.

The ancient tales fascinated her. She brushed biscuit crumbs from the pages telling of where, in the 1470s, the old Odrana Gate was torn down and the Powder Tower commenced. She sipped cooling tea while considering the stories of places she'd seen, but after three more chapters she gave in to brain fade, laid the book aside and slipped easily into sleep.

Waking to insistent tapping on the door, Gillian called out, 'Just a minute,' and scrambled out of bed.

'Sorry, slept so well,' she said to Karla after she'd opened the door.

'Mountain air. It is very good for making a person sleep.'

Gillian accepted the tray of food. 'Ta. You've gone to a lot of trouble.'

'A good start for having a busy day.' Karla waved her hand towards the sky. 'We have sunshine again. It is nice to walk. Enjoy the eggs.'

Half an hour later, Gillian stepped out into the sunshine, ready for an uphill walk to Vysoké. The bitumen road meandered past many cottages along a border of the Sudetenlands annexed by Hitler in 1938 – returned later to form part of Czechoslovakia. She found it difficult to relate this peaceful road of dips and slopes to the controversy that led to the Second World War.

Her recently-attained contentment put aside those battles and welcomed the peace from her own struggles. She hummed indistinguishable tunes, and absorbed the intriguing differences between the Czech countryside and the flat wide paddocks of Western Australia.

Arriving at the small town, she sat on a bench in the lawn area of the square, and after a drink of water, checked her phone, hoping for a message from Max.

Since sending him a text yesterday, she'd checked for a reply at least five times.

He's busy. Sorting out world problems, she told herself, before sighing and endeavouring to convince herself it didn't matter.

Now as she considered her options for lunch, she enjoyed watching the busyness of the small town.

Unable to resist eating at the restaurant called, Restaurace Pension Crazy, she chose pizza and Pilsner, and enjoyed both to the last mouthful.

With her stomach protesting on quantity, she wandered through the nearby streets, but returned to the square and browsed through several shops before being entranced by a modern plant nursery and gift shop.

'You look like you need some help.'

Gillian turned slowly towards the pleasant voice. 'Um, I … Oh, the shopping. Are these made of wood?' She extended her hands holding two miniature doors.

'Yes. They are made in Germany. They are very, ah, cute. No?'

Twisting both hands back and forth to further scrutinise the miniature doors, Gillian nodded her agreement.

'They are fairy doors.'

'Really?' Gillian's raised eyebrows gave away her surprise.

'You can see here. The tag. It will explain.' The assistant leaned forward and lowered her voice. 'They fulfill wishes for special people.'

Gillian placed one door back on the shelf and read the tag attached to the other.

'I hear,' the assistant whispered, 'If you leave the little door open at night, they come and do some housework.' Loud laughter replaced her soft voice, and Gillian spontaneously joined in.

'Well, I'll have to have one.'

'Which one do you think?'

'Let's see.' Gillian held the item at arm's length. 'Maybe the orange one. Yes, it's even more cheerful than the blue.'

The young woman took the door and held it near Gillian's face. 'For sure. It is more like you.'

As Gillian watched the trinket being wrapped, she asked, 'Why did you say it is more like me?'

'Ah, it's the fairies who hide behind the closed door.' She grinned. 'They are the ones who choose. You are happy, are you not? So, the orange fairies tell me it is for you.'

'Can't argue with the fairies.' Not today.

On her way to the door, Gillian considered a glass bowl and a Kucha bookmark, but left the shop satisfied with her one purchase, and headed for the cafe.

In between luxuriating over a creamy iced coffee, savouring the taste, Gillian unwrapped her purchase and inspected it again. The palm-sized door, surrounded by a carved doorjamb and lintel, a panelled front and a brass doorknob, had a burnt-orange backing board.

The tag disclosed the procedure for ensuring the owner of the fairy door would have their wishes granted: *Clear the mind *Breathe deeply *Whisper your wish *Do not disclose your wish.

A voice interrupted Gillian's mind full of frivolous wishes.

'Aren't they just simply too divine.' A thin woman with a sun-burnt nose pointed to her huge tote bulging with parcels. 'I got some for my daughters, and their friends.'

Gillian looked up. 'I'm sure they'll like them.' She gathered her purchase and its wrapping off the table. 'I indulged. It's for me.'

Dropping her bags at her feet, the woman asked, 'Could you put up with some company. I sure could. Been slogging endlessly around the city earlier, then this delightful town. Need a rest before we push on.'

Realising it would be rude to refuse, Gillian removed her backpack from the seat.

Now free from her parcels, the woman sat on the cleared chair, uttered a deep sigh and introduced herself. 'Betty. I'm Betty. From Seattle. You heard of us? Top left of the good ol' USA. It's almost Canada, but don't you dare call us Canadian.' She chuckled. 'Mostly it's them who don't like being labelled

Americans. Personally, I don't give a damn.' Betty squinted as she asked, 'You a local?'

Gillian shook her head.

'English?'

'No, Australian.'

'Just visiting?'

Not able to get more than a nod in before Betty recounted her four days in Prague, the "blessed nuisance of having a tiny hire car", Jerry's enthusiasm for trying a beer at every possible venue, and her hope for an uneventful trip to their next destination. 'We're to go through to Jab-lon-ec – think that's it,' she said. 'We have something booked. Jerry will know. I just do some shopping and, he sorts the rest out.'

'Is he at the pub – hotel?' Gillian managed to ask.

'God bless him. He's sure the Pilsner will be different in the countryside. I told him it wouldn't. Anyway, jolly good thing I can drive.'

After slurping the last of her drink, Gillian light-heartedly apologised for the impolite noise. 'Can't resist the last bit.'

'Can't waste it.' Betty pointed to her parcels. 'My eldest daughter will love the little door I got for her. Her grandfather taught her everything she knows about carpentry. She's an artist, you know. Does all sorts. Been doing some sculpturing. Wood. Yeah, she'll love the door. Won't be about the wishes for her. Too pragmatic. Gets on. Does what's necessary. But the younger one ...' Betty smirked and looked to the heavens, 'They'll be flat out with her list.'

'It's a pity wishes can't come true.'

Betty sucked in a quick breath. 'Don't say that, my dear. Life can surprise.'

'Yeah, I know all about surprises.'

'Well, there you go. It might be your turn next to get something truly special. Think of the fairies dancing around, looking for someone to surprise with something nice.'

'Perhaps.'

They sat with their own thoughts before Gillian re-wrapped the fairy door and reached for her backpack. 'I must get going. It's been nice talking to you, Betty.'

'Well, I did most of the talking, but thanks. My feet certainly enjoyed the rest. Are you getting the bus?'

'No, I walked.'

'Walked.' Betty looked to the sky for inspiration. 'From where?'

'Where I'm staying. It's about forty-five minutes.'

'Phew! You must be fit.' Betty sighed. 'If you feel like being a sardine, we can give you a lift.'

Gillian stood. 'No, no. It's fine. Have to walk off all the calories.'

'Well, okay.' Betty chuckled, put her hands over her stomach. 'I'm happy to have any extra on my skinny hips. That's for sure.'

'Lucky you. And, thanks for the chat. Have a safe trip.'

'Appreciate that. I hope your fairies do their job.'

As she trundled downhill towards *Siesta Haven*, the parcel tapped against Gillian's back, as if reminding her it was there.

I know. Silly thing to buy. But it is cute. And you don't have many souvenirs. *No, didn't want dust collectors.* While this will only collect unwished wishes. *What?* Well if you wish a wish and don't open the fairy door, how can it come true?

Gillian rolled her eyes, convinced arguing with herself was madness.

I'm done with wishes. Really? *Yep.* Really! *Pragmatic – that's what I'll become. Pragmatic? Yeah, like Betty's daughter.* Hah! *Get on with life. Without expectations.* Aren't expectations just the cause of failed wishes? *Maybe, but wishes— No. I'm going to be pragmatic.* Yeah, right. *Yes. Rational. Logical.* You! *I can do it. I will do it.*

Determined to spend every last minute in the mountains with cheerfulness, Gillian skipped a few steps, plucked a daisy-like flower from the road's edge – feeling immediately guilty – wondering if the picking of wildflowers was illegal here as it is in Australia. She waved at a woman sitting on a front porch, stopped in amazement when spotting a deer grazing, and stood in awe at the views across the valleys. Heading towards her home of a few more hours, she slowed her pace and drank the last drop of water from her bottle.

After returning the container to her back-pack, she paused, looked once more past the gardens and tall trees.

She stood, mouth gaping, hardly believing her incredulous eyes. 'Oh, holy heavens.'

In a shallow valley dipping to the left stood three cottages, all reminiscent of the picture on the wall of the travel agency which had sparked her trip.

She held her bottom lip in her teeth, sucked in a deep breath, letting it out slowly, before shaking her head in awe.

'There's my cottage – three ‒ "my cottages".' She chuckled. 'Well, that's it. No wonder I love this place.'

Wrapping her arms around her body, Gillian rocked to the sound of an internal hum as she soaked up the difference between the little cottages and the mountain. So cute. So large. And yet in harmony. Her eyes followed a narrow path that disappeared several times only to reappear as it snaked its way to the top. The cottages, linked to the mountain top by a single winding path, made her believe a struggle could be worth it. *I just have to keep going. You are already doing that. Yes, I am, aren't I?*

With several photos and a lightened step, she strolled back to *Siesta Haven*, satisfied with the state of her emotions.

After showering and packing her few things, she knocked on Karla's door.

'Hello. It is not time,' Karla said with a frown.

'No.' Gillian shrugged. 'Not quite. But I'm packed. I want to go to the top of the hill again. You know, have a last look. Didn't want you to think I would be late.'

'But I have made you cherry cake. I thought for coffee before we set out.'

'How lovely. Then I'll be back in time.' Gillian grinned. 'Can't waste a good cherry cake.'

'You go and enjoy. Cake you can take with you.'

Gillian turned, waved her upturned hand towards the slope behind Karla's home. 'I want to soak this up. One more time. I won't ever come back.' She dropped her hand and smiled ruefully. 'I won't be long.'

'Two hours, then we must go,' Karla said. 'The bus will not wait. You take time, for now. Enjoy the mountain.'

Gillian's legs threatened to boycott another huff-and-puff walk, but she lumbered up the slope and sank onto a grassy spot under a tree. Last time she was here, the enormousness had overwhelmed her. This time it seemed familiar, comforting – although the smallness of one human in this vastness still marvelled.

She lay in the shade, emptying her mind as best she could, but Patrick's presence hovered. She pushed away the thought of

Sienna giggling and bragging about running across a mountain top. Gillian told Patrick it was her mountain – he could own another.

So, wait a while, my lovelies. Let me have this moment.

Once her muscles had recovered she noticed the grass prickling her arms. Gillian rose, rubbed her arms, stretched and sighed loudly.

After walking to where the land fell dangerously away, she stood and absorbed the scenery, the remoteness, and the calmness of nature.

This is ... this is what I have to recall when all else fails. Me, nature and ... yes, me, nature and possibilities.

She blew out a loud breath, nodded several times, and turned towards *Siesta Haven*. 'Time to eat cake.'

As they sat on the veranda, nibbling cake, washed down with ice-cold juice, Karla asked about Australia, Perth, ocean beaches, and tried to imagine no snow-topped mountains, or travelling thousands of miles without having to show a passport.

When they drove to Vysoké for the 5.30 pm bus to Prague, Gillian thanked Karla for her hospitality. 'It's been great. I've loved every minute,' Gillian said.

'Prosím.' Karla glanced at her passenger. 'You seem ... lifted. Is that a word for your spirit?'

Gillian fiddled with the seat belt. 'Lifted? Yes, it's a perfect word. This place has lifted my spirits.'

'I am very glad.'

'You see—'

Karla interrupted Gillian. 'Your secret ... you can keep. I don't need to know.'

With her head lowered, Gillian sighed. 'It's okay. I'm now able to tell of Patrick and Sienna – my husband and daughter – with some joy. Couldn't for so long.' As the last few kilometres slipped by, Gillian shared brief elements of her last twelve months.

After they eased into a car parking space, Karla took the keys from the ignition and waved them towards Gillian. 'Going places often needs a key – either locking the door of the past or opening the door to a new day. Maybe your time here will – somehow – be a key to unlock a new journey.'

Embracing like old friends, they promised to stay in touch, but also knowing emails would become spasmodic in the months to come. Then Gillian boarded the bus back to the last days of her time in Prague.

The sound of her phone startled Gillian out of a nap. She swivelled her neck from the uncomfortable position against the coach window, and reached for the mobile.

Can we do brunch on Sunday?

Balancing the phone on her knee, she watched the scenery race by while gathering her thoughts. The passenger next to her glanced sideways, smirked as if to say, phones! An annoying necessity.

Gillian let the screen turn black.

Will be nice, she thought. Brunch, yep. And you can tell him. Go away. You have to resolve something. Is there a solution? There's always a solution. I guess. I just don't want to hurt Max. And what about you?

Gillian snatched at the wobbling phone as she sucked in a reflective breath. First rolling her shoulders, then stretching her neck again, she tapped the screen, and replied. *I'm on the bus going back to the city. Are you in Prague? How were the spies and secrets? Brunch would be nice. What time? Where?*

The phone pinged immediately.

Still in Germany. On a break. Plot continues to thicken. Is it false news or calculated insight? Unsure. Probably both. Give anything to be on that bus. I'll come to your place. Nine. Maybe walk to the park café. Anywhere will be a significant change from grappling with secrets and spies.

With a chuckle about their ongoing banter over cloak-and-dagger meetings, she typed. *I'll be ready. See u then. With a bit of luck I'll be free all day and ready to be at your service.*

It took her a while to settle on the ridiculous "thumbs-up" emoji – hoping there was no unintended inference.

She tucked the phone into her backpack under her feet, wriggled back into the seat and resumed the stare of a captive audience at the rushing trees, an occasional road-side building and the passing vehicles.

The countryside gave way to ever-spreading paneláks of suburbia. Leaving behind those high-rise concrete boxes, the coach skirted the city and pulled into the final stop.

Glad to be out of the coach and stretching her legs, she walked the length of the platform while waiting to catch the train back to Prosek.

Choosing chicken and noodles from a fast-food outlet, she wandered back to her unit, ready for an early night.

After reheating the meal, she ate slowly, half-heartedly twirling the noodles onto the fork. Dropping the undesirable cold portion into the bin, Gillian considered the items in her fridge. Only the Edam cheese appealed. With a mug of tea, a few crackers and the cheese on a plate, she settled on the couch, food and drink on the coffee table, and turned on her phone. Dozens of photos of the two days in Vysoké sprang to life and she welcomed the calm of her two days in the mountains.

Patrick would like to see ... Gillian grimaced, and pushed aside the impossible thought. Petra. Yes. I'll show her. I'll certainly be showing them off to Esther. And Sandy. Yep, and Mira.

 Dressed in her pyjamas, she transferred the recent photos onto her laptop, dating and naming each one, occasionally pausing with recollection, chuckling over the one she'd taken while lying flat on her back on the mountain top – capturing nothing but one curly cloud in a sharp blue sky.

With the photo of the three houses nestled below the mountain still open, Gillian placed the laptop on the floor and flopped back into the couch, folded her arms and sighed. With a flash of the memory of when she'd stood at the promotional poster, wondering about one small cottage being held safe in the arms of a massive mountain, a flow of satisfaction seeped into her.

I achieved something. Well done. Yeah, I feel pretty good about that. Just seeing a house and a mountain? Get stuffed. What did I say now? If you must know. It wasn't just a house and a mountain. It was about me achieving something – anything. And on my own. And getting out of my comfort zone. And ... And what? What's the other "and"? Well, I felt good. Up on that mountain. In the café. Betty. Karla. The lovely lady in the gift shop. It felt ... normal. Normal? Yeah, bloody normal. And I haven't felt that for a long time. Good for you. Shut up. I'm going to bed.

Enormously tired, but unable to drift off, Gillian reminded herself of her home in Perth, mentally walked around its garden, imagined new furniture in a freshly painted family room, and finally resorted to counting. She refused to count sheep, but the stupid kangaroos kept hopping anywhere but over the barbed-wire fence.

Surprised at having slept well, despite the initial tossing and turning – and uncooperative kangaroos – Gillian woke with an enthusiasm she didn't want to place on Max's Sunday brunch invitation.

After showering and dressing, Gillian left the building, walked through the park, acknowledged her cheerfulness, as she concentrated on soaking up last images of Prosek.

She touched orange poppies and ran her hand over the seeded tops of the long grass – probably weeds. The aroma of coffee from the cheerful café she'd often visited tempted her to stay awhile. After chatting to the staff, she bought a take-away cup and sipped slowly as she passed the shopping centre that had caused her so much early angst, but had provided friendliness more recently. She turned her nose up at the odd smell of the low-hanging branches of a chestnut tree, then took a photo of the candle-like flowers. On her way back to her unit Gillian added to her large file of photographs, taking several shots of the Metro, the flowers near the intersection, a close up of a poppy, the streetscape and its adjoining buildings, a cherry tree, a church down a side road, an incomplete building, white clouds against blue sky, another tree, another poppy. She zoomed in on the letterboxes, snapping number fifteen, the buttons for the lift and finally the door handle of her fourth-floor flat.

After cringing to the clatter of her keys in the revolting planter, Gillian dropped her bag on the couch.

So many things to do, but one thing relied on something else being completed. She couldn't wash her sheets – she needed them tonight. Same with packing – most items not already in the suitcase would be required tomorrow or the next day.

She emptied a packet of the last three chocolate biscuits, took a bite from one, then deciding she'd wait for brunch, threw all three biscuits into the bin. She brushed her teeth, combed her hair, put a few considered items into her handbag, picked up a novel with its page 36 corner turned back and waited for Max.

At 9.30 her phone rang. She put down the book, glad to have a reason to stop reading when her lack of concentration had caused the characters to become muddled. 'Hi, Max, what's up?'

'I'm sorry, but I'm still in Germany. I'm not going to get back today.'

'Why?' Gillian rolled her eyes, waited for him to continue.

'Things haven't worked out. The spies are playing up.' He forced a laugh, then paused before becoming serious. 'After the cancelled trip away, I wanted at least today to be special. Something you'd remember. Now you probably will, but for the wrong reason.'

'It's okay,' Gillian said, aware that her voice held an edge of displeasure.

'No, it's not, but not a damn thing I can do about it. I should be able to get back and take you to the airport.'

Gillian shrugged, wandered around the room, stopping at the window. 'Really, Max, it's okay. I've already booked a taxi.'

Max grunted. 'Please, Gilly, let me see you before you go.'

'Are you sure you're going to get back in time?' She watched a car hurrying through amber traffic lights. Going to their planned Sunday destination, she thought.

'I should be finished here in the next hour or two.' Max called out to someone before adding to Gillian, 'I'd much rather be enjoying your company. I was looking forward to finding your cottage. Then at least taking you to brunch.' He grunted loudly. 'Sometimes this business sucks, but ... I've got to go; they're heading back into the meeting. Please, Gilly, let me pick you up on Monday.'

She heard him tell someone he was on his way. 'Max—'

'I'm being called. Text me your flight details.'

'Max, I won't cancel the taxi until you're back in Prague.'

'Fair enough. And, Gilly ...'

'Yes.'

'I miss you.' He remained silent for a moment, then whispered, bye, and hung up.

Gillian held the phone away from her ear. 'Bye.'

She leaned against the wall, her thoughts jumbled between annoyance and relief. *Well, there was no romantic country trip. Now no romantic brunch.* At least you don't have to battle your conscience. *Conscience? About what?* You know, how the day would end. *Perhaps, but so?* Bedroom! Expectations. *No worry there, the sex would be good.* Yeah, but what about the implications. *Like what?* Commitments. *No way.* Yes way. *Really?* You're leaving. He'd expect to talk about the future. *There's no future for us.* Really? You really think you're going to just love and leave. *Damn!*

Gillian stalked into the bedroom, grabbed her handbag and moved towards the door. Deciding to see Hana and then leave the rest of the day to work itself out, she slammed the door and ran down the stairs.

After peeping through the security window, Hana opened the door wide and exclaimed, 'Ahoj, Gillian. Myslela jsem, že už jste odjela. Pojď dál. Udělala jsem kávu a teď ji nemusím pít sama.' (Hello, Gillian. I thought you were gone already. Come in. Come in, I have a pot of coffee ready. Now I don't have to drink on my own.)

Gillian chuckled as she let Hana gently prod her towards the kitchen. Then Hana put her hands over her cheeks, frowned and said, 'Hel-lo. Is Gillian feeling happy today?' She held out her hands with the palms up, shrugged and spoke slowly, 'English. Hel-lo, Gillian.'

'Hana, how wonderful. Yes, English. Gillian is happy.' She pointed at Hana. 'Hana, dobré?'

They hugged amid giggles and repeated greetings in Czech and English, each woman trying to get the inflection of foreign words correct.

Hana rang Elena, and demanded she act as a final interpreter.

Elena told Gillian her grandmother had practiced speaking a few words of English, determined to greet Gillian in her language at least once.

'She did it perfectly,' Gillian said. 'But only after such a lot of Czech I thought she'd forgotten I didn't have a clue what she was saying.'

While the younger women chatted, Hana tapped Gillian on the arm repeatedly, asking for Elena's translation. The three-way chat became confusing and after a while Hana resorted to filling mugs with fresh coffee.

'Elena, can you remind your grandmother I will be dropping off some things tomorrow morning. There'll be some food. I've arranged to leave the linen and the kitchen things in my flat. I bought the cheapest, and I'm sure Hana has enough, but can you ask if she would like them anyway.'

'It is okay for you to do that,' Elena said. 'She will be home.'

'Thanks, Elena. For everything. And please, let Hana know she made such a difference to my life here. I wouldn't believe we could get on so well.'

'Yes, she is so much older. Not usual friends.'

Gillian looked over at the older woman who smiled as she put petite bread rolls onto a plate, nodding her head as if she understood everything Gillian was saying. 'No, Elena, it's not because of our age. It's the language. I have never had to mime so much, work so hard at explaining without language.' Gillian chuckled. 'It's been hard, but rewarding. I want you to make sure you tell Hana how much I appreciate her kindness. Tell her I'll always remember her.'

'That is nice,' Elena said. 'I will tell her. She is sometimes lonely. You have made her less so. It is sad you are going.'

'It's time I went home.'

'When is the time tomorrow?'

'My flight is four thirty. In the afternoon. I have to be at the airport much earlier of course.'

'Good. I'll tell my grandmother. Can I speak to her now?'

Gillian handed over the phone and watched intently, listened offhandedly, heard her name several times and smiled when Hana glanced at her.

After finishing the call, Hana sat down next to Gillian. 'Je mi líto, že odjíždíte.' (It is sad you are going.) Accidentally brushing the corner of a cabinet with her fingertips as she imitated an aeroplane, Hana then pretended to cry.

Gillian accepted a buttered bread roll. 'Me too.'

They finished their drinks in silence, each woman wondering how they could convey their thankfulness for the brief friendship. Gillian stood up. 'I have to go.' She pointed to the door.

Still in an embrace, Gillian wiped away a tear from Hana's cheek. 'Dobré. Hana, it's all good.' Determined to get away before she too succumbed, Gillian stepped back, picked up her handbag and waited for Hana to open the door.

'Bye, Hana. Bye, my friend.'

Hana waved until the lift door closed. Gillian sighed as she entered the common ground outside the units. 'Damn, it's all much harder than I thought.'

With the rest of the day to fill, Gillian rode the Metro to Letňany, then the bus through to the shopping centre, and considered seeing a movie. With no enticing entertainment, she wandered the malls knowing she was timewasting and nothing more. She bought a Macca's thick-shake, enjoyed each mouthful and noisily slurped the last drop. With a bloated stomach, Gillian browsed racks of clothes and a bookstore.

After seeing her disappointing reflection in a window, she entered a hair salon and requested a full treatment. The young receptionist spoke hesitantly in English, but expressed each hairdressing term confidently. Gillian relaxed and spent a blissful time being pampered by delightfully silent attendants. They offered complimentary treatments in the same shop and Gillian emerged with manicured nails, refreshed skin, along with blonde highlights in her trimmed hair.

Ah, now, maybe I should update my travel clothes, she thought as she entered a department store. She held a red t-shirt against her chest. 'Mm, okay.' *But you're going business class.* Yeah, so. *Go up-market, girl. You know, something really chic.*

Her feet ached for a rest after she had browsed, tried on, selected many items, and then scanned her credit card – several times, in the last hour. She not only had new jeans and a distinctive top, both of which cost the sum of an airfare from Perth to Melbourne, there were matching bra and panties, scarf, nail polish, notebook, phone cover and a ridiculous pair of multi-coloured earrings in her bulging shopping bag.

She ordered a flat white, and a chicken and tomato sandwich from a cheerful attendant in the food hall. She slid onto a wooden chair and eased her feet from her sandals. *I'll have to repack,* she thought as she balanced her bags on another chair.

With her newly purchased outfit on a hanger in the wardrobe, Gillian put aside the matching underclothes, onboard essentials, and packed the remainder of her clothes. Halfway through sorting out bathroom toiletries she returned to the bedroom, picked up her phone and read a message from Max.

Finally! All the spies can go home to leak new secrets. Joking aside, business has been successful. There's a bit of backslapping to get through. Probably some beer to be consumed. Trying to get a late flight tonight. See you tomorrow.

Okay, that's good, Gillian thought. *Have a safe trip. Let me know. I need to be at the airport by eleven.*

Should be fine. Will text. And, Gillian, sweet dreams.

Annoyed to have to go out again to buy something moderately healthy for dinner, because her fridge was empty, Gillian strode to the shops, bought sliced ham, a crusty roll and a prepared salad, and hurried back.

Half-way through preparation, she waved the knife in the air. 'We go back a way, don't we Knife.' She made the knife nod. 'Well, our relationship is over. You'll be just Ordinary Knife and I'll be ...' She cut the roll in two. 'Who knows what my label will be. Not Mummy. Not Wife. I'll have to find another title.' She placed the knife in the sink and the filled roll on a plate.

Walking to the couch, she sat, nibbled the roll. 'Just what the doctor ordered.'

With the meal finished and chores completed, Gillian resorted to an electronic jigsaw, several games of Solitaire, before rechecking her packing.

Sleep came easy, dreams were few. She woke once, rolled over, thought of Max, Petra, Patrick, Sienna ... drifted back to sleep.

Monday, Gillian woke seconds before the alarm shouted seven o'clock. She slapped at the clock and kicked her legs free of the sheet. *Right*, she thought, *I'm going home today.*

She grinned, then the smile slowly disappeared. I guess I'm ready. Ready as you can be. Yeah, I suppose. Well, lots to do. Get up first.

After showering, dressing in her new jeans, but with the t-shirt she'd worn yesterday, Gillian checked her phone. No messages. Max hadn't contacted her and she had no idea if he had managed a late flight or was still in Germany.

She put the phone down, refolded a spare t-shirt in her carry-on, then sat next to the open suitcase on the bed. She picked up the photo of Patrick and Sienna from the bedside cabinet, hoped the love in her heart would reach them. *I'm coming home*, she told them before tucking them safely between the folds of the long dress she'd bought for her evening with Max.

Heading for the kitchen, with her phone in one hand, she dropped a slice of bread into the toaster and poked the switch on the kettle into a response.

Standing by the window, reverently soaking in the view, the popping toast made her jump. Leaving her phone on the counter, and with tea and toast prepared, she leaned against the kitchen bench – heightened anticipation not allowing her to relax enough to sit. In between eating toast and vegemite she texted Esther.

I'm awake. Getting ready. Will let u know if any delays occur. See u soon. XX

Esther's instant reply surprised Gillian, and she tried to calculate Western Australian time as she read.

Will be good to have you home. Will check the ETA before I leave for the airport. Travel safe. XX

Thanks. Gillian answered. *Not looking forward to the long flight, but at least I'll be in the front of the plane.*

Ignoring a beep from her phone, she paced between the kitchen and the window while finishing her toast. Then, with the mug of lukewarm tea, she perched on the edge of the couch as the mild anxiety of anticipation changed into excitement.

When her phone beeped again, Gillian assumed Esther had replied, probably with sarcasm, to her mention of travelling business class, so she grinned a cat-that-got-the cream smile, and decided not to reply.

With her once-used shopping trolley packed with items for Hana, Gillian poured the last of the milk down the drain and wiped the fridge shelf clean. She strolled around the unit, sipping her drink, checking that the drawers and cupboards were empty. Her phone beeped again. She returned to the kitchen, flipped open the phone. 'Ah, Max, about time.'

Are you still at the unit?

She was about to answer when she noticed it was he, not Esther, that had texted earlier. She swiped back to his first message.

Back in Prague. At the airport. Can I come to you?

'Okay.' Her mind jumped in several directions. *I do want to see him before I go.* It may complicate things. *Things?* He's bound to ask about the future. *I suppose so.* And what's the answer? *I don't know. It's all too hard.*

The phone rang and she almost dropped it. 'Hi, Max. Sorry I was just about to answer.'

'Is everything okay? I mean—'

'Yeah, I thought it was Esther texting.'

'Esther?'

'Well, she's going to pick me up at the airport.'

'Of course.' A pause; then, 'I'm back in Prague. You can cancel the taxi.'

Gillian sighed silently. She knew she couldn't turn down his offer. 'Sure. That's great.'

'Gillian, I'm so sorry our last few days didn't turn out as planned. I was looking forward—'

'It's okay. Really. I understand.'

'Maybe, but I was looking forward to it. However, changing plans at the last minute is not unusual in my job. Comes with the territory I'm afraid.'

'It's—'

'I'm in a taxi at the moment. Be back at the embassy in about ten minutes. I can get to your place in about thirty. Maybe we can go for coffee. You still have time, don't you? Then I'll drive you to the airport.'

'S'pose. I still have to take some stuff down to Hana. That shouldn't take long.' She tipped the last of her tea down the sink, imagined one last look at Prosek; imagined one last walk on foreign soil. 'Probably do with a walk before the long sit.'

'Right, see you in about a half hour.'

'If I'm not here, I'll be at Hana's.'

She pushed the phone into her pocket, then removed yesterday's t-shirt and headed for the bathroom. After cleaning her teeth, applying more deodorant, putting on mascara and brushing her hair, she slipped into the recently purchased top and checked her image in the bathroom mirror. 'Expensive does have an edge.'

Pulling the loaded shopping trolley behind her, Gillian exited the lift and approached Hana's flat.

Hana opened the door and enthusiastically hugged Gillian. 'Ještě nejsi pryč!' (You have still not gone!) She released Gillian and ushered her forward. 'Elena říkala, že přijdete. Máte čas jít na chvilku dál? Jsem smutná, že odjíždíš.' (Elena said you would come. Have you time to stay for a while? I will be sad when you go.)

Gillian pulled the trolley through to the kitchen, opened the top and took out a jar of vegemite and placed it on the bench. She grinned as she said, 'It's the ultimate Aussie spread.' She pretended to dip her finger in the vegemite and eat it. 'Yum.'

Hana shook her head. 'Zeptám se Eleny.' (I'll ask Elena.)

'Dobré. It's really dobré.' Gillian laughed as she picked up the biscuits sitting on top of containers of half-used items in the trolley. She pointed at the trolley and then at Hana. 'For you.' She leaned over and pointed at one wheel. 'This doesn't squeak. No one will hear you coming.'

Hana frowned. 'To je pro mě?' (It is for me?) After tapping the trolley's handle, she placed her hand over her chest. 'Ano?'

'Ano, yes, for you,' Gillian agreed. 'I have to go. If only I could tell you how I feel.' She took Hana's hand, squeezed it gently, then held it to her cheek. 'Thank you. Děkujiu.' She wiped away tears, and watched Hana's lip tremble, before she too had to wipe away tears.

They walked to the door, embraced again, then Gillian ambled towards the stairs. Before stepping beyond Hana's sight, Gillian turned and waved, ignoring the tears slipping over her chin. Hana closed the door softly, the click of the lock reverberating beyond its capability.

Gillian stood at the base of the fourth-floor stairs, put her hands over her face and sighed. 'So hard.' She wouldn't forget Hana's friendship. 'Despite me being a cow. Or am I the horse?' she said as she ascended the flight of stairs.

Max arrived as the tumble dryer finished the sheets and towels. Hana didn't want them so Gillian planned to leave them for the next tenants.

'Come in. I'm almost done.'

Max stood at the door, looked Gillian up and down. 'You look great. New haircut?'

Gillian made her hair swish as she shook her head back and forth. 'Yeah, thanks. A girl can always do with a compliment.'

He took her hand as they walked towards the lounge room. He placed his briefcase down before saying, 'Wish I had many more chances. To give you compliments, I mean. Sorry about the weekend, and yesterday.'

She shrugged. 'Shit happens. And, it worked out quite well. Me, mountain, little house – accomplished. Just a shame ... you know.'

'Perhaps next time.'

Gillian tugged her hand out of his; turned quickly. 'Please don't say that. I won't be coming back.'

Max hunched down on the sofa, let out a long breath. 'No, I guess not.'

She stood with her hands on the back of the sofa, a millimetre away from his shoulders. 'I have to finish up. Then we can go for that walk.' When he didn't answer, she added, 'If you still want to.'

He swivelled around. 'Certainly. I could do with getting outside. The last few days have been quite stressful.'

Raising her eyebrows in mock surprise, she asked, 'Is that why you have your briefcase? Is it full of deadly secrets?'

He stood. His eyes held mischief. 'Dark secrets and mind-blowing mysteries that you, as a mere mortal, aren't to be trusted with. I'll leave it here for now.'

'I like mysteries and, I'm quite trustworthy. You can tell me.' She poked Max in the ribs. 'I promise not to tell anyone?'

'Maybe.' His smirk broadened. 'You'll just have to wait and see.'

She raised her eyebrows, put her hand on her hip, grinned back. 'How mean of you. Just when I thought you might trust me with all the state secrets.' She stepped towards the bathroom.

'Not yet. But, meanwhile, is there anything I can do? We need to watch the time.'

'I'm almost done. I just have to fold the stuff from the dryer.'

'Want me to do it?' he asked.

'Yes, please. If you could get them out. And, you'd better check I haven't missed a sock or something. I can't reach the back.'

They strolled through the park, holding hands, joking about the first time they'd met, recalling the events they'd shared. Deciding to skip coffee, they wandered back.

'I'm going to miss this park,' Gillian said.

Max pulled her towards him, wrapped his arms around her waist and asked, 'Is that all you're going to miss?'

She looked into his eyes, held for a moment then looked down at her feet. 'No, that isn't all.'

With one hand on her chin he forced her to meet his eyes again. 'I'm going to miss you. A lot. We have to stay in touch.'

'I …' Her eyes flicked between Max's eyes and his mouth. 'Yes, but …'

'It's okay,' Max whispered. 'No pressure. Just keep in touch. We can't know the future. Even—'

Gillian stepped away from him. 'Please, Max, don't …'

He took her left hand, entwined their fingers. 'Okay, I won't. Let's just … go.'

They walked in silence until they reached the stairs at the block of units.

'What time do you have to be at the airport?'

'Eleven.'

'We should go.'

As he followed her up the stairs, Gillian sensed his eyes on her legs and on her denim-covered rear. Compelled to straighten her top before searching her bag for the keys, she spoke to cover her embarrassment, 'They're here somewhere.' She turned; experienced a flush of embarrassment as Max's eyes left her chest and reached her face.

They entered her unit in silence. He stood, leaned against the lounge-room wall and waited while she gathered the last-minute items from the bathroom.

This is too difficult, she thought as she added lipstick and a dash of perfume. I shouldn't have cancelled the taxi. With her cosmetic bag in her hand, she sighed and moved towards her luggage on the sofa.

'All set?' Max asked.

'Think so.'

'Right, let's go. I can take the suitcase.'

Music from a local radio station filled the silence on the way to the airport. Gillian tried to empty her mind of the emotions threatening to turn into banal chatter. Max sounded like a tourist guide as he pointed out several historic buildings on the way. Gillian's interest disintegrated and she only managed a quick nod or an insignificant comment in reply.

As they approached the entrance to the airport Gillian said, 'Max, you can just drop me off. I mean you don't—'

'Yes, I do.'

'It's just that ... well, I find it's anticlimactic. You know ... sitting around until you can finally go through. Rather kills the goodbye. Don't you agree?'

Max slowed the car, pulled into a parking spot. 'No, I don't.' He turned and looked at Gillian. 'But ... if you want to get rid of me ...' His slow smile teased her to answer in the negative.

'Max, it's not that.'

'No? Well, what say I make sure you really want to leave, then …' He grinned as he tapped her on the knee. 'once you're checked in, let's have a drink. After that, I'll tear myself away and you can browse the duty free.'

'Deal,' she said as she opened the car door.

Once through the formalities, they chose drinks and settled into soft seats of the business class lounge.

'Cheers. Here's to an uneventful flight.' Max clinked his glass against Gillian's. 'Na zdraví, as they are want to say in Prague.'

'Na zdraví,' Gillian repeated. 'At least I've remembered that Czech.'

'Most do.' He placed his glass down. 'What's the first thing you're going to do when you get home?'

'Mm.' Gillian hesitated. 'Well, after the necessary bits and pieces, probably catch up with my friends. Sandy's getting married. Mira's pregnant. Yeah, probably have a long session over wine. I'm sure Esther will have a hundred things to brag about.'

Max nodded slowly, ran his finger around the top of his glass. 'Are you going to be okay with that?'

'Oh, I'm quite used to my sister's bragging. All warranted really. She raises so much money for charity and—'

'No, I meant with your friends. A new baby? A husband?'

Gillian took another mouthful of wine, swilled it across her tongue, and swallowed it. She glanced at Max, saw the care he had for her. 'I think so.'

'Has your visit here helped?'

Quick flashes of Izzy skipping down the street, of Petra and Ivan singing Happy Birthday to their daughter, of the yellow dress she bought for an unknown child, made her suck in a quick breath before replying. 'I can only hope I can share Mira and Sandy's happiness without ruining it. But, yeah … I guess I've become stronger. At least on the surface. Isn't that all we can do. Bluff our way through life.'

'I don't believe that, Gilly. Anyway, true friends won't want that.'

'I suppose. But you can't tell me you've never pretended one emotion to cover another.' Her brow wrinkled as she waited for his answer.

'Actually, you're right. I have to do it all the time. Some situations are deplorable, and I have to just ignore the emotion of it and get on with the job.'

'There, see. That's what I mean. I'll just get on with the job of enjoying their special time.'

Max drained the last of his beer. 'Do you want another one?'

'Nup, I'll just finish this one, thanks anyway, but you can have another.'

'Maybe a coffee instead. Haven't got a driver today.'

They watched people filling their plates and glasses with freebies, listened casually to the never-ending announcements and let the minutes pass without talking.

'You will keep in touch?' Max asked softly.

'I guess.'

'Gillian, please. I thought we had something special. Something that could grow. Was I wrong?'

She reached out and placed her hand over his. 'We did.' She stroked his fingers. 'But, how can it grow? I couldn't live here. You have your job. It can't work.'

He turned his hand over and gripped her fingers in his. 'But if we stay in touch, who knows. Maybe—'

'Max, don't make it any harder for me. It wouldn't work. I still have to figure out my future. Patrick would come between us. Even Sienna. Someone told me grief is just love with nowhere to go. If that's true, I have to find a place for them. I know it sounds corny, but I do. Once I've worked out how to have them in my life, without too much pain, I can move on. I couldn't expect you to—'

'It's okay. I understand. But I'm going to email you. I'm sure you'll want to know how Anna Schroeder's going with that recipe you swapped. And Luis, you remember, the Chilean, the next time he's in Prague he's bound to ask about you.'

Gillian chuckled. She had Anna's recipe for sauerkraut in her phone, and would be trying it out on Esther. 'Email's okay.'

'And Gilly, I'm due for holidays. I usually go back to Adelaide, but might even take them in Perth. You wouldn't turn me away, would you?'

Downing the last of her coffee, Gillian briefly wondered about her reply, but answered confidently. 'No, of course not.'

'Good, now it's time for me to go.' He stood, reached for his briefcase tucked next to his legs. 'I have something for you.'

'Oh?' She chuckled. 'Some top secrets? At last!'

'Not exactly. But I hope you like it.' He reached in and took a large gift bag from the briefcase. 'I know you took a million photos, but I wanted you to have this anyway.'

Carefully taking the paper bag, she peeked in. 'A book.' She lifted out a beautifully bound book. 'It's gorgeous.' Placing the book on her knee she flipped open a page, stared at the glossy picture before slowly turning more pages. 'It looks old.'

'Yes. I've had it a while. Hope you don't mind a pre-owned gift, but I thought you'd love it. It has a lot of Prague's traditional buildings, some with the sort of doors you've been collecting.'

Gillian ran her hand over the page, the shimmering paper reflected the grandeur of Prague Castle. 'I love it.' She placed the book on the table, stood and hugged him. 'Thanks, Max. It's perfect. And thank you, for everything.'

One of Max's hands remained on her hip while the other hand caressed the nape of her neck. She leaned into him, tilted her chin up and kissed him. His hand reached her hairline and he didn't let go until after a long lingering kiss. 'I'll miss you,' he whispered.

She stood back and picked up the book, held it against her chest. 'Yes,' she said, 'and I'll miss you. You've made me see … I'm not sure what, but perhaps I can now understand how one can share a heart. I guess … well, thanks, Max.'

He picked up his briefcase, stood as close as he could without contact. 'Prosím. My pleasure. I'd do it again in a heartbeat.' He shifted a strand of hair from across her cheek. 'I'll go. Before I'm begging you to stay.' He grinned. 'We ambassadors are taught not to beg. And my non-begging negotiating skills have let me down.'

Gillian had a moment where she wanted to grab him, make him beg her to stay, but he spoke again. 'You need to go home and be with your memories. Let Sienna and Patrick settle.'

She remembered her promise to take flowers to her husband and daughter's grave. She looked intently at Max. 'Yes, I do. You're right.'

He kissed her again, this time briefly. He turned and walked away. Her eyes travelled over the back of his crinkled shirt, lingered on his striding hips. A flash of a future with him hit: intense conversations with dignitaries, visits to far off places, security guards, Aussies needing guidance – she blinked; the illusion vanished.

Max turned again and waved, then he was gone. Her hand dropped from a reciprocal quick wave.

She recalled his gallant acceptance of Patrick still being a part of her every day, and the tender moments they'd shared. It was nice. Nice! Come on girl. It was more than bloody nice. Yeah … it sure was.

She pulled a tissue from her bag, but the tears didn't come. Tucking the tissue into her sleeve, she looked more closely through the book, reading the descriptions, smiling as she recognised some of the featured buildings. The glowing night-time shot of Charles Bridge brought back memories of a shared evening stroll: the earrings with a spot of a pearl he'd insisted on buying for her, the Bratwurst and sauerkraut roll they'd enjoyed, the shared laughter, the kisses … Yes, definitely more than bloody nice.

In the last forty minutes before the boarding call, Gillian meandered through the duty-free shops. She bought three-for-the-price-of-two blocks of chocolate and a book of Sudoku. Ignoring the countless trinkets, perfume and makeup, she considered buying a beige and aqua Prada handbag. After returning twice, she decided to treat herself one more time. 'Time for budgeting when I get home,' she told the assistant.

'One should have at least one Prada bag in one's lifetime,' he added after asking if she'd like it wrapped.

'No, I think my old one will fit in my hand luggage. I'll take it as it is.'

While she transferred her bits and pieces from her old handbag, he removed the tags. As she took the receipt, he dropped a tiny sample bottle of perfume into her hand. 'On the house,' he said. 'It might come in handy if you score a not-so-pleasant travelling companion.'

Armed with her purchase and her hand luggage, Gillian headed for the lounge again and waited for the boarding call.

Gillian cursed the interruption of Dubai – she just wanted to get this last leg over and done with.

The lounge provided a calm waiting environment, and she browsed the never-ending food offerings twice before choosing some dates and a glass of water.

Boarding proved uneventful and she settled down with earphones providing classic music – perfect for distracting cabin noises and encouraging relaxation.

Sleep came in bursts, as did the eating and the miniscule walks to ward off any threatening blood clots. While she reminisced on her time in Prague, the dot on the screen labelled Perth, crept closer.

Gillian woke to the gentle verbal nudging of the flight attendant. 'Excuse me, Mrs Middleton, would you like some lunch, we're not far away now.'

'Oh.' Gillian blinked, looked up at the voice. 'Yes, please.' She removed the headset sitting lopsided on her head, and sat up straighter. 'Did I drop off again?'

The flight attendant smiled. 'Yes, I'm afraid you did. But never mind, you'll soon be back home and able to sleep as long as you want. Now, we've got chicken and mushroom tortellini, or a lamb curry.'

'The lamb, please.'

'And coffee or tea this time.'

Gillian chuckled. 'I think it'd better be coffee.'

'Done. It shouldn't be long. Is there anything else for now?'

'No … but wake me if I fall asleep again. I want to watch the descent.'

Gillian unhooked the contraption, forced it between the two scrunched-up magazines in the storage pocket. The window revealed blue sky in between a mixture of smoky-coloured clouds with dark tips and misshapen ivory-coloured masses.

After finishing the meal and taking her time over the coffee, Gillian leaned back in the seat, closed her eyes. She wasn't sleepy, but she wanted to think through her stay in Prague again.

If only this had been a holiday for the three of us, Gillian thought. *We'd be talking about the things we'd done. Patrick would be planning a return, saying he'd always wanted to travel abroad. I would've laughed at him, reminded him it was he who never wanted to go this far from home. Then within minutes he'd be talking of going to Paris, Madrid, Rome next year. I'd be saying, I told you so. He'd nod and say he didn't know why they hadn't done it before. Sienna would be itching to get home and tell her tales to anyone who would listen.*

Who will I tell? What will I tell?

Mira? The epitome of kindness. Her questions will be general. Not asking any awkward, personal ones. I'll have to tell her about Petra's new bean, of course – or did I already?

I know what Esther will ask. Did you achieve anything by running away?

Did I? Gillian rolled her head around, opened her eyes and checked the scenery. Clouds buffeted each other for room in the decreasing blue sky. Still a few small cotton-wool ones, but mean and nasty shapes threatened to ruin their run into Perth.

Closing her eyes again, she listened to the calming, consistent engine noise.

Did I? she thought again. *Did I achieve anything? Let's see. I had a break from Esther's prodding.* Yes, but she's your sister. Who else should prod you?

Gillian remembered Morgan saying, 'You don't have to explain stuff to a sister.'

Not quite true with Esther, but, yes, there's background, bloodline, past history that makes for familiarity. And Lettie's advice to speak up; to tell Esther exactly what I do want.

Esther's offer of a joint holiday in Singapore meant a lot to Gillian. Singapore? Perhaps the sights, the shopping, would be a distraction while we re-connect.

Could they be better sisters now they were both widows? Gillian wondered if grief would at last bring them closer. Time will tell. Especially the few weeks when we'll be living together.

She imagined Esther explaining the plusses for continuing to live in one house and rent the other. No way. But she did see them both growing old, disagreeing over memories, laughing over childhood nonsense, sharing more time.

She chuckled loudly, opened her eyes, glanced around, glad of the empty seat opposite, happy not to have to explain her thoughts.

And what about Sandy? Gillian brushed away a crumb from her chest. *She'll want to know about the shops ... no, the fancy boutiques. Well ... after she's told me the finer details of the Magnificent Murray. And, she'll be the one to ask about Max.*

What will you tell her? As little as possible. *Not about his floppy hair, his large hands, his diplomatic nodding when you spoke of Patrick. Especially when his hands were ...* No! Well, I might. Shouldn't think I could tell Mira ... or Esther. *What else might you tell Sandy?* Mm. *Come on, you have to be prepared.* Well ...

Will you keep in touch? With Sandy? Of course. *No, stupid, with Max.* I said I would. *Yeah, but will you actually communicate with him. Not just politely answer his emails.* Maybe. *Do you think of Max more than Patrick?* NO! *Are you sure?* It's different. If I think of Max it's not the same as I think of Patrick. *Of course not. Patrick's dead.* Don't say that. *He is.* Yeah, but it sounds so final. *Like it's not!*

Gillian had been picking at a small catch in her fingernail while arguing with her alter ego, now she pulled a piece of nail free, immediately furious with herself.

Stop it! Stop it. Her throat tightened, she unscrewed the top of a drink bottle and swallowed the last drops. She let the empty bottle and cap fall to the floor. Refusing to let tears surface, she thought of the last time she'd seen Patrick. He'd leaned forward and kissed her, ran his finger over her cheek. He said, 'See you soon, darling. Have a nice time.'

And after returning Siena's cheerful wave as the car pulled away, she'd hummed as she went back into the house, determined to make the most of the "me" time they'd given her.

'Me,' she whispered. 'Me time. Too much of it now.'

She thought of the times she'd spent with Max. How he'd been so accepting, so obliging; happy to let her have her moments when the pain hit. Not many men would. *Yeah, but it was just a holiday fling.* Really? *Yeah. Can't be more than that.* Why not? *Prague, Perth.* 'Der.'

She grinned as she realised she'd said the silly word aloud. She folded the rug, placed it neatly on the seat across the aisle, slipped her feet back into her shoes.

Me. Max. No, it couldn't work. But it did show you ... *Yeah, possibly how to get hurt again.* Well, no pain, no gain. *I've plenty of pain. Where's the gain.* You're right, sorry. But, Max. *Yeah. I guess I could see ... in the future ... maybe. If the pain eases a little more. Petra said it does.* She did, but she also said not completely. You just have to be strong. *Yes, but ...*

The flashes of the past would still be everywhere: hiding in the purple lavender, reminding her of the times Sienna had filled a basket of the blossoms; when she'd peeked out from behind the couch pretending to be the cat she'd wanted; when Patrick and she had cuddled up in front of a movie; the kitchen where they'd made scones; the bedroom where ...

Gillian prodded the screen, shifting her thoughts as she watched the miniscule plane heading across the map towards

Perth. 'Perth,' she whispered, 'Home without them.' Perhaps, just perhaps I'm a little stronger, now.

Gillian hoped she'd be able to use the memories, scattered throughout her home, like a blanket, wrapping up the past, keeping her comforted.

The captain's voice interrupted her thoughts. 'All crew, please prepare for landing.'

A singer's voice, Gillian thought. *A bit like Patrick's. Darling Patrick. Can I really be strong enough to survive without you?* Petra showed you how it's possible to surround the pain in memories. Like a scar healing a cut, making the skin stronger, a mark of acknowledgement. *Yes, the bigger the cut, the longer it takes to heal, but it ends up stronger. Doesn't mean you can't run your hand over the scar, remember how it happened, how much pain endured before the healing.*

Gillian tipped her head back, closed her eyes again, imagined Patrick cuddling Siena, both of them smiling. *They're all good,* she thought.

The plane rocked as it hit a pocket of air. Gillian's eyes flew open, the image of her loved ones disappeared instantly, but as the plane stabilised, she sighed. *Nothing more I can do for them. They're all good. Whatever, wherever. Now it's up to me.* She ran her finger around the pearl in her earring. *Maybe ... who knows ... perhaps ...*

The captain's voice interrupted, 'Please make sure your seatbelts are tightened. Some turbulence may be experienced.'

Yes, Gillian thought. *There's bound to be turbulence, but I'm prepared.*

Her smile broadened as she enjoyed the unintentional advice. She gave a quick salute. 'Aye, aye, captain.'

Forty minutes later, as she bid goodbye to the smiling crew, she imagined she could smell eucalyptus. She snapped a picture of the aircraft's door and went on her way.

From the Author

So many doors have opened to me since 2008 when my writing adventure commenced. These figurative doors have revealed people I needed and exposed experiences which enhanced my life – I'm grateful for each and every one.

My heartfelt thanks to Jennifer of Daisy Lane Publishing who understood how special the setting for this story is to me – and for indulging my attachment to Czech doors.

In 2012, not long after our youngest grandchild was born, hubby, Graeme, and I visited our Prague family. We spent time behind the baby stroller, walking the streets, absorbing the character and beauty of the suburbs of Prague. Entranced by the variety of doors, we photographed many—elaborate doors, ugly doors, ancient doors, broken doors, fabulous doors—and in subsequent trips, added to this electronic collection, now over 150.

With, Elaine, my friend since 1951, hounding me to do something with these photographs, I added the intrigue of doors to an emerging theme for my next novel. Not quite what Elaine had in mind, but I hope she enjoys the result.

As the word count built, my wonderful writing buddies read snippets, chapters, and encouraged me to continue – several reviewed the completed manuscript. Without those from Gosnells Writers Circle and Women's Writefree Writing Group, the door might have closed long before Gillian's time in Prague created anything significant. I thank you all.

The journey of Doors of Prague had been on a slow road and several people regularly asked, 'Is it out yet?' One such person, Margot Wilkin, while not a writer, agreed to read the latest draft in November 2018. I appreciate her thoughtfulness, her valuable insight and suggestions. Thank you, Margot.

Huge thanks to Lynne Tatam for the sketch used as chapter headings. Love it.

When, Hana, a non-English speaking character, befriended Gillian, I created a situation outside my skill-set, and one not viable through an on-line translator. My wonderful daughter-in-law, Šárka, spent many hours translating my words into believable Czech, and making Hana more realistic.

In short, Doors of Prague would not have been feasible without her. I am truly grateful. Děkujeme, Šárka.

My family, the ones in Prague and those in Perth, have always supported me, and that means the world to me. Sharon, Lindsay, Glen, Šárka, William, Ellen and Ben – love and hugs – mx.

Graeme always has the dubious honour of being my 'first reader' and often perused ongoing drafts – and yet he's survived. Together we experienced the Czech Republic as more than a tourist destination – one where our hearts are bound. I hope it shows between the fiction of Doors of Prague. Thank you. I love you.

I trust those who read Doors of Prague understand that the underlying emotion is the value of friendship. Gillian would not have survived without friends who opened their door and gave her hope. And neither would have I.

To all my friends – new, old and ones I have yet to meet – may the next door you open bring you contentment.

The following is a collection of those elaborate doors –
ugly doors, ancient doors, broken doors, fabulous doors –
photographed by the author in 2012 in several areas
of Prague.

ABOUT THE AUTHOR

Barbara Gurney is based in a southern suburb of Perth, Western Australia.

Her writing is described as lyrical with strong narrative. News items often influence her poems while over-heard life experiences are hidden in short stories.

Barbara enjoys creating characters worth remembering – bringing emotional connection between her fictional people and readers.

For more information and to view Barbara's work contact her at www.barbaragurney.webs.com